Vigil

Vigil

CECILIA SAMARTIN

Washington Square Press
New York   London   Toronto   Sydney

Washington Square Press
A Division of Simon & Schuster, Inc.
1230 Avenue of the Americas
New York, NY 10020

First Washington Square Press hardcover edition July 2009

WASHINGTON SQUARE PRESS and colophon are trademarks of
Simon & Schuster, Inc.

For information about special discounts for bulk purchases,
please contact Simon & Schuster Special Sales at
1-866-506-1949 or business@simonandschuster.com.

The Simon & Schuster Speakers Bureau can bring authors to your live event.
For more information or to book an event, contact the Simon & Schuster Speakers
Bureau at 1-866-248-3049 or visit our website at www.simonspeakers.com.

Designed by Jill Putorti

Manufactured in the United States of America

10   9   8   7   6   5   4   3   2   1

Library of Congress Cataloging-in-Publication Data
Samartin, Cecilia.
   Vigil : a novel / by Cecilia Samartin.—
   p. cm.
   ISBN-13: 978-1-4165-4952-9 (alk. paper)
   ISBN-10:   1-4165-4952-8 (alk. paper)
   1. Women immigrants—Fiction. 2. Salvadorans—United States—Fiction.
3. Women refugees—El Salvador—Fiction. 4. Nannies—Fiction. 5. Upper
class—Fiction. 6. Problem families—Fiction. 7. Domestic fiction. I. Title.
   PS3619.A449V54 2009
   813'.6—dc22
                                        2008040487

For my soul children
Sarah, Matthew, Jack, Lucy,
Caroline, Catherine, and Holden

It often happens that those who spend their time giving light to others remain in the darkness themselves.

—Mother Teresa

Vigil

O_{ne}

AS THE SUN ROSE, Ana watched for Dr. Farrell's car from the second-story window. An orange glow had begun to bleed across the sky, and the shadowy shapes that moments earlier looked like sinister creatures ready to pounce were transformed into the benign shrubs and trees of the garden. As everything became infused with a soft silvery light, Ana waited for that mystical sense of hope to ease into her soul as it always did when she saw the sunrise. But on this morning the cold she'd awakened with remained untouched. Instead of receiving the gift of a new day, she felt as though she'd been robbed of what had become most precious to her—time.

Moments later, Dr. Farrell's headlights flashed through the gate, and Ana rushed downstairs so she could get to the door before he rang the bell. She wanted to prevent hearing its deep melancholy tones echoing throughout the house at such an early hour, yet she was unable to prevent the aching in the pit of her stomach. The only way to muffle the dread was to once again remind herself of the miracles modern medicine could achieve. Doctors reattached severed limbs and transplanted organs from one body to another, and if caught early enough, they were even capable of curing cancer. When she thought about it in this way, it seemed perfectly rational, even sensible, that she remain hopeful. Perhaps the reason Dr. Farrell was stopping by so early was that he was eager to tell her of a new treatment he'd heard about and he didn't want to waste any time getting started. But when Ana opened the door, just as he was preparing to ring the bell, and looked into his defeated eyes, took in the stoop of his shoulders and the descending curve of his mouth, she knew that they'd finally reached the end.

A few months ago this revelation would've been a total shock to anyone who knew her beloved. He'd always been a supremely healthy and robust individual and Ana secretly believed that he'd been blessed with superhuman strength that made him immune to the petty ailments plaguing lesser mortals. Yet this was little comfort as she listened to Dr. Farrell.

She nodded silently as he explained the results of the most recent lab tests following this last round of chemotherapy. Adam hadn't responded to the treatment as they'd hoped, and another growth had been discovered along the base of his spine. It had begun to infiltrate the bones of his hips, and before long he'd lose the use of his legs and his most basic bodily functions. Behind thick glasses Dr. Farrell's eyes grew misty as he said that all efforts should now be directed toward keeping him as comfortable and pain free as possible and that Ana needed to take care of herself as well.

"These final days are always hardest on the caretakers," he

said. That's how he referred to her, but she wasn't offended, because she understood that Dr. Farrell was relying on his professional jargon to maintain his composure. He'd been one of Adam's oldest and dearest friends.

Ana wavered on her feet and Dr. Farrell took hold of her shoulders to steady her. "Are you okay?" he asked.

"Yes, I'm fine," Ana replied.

"You don't look fine. You've lost more weight."

"Not much," Ana replied, trying to dismiss it.

"You can't afford to get sick now, Ana. After I leave I want you to lie down and rest. You look as though you haven't slept in days." Although she was over forty, and her short, dark hair was laced with streaks of silver, at that moment she appeared as vulnerable as a lost child.

"I will," she replied softly.

"Have you spoken with the kids recently?"

"I spoke with Jessie yesterday. She should be arriving today."

"And Teddy?"

Ana lowered her eyes, unable to hide her disgrace.

"I'll call him," he said. "I'll make time this morning."

Ana looked up, her eyes clear and focused once again. "Tell him that his father needs to see him now more than ever."

"I will," Dr. Farrell said, glancing at his watch. "I arranged for the nurse to come by this afternoon, but I'll be back first thing tomorrow morning. I don't have any surgeries scheduled, so I'll be able to stay longer." He squeezed her shoulders with fatherly affection. "Actually, before you lie down, I want you to eat something first. Can you do that for me?"

Ana's stomach turned at the mere thought of food. Ever since Adam had stopped eating she too had been unable to eat, and when the chemotherapy treatments caused him to retch, she felt like doing the same. Nevertheless, she assured Peter that she'd eat something right away, and then waited until his car drove out of the gates to go back inside.

Numb and depleted as she was, it took every ounce of her strength to climb the stairs she'd bounded down moments earlier when she thought there might still be hope. Now she feared that she'd slither back to the bottom if she didn't deliberate every single step. Even so, her feet faltered once or twice and it seemed that she'd never reach the top. Every step brought to mind all there was to do, to prepare and plan for.

When she reached the last step, she looked about in a stupor, as if she hadn't spent the last twenty years of her life in this house. If someone were to ask her where she was or even her name, she might not have known how to answer.

Taking firm hold of the banister, she peered down the long corridor. It undulated before her like an endless snake, and there were so many doors to choose from, but somehow she managed to find the one behind which Adam slept. And with small, well-practiced movements she entered the room, and the heavy, stale air of the sickroom brought her back to her senses.

She approached the bedside and gazed down at him. Nestled among so many pillows and blankets, he looked impossibly small and tender to her, more like a newborn beginning life than a man on the brink of death. Surely there was still time for them. Perhaps even more time than Dr. Farrell knew.

Inspired by this consoling thought, Ana smoothed out the

blankets. She rearranged the collections of pills on the night-stand, and then passed her hand gently across her beloved's brow. His eyelids softly fluttered, letting her know that he was aware of her presence, and she smiled.

She lowered herself into her chair by his bedside and folded her hands on her lap. She closed her eyes and her lips began to move in silent prayer. As sunlight streamed in through the bedroom window, her agony began to ease with its warmth, but then she remembered what Dr. Farrell had just said, and the aching in her stomach resurged. She tried to overcome it with prayer, but it pounded and wailed, creating such a hideous clamor inside her that it overwhelmed her orderly chants and left her feeling hopeless again. Without her natural optimism to buoy her spirits, she sank deep into a bleak and all-too-familiar place.

"I don't want to be left behind again," she murmured. "Please, I don't want to live without him."

A voice straining to be heard above her anguish answered her, although later she would question whether she'd been dreaming. "You must look back on where you've been to know where you're going," it said.

"What difference does it make? The past doesn't change the present or the future."

She waited for an answer, and when it didn't come the deathly silence spread over her again, stealing away her breath little by little. After some time she opened her eyes and tried to clear her head and calm her heart, to prepare for this parting that she feared was beyond her strength to endure. But weak as she was, she couldn't resist the call to "look back," and found herself pushing and pulling on this pitiful patch of time she'd been given with a newfound conviction. Perhaps she'd be able to stretch it beyond its limits until it frayed and tore along the seams of her understanding. Then she'd be able to weave it all back together again, thread by precious thread, to create a new understanding of herself and her life.

Her body melted into the chair, and her face became slack. "What else can I do but remember?" she murmured. The sound of her voice caused her beloved to shift his head slightly toward her, but she was too caught up in her memories to notice.

"You ask too many questions, *mija*," Mama said, glancing up from her sewing with a critical eye.

"I just want to know what he was like. Was he short, or tall? What color were his eyes?"

"Your father isn't a man worth remembering. The less you know about him the better," she snapped.

But often she'd break down and tell me about him when she felt most frustrated with life. When the few chickens we kept in the yard were stolen, leaving us without meat or eggs for months, she scorned him lavishly. And when she smashed her finger while repairing the roof during a particularly heavy rainstorm, his name along with a colorful assortment of foul-mouthed descriptions erupted from her mouth with every whack of the hammer, filling her with strength and conviction, and reminding us both that we wouldn't be defeated by his absence. Quite the contrary, at those times I was grateful that we didn't have a "foul, lazy drunkard who couldn't find work in the day or his way home at night" to deal with.

When my mother calmed down, she'd also blame herself as she bemoaned my father's innumerable faults. "I was the greater fool to believe that a man's sweet words and caresses could ever ease the harsh realities of life."

In the village where we lived there was no electricity or running water, and when the rainy season came it wasn't unusual for several of the huts to wash away in a torrent of muddy water. For weeks afterward children combed the banks of the muddy river in search of clothing and pottery they might exchange for a few coins if they were lucky. In our world harsh realities were as common as mosquitoes on a hot humid night, and it was ludicrous to imagine life without mosquitoes.

My mother wasn't alone in her predicament. Many of the women in our village had been left by their husbands to raise their children alone. And there was little hope for those who'd managed to keep their men under their roofs a bit longer than the rest.

"It's just a matter of time before your *tía* Juana finds out that Carlos isn't hiding out in the hills to avoid the National Guard. He has another woman, and a whole other family besides," my mother said. "And then she'll know what I knew the minute I laid eyes on him."

"What's that, Mama?"

"That he's a smiling scoundrel who'll never change," she answered with a dismissive little shrug.

"Have you actually seen him with the other woman?" I asked.

"No, but I see it in the way he looks at every woman who crosses his path. And if I were blind, I'd be able to smell it on him too." Her dark eyes burned with an inner fire. "Sometimes I wish I didn't see as much as I do."

Mama had predicted too many calamities for me to doubt
her. She was a practical mystic who was able to assess the circumstances before her and understand in seconds what it took others
weeks, months, or even years to understand. Unlike many of the
other women who'd suffered, she'd learned from her mistakes and
had found a way to transform her agony into wisdom—wisdom
she applied to her own life, time and time again.

"Why won't you say hello to the man from town who smiles
at you, Mama? Don't you think it would be nice to marry a rich
and handsome man?"

Mama briefly thought about this. "Sometimes I think it
would be nice, but . . ." She clucked her tongue the way she did
when she shooed the chickens out of the house. "The truth is
that you're more than enough headache for me," she said with
a teasing smile.

A continuous flow of human drama played around us, con-
firming Mama's discerning view of humanity and providing
us with a kind of sordid entertainment as well. One time I remember well, I was walking home from the market when I saw
our neighbor Dolores throw herself at her husband's feet. He'd
been away hiding from the National Guard in the hills for some
time, and it was well known that in his absence she'd made extra
money by cooking and cleaning for the same wealthy man who
always smiled at Mama. It was also well known that Dolores's
husband was a very jealous man, and that the mere thought of
his wife in another man's house would drive him mad.

She threw herself at his feet, sobbing while he frowned as
though his shoes had been wet not by a desperate woman's tears,
but by a urinating dog. I was afraid that he'd kick her face away

but he ordered her back into the house instead, and she immediately scurried inside, grateful, it seemed, that he hadn't struck
her. Then he took his machete from his belt and began to throw
it against a nearby tree, again and again, each time striking his
mark with alarming accuracy.

Mama nodded, listening to the impassioned recounting of
what I'd just seen and heard. "Do you think he's going to hack
her up with his machete?" I asked, horrified.

"No," Mama replied. "She'll lose her life little by little, not
all at once."

I wasn't sure what she meant by this, but a few days later we
saw Dolores at the market, both her eyes rimmed by the most
spectacular shades of purple and blue I'd ever seen. They were
so swollen that it was a wonder she could see the peppers she
tossed into her basket, and I noticed that her basket was full of
vegetables and a freshly killed chicken besides. Apparently, after beating her soundly, her husband had allowed her to spend
the money she'd earned.

"You see," Mama whispered, sad for Dolores, but nonetheless pleased to have made another accurate prediction, "if Dolores wants to keep working for that rich man, she'll have to pay
with bruises and broken bones. And one day, when there are no
bones left to break, or eyes left to blacken, he'll kill her once and
for all."

"That's terrible, Mama. We should warn her so that she can
get away from him now before it's too late."

Mama shook her head. "It's no use, *mija*. Look at her. She's
happy that today her basket is full and her husband is home. She
can't see beyond that."

It was only after the day was done and we lay in our hammocks listening to the night sounds, the scuttle and cries of the creatures that lived in the jungle nearby, that my mother allowed herself a romantic thought or two completely lacking in practical wisdom. At these times she'd whisper to me in a dreamy voice full of possibilities, "Let's imagine, *mija*. Let's imagine that we're floating on a little boat in the middle of the ocean far away from here, and that millions of stars are twinkling above us, and that just as many colorful fish are swimming below us." Or, "Let's imagine, *mija*. Let's imagine that we're sleeping in a magnificent house with enormous glass windows and tile floors, and in the morning we'll wake to the sound of guitars softly strumming."

Every night lovely images like these colored my dreams, and because of them, no matter how many harsh realities I encountered during the day, I never had trouble sleeping.

My favorite playmate was my cousin Carlitos. We most enjoyed playing down by the riverbank, where the mud could be sculpted into all manner of objects for our amusement. Sometimes, when we were still too young to be embarrassed by our nakedness and the river was high enough to reach to our waists, we'd strip and cake our bodies with layer upon layer of mud until it was impossible to know who was the girl and who was the boy. If we should happen upon anyone who knew us, we'd challenge them to guess, and laughing hysterically, we'd jump into the river and wash ourselves clean just to prove how wrong they were.

I often wondered how it would be when Carlitos grew up and became a man. Would he be like his philandering father or the other men in the village who beat their wives? It didn't seem possible that sweet, lovable Carlitos could ever be like that, and it occurred to me that if I ever hoped to get married, I could spare myself quite a bit of suffering by marrying him. I suggested this to Carlitos, who, just as I expected, thought it was a fine idea, and one afternoon after we'd been playing by the river, we approached our local priest and asked him to marry us right then and there.

"I'll be honored," he said. "In about ten years."

"We don't want to wait that long," I declared, and Carlitos took my hand, which I found very touching.

The priest laughed, and then considered us more seriously. "You are still too young to get married, but I will give you a premarital blessing," he said, and placing his hand on our mud-splattered heads, he muttered a quick prayer. That was good enough for the time being, and Carlitos and I ran around for days telling everybody we were husband and wife until we grew tired of it and invented a new game.

The only man Mama respected was Monsignor Romero. But then again, everybody in our village not only respected but revered him. He was the archbishop of our country, and when civil war broke out many of his own kind turned their backs on him, but he never turned his back on us. He openly condemned the violence that was taking place in villages like ours all over the country. At that time people needed to hear him speak more than they needed to eat, and they gathered around any working radio they could find. Mama told me that listening to him helped her understand that every human being has the right to live with dignity no matter how poor they might be, and that to do this they had to organize themselves.

As difficult as it was for me to understand the trouble that happened between men and women, it was nearly impossible for me to grasp this bigger problem involving soldiers, presidents, and priests. I hadn't seen the fighting with my own eyes, but I'd heard about the killings taking place and noticed that more young men were disappearing from the villages. When I asked Mama about it, she told me that because of their physical strength and foolishness, men were the ones who fought in wars.

Feeling rather like a mystical apprentice, I offered my own philosophical tidbit for her to ponder: "Maybe this is why men are sometimes cruel to women—because they are the ones who must go to war."

Mama looked up from her sewing with a start, her eyes still as her mind turned over what I'd said. I felt that I was on the brink of possessing the same illumination that gifted her, but then she dispelled my vision with a quick shake of her head. "You have it backwards, *mija*. It's because the men are cruel that we have war in the first place," she said, turning back to her work.

If Mama said the war was all around us, then I knew it had to be true, but life in our village appeared relatively unchanged because of it. The adults continued to work on the coffee plantations nearby as the children attended to their chores and went to school. In the evenings the women cooked while the men that were left gathered in the square to drink. Most days it wasn't unusual to walk into our own small hut and find the table in the center of the room draped with rich fabrics of vibrant purples and blues trimmed with intricate gold embroidery and to hear the gentle rhythmic sound of my mother's sewing machine.

Aside from her philosophical talents, Mama was also the best seamstress around for miles, and the local parish priests always brought their mending to her.

My father's only saving grace was that before he disappeared he'd given my mother a magnificent sewing machine complete with a foot pedal and a carved wooden cabinet beneath. I was fascinated by the glossiness of the black machine that my mother regularly polished with a soft cloth, and I often ran my fingers along the pretty floral carvings that decorated the doors of the cabinet below. Ours was the only sewing machine in the village, and my mother said that my father had probably stolen it, but this didn't seem to bother her too much, and she never attempted to find its rightful owner.

It was a wonder to see our simple hut contain such magnificent colors that shimmered with their own sacred light, and when I touched the fabrics I imagined that this is how it must be to touch an angel. I felt privileged to get this behind-the-scenes glimpse at God's glory, and of course I was very proud to have a mother who was deemed worthy of mending such splendor. One of my favorite pastimes was to watch her work at her sewing machine as the needle valiantly marched toward its destination, occasionally holding the fabrics for her when she asked me to help, and learning how to sew myself, although never with her precision and finesse.

Sitting straight in her chair as she worked so that the tip of her long, black ponytail just swept the dirt floor, she often told me of her dream to one day own a little dress shop. "People will come from all over to buy the pretty clothes I make. Or else, they'll bring clothes for me to alter when they get too fat or too skinny. They'll pay me well, and I'll be able to save enough money to buy a house for just you and me. This house will have running water, electricity, and a tile roof that doesn't rattle when it rains."

These dreams sounded wonderful to me, and when she showed me her excellent work it seemed very likely that they would one day come true.

"Is this what you see in your future, Mama?" I asked, hoping that her powers of prediction might apply in this as well.

Mama shook her head sadly. "I can't see things for myself. If I could, I would never have taken up with your father. Of course," she said brightening up, and giving me another one of her rare smiles, "without him, I wouldn't have you."

When Mama was finished with her mending I'd help her fold the long robes and put them away, always careful to keep the corners tight and to fold along the seams. This wasn't easy as we were both small and needed to each stand on a chair to keep the fabrics from touching the floor. Then she would store them in the carved cabinet beneath her sewing machine that she reserved for her best work. She was certain they wouldn't get dusty in there, and my cousins and I knew that tampering with anything in Mama's sewing cabinet would lead to swift and certain punishment.

Regardless of how much our tin roof rattled when it rained, I lived happily beneath it with my mother, my *tía* Juana, and my four cousins. Life was usually peaceful, but eventually, just as Mama predicted, *Tía* Juana found out that her husband was cheating on her and she threw him out, saying that she never wanted to see him again and that even if he was the last man left on the planet, she wouldn't allow him to lay a finger on her. Even so, every once in a while *Tío* Carlos would show up and sleep with *Tía* Juana in her hammock until she threw him out again.

We slept in hammocks behind blankets that we strung up from the ceiling for privacy, and at night when he was with us I sometimes heard him and my *tía* Juana groaning and breathing heavily from behind their blanket. If the moon was full, I'd peek between the spaces in the blankets and catch glimpses of them with their arms and legs twisted around each other as though they were wrestling.

"Go to sleep, *mija*," Mama whispered when she saw me spying on them. "Do you want cockroaches crawling in your ears and out through your eyes?"

"No, Mama."

"Well that's what happens to people who spy."

I lay back down in my hammock next to her, as worried about *Tía* Juana as I was about the cockroaches. "This time I think they might kill each other," I whispered.

"He won't kill her," Mama replied. "This is what men and women do together at night. It's a private thing."

"Why do they do this private thing?"

"This is how they make babies, and also how they try to forget about them, if only for a few seconds," she replied with a cynical chuckle.

"I don't understand, Mama. Why do they want to forget?"

"Enough questions for now, *mija*. Now go to sleep."

But sometimes it was impossible to sleep with so much

carrying-on, and a strange sound that reminded me of the slapping and slurping sounds Carlitos and I made when we played with the wet mud by the riverbank. Private as this business between men and women was, I thought that they should've been much quieter about it. And if *Tía* Juana should explode in a fit of rage and start yelling at the top of her lungs about the new women he had and the other children he'd fathered, then nobody slept, not even Carlitos, who everybody joked could sleep through an earthquake.

Tío Carlos wasn't the sort of man who'd beat a woman to control her. Instead, when *Tía* Juana accused him he hung his head and nodded, as though genuinely ashamed. Then he'd go away to the hills or to the other woman's house and be gone for weeks. Many people considered him to be weak and not worthy of respect because of the way he tolerated *Tía* Juana. During festivals, when the men gathered around to drink their *aguardiente* from small jugs they passed between them, rarely was he invited to join them. Even so, my cousins were always happiest when he was at home, and I have to admit that even though he wasn't my father, I felt a mysterious sense of completeness when he was home as well—a sense that we'd borrowed a dream from another life and made it our own.

I secretly envied my cousins for knowing who their father was. And no matter how bitterly my mother and *Tía* Juana criticized him after he'd gone, when I came home in the afternoon and didn't find *Tío* Carlos sitting at the table or napping in the hammock strung up outside the house, I missed him, and imagined that he'd gone to meet my father deep in the mountainous jungle. In my vision they both had guns strapped to their bodies and together they fought off the evil that plagued our land. One day they would return to the village as heroes, redeeming not only themselves but all men, so that even my mother would have no choice but to welcome them home. Of course, this was a bit of wishful thinking I was reluctant to share with her.

One night I was lying in my hammock when *Tía* Juana came home, breathless and sobbing so hard she could hardly speak. At first I thought that she'd finally run into *Tío* Carlos in the company of his other wife and children. During her raging fits I'd often heard her say that if this ever happened she'd hack them up with the machete she carried at all times for just that reason. But as I listened, I soon realized that her upset had nothing at all to do with *Tío* Carlos, but with the war. Mama and *Tía* Juana usually spoke softly to each other when we slept, but their horror was too great and our house was too small to keep us from hearing what they had to say.

Tía Juana's voice was shaky as she recounted what she'd heard on the radio during her Bible study meeting, that Monsignor Oscar Romero had been gunned down on the altar of his church immediately after giving his homily. The only man who had the courage to stand up to presidents and generals and the entire world and to publicly condemn the murder of the poorest *campesinos* in our country was now dead, and there was no one left to defend us.

After *Tía* Juana finished telling Mama what she'd heard there was only silence. Trembling, I got out of my hammock and peeked behind the blanket. Mama was sitting very still and staring off into space, as though she could see beyond the walls of our hut, through the jungle, and over the hills into the future. *Tía* Juana lay her head on the table, and the only movement in the room was the flickering flame of the kerosene lamp that created a gruesome pattern of shadows and light in the room—as though the demons of hell were dancing with delight at having heard the news.

The next day when Mama and I were alone in the house, she emptied out her sewing cabinet with the brass hinges. Then she directed me to get inside. Although I had no idea what she was up to, I did as I was told. It was a tight squeeze but if I brought my knees up to my chest and lowered my head, she was able to close the doors without too much difficulty.

"Can you breathe?" she asked.

"Yes, but it's very uncomfortable," I replied.

"That's okay. As long as you can breathe. That's all that matters."

When I asked her why she had me do this she didn't answer, but I saw the same fear and resignation in her eyes I'd seen when she heard about Monsignor Romero.

The pain of the Monsignor's murder was abated by the presence of a new village priest, who came from San Salvador. He also spoke boldly and made people momentarily forget about their fear, and believe that life could be better if they didn't give in to it. "Peaceful organization is your right," he'd say, and the villagers cheered. He'd slam his fist on the pulpit and cry, "Politics should never take precedence over human life!" and the villagers roared their approval.

Like the other priests, Father Lucas often came to our house with his sewing work for Mama, and although he always had a smile for me, I felt intimidated by him and feared that if I looked into his eyes for too long, he'd be able to see the imperfection of my soul in all its gruesome detail. He and Mama and *Tía* Juana would talk about many things, and with their help he began to organize community meetings, some lasting until long after my cousins and I had gone to bed. When they returned to the house their spirits were always high, but I wished that these meetings would stop, or at least that Mama wouldn't attend and would stay home with me. When I asked her to stop going, she scowled at me. "We have to be brave, *mija*. It's the only way to survive this war that's all around us."

All this talk of courage and organizing and new order made very little sense to me. I knew that I would never be courageous like my mother. I was a simple coward who didn't like hearing so many stories about death and martyrdom. They didn't provoke anything in my heart but fear. For the first time I had difficulty sleeping, and if I should dream at night, it was always about escape. I'd run for miles into the blue-green jungles that blanketed the mountains around us. I'd run through the darkness, beyond the fear and the need for courage and resilience and vigilance, to the place where there is only quiet and peace.

One night I was awakened by an eerie howling sound. It wasn't unusual to hear stray dogs in the night, and sometimes even coyotes calling to one another from the mountains, but this howling was different, as though the animals were closing in on us from beyond the jungle. It caused me to sit up in my hammock and listen more carefully. My mother was also awake, her ear tuned to this mysterious sound. She whispered to me so the others wouldn't hear. "Go to sleep, *mija*, it's only the dogs. They must be very hungry tonight." I did as I was told, but I woke up several more times throughout the night, and when I looked at my mother's face, her eyes were always open.

Very early the next morning, before the sun came up, there was a great commotion in the village. A group of National Guard soldiers had arrived and were demanding that everyone report outside to the square. Those who didn't obey would be shot on the spot. My cousins began to whimper and scamper about as *Tía* Juana fussed and barked orders of her own. Carlitos shoved my shoulder as he got dressed to get me moving, but I was too frightened to leave my hammock, and I waited for instructions from my own mother.

Tía Juana corralled her brood and headed out the door. Before she left, she turned to my mother, who still hadn't made any preparations to leave, and said. "For once, do as you're told, Maria. Don't be a fool."

I was preparing to get out of my hammock and follow them out the door when my mother stopped me with a hand to my shoulder. Without a word she led me to the sewing cabinet that she'd already emptied in the corner of the room, and I saw the beautiful robes of the priest she'd been mending lying on the dirt floor. I began to quiver with fear.

"Let's imagine, *mija*," she said. "Let's imagine that we're birds and that we've found a place to rest. Here you will be safe until I come for you again."

As I looked into my mother's eyes, the commotion outside

grew faint, until finally, I couldn't hear it at all. I heard only her voice, speaking gently and calming my fears. I climbed into the cabinet that she held open for me, crouched down, and pulled my knees up to my chest. As she closed the doors, I stuck my hand out to stop her and said, "Mama, I'm afraid to be alone. I want to be with you and the others. But mostly, I want to be with you."

"I will always be with you, *mija*," she said. "Now you must be quiet. No matter what you hear, you mustn't leave your little nest until I come for you."

"And when will you come for me?" I asked.

"Soon," she said, "very soon." Then she closed the doors and threw the robes over the sewing machine. I heard her footsteps as she ran out the door of our hut toward the square.

I don't know how long I waited, perhaps an hour, maybe two. Soon my back began to ache and I felt the excruciating need to stretch my legs and straighten my neck, but it never occurred to me that I could leave the cabinet. I was to wait for Mama as she had instructed. She would return for me, of that I had no doubt.

From inside the cabinet, with the robes draped over the top, I could hear very little of what was going on outside. A couple of shots rang out, but that is all, and the frantic commotion seemed to have calmed. Perhaps the soldiers had left and I would soon be allowed to leave my hiding place. I had almost convinced myself that this is what had happened when I felt the ground beneath me vibrating through the cabinet. Someone was approaching the hut, but these were not my mother's light and agile footsteps. These were the heavy plodding footsteps of an angry soldier.

All at once, the light wooden door was kicked open with such a force that it crashed against the wall of the hut, causing the roof to rattle and several items to fall off the shelf and shatter on the floor. How many times had my cousin Carlitos done the same? And how many times had *Tía* Juana spanked him for it?

I closed my eyes and stopped breathing in an effort to stop trembling. I imagined myself to be even smaller than I was. I was no longer a baby bird waiting for her mother to return, but an egg unable to breathe or move or to make even the slightest sound. Through my shell I heard the intruder's breath deep in his throat, his grunts as he tore down the blankets one by one from the ceiling. Beyond the hut and through the open door I heard the soldiers outside laughing and jeering like drunken fools throwing stones at a stray dog, and cheering when the stone met its mark. The bleeding hound limped off whimpering as it prepared to die alone. I would never understand how suffering and death could ever be so amusing, and all at once a knowing seeped in from the darkest recesses of my soul and I became aware of the pitiful sounds of women and children, my mother, my aunt, and my cousins weeping, gasping and begging for their lives. I saw them kneeling on the blood-soaked earth, some with their eyes turned toward heaven and others staring straight ahead. One by one the shots rang out, and they fell over one another until nobody was left standing. And then I heard a howling wind blowing through a cold, barren landscape without trees or mountains or valleys. And a river trickled forth from the wound in my heart. It bled through everything I'd ever known, ever hoped for or believed in.

The soldier kicked over the chairs and the only table in our hut, ripped the hammocks from the walls, and swept everything off the shelves, sending the world I knew and everything within it crashing to the floor. He crushed the remnants of my life under his boots, but he never laid a hand on the sewing machine and cabinet in the corner, covered with rich fabrics of purple and gold.

He left for the next hut, and I was engulfed by a bitter silence.

I don't know how much longer I remained in the darkness with my knees pressed against my chest, my head bent over the whole of my body. It could've been days, or maybe just a few hours. All I remember is that my arms and legs were numb and I was only able to breathe in short, shallow breaths. Every time I thought of leaving my hiding place, I remembered my mother's words. No matter what I heard or what happened, I was to wait until she came for me. We whispered to each other as we swung in our hammock that was strung between heaven and earth.

"When are you coming back for me, Mama? What do I do until you return? Where are you now? Why aren't you here with me?"

"You must be patient, *mija*," she said. "And you must remember that I will always be with you. Always."

I heard footsteps approaching from far away and a familiar voice, but my senses were so distorted that at first I was unable to recognize the sound as human. Eventually I realized that it was a man, calling out, looking for people. It was Father Lucas! Dear Father Lucas. He'd gone to San Salvador for a few days, and now he was back. Surely Mama didn't mean for me to hide from Father Lucas.

He called out again in a plaintive, shaky voice. "Is anybody here?" he said. "If you can hear me, answer me." I wanted nothing more than to answer by springing out of the cabinet with both arms outstretched, but I was nothing but a paralyzed, compressed mass of flesh and bone, and I couldn't even be sure if my eyes were open or closed. Somehow, I managed to wiggle my big toe and was able to edge it to the side of the cabinet. The movement of my toe loosened my foot at the ankle, and I was able to make a faint tapping sound that grew louder and steadier, but still I was unable to speak. My throat had frozen shut, and when I attempted to reply to Father Lucas's desperate plea, I made a peeping sound that wouldn't have passed for even the squeaking of a mouse. But miraculously, the robes were swept away from over the sewing machine and the doors of the cabinet slowly opened. "Ana, is that you?" he asked.

I was unable to move, and since I was unable to speak as well, I answered him with my thoughts. "Father Lucas, I've been waiting for my mother to return. She told me to wait for her no matter how long it took, but I don't think I can wait any longer."

"Sweet Mother of God," he exclaimed, and then he reached in and pulled me out of the cabinet, as though he were delivering a deformed and hideous infant into the world. Gathering me to his chest, he covered my face with his hand and carried me out of the hut, but through spaces between his fingers I caught glimpses of the bloody corpses that lay all around the village. They were scattered about like laundry that had blown off the line during a violent storm. One boy wearing a single white tennis shoe had his hands tied behind his back. His stomach had been split open so that his intestines spilled out over the ground where he lay like a shiny mass of enormous pink and blue worms. I instantly knew it was Manolo because he was the only boy in the village who owned a pair of white tennis shoes and was the source of much envy because of it. I shut my eyes tight and clung to Father Lucas, no longer wanting to see the horrors beyond his fingers, but I would remember that one twisted ankle and white tennis shoe for the rest of my life.

Muttering unintelligibly like a madman, Father Lucas carried me along the road to the village church and down the aisle, where he laid me before the altar. He knelt next to me trembling and clenching his teeth as he pressed his bloodstained hands against his forehead and then mine several times back and forth until both our faces were covered with blood and dirt. The tears streaming from his eyes created trails down his cheeks and throat, moistening the edge of his bloody collar. "Your mother told me that if anything should happen, I was to look for you beneath the cloth of the church. I didn't know what she meant, and I told her not to worry, that nothing would happen. How could I be so wrong, Ana? How could I be so wrong?"

He turned away from me to face the altar and he continued to weep and pray for a very long time as I lay like a fetus beside him.

Two

WITH BLEARY EYES, ANA glanced at the clock on the night-stand and was startled to see that it was nearly eight o'clock. She'd been sitting in the same chair without moving for over two hours, and when she rose and leaned across the bed to look into her beloved's face, a hot twinge shot up the length of her spine. She dismissed it when she saw that he was no longer resting comfortably. Tiny fissures of strain were forming around his eyes and mouth, and every breath he took was a saw moving across his ribs. The pain medication she'd given him a few hours ago was obviously wearing off. As soon as he opened his eyes and was alert enough to swallow, she'd administer another dose. She reached for the pills among the forest of containers on the nightstand. Although she kept them well organized, she always double-checked the labels just to make sure.

She opened the containers, took the pills out one by one, but kept them in the palm of her hand. She longed to exchange a precious word or two with him before he succumbed to the medication, which always made him sleepy.

Her mind turned back to the prognosis Dr. Farrell had delivered just two hours earlier, although it seemed like long enough ago to have rendered it strangely unreal. He was unquestionably an excellent doctor and a wonderful friend, but it wasn't the first time he'd been wrong. And wouldn't anticipating death provoke it to come sooner than necessary?

Ana felt a familiar heaviness gather behind her eyes, causing her vision to blur. With her free hand she began rubbing her temple in a vain effort to stall the migraine she knew was coming. Over the years, she'd learned to manage these headaches by imagining her pain as a beautiful twisting vine that grew through and around her, purging her of self-indulgences and reminding her that in this life there is no escape from suffering. No matter how far you may run or how deeply you dig in your heels, there is no escape.

As the headache gathered strength and prepared for its final assault, Ana pondered why God saw fit to once again take away the most precious human being in her life. She knew it was a selfish question, but she was unable to detach herself from its mystery as she gazed at his emaciated form on the bed. She took in the feeble torso and limbs that had once been so sturdy. She studied the gaunt face, and eyes that appeared to be slowly sinking into his head. Could this be the same man with whom she'd laughed and cried for so many years? Was this the same man who could lift her up over his head as though she were a rag doll? It didn't seem possible.

When Adam opened his eyes, Ana smiled. She hadn't seen

those dark crystalline orbs for several hours, and it was a wondrous thing. As weak and dim as they were, they still filled her with inexplicable hope.

He wanted to speak, but it took him several moments to focus and gather enough energy to do so. Ana's hand formed a fist as she willed with all her might that his strength not fail him. There was so much they still needed to say to each other. He licked his lips and she nearly dropped the pills on the floor as she reached for a glass of water to moisten them. Her hand trembled as she brought the glass to his mouth, and she worried that she might spill it all over him before he was able to take a sip.

"Ana," he whispered, "I'm glad you're still here."

"Of course I'm here. Where else would I be?" she said, smiling.

He closed his eyes. "I dreamt that you left me."

"I will never leave you."

"In my dream you were dancing and climbing trees."

Ana took his hand and brought it to her lips. "This is where I want to be, not dancing or climbing trees."

When he opened his eyes again, they appeared to be cast in a different light, as though a gray sky were reflected in his gaze. "I want to dance, and climb trees with you, and . . ." He took a deep, labored breath and was unable to finish his thought.

"Yes, I know, my love, I know," Ana said, pressing his hand to her cheek. She tried to sound cheerful when she added, "Jessie's plane gets in this morning, and Teddy will come too. I know he will."

He nodded and shuddered as he inhaled, trying to fight against the encroaching agony that would soon overcome him.

Ana knew that if she didn't give him his medications immediately it could take hours to bring his pain back down to a manageable level.

She showed him the pills in her palm and placed them on his tongue one by one. Adam eased his head back into the pillow and fell asleep almost instantly. She waited for his breathing to become regular, transfixed by the rising and falling of his chest, until she was able to lean back in her chair and relax just a little, certain that he was resting peacefully and painlessly. As she too became filled with peace, she resolved that she would do whatever necessary to ensure that her beloved saw his son again, held him in his arms, kissed him, and told him how much he loved him.

With that thought firmly in place, she stood and walked toward the window, amazed that her migraine was almost gone. Her gaze stretched across the expanse of the walled garden below. Every day it seemed different to her. The green of the trees and the grass was just a shade brighter or darker, depending on the quality of light that cast upon the leaves. The roses bloomed with cheerful new faces, and the azaleas appeared to quiver with the promise of spring.

Ana thought back on Adam's dream and frowned. Perhaps she should've told him that she too wanted to climb trees and dance with him as he did with her. This would've been the best thing to say, and she resolved to keep her mind clear and to stay focused on these moments that were passing far too quickly. Even so, she was unable to stop the images and sounds that assaulted her. She yearned to muffle them and vanquish them completely, but the past and the present were colliding in her head like a jumbled drawer of needles and pins that mercilessly pricked at her fingers whenever she attempted to reach in for just one.

During the weeks that followed the massacre, I was neither dead nor alive. I hovered in a gray limbo, devoid of all thoughts and feelings, sounds and colors. I drifted in and out of consciousness. Although I realized that I was walking and moving around, breathing, and putting food in my mouth, eliminating the waste from my body, scratching my nose, and coughing from time to time. The only part of me that was still alive was the most primitive part, resilient in the face of the worst evils of man. I feared that the rest of me, the soulful part, had gone to sleep forever.

Father Lucas had taken me to a makeshift orphanage before heading back to San Salvador. It was occupied by children of all ages who'd lost their families in the death squads, as I had. The most recent arrivals were vagrant ghosts floating in and out of the rooms and the yard without purpose or direction. Some of us could sit for hours in one spot, not bothering to move even if it should start raining over our heads. If we were to look up with our mouths open, we could surely drown. In some cases, children who were old enough to eat independently needed to be spoon-fed, or force-fed because not even hunger motivated them. This went on for several weeks, and eventually some of us began to thaw, and the blood started to flow through our veins, although some never recovered.

But in some ways, this return to life was worse because I was able to direct my own thoughts again, and when I thought of my mother and Carlitos and *Tía* Juana and all my cousins, an excruciating pain spread over the whole of my body, as though my limbs were being torn from their sockets, as though my flesh were being ripped away from my bones, and I would only wail and moan for hours until I was too tired even to breathe. In this place there was only the hollow and agonizing question I would ask myself a hundred times every second of my life so that it became the very essence of my being: "Why? Why were my mother and all my family dead? Why had every man, woman, and child in my village been brutally murdered?" And even more difficult to comprehend, "Why was I still alive?" "How could this be?" I asked myself over and over again. "How could they be gone? Why did God take them from me?" There was no answer that could ease my agony. I was alone, and I would mutter for hours, "I am alone now. I am alone now," not because I was at peace with the idea, but because I understood it. As it had been when I would open my eyes in the middle of the night to find that I was the only one listening to the night sounds, and watching the moonlight glow through the slats of our hut while everyone else slept, this is how I imagined it would be for the rest of my life.

Like me, all of the children came from humble villages and were accustomed to few comforts. But even for poor children, the conditions were difficult to endure. There weren't enough hammocks to accommodate everyone, and we slept three or four together depending on our size. Many more of us slept on

the floor, and this was especially unpleasant because of the ver-
min that crept through the night.

I was lucky to have been situated in a hammock with two
other girls. One slept soundly, but Teresita cried herself to sleep
almost every night while calling out for her parents. We all
cried, but Teresita didn't give way to exhaustion after an hour or
two like the rest of us; she cried until dawn glowed through the
gaps in the walls. Although she was bigger than me, I sang her
the lullabies my mother sang to me, sometimes through most
of the night. Teresita's nightly vigil depleted me, but I always
felt grateful when she laid her moist face on my shoulder and
implored me to sing to her again. She reminded me that in spite
of everything we'd lost, we were still human beings who could
be comforted and offer comfort to others.

Food at the orphanage was scarce, and fights often broke out
when it was time to distribute the measly portions of beans and
corn tortillas, especially among the boys. They were angrier
than the girls and didn't cry as much. If one boy were to look
at another with the slightest hint of aggression in his eyes, or if
he was bold enough to take the largest ear of corn, he would pay
for it with a beating, if not at that moment, then later when we
weren't being watched.

The priests and nuns who looked after us spent most of
their time breaking up fights, cooking tortillas, shoveling dirt
over the latrine, and shuffling us off between the few huts that
comprised the orphanage compound, as though to trick us into
believing that we were not truly confined. Because of the certain death we'd encounter, we weren't allowed to go more than

a few hundred yards beyond the huts where we slept. Despite the harsh conditions, no one, not even the toughest boys, dared to disobey.

But when all was quiet, I often stood at the perimeter of the compound to gaze at the dense blue-green jungle that blanketed the hills as far as the eye could see, endless, beautiful and menacing all at once. At these times I sometimes heard my mother's voice in the wind that swept through the valleys over the jungle trees. "Do not be afraid, *mija*," she said. "Even if you can't see me, I can see you." And I held my breath and felt her embrace in the warmth of the sun, and for a brief shining moment I sensed her strength within me, but when I exhaled she was gone again.

The intense logging that had carved out ugly brown patches into many of the mountainsides was not visible from there. It was hard to imagine that deep within the mysterious and tranquil shadows of the jungle, rebels and guardsmen were at war, shooting at one another with their guns or hacking away at one another with their machetes. And I wondered what the jungle creatures, the birds in the trees and the snakes slithering along the ground, thought of the turbulence that had infected their world. Were they as afraid as we were, or were they able to find a safe and imperceptible place to hide until the war was finished? I hoped so, and prayed that even the rattlesnakes that had always frightened me would find snug little holes where they could wait out the war in peace.

Sometimes the sounds of battle reached the orphanage, and I quickly ran back into the hut and retreated to the farthest darkest corner I could find. I was no longer a little girl, but a brown beetle that I figured had to be the creature farthest from harm's way. How wonderful to be a brown beetle that could at that very moment scurry beneath the feet of murderers without being noticed. "I wish I could be brave like you, Mama, but I'm only a coward. Forgive me, Mama. Forgive me."

And the soft hush of her voice filled me with peace, and eventually I was able to leave the dark corner of the hut.

Most of the priests and nuns who looked after us were not accustomed to the harsh realities of rural life in El Salvador, and it seemed to me that some were even more broken than we were. Many had come from fine city homes in other countries, motivated by the noble goal of rescuing us from ourselves. But I doubt they expected that being heroic could be so unglamorous, that it would require them to defecate only a few yards from where they slept and to pick the worms out of their food.

As we watched the sisters and priests amble about between their chores, their heads bowed as they went, I noticed that one of the sisters was not as sullen as the rest. She had a spring to her step, she ate the worms in her bowl with gusto like the rest of us, and when she shoveled fresh dirt over the latrine, the most unpleasant chore of all, she often whistled. Sister Josepha came from the United States and spoke Spanish with a heavy accent we all found amusing. When we laughed at the way she said certain words, she'd laugh along with us and never became angry or accuse us of disrespect like some of the others.

It felt good to laugh. When this piece of dormant humanity stirred within me it filled me with newfound energy. Whenever

Sister Josepha mispronounced a word, I felt that it was my duty to correct her, and sometimes I'd correct her so often that she'd prop her hands on her hips and say, "Ana, you're a wonderful teacher but don't you think you should give your student a break every now and again? *Un descanso?*"

She was small and stout, and she had a round head that looked even more so because of the wimple she wore from the moment she woke in the morning to the moment she went to sleep at night. I loved the way her curly brown hair peeked out of the edges like a crust, making her face look like a thick *pupusa*. I did everything in my power to be near her and it was a mystery to me how every child in the compound wasn't glued to her side as I was. Didn't they feel the healing that emanated from her, the warmth, the hopefulness? She was the only one among us who was fully alive, breathing deeply while the rest of us gasped for air.

No matter what Sister Josepha was doing, be it sweeping the filth out of the huts, stirring a pot of something at the outdoor kitchen, or shoveling dirt over the latrine, should she look to her right, she was almost certain to find me standing there waiting, simply waiting for her to notice me. But I wasn't as passive as I looked. Her right elbow belonged to me and if someone had attempted to take it from me, I would've fought for it as fiercely as some of the boys fought for their food. Sometimes, she'd ask me to help her; at other times, she just let me stand there doing nothing. But even doing nothing was something, so long as I was near Sister Josepha.

As constant companions, we had plenty of time to talk, so I asked her why she'd become a nun, and if it was because she knew that life with a man would lead to nothing but heartache. This brought a bemused smile to her lovely round face. "Of course not," she said. "I was in love once, believe it or not, but when God spoke to me and directed me to follow him, I had to listen and obey."

"God spoke to you?" I asked, intrigued. "With your ears all covered up, it must've been difficult to hear him."

Sister Josepha laughed. "No, no, silly. When God speaks to you, you don't hear him with your ears," she said, pointing to the side of her head. "You hear him with your heart."

"Is that like smelling with your eyes and tasting with your nose?"

She laughed again, which pleased me greatly because her laugh made me feel as though all the angels in heaven were smiling upon me. "Something like that," she said, giving my ear a playful tweak.

It wasn't a surprise to any of us that back in the United States Sister Josepha had been a teacher, because she had a way of talking that made you stop whatever you were doing just to listen. After the chores were done we often gathered around to hear her explain the war, and as the pieces slowly came together, things started to make sense to me.

"The war that is killing your people and destroying your land isn't really your war," she said. "This war belongs to the Soviet Union and to my country."

At first we didn't understand how this could be true when we hadn't seen people from any of these countries she mentioned. We'd seen only El Salvadoran men and boys wearing soldiers' uniforms, but she explained that while the Americans and the Russians didn't fight the war themselves, the Guardsmen were trained and supported by the Americans, and the Rebels by the Soviet Union and other communist allies.

One of the boys said, "It's like a soccer game. Don't you want your country to win, Sister Josepha?"

"There are no winners in this kind of game," she replied sadly.

Another boy said, "My father was killed by the Guard because they thought he was a communist. When I'm older, I'm going to kill all the Guard so that the communists win the war." He raised an angry fist in the air, but could hold it only for a few seconds before breaking down in sobs.

Sister Josepha rushed to embrace him, and the boy wept on her shoulder for a long while as we looked on. "Forgiveness and understanding is the answer, little one," she said over and over until he was still and quiet against her breast.

Sister Josepha removed her wimple and veil only at night before she went to sleep. She carefully hung the stiff white fabric on the hook next to her hammock and brushed off the dust that had accumulated over it throughout the day with a cloth she kept tucked into her sleeve. I could tell she was uncomfortable to have us see her short brown hair that looked like tiny snails stuck to her head, but there was no way to avoid it as the sisters and priests slept in the same huts with the children. She never lay in her hammock in the daytime, but one afternoon she excused herself after announcing that she wasn't feeling well. As her constant companion, I knew better than anyone that she'd been feeling poorly for several days and had spent quite a bit of time behind the trees where the latrine was located. I maintained enough distance to give her privacy, but I was close enough to hear the blustery sounds of her stomach upset, which I still considered strangely holy when coming from her.

I stood guard outside her hut when she went in to lie down, and waved away the children who tried to enter, explaining that Sister Josepha was ill and needed to rest. After a few minutes I became anxious and went in to check on her. I was relieved to find her soundly asleep and snoring lightly, her wimple and veil hanging on its hook as usual. I felt suddenly compelled to remove them from the hook, and without thinking about it, tiptoed over to the small mirror at the far end of the hut. I put the wimple over my head as I'd seen Sister Josepha do countless times, and then draped the veil over the top, allowing the fabric to fan across my shoulders. I stared at myself in the mirror for a very long time, mesmerized by the sight of my face that had been transformed from plain and unremarkable into something angelic. I saw the great sadness in my eyes, and my mouth set straight with resolve. Crowned as I was, my banal misery had been elevated to a sacred kind of suffering. All at once, I'd taken several steps up the ladder leading to heaven and put a remarkable distance between me and the calamity of my species. I had no doubt that I was staring into the face of providence.

I felt a hand on my shoulder and saw Sister Josepha's reflection behind me. I'd been so captivated that I hadn't heard her wake up or walk across the hut toward me. "Ana," she said, her face shining. "You look . . . you look beautiful."

Tears sprung to my eyes. I was ashamed that she'd caught me with her precious wimple, but also stunned by what she'd said to me. Never in my life had anyone told me I was beautiful.

I removed the wimple and handed it back to her. "I want to be like you, Sister Josepha. I want to be a teacher and I want to be the bride of Christ and no other."

Sister Josepha embraced me. "Thanks be to God," she said.

Following my revelation, Sister Josepha and I became even closer than before, and at night after I'd sung my lullabies to Teresita, she'd allow me to sleep with her in her hammock. I curled up beside her and tried very hard not to be a disturbance. But sometimes, if she was still awake, she would encircle me with her arm as my mother used to do, and she'd say, "When the war ends we'll all be free of this misery. Let us pray for a quick resolution to the war, Ana."

"Yes, Sister. Let us pray."

"And you shouldn't feel guilty about surviving when so many others have died. These matters are up to God and not us."

I accepted her words gratefully, the way Teresita accepted my lullabies. I would never know for certain why God chose me to live, but if nothing else, my ignorance about such things and my submission to the mystery of my survival created a willing servant, and I understood that my life was not my own.

After several nights of this talk, I realized that Sister Josepha felt badly because she was unable to single-handedly stop the war. Dear Sister Josepha. I wanted to take her sweet *pupusa* face in my hands and tell her not to worry about such things anymore, that it was like trying to count all the stars on a moonless night, an impossible task that would only keep her awake.

"I would like to leave this place and go to your country," I said to change the subject. "Let's imagine that we're two birds flying over the sea and the mountains and valleys on our way there."

"I'm surprised you'd want to go to the United States after all I've told you."

"I don't understand all the politics you teach us, Sister, but I think it must be a wonderful place."

"Why?"

"Because any place you come from has to be wonderful."

She kissed the crown of my head and said, "Someday, I will take you there."

One evening as I slept next to Sister Josepha, I was awakened by a horrible and familiar sound. This time I had no doubt about the source of the howling, and immediately turned and shook Sister Josepha awake. She was unconcerned and thought, as I had the first time I'd heard it, that it was nothing but feral dogs or coyotes calling to one another. As we listened, the howling got louder and I began to shake and whimper with fear.

"Even if it is the Guard, they won't bother us here," Sister Josepha said, trying to calm me, but I was pulling at my hair and felt that all the terror I'd suppressed while hiding in the sewing cabinet was bursting out of me all at once.

"They'll kill us, Sister," I cried.

"Quiet," she said. "You'll upset the others."

I repeated more softly, "But they'll kill us. We have to hide."

Sister Josepha didn't move, but she was pensive. I could only hope that she was listening to God's voice in her heart. Suddenly she sat up and swung her legs out of the hammock as she reached for her wimple. In no time she was fully dressed and lacing up her shoes. By then, the howling was so close that I was certain the soldiers were only a few hundred yards away.

"If they are soldiers as you say, I'll go speak to them and explain that there are no rebel guerrillas here, only children," she said. "And if they're hungry, I'll give them something to eat."

It was foolish to think that sensible talk and a plate of food could ever combat the evil that possessed these men. They were hungry for blood, and they wouldn't return to the hell that had spawned them until they'd had their fill of it. Already I could sense the pounding of their boots out on the road, the rattle and click of their weapons, their sniggers and jeers. "Don't you hear them?" I asked, still trembling.

"Try and calm down, Ana. I want you to wait here while I—"

I grabbed her sleeve midsentence and I pulled her through the hut of sleeping children, and out the door toward the back of the compound where the latrine was located. We weren't spotted only because our hut was the farthest from the road. I had every intention of pulling her deep into the jungle, but Sister Josepha took back control just as we reached the perimeter of the compound and pulled me behind the tree where the latrine was located. The stench was overwhelming, but this is where she insisted we wait. She whispered sternly, "Once you're satisfied that all is well, we'll go back. I just hope we didn't wake the other children."

From behind the tree we could see that there were about ten soldiers in all. Some were leaning on their guns while others urinated into the well, chuckling and shoving one another playfully. One man became annoyed when his boot was splattered with urine and he kicked dirt at the one who'd splattered him, who in turn spit at him, causing those watching to laugh out loud. If we ignored the guns and the uniforms, they could've been boys playing among the coffee trees on their way home from school. If their mothers caught them behaving in such a fashion, they'd be in for a spanking or worse.

Then we saw one of the priests come out of his hut to address the soldiers. The sight of gray hair gleaming in the moonlight let us know that it was Father Anselmo, who was in charge of the orphanage. We were too far away to hear his words but we could see that the men were listening to him because they were no longer leaning on their guns and had started to walk toward him and gather round the way we gathered around Sister Josepha.

As Father Anselmo spoke he lifted his hands in a desperate plea, and all at once the soldier standing behind him lifted the butt of his rifle and struck him hard on the back of his head. Sister Josepha gasped as he fell face forward on the dirt and the same man who'd hit him placed his foot squarely on the old priest's back. Father Anselmo's arms and legs flailed about pitifully, reminding me of a lizard after it had been speared by a sharp stick. Often the poor creature lingered and squirmed long after the boy who'd speared it lost interest, but I was always quick to end its misery with a large rock. Standing behind me now, Sister Josepha's arms encircled me.

Some of the Guardsmen drifted away and began to pass out cigarettes among them. The soldier standing over Father Anselmo became momentarily distracted by this, and the old priest was able to arch his back in an effort to stand, but the guard brought his foot down hard, and the old man crashed back to the ground. He started flapping and thrashing again, and the guard bumped him on the head with the butt of his gun a few more times to quiet him down. Then he called out to his companions, pointed his weapon at the priest's head, and pulled the trigger, after which the squirming instantly stopped.

Sister Josepha jumped at the sound of that single fatal shot and squeezed me so hard I could feel her heart thumping wildly against my back. She began to mumble frantic prayers just as another soldier appeared with the young nun who slept in the hut next to ours. Sister Roberta was fair and slight, and so quiet that I often wondered if she'd taken a vow of silence. The soldier was dragging her roughly by her arm toward the other men. In one swift motion he ripped off her modest dress, as though it were made of paper, and pulled off her undergarments, until she stood naked before the men. She tried vainly to cover her breasts and genitals, but the soldier whacked her hands away with the barrel of his gun. She wailed, and the trembling of her pale thighs was visible even from a distance.

Sister Josepha shrieked in horror just as the men exploded with a cheer and began to drop their trousers. She grabbed my arm and pulled me away, but not before one of the men turned to look toward where we hid. I'll never forget his eyes, like bleeding scabs that will never heal.

We ran deep into the darkness of the jungle, but I had no doubt that they were after us. We'd been spotted by one, and surely the rest had heard Sister Josepha's scream. They would never allow any witnesses to their terror survive. They were stronger and faster and knew the jungle well. They were probably just a few steps behind us and soon they would catch us, brutally violate us, and kill us like dogs. I was certain that I could hear them thrashing through the jungle behind us, but I was also strangely fortified. Deaf to the children's screams, the gunfire, the jeering, and all the horrifying sounds of war, I heard only the howling deep in my soul as my arms and legs moved in torpid spasms through the undergrowth, desperate to get away and nothing more. The dense sounds of the jungle and the thickening presence of nature surrounding us were more shielding than I could've imagined. It didn't scare me as before, and I embraced whatever it brought, even death, knowing that the fatal bite of a rattlesnake would be an infinitely better way to leave this world than what I'd just seen.

As we ran deeper into the jungle, the roots and low branches slowed us down, and Sister Josepha's veil and wimple were snagged so many times that she had no choice but to remove the lot and sacrifice it to the jungle that had saved us. We ran all through the night. As dawn was coming up, we could see its delicate gray light through the trees, and Sister Josepha stopped and fell to her knees. Gasping for air, she pulled me down next to her, and together we prayed for Father Anselmo and Sister Roberta and all the souls that had perished. It hurt me deeply to see sweet-hearted Sister Josepha weeping so inconsolably, as though she'd lost all faith in humanity and maybe even God. I threw my arms around her neck and clung to her, but I couldn't weep. I felt an elation I didn't quite understand. My heart and lungs were infused with a sensational power, and I felt that I could run a hundred miles through the jungle without stopping once to catch my breath. I'd escaped the howling dogs yet again, and with my precious Sister Josepha beside me, I was no longer alone.

Three

THE DISTANT SOUND OF a car door slamming caused Ana to jump slightly and focus her gaze on the farthest corner of the garden. Still at the window, she was able to see where the drive veered toward the gate and where she was almost certain that there was something moving just beyond the laurel trees. She then remembered that she hadn't closed the gate after Dr. Farrell left that morning, and she was preparing to go downstairs to take care of it when she realized that a woman dressed in a dark cloak and veil was making her way up the path toward the house. She was somewhat portly and wobbled on her feet as she walked over the gravel, but she was able to steady herself with her cane and was making slow but steady progress.

The cloaked woman emerged from under the shadow of the trees, and Ana immediately recognized Sister Josepha's round face, uncharacteristically tense as she concentrated on her trek over such uneven terrain. Ana gasped and was charged by a sudden bolt of energy. After making certain that Adam was still

asleep, she rushed downstairs and out the front door with the un-
fettered exuberance of a child. She ran swiftly and nimbly over the
gravel, waving as she went and calling out, "Wait, Sister Josepha!
Wait and I'll help you to the door." By the time Ana reached her,
Sister Josepha was smiling and squinting behind her square spectacles. Ana pulled her into such an ardent embrace that the older
woman dropped her cane, but she was chuckling and obviously
delighted to be received with such enthusiasm.

"Ana, my dear," she said, righting her spectacles that had
been dislodged during their embrace, "how wonderful to see
you."

Out of breath after her sprint, and reaching down for Sister
Josepha's cane, Ana replied, "It's wonderful to see you too, Sister. And it's a miracle that you're here because I was just thinking
about you. Just now," Ana said, pointing excitedly toward the
window. "When I saw you I was . . . I was remembering . . ."

"Didn't you receive my letter?" Sister Josepha asked, frowning as she took her cane.

"Well, yes, but my head has been filled with so many things
that I forgot you were coming today." Ana then noticed that the
driver had left Sister Josepha's small suitcase propped against
the gate. She'd bring it in as soon as Sister Josepha was settled in
her room, but for now she wanted nothing more than to spend a
few minutes with her.

Sister Josepha nodded sympathetically and took Ana's arm
as they began to walk toward the house together. "You must
lean on your faith during these difficult times, Ana, it is your
ultimate consolation."

"I try, but you know I've always been a coward."

"I know no such thing," Sister Josepha snapped. "You've survived what few people can imagine. My goodness, whenever I think back to how well you managed when I brought you here, I'm in awe. You had every reason to be angry and afraid, but you adjusted without a trace of bitterness in your heart." She smiled sweetly. "A coward could never do that."

Ana patted Sister Josepha's hand affectionately. "But you were always with me. If you hadn't been there, I wouldn't have survived anything and I wouldn't be here now."

Shaking her head, Sister Josepha stopped to catch her breath, and then she looked up to admire the great house towering before them. "God has blessed us both," she said. "And he will bless us again."

Sister Josepha resumed her slow pace up the front steps, and when they stopped again to rest, Ana said, her voice trembling, "Oh, Sister, sometimes I fear that I'm being punished for my sins, and that God is angry with me for not having done enough."

The older woman didn't respond right away, and Ana took her silence to mean that she agreed. But Sister Josepha was momentarily preoccupied with looking back at how far they'd come, and then forward at how much farther they had to go, to determine how much longer she needed to rest. She sighed and looked fully into Ana's apprehensive face. "I suppose that there are some who would disagree with me, but I believe that we are the ones who punish ourselves, not God. And," she said, taking firm hold of Ana's arm as they continued up the steps to the front door, "the path he has chosen for you may not be as obvious as you think, Ana. You must remember that he is not confined by your fears and your doubts."

"Sister, if I could see my path I'd run down the length of it as quickly as I could."

Sister Josepha shook her head. "My suggestion is that you don't go running off anywhere right now, my dear," she said.

Once they entered the house they went directly to the kitchen, where Ana prepared tea and toasted several slices of bread that she spread generously with butter and jam. Sister Josepha said a brief blessing over their breakfast, and they ate in silence as the morning light grew more vibrant around them. It was extraordinarily comforting for Ana to see Sister Josepha sitting there in the kitchen. Her presence filled the house and Ana's heart with a tranquillity that gave her momentary respite from her torment, and she was able to eat an entire slice of bread and jam because of it. Just as she did when she was a child, Ana felt that as long as Sister Josepha was near, she could survive whatever lay ahead.

When they finished their breakfast, Sister Josepha said, "I would like to see him now, if you don't mind."

"I don't mind, but his medication makes him very sleepy, and he won't be able to speak with you until he wakes up."

Sister Josepha nodded. "It isn't necessary that I speak with him or that he speak with me."

Ana led Sister Josepha upstairs, and when they entered Adam's room the older woman promptly sat in the only chair and reached into her sleeve for her rosary, twisting it around her chubby fingers as it was her custom to do. Ana knelt next to her and lowered her head. She hadn't prayed the rosary for years, but as she spoke the words of the Our Father and the Hail Mary, and as she listened to Sister Josepha recite the holy mysteries one by one, it seemed that only yesterday she'd kept her own rosary tucked into her sleeve.

After one full day and night in the jungle we came upon a dirt road that was used for transporting workers between the villages and the coffee plantations. In a couple of hours we found ourselves on the back of a truck headed for a nearby plantation, and later that day, thanks to the kind generosity of the plantation owner, on a bus that would take us directly to San Salvador.

For several weeks after our escape, Sister Josepha devoted herself to getting me out of the country. At that time, claiming political asylum in the United States after the massacres that had taken place wasn't so difficult, but the legal details and paperwork involved when traveling with an orphaned child were more complicated.

During the weeks that Sister Josepha and I were together in San Salvador as she filled out endless forms and met with officials from both countries, it never occurred to me that I would be leaving El Salvador to become anything but an American nun. I knew this even though I hadn't experienced my calling like a distant voice from heaven whispering to my heart, seducing me with angelic visions of divine ecstasy. Instead, God had grabbed me by the shoulders and placed my feet squarely upon the path toward a religious life, and I wasn't about to argue with such an unequivocal message.

Finally, the day came when I boarded a plane with Sister Josepha bound for the United States. I kept my eyes closed and my face pressed against her as I prayed during most of the flight, certain that at any moment the plane would fall out of the sky. Even before we landed, I knew that my life would change dramatically, but I wasn't prepared for how different it would be. Naturally, I'd heard that in the United States luxuries such as indoor plumbing and electricity were common, but to see it with my own eyes was astounding. At home, only the rich plantation owners or the professionals who lived in the city enjoyed such comforts, but here they were available to everyone.

The first day I bathed indoors, I wondered what my mother would've thought to see me standing beneath an endless stream of warm water as I washed myself clean. She might've considered it a waste because at home the water that remained after a bath would've been used to water the small vegetable garden that grew behind our hut, but here it disappeared down the drain forever and I had no idea where it went. How Carlitos would have enjoyed walking into a darkened room only to flip a switch on the wall and see it suddenly filled with light. No doubt his eyes would've widened with wonder, and then he would've laughed as he switched the light on and off, not stopping until *Tía* Juana smacked him on the side of the head.

As amazing as these comforts were, even more amazing to me was how quickly I adjusted to them. In only weeks I couldn't imagine how I'd ever lived without electricity and indoor plumbing, and this provoked an aching in my heart because it pained me to think that my family would never know these wonders for themselves. For the rest of my life whenever I saw water flowing freely from the faucet I would think of them.

Soon after we arrived in Sister Josepha's home state of California, she found a school for me near her convent in Los Angeles, but shortly thereafter informed me that she'd been reassigned out of state and that I would continue living and studying at the all-girls Carmelite school, the same school she had attended. I was deeply saddened to be separated from her, but as far as I was concerned the convent was my new home, and to stray from this place would've been like disobeying my mother when she ordered me into the sewing cabinet. I didn't entertain the idea even for an instant. I devoted myself to learning English, to preparing myself through studies and prayer for the next phase of my life, and the early years passed quickly.

Although some of the other girls and I lived at the school during the week, the sisters allowed me to visit my friends and their families on some weekends, so in this way I was exposed to bits and pieces of life beyond the protective walls of the convent. I found it interesting, but it never occurred to me that the loud and colorful world where the other girls lived could ever be mine. It was a messy, sprawling, cluttered affair that spun around in many directions all at once. It was a world filled with complaints about parents, gossip about friends, and unceasing devotion to beauty, with particular attention given to the size of various body parts and the styling of one's hair. And although ours was an all-girls school, there was an ever-present fascination with the opposite sex.

They tried to include me in this talk, and I did my best to follow, but I always felt awkward and out of place. I was as hesitant as one is when presented with an exotic and unidentifiable plate of food. You might try it once or twice for the sake of politeness, but if you find it unappetizing you certainly don't serve yourself a heaping plate of the stuff. It didn't nourish me. It was an adventure for my palate and nothing more.

And so I hovered about the periphery, aware enough to know that my place was to listen and to try my best to absorb the unique flavors of this other world, but their talk and worries about boys and clothes seemed rather silly. When all was said and done, they still had their families and their secure and comfortable homes where they'd sit around the table together and laugh and talk about their lives as I remembered doing with my mother and my aunt and cousins. When you had all of this, what was there to worry about?

Sometimes I wondered if I would ever become infected with this strange but somehow wonderful disease, for despite all of their dramatic suffering, I could see that they were happily sick with it. But I came to accept that I'd acquired a mysterious immunity. Whenever I returned to the convent after one of these weekend visits, I felt such a sense of relief wash over me that sometimes I'd start weeping uncontrollably. This I understood as my soul's joy at finding itself home again. I desperately needed the quiet structure of the convent, the peaceful predictability and the continuous presence of God that Sister Josepha had always said would never disappoint me. In this place I couldn't hear the howling or the profane laughter of the National Guard. I couldn't hear the desperate cries for help, the agonized wailing of mothers beseeching God to intervene and save their children. There was no need to call out for God to find me here because he was always present, like the flickering candlelight and the fragrance of incense that permeated the air.

I now had my new holy family, and the thought that one day I'd be referred to as "Sister" filled me with wonder. I'd never been anybody's sister before, and I considered it the most beautiful word known to man. And to think that my sisters would be women from all over the world and all backgrounds, black, white, Asian, and Hispanic. I marveled that there were a few sisters from India as well. How I longed to be a member of this international community that revered and dignified all individuals equally. Once these dear ladies donned their habits, they were one in the eyes of God, although their faces shone more brightly and more distinctly than ever.

During my junior high and high school years, Sister Josepha and I wrote to each other frequently, and I relied on her to keep me informed about what was happening in El Salvador, as watching too much television, even news programs, was highly discouraged at the school. She informed me that after years of denying that the village massacres had happened, the El Salvadoran government, as well as the United States, were admitting that some human rights violations had taken place. Investigations had begun, but the conflict between the U.S.-backed ARENA party and the rebel FMLN party continued, and the innocent were still dying. My first sunrise prayers were always for the families who struggled to survive in the midst of poverty and war. And as always, I rededicated my life, my every breath, to those who had already died.

With the exception of the year she had knee surgery and was required to stay off her feet, Sister Josepha and I saw each other almost always during the Christmas season. The order had moved her to a Catholic school in New Mexico and she was teaching social studies there. She was quite happy, although she hoped that she would soon be given the opportunity to open her own school for orphans from the Indian reservation. She encouraged me to join her once I finished my religious and academic studies, and I hoped that the order would consider it as magnificent an idea as I did. Often I pictured Sister Josepha and me working side by side while wearing our holy uniforms, for by then I'd be a consecrated servant of God. This image filled me with such joy that I avoided thinking about it at night, as my anticipation didn't allow me to sleep and I'd stay awake for hours.

The week following my high school graduation, I was delighted to write Sister Josepha to inform her that I would soon begin my own postulancy with the Carmelite Order of the Holy Family and that I would embrace the vows of chastity, poverty, and obedience with all my heart, just as I promised her I would all those years ago. I received a card from her the following week. It was a beautiful card that depicted a shining golden cross and a young woman in a white veil kneeling before it, her face subtly illuminated by the light of the cross. Sister Josepha had taken the trouble to find a card with a picture in which the novice had a dark complexion like me, and she wrote that I was her spiritual daughter and would always remain in her prayers. This is the only card in which she didn't include news of home, although I was aware that the peace talks between the El Salvadoran government and the FMLN rebels had broken down. I was nonetheless hopeful that soon God would confer the peace I'd found in my own life upon my country. Only this could lightly ease my guilt over having escaped the horrors of war, for it seemed to me that the painful ugliness of my past had finally been overshadowed by this beautiful if hazy notion of heaven on earth. Surely, with time, my vision would gain clarity and strength and my present life would be filled with nothing but the splendor of God. And then, finally, the evil of politics and the cruelty of man would be swallowed up by the unfathomable peace and beauty of God's love.

During the first two years of my novitiate, I fell smoothly and effortlessly into the structured cadence of convent life. At five in the morning, when the prayer bell rang, my eyes were already open. I was only too eager to rise from my bed and experience another dose of peaceful bliss, another day that would put healing and distance between me and my past.

I believe that my superiors were as happy with me as I was with them. By then I'd lived with nuns for so long that I knew better than anybody how to walk as though I were floating on a cloud, and how to maintain custody of the eyes, taking care not to assault anyone with my probing stare should I pass them in the hall or on the stairs.

When I graduated from the lighter veil of the postulant and was finally able to wear the heavy white veil worn by a true novice, I was overjoyed. I adored my new veil and took great pleasure in the feel of its weighty drape across my shoulders. When I removed it in the evening and glanced at my shorn head, plain, long face, and somber eyes in the mirror, it seemed that I was looking into the face of a stranger, or perhaps I was looking at the hapless state of my soul without God's strength to guide me. Whichever it was, I kept these encounters as brief as possible.

Over time I came to understand that I'd been born to this life, and often while I was deep in prayer my thoughts turned to my mother. I saw her wise eyes watching me and I could tell that she was pleased to see that I'd avoided the pitfalls she'd warned me about in this life. Perhaps God had been speaking through her and this was the path she'd been directing me toward all along. And while kneeling for endless hours ensconced within the quiet of the sanctuary with the rosary wrapped around my fingers, I was able to understand that without the tragedy of my past, I never would've met Sister Josepha, and I never would've come to the United States, and I never would've received such a fine education and learned to speak English as well as I did. No doubt, my mother would've been quite happy with this development.

"I hope you can see me, Mama," I whispered. "I hope that my service and dedication to God is enough for all that you suffered and lost."

First and second year novices were rotated between the most menial chores at the convent, which included cleaning, laundry, and kitchen duty. My first assignment was in the kitchen, and although this required me to get up an hour earlier than usual, I relished the opportunity to chat with the other sisters as we prepared the meal. I enjoyed the sounds of the kitchen, the plates clinking, the rush of water in the sink, the smell of bacon frying, fresh bread baking, and coffee brewing. All of this commotion reminded me of village life, and by then my soul had healed sufficiently to endure the memory.

Breakfast commenced and concluded with a prayer and was eaten in silence. Lunch and dinner were structured in a similar fashion, except that sometimes at the dinner hour spiritual music was played over the speakers and one of the sisters or perhaps a visiting priest might edify us with a reading while we ate, always in silence.

The days proceeded in this peaceful and predictable fashion from the moment we woke in the morning until we lay our heads on the pillow at night, with rare interruptions. This endless flow of tranquillity was as amazing to me as the turn of a faucet. To see clean, clear water running on and on from a spigot always gave me pause to reflect upon God's boundless generosity and benevolence.

In the distance, I often heard the wail of an ambulance or a police car siren, and the rumble of traffic, but by the time these sounds reached over the wall through the garden and into our cloistered life, they were softened to a mere suggestion. It was nothing but a faint reminder of the chaotic world outside the convent walls and nothing to worry about. Infinitely more disturbing was the barking of Sister Olivia's little dog, Muffin. Muffin was a toy poodle the color of clarified butter, and for some reason she didn't bark at squirrels or cats. She barked only when men entered the convent, and she didn't stop barking until they left. The other novices and I sometimes joked about how Sister Olivia had managed to train her little dog to be frightened of men.

Whenever we would hear Muffin's yapping, we knew that at least one boy or man was somewhere on the grounds. On Wednesday afternoons we always assumed it was the gardeners, but at other times we'd pause in our chores and wonder who it might be and how long he'd stay. The week the Franciscan seminarians arrived for their yearly retreat, Muffin was so upset by such an overwhelming masculine presence that she wouldn't stop growling and snarling. Eventually, she had to be shut away in Sister Olivia's room because even the most patient of the sisters became annoyed.

The seminarians were about my age, between eighteen and twenty-four, and I often watched them file into the chapel from the kitchen window as I peeled the potatoes and carrots they would be having for their lunch. Some were short and squat, and others were quite tall with broad and muscular shoulders like field hands. They walked swiftly, looking more like soldiers than priests, and I wondered how education could temper this seemingly masculine and ungodly energy, and how many would actually allow themselves to be tamed.

One afternoon as I watched them, the girl working next to me said, "Excuse me, Sister, but if you continue to peel away at that potato, you'll have nothing left." I stopped and looked down to see that I'd whittled the potato down to the size of my thumb. I blushed, and as I continued to work I was careful not to look out the window at all, not even a peek.

As I approached the second year of my novitiate, I was relieved from my duties in the kitchen and reassigned to the less agreeable cleaning detail, but I didn't mind, because I was given the additional responsibility of looking after the children at the Blessed Mother preschool. I didn't think I'd love it as much as I did. The playful and innocent energy of the toddlers was contagious, and I spent most of the day laughing. When the mothers came to pick them up at the end of the day, I described their children's antics, highlighting how clever they were and how distinct their personalities.

"You have a gift, Sister," they'd say. "It seems that you know our children even better than we do."

I colored upon hearing this. We were not encouraged to indulge ourselves with too many compliments. "A mother always knows her child best," I replied with a bow of my head.

"But my son responds to you much better than he does to me. When you speak to him he actually listens," she replied.

Another mother added, "What is your secret, Sister? Tell us so that we can try it at home."

"I don't have any secrets," I replied. To me it was very simple. I enjoyed playing with the children and they enjoyed playing with me. If they broke a rule or were unkind with another child or a staff person, I would gently remind them of the rules and praise them when they behaved properly. It was never more complicated or mysterious than that.

"Please advise us, Sister. How can we get our children to be more obedient?"

"I'm not sure what to advise," I said, uncomfortable in the role of expert.

"Oh, you must have some advice," they said, gathering round.

I strained to come up with something, and finally what came to me was this. "I suppose that there is great power in gentleness," I said.

At first they didn't seem to understand my meaning, and then their eyes softened with wonder.

One woman said, "That makes sense to me, although I can't tell you why."

Another asked, "Do you think this gentle approach would work with our husbands as well?"

The woman standing next to her said, with a smug smile, "I doubt it, Paula, your husband's probably more difficult to manage than your son." And we all laughed.

On most afternoons you could find me standing in the parking lot surrounded by a circle of young mothers as they talked about their lives and their troubles. I was surprised by how similar these modern women were to the simple women I'd known in my village. And the problems they had with their men were similar too. A few even confided privately that their husbands were engaged in extramarital affairs. When they asked me what I thought about this, I didn't hesitate to offer an opinion. "Men are born with one foot on the road to corruption," I said. "And trying to change them is even more difficult than enduring them."

There were no smiles following this sober declaration, and one woman asked, "Then what is the answer?"

It felt as though my mother's voice had lodged itself in my throat and that her mystic nature had possessed me. "Acceptance," I replied. "Acceptance or retreat."

Eventually my turn came to serve the gardeners, or "the boys" as the sisters referred to them, although several were well past fifty. They ate their lunch at the convent in a room off the kitchen reserved for lay visitors. Most of the sisters didn't like serving "the boys" because they were messy and loud, and although they made an effort to moderate their brusque manners around us, they could still be off-putting. But I secretly enjoyed serving them. For one thing, I was one of the few sisters who was able to converse with them in Spanish, as the other Spanish-speaking sisters were much older and would never be assigned such a menial task. But it was more than this. I was intrigued by the animalistic gusto with which they ate. I remembered when my uncle would come home after a long hiatus in the hills and how he was so intent upon every bite of food that he was unable to say a word until he cleaned his plate.

I was fascinated by their thick forearms that they rested on the table as they ate, and the dirt under their nails, and their rough clothes and heavy boots. The odor from their bodies was a spicy, earthy smell I found intoxicating, and almost as mysterious as the incense that smoldered near the altar. And the way they laughed so unfettered and free, sometimes pounding their hands on the table and leaning back in their chairs, reminded me of the children in my class. Often I'd find myself smiling along even when I didn't have the slightest idea what they were laughing about.

One of the younger gardeners often smiled and winked at me when I served him, and one day he was bold enough to say, "Sister, I think that you're far too young and pretty to be a nun."

"I may be young," I replied placing a bowl of spaghetti in the center of the table, "but I am not pretty."

"Oh, but you are." He turned to his right. "Don't you think she's pretty, Julio?"

Julio blushed and elbowed the young man sharply in the ribs. "You must excuse my brother, Sister. He has very little sense in his head."

Later while I was collecting the dirty plates and Julio was not around, the young gardener approached me again. "If you weren't a nun, I'd take you out dancing. Have you ever been dancing, Sister?"

I was shocked and fascinated by the question, and nearly dropped the armload of dishes. This young man was as foolish as he was courageous. It's true that I wasn't officially a nun yet, but he didn't know that.

"I think . . . I think you should listen to your brother," I returned, and I heard him chuckle as I walked back to the kitchen. My heart was still beating fiercely as I sunk my hands into the warm soapy water, and despite my better judgment, I found myself thinking about how it would be to go dancing with this young man. Beyond the convent walls there was the madness of a violent world, but there was also dancing, and there were parties where women dressed lavishly while elegant men escorted them through this dangerous labyrinth. Outside the walls there was music that made you forget yourself and your holy obligations, and there was the erotic pleasure of physical love. I recalled the vision of my uncle and aunt, their bodies twisted through and around each other like the knots of the hammock, and I wondered if this experience of love was worth the sacrifice of peace. I wondered about this sometimes even as I prayed.

I felt ashamed for enjoying the young gardener's attention. And even after my assignment serving "the boys" had ended, I thought of him whenever I heard the blowers howling out in the garden, and I imagined how it would be to run my finger along the thick vein that ran from the inside of his wrist to his elbow. At night before I fell asleep in my cell, I sometimes searched for this same vein in my own arm, and as I searched,

I thought about the young gardener who wanted to take me out dancing.

One afternoon my superior, Sister Pauline, ushered me into her office. A few days earlier I'd made an official request to take my first temporary vows, and I assumed that she wanted to speak with me about this, as she did with every novice. After taking these vows, I would have to wait another two years before making another such request, which at the age of twenty-one felt like an interminable amount of time to wait. But in the meantime I'd be allowed to wear the dark brown and black habit of the fully professed nuns, although my veil would remain white. How I longed to send Sister Josepha an updated photo of myself in my new vestments.

Mother Superior and I had had many edifying conversations in her office over the years, and I welcomed the opportunity to learn from her wisdom. As always, she leaned over her desk and clasped her hands before her as her black veil fell across her shoulders in an authoritative sweep. All the while she peered at me through her rectangular spectacles in that singular way that made me feel as though she knew me better than I knew myself. She stared at me for a remarkable length of time without moving a muscle, her expression a frozen mask of scrutiny. This could be quite unnerving for those who didn't know her, but I'd experienced this inspection from her many times before and long ago realized that in her position of authority, Mother Superior was not required to observe custody of the eyes. Eventually she pointed to a chair facing her. "Please sit down, Sister," she said gently.

I lowered myself into the chair, aware that my knees had started quivering and my intuitive fear was beginning to gather like a storm in the pit of my stomach. This fear that had been awakened as a child had been dormant for years, but it hadn't lost its potency. Already I felt myself breathing in tight little gasps as I clutched my hands one to the other, certain that this conversation would be different from the rest.

Mother Superior bowed her head before looking back at me, her gaze firm and resolved. "I've been thinking and praying very hard about this, and I've come to the conclusion that it would be best for you to take some time away from the convent."

Her words hit me squarely in the pit of my stomach, leaving me quite breathless. How could she be asking me to do such a thing, to act against the deepest yearnings of my soul? "I . . . I . . . don't understand."

She sighed and closed her eyes as though to listen to a voice deep inside her. When Mother Superior spoke from this place of inner knowing, pure light shone forth from her mouth, and there was no denying her that power derived from contemplation and wisdom, and I braced myself to receive it.

"Ana, in this life we are preparing for death, the moment when we will look into the face of our creator. But we must not mistake life on earth with the eternity that lies beyond."

In response to my befuddled expression she continued. "I sense something in your demeanor, a curiosity and a yearning that distracts you from your focus on our beloved Savior."

Breathing hard, I sat on the edge of my chair and placed my hands on her desk. "Mother Superior, forgive me, but I don't know what you mean. With . . . with all due respect, all

I care about is God's will for my life. I want only to serve him as humbly and obediently as possible." I sounded desperate when I should've been serene, but it was impossible to compose myself.

"Curiosity isn't a bad thing, Sister," Mother Superior continued. "Before you can find the answers you need, you have to ask the questions, and I don't believe you've done that yet."

I felt every muscle in my body stiffen. "But I don't have any questions. And all I want is to live here with you and the other sisters. You are my family."

Mother Superior studied me for a few moments longer, trying to discern my motivation, and then she gave up a beleaguered sigh. "Dearest Ana, you were a mere child when you came to us. You needed a home, but unlike the other novices, you've never lived outside our community. And I believe that this may be at the heart of your dilemma."

I wanted to dismiss everything she was telling me as nothing but the ranting of an overly protective mother, but I couldn't deny everything she said. The truth is that I'd always seen myself as a lost bird with broken wings that happened upon a beautiful flock that nurtured me as one of their own. My wounds had healed within the tranquillity of their world, and now I was being pushed out of my nest, but I didn't want to leave. This was my home.

"Sister, I . . . I cannot leave the convent." Tears sprung to my eyes, and I hastily wiped them away with my sleeve. "Where would I go? What would I do?"

Sister Pauline's expression softened somewhat. Although she was not typically impressed by tears, she knew that I wasn't one to shed them ingenuously. She handed me a tissue from the box on her desk. "I understand that this will be a challenge for you, but I am quite certain that it is one you must face. And if it's God's will that you proceed with your commitment to a religious life, then taking time away will not alter his course for your life. Quite the contrary, that will only strengthen it, and you will be able to proceed with an unencumbered spirit."

I knew that it was not only useless, but also unwise to argue with my superior about a matter so integral to my formation. If the Carmelite sisters were to accept me back into their fold, I would need to demonstrate not only devotion but obedience as well.

I bowed my head and sniffled. "I will do whatever you ask of me, Mother Superior."

"Very well," she said in a lighter tone. "As I mentioned earlier, I've been thinking and praying about you for a long time, and just yesterday it came to my attention that a family well known to our parish church is looking for a nanny."

"A nanny?" I echoed.

"Yes, and considering your obvious talent with children, I think this opportunity would be perfect for you."

My apprehension eased a bit, as I never tired of hearing about my abilities with children. Then it occurred to me that my unseemly pride was apparent and concerning to my superior. Perhaps she complimented me to test my character.

"Thank you, Sister," I replied, lowering my gaze in an effort to appear as humble as possible.

"Mr. and Mrs. Trellis are looking for the right person to care for their small boy. Their present nanny had to go to Mexico because of a family emergency, and Mrs. Trellis is expecting another baby shortly, so naturally they're anxious to find a replacement as soon as possible. The assignment shouldn't last more than six months, ample time for you to think and reflect, wouldn't you say, Ana?"

"Yes, Mother Superior," I said.

"The Trellis family has quite a legacy," she said, and then went on to trace their illustrious lineage and to highlight the charitable contributions they'd made to the convent, to the church, and to other community organizations. I listened with half an ear as I struggled to understand how in just a few minutes everything in my life had changed, and why it was that all of the changes in my life had been so brutal and abrupt. In truth, I was feeling quite sorry for myself.

"Sister, are you listening?" Mother Superior asked.

"Forgive me, I suppose that I'm feeling a bit overwhelmed by all of this."

"Of course," she said with sympathetic bow of her head. "I'll relieve you from your duties in the preschool this afternoon so that you can rest and start organizing your things."

I would've much preferred to spend the rest of the afternoon with the children, but I bowed my head and mumbled my gratitude instead. Mother Superior dismissed me, and as I dragged my feet back to my cell, I wept into my sleeve so that the other sisters wouldn't notice. If they had asked me what was wrong, I wouldn't have known how to explain that once again my life was about to change without my consent.

✳

When Sister Josepha and Ana had finished praying, the older woman carefully gathered her rosary together and tucked it back into the pocket of her sleeve. As she did so, the beads made a pleasant clacking sound that filled Ana with nostalgia and melancholy. It seemed to her that the prayers had been able to stop time, or at least slow it down a bit, but now the world was back to moving at a dreadfully brisk pace.

The two women left the still-sleeping patient in his darkened room and went out to the corridor, where sunlight was streaming in through the windows overlooking the garden. As Sister Josepha passed by the window, she paused to admire the sight, squinting as her eyes adjusted to the bright light outside. "What a beautiful and restful place. We should make some time for the garden today, Ana," she said.

"I'd like that, but let me show you to your room so you can rest. I hope you'll be able to stay longer this time," Ana said, remembering that her previous visits had always been far too brief.

"I'll stay as long as you need me," she replied.

Relieved to hear this, Ana led Sister Josepha to the room that she herself had occupied for many years.

"Such luxury," Sister Josepha said when she entered. "How many cells would fit in this space, nine? Ten?"

"More or less," Ana replied with an awkward smile. Sister Josepha was obviously tired, and it would've been appropriate for Ana to leave at that point, but she remained where she was, her sense of propriety suspended by her worry. "I wonder what you would advise . . . ," she muttered.

"What was that, Ana? I'm sorry, my hearing isn't what it used to be."

Ana leaned against the wall, her small face contorted by the great suffering that made her look older than her forty-two years. "Sister, what would you advise someone who must choose between honesty and love?"

Sister Josepha's eyebrows came together in a sharp V. "I'm afraid that I don't really understand your question, dear. You're going to have to be a little bit more specific."

Ana tried to find the words to articulate the tangle of thoughts and feelings tormenting her, and all the while she hesitated, fearing that it was a mistake to have brought up the issue at all, but she valued Sister Josepha's opinion greatly. "What if . . . what if the only way you knew how to express your deepest love for someone was to be dishonest with him or her, what would you do?"

Sister Josepha lowered herself down to the edge of her bed with a sigh and placed her cane on the bed next to her. "Ana, are you in some kind of trouble?" she asked, her lips pursing in nervous little spasms.

Ana shook her head, feeling suddenly faint. "I have a difficult decision to make and it's hard to explain it all right now."

"I see," Sister Josepha said as she fingered the hooked handle of her cane. She took a deep breath. "Well you know as well as I do that under normal circumstances love without honesty is impossible, but my guess is that you're not dealing with normal circumstances, am I right?"

Ana nodded.

"Then you should remember that with God nothing is impossible."

"Thank you, Sister," Ana replied with palpable relief.

"But you must be careful, Ana," Sister Josepha continued. "If you're contemplating dishonesty, then perhaps you are the one who is being deceived."

"Yes," Ana muttered. "I know I must be careful."

"You know," Sister Josepha said, smiling fondly, "when you left the order all those years ago, something told me you wouldn't be returning, yet I had no doubt that you'd find your way. The same is true now, my dear. When life takes us beyond the path we've envisioned, we are reborn."

Ana considered the older woman dubiously. "I hope you're right, Sister," she said.

Sister Josepha clasped her hands together and lowered her head for a moment. When she raised it again, her eyes were shining. "I know that it's been hard for you to separate from the Trellis family, but perhaps the time has finally come for you to leave here and work with me in New Mexico."

"You know I've always dreamed of working with you," Ana said, allowing herself to get momentarily swept up in the thought. "Yes, perhaps you're right. I'll think about it and pray about it."

"And I have no doubt that your prayers will be answered," Sister Josepha replied so cheerfully that in spite of everything, Ana couldn't help but smile.

Four

ANA WENT OUTSIDE TO collect Sister Josepha's small bag that she'd left against the gate earlier. It had probably been too difficult for her to manage on the gravel with her cane and bag at the same time. As Ana walked across the garden, she became aware of the clear brilliance of the morning and the birds' sweet chorus signaling that it would be a glorious day. Already the sun had risen high enough to settle itself within the highest branches of the oak tree, like a glowing owl watching her. In an hour or so it would hover over the camellia tree, but Ana didn't intend to linger. She knew that Adam would soon be awake and she wanted to be by his side when he opened his eyes. The mere thought that he would wake and find himself alone was unacceptable to her, and she hastened her stride.

After leaving Sister Josepha's bag by her bedroom door, Ana immediately returned to her beloved's side. Sun spilled in through the open window, making the room far too bright, and as Ana drew the curtain she was startled by her reflection in the mirror. She stepped in closer, cautiously, as though approaching a ghost, and then all at once the illusion was lost. This woman with silver framing her thin face and deep shadows beneath her eyes was far too old to be her mother. Her mother had been a vibrant, sharp-eyed woman with astounding reflexes and strength to match. Ana imagined that had her mother lived to a ripe old age, she would've kept herself busy sewing dresses to sell at her store, and decorating the front window with the prettiest of her creations. She would've swept the front steps several times a day while waving to passersby. Perhaps this was her heaven.

Ana turned away from her reflection, realizing that she looked not only old but unkempt. For the last couple of days, she hadn't left her beloved's side even to shower. After making certain that he was still asleep, she quickly showered and returned with a pan of warm water and a washcloth. Adam hovered between sleep and wakefulness as she tenderly bathed, powdered, and changed him into a fresh pair of pajamas. He cooperated silently with what she knew had to be a great indignity, but she also knew it would be worse for him if anyone else performed this duty. He sighed when it was over, but Ana could see he was much more comfortable and alert, as he usually was after his bath.

He looked up at her with grateful and luminous eyes while Ana proceeded to comb his hair, marveling at the beauty of the silver threads gleaming through his dark hair.

"Am I going to a party?" he asked hoarsely.

"Yes, why not?" Ana replied, matching his playful smile. "And when I'm finished combing your hair, I'll comb my hair as well and go with you."

He shook his head sadly. "I'm afraid that to this party I must go alone," he said.

Hearing this, Ana stopped what she was doing. He lifted his hand toward her in a gesture of sympathy, but he lacked the strength to reach her, so Ana came to his side and pressed her cheek to his hand.

"Forgive me," he whispered. "I say foolish things sometimes, and I'm afraid I'll drive you away."

"I won't ever leave you," she said. "I promise."

"But you were eager to leave me once."

Ana stood and resumed combing his hair. "I wanted to leave the situation, not you."

"Because you were frightened of what might happen between us," he said.

"Yes, I was," Ana replied.

At this, his shoulders started to shudder, and Ana became alarmed that he might be having a heart attack. Dr. Farrell had warned her that in his weakened state this could happen. But when she looked into his face, she was amazed to see that he was laughing. The dear man could barely garner the energy for it, but his illness was unable to suppress him.

"What's so funny?" Ana asked, forcing a smile, even though she felt like weeping.

"*You* are," he replied. "When I think of how you used to look at me with those big round eyes of yours." The smile left his face. "Are you still afraid of me?"

"No," Ana whispered. "You know I'm not."

Satisfied with her answer, he eased his head back down to

the pillow and closed his eyes. His breathing grew steady and even again, and the muscles of his face became flaccid.

"As long as you're with me I'm never afraid," Ana said more loudly, but she couldn't be sure that he'd heard her. She waited for a moment to make sure that he hadn't just dozed off for a few seconds, and when it was clear that he'd fallen into a deep sleep, she arranged the blankets up over his shoulders and sat in her chair to wait until he woke again.

The taxi came to take me away from the convent as the bell for morning mass was ringing. Sitting primly in the backseat, I saw my reflection in the rearview mirror and was struck by how different I looked without my veil, like a grim prepubescent boy. I would dearly miss my veil. I felt wise and serene while wearing it, but obviously neither wise nor serene enough. I thought of how smoothly I'd learned to walk through the convent corridors. My movements were always slow and deliberate, so that when I picked up a utensil or a book, it appeared as though the Holy Spirit were lifting the object rather than my mortal hand.

My only hope was that the next six months would go by as quickly as my postulancy and that I'd stand before Mother Superior more chaste, more obedient, and more committed to poverty than ever before. She would see the holiness beaming forth from my body like a light from within. Perhaps I would levitate before her very eyes as I spoke to her of my love for the Lord, or I would be blessed with the holy stigmata. With eyes filled with eternal sorrow I'd show her the bloody wounds on my hands and feet. Surely that would convince her.

I glanced at my bare head again in the mirror and was reminded of Sister Josepha on the night that we ran through the jungle for our lives. As on that night, my body shivered, sweat poured down my sides, and I was unable to calm myself with thoughts of holiness.

We'd been traveling for ten or fifteen minutes when my mind turned to the prospect of meeting the Trellis family and moving into their home. In my small suitcase I had packed basic toiletries, some undergarments, another blue smock dress (I was wearing the other one), two white blouses, a nightdress, and a navy blue sweater. In a soft voice, I rehearsed how Mother Superior had told me to introduce myself.

"Did you say something, Sister?" the cab driver asked, peering at me in the rearview mirror.

"No, excuse me," I replied, embarrassed that I'd been caught talking to myself.

"Where are you from, Sister?"

"I'm from El Salvador," I replied, happy for the distraction from my worries.

"Ah, Salvadoreña," he replied, and he switched to Spanish. "I have neighbors from El Salvador. They were very glad to get out when they did. They say things are worse than ever."

"People continue to suffer," I sadly agreed.

"I hear that aside from the killings, they are stripping the jungles from the mountains and that when it rains the rivers are nothing but mud." The driver flashed sympathetic eyes in the rearview mirror. "I sure hope you don't have family there."

As always, talking about El Salvador and thinking about the past filled me with shame and self-reproach. While other immigrants I knew relished every opportunity to talk about home and remember, for me it was very different, so I answered hastily that I didn't have any family left and changed the subject. "Where are you from?" I asked.

"I am from Merida," he replied, lifting his chin so that I could clearly see his murky smile accented by a few gold teeth in the rearview mirror.

"Ah, Merida. They say it is very beautiful there."

"Yes, it is beautiful, but everyone is very poor," he replied, shaking his head.

"Do you still have family there?"

At this he brightened up. "Yes, I do. My mother and father are still living but they are very old, and I have five sisters and three brothers, all with children of their own. I have so many nieces and nephews that I lost count. I think there must be about thirty of them."

"Heavens, and all still in Merida."

"Yes," he said, placing his right hand over his heart. "I am the only pioneer."

During the remainder of our journey the driver told me about the various sins that his brothers and sisters had committed. They included theft, extortion, and copious amounts of adultery and fornication. "I'm not sure," he said, "but I wouldn't be surprised if my brother killed a man too. They won't tell me because they know I'll get angry. I'm the only one who isn't completely lost to sin, Sister. I never miss mass on Sundays," he said, looking at me earnestly.

"I have no doubt that God will reward you," I replied.

He nodded happily. "I hope you're right, Sister."

Mother Superior had told me that the Trellis house wasn't far from the convent, and before long the taxi slowed as we drove down a tree-lined street. We eventually stopped before an elaborate wrought-iron gate, such as I'd seen only at graveyard and church entrances. We turned up the drive and continued on until a grand house came into view. The driver whistled through his teeth.

As we drove closer, we could see that the mansion was of a Spanish style, reminding me of the elaborate haciendas that belonged to the coffee plantation owners of my country. It was flanked by many graceful arches and crowned with an elaborate red tile roof that reflected the soft glow of the morning sun.

All around us the garden exploded with color. Flowers of every kind glistened with morning dew, and the trees stood like sentinels saluting us. All was meticulously maintained. The flower beds were tidy, and the lawn was a flawless green carpet. Although much more expansive and elaborate, it all wasn't so different from the convent I knew so well. I had no doubt that within this beautiful sanctuary it was possible to forget about the ugliness of the outside world. Thinking about it this way helped me to breathe a little easier.

The taxi fee having been previously paid, I thanked the driver for his excellent services and watched him drive away over the white gravel drive and out the gate, feeling as though I'd seen the last of a dear friend. With my small suitcase in hand, I became aware of the breeze on my bare scalp and exposed ears, and I began to shiver. Feeling smaller than a speck, I turned and walked toward the house, every step loudly crunching into the gravel. I knew that Mother Superior had informed the Trellis family I would be arriving early, but still I feared that I'd wake the inhabitants of this grand house. By eight o clock in the morning the sisters would've been up for hours, but this wasn't the case elsewhere. I suspected that wealthy people slept in late, and perhaps missed the mornings altogether.

As I proceeded toward the front door, I tried to stand straight in case someone was watching me through one of the many windows. "Never assume that you're not being watched," Mother Superior had always told the novices, "because you are, if not by human eyes then by the angels and saints in heaven, who look down on us from time to time." And so, mindful of my posture and focusing on how I would introduce myself, I approached the front door, a tangle of nerves.

I lifted my hand to ring the bell, but hesitated when I noticed that the intricately carved door looked like the entrance to heaven itself. My hand drifted away from the doorbell, and I ran my fingers along its multilevel grooves and valleys as though it were a mysterious instrument. Standing so close, I couldn't make out what it was, but when I took several steps back, I beheld two beautiful peacocks with their tail feathers fanning out behind them. The smaller, more demure female was sheltered by the imposing male, whose great fan of glorious feathers enveloped them both. I'd never seen anything like it and I could've stood for quite some time admiring the artistry of the carving, but I couldn't delay any longer. I stepped forward, straightened my shoulders, and rang the bell.

A series of deep melancholy tones echoed through the house, and I expected to wait several minutes before anyone came to the door. I'd sit on the front step and wait until noon if need be, but I wasn't about to ring the bell a second time and risk appearing impertinent. Moments later, however, the door was opened by a gray-haired little lady with bright blue eyes that glittered from her ruddy face. She wore a blue velvet dress with a lace collar beneath a white apron, and white tennis shoes and socks. "Are you Ana?" she asked brightly.

"Yes. Sister Pauline, my Mother Superior, sent me," I replied, completely forgetting my introductory speech.

"Well, I'm Millie," she said, with a warm and welcoming smile. "I'm the official greeter, but when I'm not greeting visitors you'll usually find me in the kitchen." She opened the door wide for me to enter. "Please come in dear. Oh my," she said eyeing my small suitcase with concern. "Is that all you brought?"

"Yes, but I don't need much," I replied.

Her face fanned out into a brilliant smile. "Very well," she said. "Please follow me, Ana."

As she led me through the house, she spoke about how much the family had been anticipating my arrival, and how delighted she was that the convent had been able to provide them with someone. This helped me to relax a little, and as she chattered on I admired the hanging portraits of people I assumed long dead, and the massive dark furniture that loomed in the corners. The house looked very much like a church. There were several stained-glass windows as well, but they weren't made with the typical church colors. These were more delicate, and I actually thought they appeared the way celestial windows should be—filled with more light than color. Against the whitewash interior of the house, shafts of muted color glowed everywhere, and as we walked down one corridor Millie's gray hair changed from blue to yellow and burnt orange before reverting back to gray again.

"You're younger than I expected," she said, glancing back at me. "Flor must be twice your age. She's the nanny who was here before."

I wasn't sure how to respond. Was this good, or bad? "I'm older than I look," I replied, deciding that in this situation maturity would be considered an asset. "But people think I'm younger because I'm small."

"Really? That doesn't work for me anymore." She chuckled, and then stopped to face me, her happy mood suddenly deflated by a sobering thought. "Do you think you can handle an extremely willful child?" she asked.

"That is my gift," I replied, embarrassed to have complimented myself so boldly. "That's what they tell me, anyway," I corrected.

"We'll see," she replied with an offhand shrug and then continued down the hall. "I'll show you to your room first, and then Mr. and Mrs. Trellis would like to meet with you in the study. Teddy's about somewhere. He wakes up very early. In fact, sometimes I believe the child never sleeps," she said in an exasperated tone.

"Teddy?"

"Theodore, the child you'll be looking after," Millie said. "But everyone calls him Teddy."

As we continued to make our way through the house, I tried my best to focus on the general floor plan. If I was to be shepherding my little flock of one about such a huge area, I'd have to know where I was.

Millie led me through several formal rooms, all of them elaborately furnished with the same oversized furniture. I'd never seen so many sitting rooms with fireplaces, and could only imagine the black cloud that would hang over the house if they were all burning at once. We continued to walk upon once-lustrous carpets now dulled by years of footsteps, and I noticed that in some places the carpet had worn through, revealing patches of the plain weave underneath. Toys were scattered about here and there, leaving little doubt that Teddy had free reign of this enormous and fascinating playground.

"Has the Trellis family lived here for very long?" I asked.

"Since the beginning of time," Millie replied with a flutter of her hands. "The house was built by Nathanial Trellis when there was nothing else around here but open fields and orange orchards. Nathanial Trellis was Mr. Trellis's great-great-grandfather. We passed by his portrait just now. He was the old man with the white beard and the pipe."

"Yes, I think I remember him," I replied, not at all certain that I did.

"He was an extremely religious man and very generous with the church. He made his fortune in the railroad business, and then a bit of horse racing on the side. Unfortunately, his sons and grandsons inherited his love of horses and gaming more than they did his religiousness, and countless acres were sold off over time to pay for gambling debts and who knows what else."

We passed by another elaborate living room somewhat different from the others in that it contained enough couches and chairs for at least thirty people to sit, and in the corner, near a row of enormous arched windows, stood a grand piano. In the convent there were two spinets, but I'd never seen a grand piano before and I marveled at the instrument's size, the fine black polished wood, and the magical aura it exuded. While gazing at it, I could almost hear the music drifting in from the past.

"This piano is a rare gem," Millie said. "It's a Steinway over a hundred years old, and crafted by Henry Steinway himself. I'm sure it's worth a fortune."

"Does anyone play?" I asked.

"Not anymore," Millie said, turning away, but not before I noticed the regret in her eyes.

"Maybe Teddy will be interested in taking lessons someday," I offered hopefully.

"Perhaps," Millie said, but she seemed eager to get on with things, and led me to an enclosed flight of stairs near the back of the house. "We could've gone up the main staircase as well, but I like to use these service stairs—they're quicker."

"Is your room up here too?" I asked.

"It used to be, but when my arthritis started flaring up I had no choice but to move downstairs. My room is near the kitchen."

As we climbed the stairs, Millie informed me that my room was next to the nursery, which used to be next to Teddy's parents' room, but that they'd moved the nursery to the east wing of the house when Mrs. Trellis's pregnancy advanced to the later stages. "Teddy fell into the habit of climbing out of his bed in the middle of the night and getting into bed with his mother and father. Mrs. Trellis wasn't able to get much sleep because of it."

It was evident once we'd reached the second floor that the

service stairs continued on to a third floor. These stairs were similar to the stairs we'd just climbed, but it appeared that the wood hadn't been cleaned or polished in many years, and the walls enclosing the stairway were stained with years of grime, upon which I could see the imprint of many little hands.

Millie noticed my interest as I hesitated and peered up into the darkened stairwell. "There's nothing much up there but a bunch of old junk and furniture," she said with a dismissive wave of her hand. "I've been meaning to have it all cleaned out and closed off, but I never seem to find the time."

"Is it the attic?" I asked.

"Not really," Millie replied, uncomfortable again. "One of the rooms is used for storage, but most of the third floor is where the servants' quarters were located many years ago. My room used to be up there too," she said with a nod. "But things have changed quite a bit since then. Now we have a cleaning service that comes in twice a week, and I'm the only live-in. Of course," she said smiling again, "now you're here as well, and I couldn't be happier."

As we made our way down the corridor toward my room, I slowed to admire the view of the courtyard below. It was rimmed by a graceful colonnade and a menagerie of flowers, and in the very center sat a sparkling pool, the bottom of which had been decorated with a colorful mosaic of the same two peacocks I'd seen on the front door. Small currents in the water made it appear as though the magnificent birds were waving their feathers at us.

When Millie saw me admiring the pool below, she said, "A few years ago that courtyard was featured in *House and Garden* magazine. Oh, what a fuss they made. Photographers milling about everywhere, designers and journalists acting as if they'd stumbled upon the Garden of Eden, when after all, it's only a courtyard with a pool."

"But it's so beautiful," I said, transfixed by the blue-green feathers glistening beneath the water. At that moment a woman emerged from beyond the portico. She wore a black kimono and slippers, and her auburn hair was pulled back into a bun at the nape of her neck. She pushed the silken robe away from her shoulders and let it fall to her feet, revealing a black maternity suit underneath. It was a wonder to me how she could look so graceful with her belly bulging as it was. It was the length and proportion of her limbs, the exquisite curve of her shoulders and throat. She kicked off her slippers and stepped toward the pool. She raised her arms while bending at the knees slightly and dove in without so much as a splash.

Millie shook her head and muttered, "Mrs. Trellis knows that she shouldn't be exerting herself like that." We watched as the woman swam the length of the pool and back again without stopping. Once in the shallow end, she stopped briefly to smooth the hair away from her eyes and then resumed her laps. Her arms and legs moved smoothly through the water, giving the impression that she was being pulled by an invisible tether from one end to the other. It seemed that if she wanted, she could go on swimming forever without tiring.

"I'm sure you can use the pool whenever you like," Millie said kindly.

I tore my eyes away from Mrs. Trellis. "Thank you, but I . . . I don't know how to swim," I replied.

"My goodness, I thought all young people knew how to swim. Even I know how, but I wouldn't be caught dead in a bathing suit at my age," she said, nudging my shoulder.

When we reached the nursery we peeked in to see if Teddy might be there, but all we saw was toys and clothing strewn all over the floor and furnishings. In one corner stood an elaborate Legos construction, and in the other a collection of farm animals had been shoved into the mouth of a stuffed dinosaur.

"Well, he's definitely up and about," Millie said with a nervous edge to her voice. I could only assume that she'd been the one assigned to look after Teddy since the nanny had left. No doubt she was the happiest of anyone that I'd arrived to take over. "He's probably downstairs with his father, the little dear," she said, chuckling.

My own room was remarkably spacious, with a large window facing the east garden. It had a double bed with a yellow lace coverlet, an armoire, and its own bathroom. I'd never seen such a large and luxurious bedroom, let alone occupied it. It seemed appropriate for royalty, but certainly not for a young girl who'd spent much of her childhood living in a hut with dirt floors, and then a small convent cell. I was quite overwhelmed by it, so much so that I didn't dare set my bag down.

"I hope you'll be comfortable here," Millie said.

"It's lovely but I don't need all this space, and I certainly don't need my own bathroom. Do you have anything smaller? Or perhaps I can set up a bed in the corner of Teddy's nursery."

Millie smiled as she took my suitcase and tossed it on the bed. "You'll get used it," she said, glancing at her watch. "But I think you should unpack later. Mr. Trellis stayed late this morning so he could meet you, and I'm sure Mrs. Trellis will join you as soon as she's finished with her swim."

We proceeded down the main staircase this time and Millie hobbled a bit as she went, telling me that her arthritis had a preference for her right knee and hand, which only proved how malicious a disease it was since she was right-handed. At the bottom of the stairs we made a sharp left and proceeded down a corridor I hadn't seen on my first tour. It was paneled in dark wood that gave it a distinctively gloomy feel, and a long russet-colored carpet ran its length. Millie turned and whispered to me. "Mr. Trellis can be somewhat impatient at times, so when he asks you a question, I suggest that you answer it plainly without too much fuss. He's quite brilliant and he doesn't like wasting his time."

"Thank you, Millie, I'll try and remember."

Millie continued, her anxiety increasing as we made our way down the hall, although it seemed that talking eased her nerves somewhat. "The senior Mr. Trellis was a renowned heart surgeon but neither Adam nor his brother, Darwin, were very interested in medicine. I think they were put off by the long hours their father worked, or perhaps by the gruesome nature of his work. I don't suppose that cutting people open, even if it is for a noble purpose, can be very pleasant. Dismembering a chicken is the absolute limit for me, and sometimes even that makes me squeamish. Anyway, Adam, Mr. Trellis to you, made a name for himself in finance, and his brother . . ." Millie smiled in spite of her nervousness. "I'm afraid that he's only managed to make a name for himself with the ladies. Oh, he's quite clever, and far too handsome for his own good, just not very focused, I'm afraid."

She chattered on in this way until she stopped before a door that was slightly ajar and knocked, her knuckles barely making a sound on the dense wood. I entered after Millie and beheld a dark, cavernous room lined with floor-to-ceiling shelves. By the faint light entering through the window at the far end of the room I saw countless books. But what caught my eye, in between and around the books, was the multitude of anatomical reproductions of the human body, as though torsos had been dismembered and then skinned in various ways to reveal the internal organs. There were also plaques and medical charts of different sizes and colors covering every inch of wall space available.

A man, who I assumed to be Mr. Trellis, sat with his back to us as he read. By the breadth of his shoulders and thickness of his neck I could tell that he was a large man. I felt suddenly anxious. With the exception of confession, I'd never been alone with a man, and I hoped that Millie would stay in the room until Mrs. Trellis had finished her swim and could join us. Still focused on his book, he turned around, revealing severe angular features and a thick shock of wavy chestnut hair that didn't appear to have seen a comb for some time. It was difficult to imagine that this coarse-looking man could be married to the refined woman I'd seen just moments ago. He seemed better suited to working in a quarry, digging ditches, or felling trees than he did to this sophisticated world. A chill overcame me, and I hoped that our meeting would be brief.

Millie cleared her throat. "Excuse me, Mr. Trellis, but the new nanny is here."

"Thank you, Millie," he said, barely glancing at her.

And to my great dismay she left with nothing more than an encouraging smile that did little to lessen my anxiety.

"Please sit down," Mr. Trellis said, waving me toward a chair without looking up.

I sat in the nearest chair and waited for him to finish his reading. I crossed my legs at the ankle and then uncrossed them. I passed my hands along my navy skirt and quickly examined my cuticles to make sure they were tidy, which they were. When he was done, he carefully marked the page he'd been reading and raised his head to look at me with dark eyes that smoldered like embers in a cave. Still, it was obvious that he was thinking about something else and was reluctant to shift his attention to me. I smiled politely and waited for him to begin, but this didn't seem imminent. He shook himself from his reverie, somewhat annoyed. "I'm sorry, what is your name?"

"My name is Ana," I replied with a polite nod.

"Very well, Ana. Mrs. Trellis will be joining us shortly. In the meantime . . . in the meantime . . ." He seemed at a loss for words as he focused and then refocused his eyes upon my face. "I'm sorry, why are you here?" he asked, his annoyance growing.

"I'm here to look after your son," I replied.

"Ah yes, I know that Millie has been making inquiries, but how did you learn of the position?"

"Mother Superior told me about it a few days ago," I replied, grateful to find that I was able to formulate a coherent sentence even though my heart was racing at a gallop.

At this, I noticed a flicker of interest mar his otherwise impassive expression. "Mother Superior? Millie didn't tell me they were sending a nun."

"Actually, I'm not officially a nun yet. I'm still in the formation process."

He smirked, apparently amused to hear this. "The formation process. It sounds like you're an amoeba." He studied me for a moment, as though I were the amoeba he was referring to. Then he stood up, his body emerging from his chair like a massive tree rising from the earth. "Did your Mother Superior inform you that this would be a short-term position?" he asked, looking down at me. "Our previous nanny, Flor, should be returning from Mexico in a few months."

"Yes, and that suits me very well."

He walked around his desk, and seated himself in the chair directly opposite me. "Really? Why is that?"

I shook my head, flustered and overwhelmed by his nearness. He looked even bigger sitting before me than he did behind his desk. "I . . . I would like to continue with my novitiate; I plan to take my vows in six months."

"Yes, of course," he said, glancing toward his desk. Perhaps he was eager to get back to his reading, and be done with this mundane exchange. "And you are from . . ."

"I was born in El Salvador, but I've been living here in the United States for over ten years."

He fastened his eyes upon me. "Tell me, Ana, why does a young woman from El Salvador choose to become a nun in this day and age?"

My mind went suddenly blank, but I was finally able to summon the response that had always seemed like the right one. "I . . . I was called," I stammered.

"Really? By whom?"

"By God."

He seemed intrigued, or perhaps he was just trying to pass the time. "Then why are you here?"

"Mother Superior told me that she thought it would be good for me."

"You mean to tell me that you've had the rare privilege of hearing directly from the Master of the Universe, and you listen to a mere mortal?"

I searched for an adequate answer while staring into his formidable gaze. I was certain that nothing I'd say would satisfy this strange man's curiosity and intellect. Suddenly I felt the muscles in my face begin to quiver, and I was afraid I might weep, but I managed to compose myself. "I . . . I . . . believe that God speaks through those in authority . . . at times . . . not always," I mumbled, feeling defeated.

Apparently disappointed with such a bland response, he leaned back in his chair and crossed one leg over the other. Again, I was discomfited by his sheer size and the potential power generated by his movements. It occurred to me that with one hand he could, with moderate effort, squeeze my throat and strangle me as I'd seen my mother do to chickens on many occasions. "Has your God mentioned anything to you about Teddy?" he asked.

"No, he hasn't," I replied.

"Well then let me inform you on his behalf," he said with a patronizing nod. "Teddy is quite a handful. He'll demand all of your attention every minute of the day that he's awake and even at times when he's asleep, as he's prone to nightmares. Millie's been having quite a time, and my wife is beside herself."

"I'm sure that Teddy and I will get on very well."

"I hope you're right," he said, reaching over for something on his desk. In the process a model of a quartered torso fell over on its side. It had been split open from the base of the throat to the pelvis, and the skin and bones were pulled back to reveal a repulsive arrangement of meaty organs, veins, and guts. I shuddered at the sight.

"My father was a surgeon, hence all the medical paraphernalia you see here," Mr. Trellis said.

I nodded and smiled politely, unable to turn away from the gruesome sculpture before me. I remembered the single white tennis shoe and the twisted foot. I saw the pink and blue intestines spilling over the dirt, and I closed my eyes.

"Fascination and disgust do go hand in hand, don't they?" Mr. Trellis asked, and I opened my eyes at the sound of his voice. "When I was a boy my father allowed me to witness a heart transplant. It's quite a sight if you can get beyond the stench. I've never forgotten it. In fact, I've come to think of it as life struggling with mortality, and from what I remember, it's a revolting struggle."

I nodded haplessly and tore my eyes away from the grisly sight.

Dr. Trellis leaned toward me so that his elbows rested on his thighs. He considered me with a most solemn expression, and I was struck by the length of his fingers, which he held together as though in prayer, fine dark hair sprouting from his knuckles. He frightened me, but I was unable to look away from him.

"It's much easier to ponder the mysteries of life and death, to meditate in prayer while kneeling in your pristine sanctuary, inhaling the sweet smell of incense, and losing yourself to the beauty of the choir. This is the antiseptic God that you worship, isn't it, Ana?"

I stared at him dumbfounded, wishing desperately for our meeting to end.

And suddenly, my prayers were answered. The door flung open and a little streak of a boy came running into the room at breakneck speed, calling out, "Daddy! Daddy!" at the top of his lungs. He flung himself at his father's immense frame and scrambled onto his lap. Mr. Trellis stiffened as he received his son's embrace and then awkwardly patted his back, clearly uncomfortable to have me witness such a tender scene. Nevertheless, parental adoration was visible in his eyes. I admired the little boy's ability to love this intimidating man with such courage and abandon.

Suddenly aware that they weren't alone, Teddy turned to look at me. He stared for a long while with his enormous chocolate brown eyes. Then all at once, his face fell into a frown. Before his father could say or do anything to stop him, the child sprung toward his father's desk, grabbed a small paperweight, and threw it at me with all his strength, but it was too heavy for his small arm and landed several feet short of its target.

"Teddy!" Mr. Trellis said, taking firm hold of his son's shoulders. "Ana has come to take care of you, and you must treat her with respect."

With mischief lurking in his dark eyes, Teddy shook his head violently and shut his eyes tight. "No like Nana."

"Teddy," his father bellowed. "You must apologize to Ana this instant."

But Teddy wasn't motivated by his father's command. Instead, he somehow managed to wriggle away from his grasp and run toward the door with the same exuberance he'd entered with moments earlier. Then he stopped suddenly and took several steps in my direction, his eyes challenging me. Yet something told me that he was more interested in the world around him than he was in his ability to make it bend and twist according to his will. When he was close enough to reach out and touch me, he said, "Nana is a poo poo and a pee pee!" And he started to laugh.

Mr. Trellis stood, looking even taller than before. "Teddy! You will not disrespect Ana in this fashion. If you don't apologize you'll get a spanking and go to your room." He took a threatening step toward his son, blocking his access to the door, and Teddy began to wail at the top of his lungs.

"No, Daddy! No!" he cried, as he scurried about the room like a mad squirrel while his father tried to catch him, but his stature put him at a disadvantage. Every time he came close enough to grab the boy, Teddy managed to dart out of reach, scrambling away from him time and time again. Mr. Trellis's face began to glow an ominous shade of red, while Teddy screeched and had the time of his life. Once or twice Teddy came close enough to me that I could've grabbed him myself and ended the chase, but I thought better of it, and instead tucked my feet in under my chair so that neither father nor son would trip.

Thankfully, the door opened and the woman I'd seen earlier in the pool entered the room.

"Mommy! Mommy!" Teddy cried, running toward her. "Daddy hurt Teddy! Daddy *kill* Teddy!"

Mrs. Trellis wrapped her arms around her son while scowling at her husband. "Adam," she said, "what's going on? He's literally trembling."

"Nonsense," Mr. Trellis replied. "That child isn't even afraid of God, and he owes Ana an apology."

Mrs. Trellis turned her beautifully sculpted head in my direction and smiled wanly. Her hair was still damp and her fair skin glowed like porcelain illuminated by candlelight. Her features retained the refined perfection of a child's, yet there was no doubt about her adult allure.

"What did Teddy do?" she asked. I was preparing to answer when I realized that her question had been directed not to me, but to her son. Teddy covered his face with his hands and buried his head in his mother's protruding belly. Mrs. Trellis noticed the paperweight on the floor. "Did Teddy throw something at the new nanny?" Teddy nodded fervently and pressed his hands more tightly over his eyes. "Daddy and Mommy have told Teddy many times that he is never to throw things at our visitors. Now Mommy and Daddy are very, very sad," she said, a pout curling her lips, but Teddy didn't respond. "Is Teddy sorry?" she asked sweetly, and he nodded against her belly again.

"There, you see?" she said, turning to her husband. "He's ashamed of himself and he's sorry."

Deflated and weary, Mr. Trellis made his way around his desk and sat down. "Let's leave it for now, Lillian," he said, nodding in my direction. "Ana's been waiting."

Mrs. Trellis's blue-gray eyes scanned me from head to toe. They were the ethereal eyes of the Madonna herself, and I felt myself squirm under their inspection.

"You seem far too young. Are you even eighteen yet?" she asked.

"Oh, yes," I replied, wanting very much to please her. "I'll be twenty-two in a few months."

She cocked her head to one side and studied me further. "Are you certain you can look after Teddy? As you've already seen, he can be quite energetic."

"I have no doubt that I can, Mrs. Trellis. I've worked in the infant and toddler center for quite some time now. And according to the mothers, I was the best teacher they had." I was surprised at how readily I was prepared to boast all of a sudden.

"Forgive me for being so direct, Ana. I know my husband will be annoyed with me for asking you this." Before continuing she glanced at him again and smiled ever so sweetly. It was impossible to imagine that he or anyone could ever be annoyed by such an angelic creature. She turned back, her expression serious. "Are you willing to protect my son with your life?"

Even Teddy, who'd kept his face well hidden, lifted his head to see and hear how I would answer.

"Lillian, please," Mr. Trellis said, frowning. "Is this really necessary?"

"Darling!" Mrs. Trellis gasped. "If anything were to happen to my Teddy, I couldn't go on living, or give birth to the child in my womb."

At this Teddy threw his arms around his mother and held her in an impassioned embrace while she stroked the fine dark hair from his forehead.

"I understand," I said, looking between Mr. Trellis's deadpan expression and his wife, who was the picture of maternal sorrow and sacrifice. "You want to know what I would do in case of an emergency."

"Yes, exactly," Lillian replied, flashing her husband a triumphant look.

I sat up straighter and said, "When Teddy is in my care, I promise you that I'll do everything a mother would do to make certain no harm ever comes to him, even if it means risking my own life." That said, I glanced at Mr. Trellis, whose aloof expression was unchanged. Then, as though disgusted by the scene before him, he turned back to his books.

With one hand on the small of her back and the other clutching her son's hand, Lillian Trellis graced me with a regal nod and said, "Very well then, Ana. It is my great pleasure to welcome you to our home."

I spent my first few days at the Trellis house following Teddy around, and as he scuttled about like a delirious little rodent with free reign of the pantry, I tried to engage him in some kind of focused play. It was the most exhausting job I'd ever had, and I was amazed that looking after one child could take more out of me than looking after a classroom of twenty or more. Teddy was curious and active to be sure, but the exhausting difference had more to do with the size of Teddy's playground. It was several acres and included three separate buildings—the main house, the guest house, and the garage, several fountains, and a multitude of rooms filled with an infinite number of places to hide. As it turned out, hide-and-seek was Teddy's favorite game, and I was constantly finding his toys in his favorite hiding places, under chairs, behind cabinets, and in hall closets. I'd also find them stuffed under chair cushions, and even dangling from the chandeliers. He particularly enjoyed tossing his lighter toys up to where he couldn't reach, like satellites that could widen his circle of exploration.

The only clear direction I'd received from Mrs. Trellis was to keep Teddy away from the pool, especially during those times that she kept the fence unlocked during her morning swims. Teddy was intrigued by the magnificent pool and often insisted that we linger nearby so he could gaze at it. "Teddy swim in pool," he'd say, pointing through the fence.

And I'd reply, "Your mama says you'll get swimming lessons very soon, and then you'll go in the pool."

He'd stamp his foot and say, "No! Teddy swim now, Teddy swim now!" It took some effort to pry his chubby fingers from the fence and distract him with something else.

Mealtime was especially chaotic. Usually, Teddy and I ate alone in the kitchen. He despised his high chair and much preferred the kitchen chairs that spun round and round on their base. I tried feeding him as he spun round, deciding that it was better than chasing him all around the house with a plate of food as Millie had been doing. Should Millie walk in on us, she'd shake her head in dismay. I thought we were making some progress, but Millie wasn't impressed.

Within a few days, I'd persuaded Teddy back into his high chair by telling him a story about a little lizard that grew into a giant dinosaur by eating in his high chair. This time Millie was impressed and she agreed to watch him for a few minutes while I tidied the nursery. On my way back to the kitchen I discovered a bizarre-looking stuffed animal resembling a skinny red monkey hanging from the pool fence. Next to hide-and-seek, Teddy's favorite thing to do was to toss his toys up over the fence and into the pool, the only spot within his immense playground where he was denied access. I unhooked it from the fence and went directly to the kitchen with the creature tucked under my arm. Millie was slouched in the chair opposite Teddy with bits of macaroni and cheese dangling from her hair and an impotent spoon in her hand. When Teddy saw me his face exploded with a smile and he reached out to me, his little fingers desperately clawing the air. "Elmo! Nana find Elmo!" he cried. I brought Elmo to him and he hugged it impossibly tight and kissed the tip of his nose many times over. Then he shoved him into my face and said, "Kiss Elmo. Elmo love kisses." I glanced at Millie, who looked at her wits' end. I could only imagine how many times she'd been forced to kiss Elmo since Flor left.

"Thanks for your help, Millie. I'll take it from here," I said and I gave Elmo a big kiss on his nose, as Teddy had. "Hello, Elmo," I said. "I'm so glad I found you. Now let's sit together and watch Teddy eat his lunch."

Teddy then grabbed Elmo and flung him across the room. He shrieked with delight when he hit the wall. "Elmo, fly," Teddy said. Then he grabbed his lunch and threw it with equal enthusiasm toward the wall, but his bowl didn't fly nearly as well as Elmo had, and it landed near Millie's feet, splattering her shoes and the floor surrounding her with macaroni and cheese.

"I think it's time for my nap," Millie said, shaking her head, and she left me with Teddy.

By my second week at the Trellis house I decided that the time had come to begin taming Teddy. It seemed to me that he had had too much stimulus, too many choices, and too little direction. I started by diminishing the size of his play area, but made it more interesting. Teddy was like a little spark jumping about, ricocheting off the walls, the furniture, the trees, and trying to ignite but never finding the intensity or heat to create a lasting flame. Only when he was sleepy did he slow down a bit, and only at these times did I sense the connection growing between us. At the beginning I'd lie down next to him wherever he decided to lay his head, which could be anywhere in the house or the garden. I felt ridiculous lying on the floor in the dining room or one of many formal sitting rooms, but at the Trellis house no one paid much attention. Should Millie encounter us on her way to the kitchen, she'd step over us or walk by without saying a word.

When he napped, it calmed Teddy to clutch two of my fingers and gaze into my eyes while sucking his thumb. He'd nod or shake his head in response to my questions, and remove his thumb to speak only when he felt particularly passionate about something.

"Is Teddy sleepy?"

He'd nod.

"Shall we go upstairs to your cozy bed?"

He'd shake his head furiously.

"If you're a good boy and sleep in your bed, then after your nap we can look for bugs in the garden."

He'd close his eyes while thinking about it, but I could tell by the grip on my fingers that he wasn't yet asleep.

"And then I'll read you your favorite story . . ."

His thumb would fly out of his mouth. "Three stories. Teddy want three stories."

"Okay, Teddy will have three stories," I replied, and he allowed me to carry him up to his room.

Mr. and Mrs. Trellis's daily routines eluded me. The only pattern I perceived was that Mr. Trellis departed for work by eight every morning, and Lillian Trellis took her morning swim almost immediately thereafter. She'd appear at the side of the peacock pool in her robe and slippers and enjoy several long and languorous laps, gliding effortlessly over the surface of the water from one end of the pool to the other. When she was finished, she emerged from the water like a siren, shook out her long auburn hair, and entered the house rewrapped in her robe. How she spent the remainder of her day was a mystery to me. Often I wouldn't catch sight of her again until two or three in the afternoon.

Mr. Trellis was usually away, and when he was home he spent most of his time in the study, sometimes until very late at night. I knew this because the corridor window just outside my bedroom door faced the courtyard, as did the window of his study. Just as his father warned, Teddy suffered from frequent nightmares and when I went to console him, I often saw a faint light glowing there. I remembered that Millie had said he was brilliant. Didn't brilliant people ever sleep?

I was careful to stay out of Mr. Trellis's way, but if I should happen to run into him, I could count on him not noticing me. Most of the time he brushed by me, preoccupied and muttering to himself.

Nevertheless, I'd always remain respectful and cordial, as Mother Superior would've expected. "Hello, Mr. Trellis. How are you today?" or, "Isn't it a beautiful day?" To which he'd usually reply with a grunt, as though I wasn't worthy of a completely articulated word or two.

If Teddy was with me, he'd let go of my hand and run as fast as his little legs could carry him and leap into his father's great arms that were always ready to receive him. Nevertheless, Mr. Trellis appeared uncomfortable with this display of affection, especially if Teddy was in the mood to shower him with a flurry of kisses all over his face. Teddy was as willful and fierce with his love as he was with his defiance, and at times his father would end these exchanges abruptly. When Teddy returned to me in tears after his father reprimanded him for being too forceful or rude, I held him and comforted him as best I could, encouraging him to be more gentle, while assuring him that his father loved him very much.

Mr. and Mrs. Trellis took their meals wherever the mood struck them. Sometimes I caught glimpses of them in the sunroom adjacent to the kitchen. At other times they ate in the dining room or even in their bedroom, which seemed very strange to me. Millie complained about having to provide "room service" at a moment's notice and often enlisted my help with carrying the tray upstairs, but I was grateful that she was always the one who entered their room. I was afraid of what I'd see if I went in there. Would they be lounging together in various phases of undress? Might I be confronted with an intimate scene that would require me to immediately avert my eyes?

One evening before dinner, while Teddy and I were crouched outside in the courtyard searching for roly-poly bugs in the dirt, I overheard them through the open window in the sunroom. "I can't bear it anymore, Adam," Mrs. Trellis said. "You leave this place every day, but I feel like a prisoner. I can't stand being shut in like this, waiting, just waiting."

"In a few weeks you'll have the baby and everything will be back to normal again. You'll see." His usually gruff voice was unrecognizably warm, almost tender.

They didn't speak for a moment or two, and then she said, "You know what would cheer me up? A party. . . . Oh please, Adam, it's been so long since I've thrown a party."

"That's a lot of work for you, Lillian. Why don't we get away for a few days instead?"

"But I love parties, and after the baby comes it'll be months before I'll feel up to it, and Ana's so good with Teddy, he won't be a problem to manage at all."

"Well . . ."

"Oh please, Adam, it would do me so much good."

All at once, Teddy startled me by throwing his arms around my neck and pressing his cheek against mine with all his strength. "What's wrong, Teddy?" I asked, chuckling.

He released me and opened his little fist, revealing three little black bugs curled up into balls. He inspected my hands one at a time, only to discover that I hadn't found any. Then he selected one bug from his collection and gave it to me. "Take care of it, Nana," he whispered in my ear. "Roly-poly loves you very much."

Later that evening, after Teddy had gone to bed, Millie and I were having a cup of tea in the kitchen. "Flor could never get Teddy to sleep this easily," Millie said, while nibbling on one of her homemade lemon cookies. "I've never seen him respond to anyone the way he does to you. Have you put some kind of spell on him?" she asked, grinning.

"Teddy's a good boy. He just needed a little bit of structure and guidance."

"Well, things are definitely calmer and more pleasant since you came."

"Thank you, Millie," I replied, very pleased to hear her say so.

She nudged the plate of lemon cookies toward me. "So," she said, "I hear there's going to be a party,"

"Yes, I heard something about it too."

"Well I think you should know that things will be a little different around here for a while. And it really isn't accurate to call it a *party*," Millie continued with a disapproving smirk. "It'll be more of a spectacle than a party, and Lillian will be the grandest spectacle of all." Millie waited for me to react to her comment, but I had no idea what she was getting at, so I helped myself to another lemon cookie.

"They met at a party in this very house. Did you know that?"

"Who?" I asked.

"Adam and Lillian, of course," she replied. "She was glued to his side the entire night," Millie said, "and she trapped him in that way that some women do."

"I'm sure Ms. Lillian never has to try very hard for men to notice her," I said.

Millie hunched her shoulders and motioned for me to come closer. "What I mean is that she got herself pregnant," Millie whispered, glancing over her shoulder. "It's the truth, so help me God. I counted the months and I barely reached seven."

I turned away from Millie's gaping eyes, feeling suddenly uncomfortable to be gossiping this way. "If that's true, then Mr. Trellis did the right thing."

"Well, I think it was a stupid and reckless thing to do. Who knows if he's even the father? He should've sent her off to the nearest convent and let the sisters look after her and her baby until he knew for sure. You would've looked after her, wouldn't you, Ana?"

It was strange to hear Millie mention the convent and the sisters at that moment. I'd been there only for three weeks, but I'd been so wrapped up in Teddy and in adjusting to my new environment that I hadn't thought of them very much at all. It seemed as though my previous life at the convent belonged to another era and to another person entirely, and this unsettled me a little bit.

I glanced at Millie, who was still waiting for an answer. "Of course we would've looked after Ms. Lillian and her baby, but every child needs a family."

Millie scoffed and popped another lemon cookie in her mouth. "Some family," she said, her mouth full of lemon cookie.

Once Teddy's schedule had normalized and he was taking predictable naps, I had more time and energy to familiarize myself with my surroundings. My favorite place to sit was at the edge of the fountain in the front garden. It was a mossy, tranquil place where the mist was transformed by the sunbeams into cooling prisms of light and color. In this place I felt as though I were suspended within a peaceful bubble where I could pray and meditate without being disturbed.

I much preferred the garden to the house, but one afternoon I decided to spend my free time exploring inside. On several occasions when Teddy was playing hide-and-seek, I hadn't been able to find him, and felt somewhat apprehensive about searching for him in areas I wasn't familiar with. Sometimes, Teddy would come down the stairs with his hands on his hips and a fierce little scowl on his face. "Nana no find Teddy," he said. As far as Teddy was concerned, hide-and-seek was no fun whatsoever unless I found him.

"But I was looking for you everywhere," I said. "Where were you hiding?"

"Up," Teddy said, pointing to the ceiling.

"In the bedrooms?"

"No. Up, up," Teddy replied with certain disdain.

I knew that "up, up" had to be the third floor, and although Millie had said that I'd never need to go up there, she didn't forbid me to go. It seemed to me that if Teddy was hiding up on the third floor, I should familiarize myself with it, and I decided to do so the first opportunity I had. The opportunity came one afternoon when the house was quiet. Mr. Trellis had gone to work as usual, and I'd overheard Mrs. Trellis informing Millie that she'd be at the hair and nail salon most of the afternoon. Teddy was taking his nap, and Millie had retired to her room after lunch for a nap as well.

I climbed the darkened service stairway to the third floor, taking care to go slowly as my eyes adjusted to the diminishing light. Cobwebs hung over the windows and down the walls like torn grimy lace. Although it was a sunny day, the windows on the third floor were much smaller than elsewhere in the house, which kept the space dark and cool. I took several tentative steps forward. The mustiness was thick in the air, and I wondered how Teddy was able to hide in such a scary-looking place. But there was no doubt that he did, for midway in the corridor just beyond one of the open doors, I spotted a bright red furry limb that I had no doubt belonged to Elmo. On my way to retrieve him, I passed several small rooms containing a few sticks of furniture that had been draped with sheets darkened by layer upon layer of dust. I shuddered to think that Teddy might have hidden under these sheets where black widow spiders could be lurking. I would ask Millie about locking these rooms as soon as possible.

I recalled how she'd told me that years ago when she was about my age, she'd been one of several maids who lived in these rooms. It was easy to imagine many servants cheerfully bustling along in their crisp aprons and caps as they went about their duties. There was even an old-fashioned contraption on the wall exactly like the one I'd seen next to the pantry in the kitchen. It consisted of a tiny bell and several glass knobs that corresponded to every room in the house. In this way the servants would know exactly where in the house their services were required. It was difficult to imagine Millie ever responding to such a summons, unless it was to throw her shoe at it.

I grabbed Elmo by his furry red paw, expecting him to be in yet another small room similar to those I'd passed, but found a much larger room used for storage. Through the murky light, I saw several stacks of books, and trunks and boxes of all shapes and sizes. Oil paintings were lined up against the wall, as well as two mannequins that had been yellowed by time, one much larger than the other. On the far shelf, my eye caught a collection of small white busts and silver cups tarnished by time, some lying on their sides. Clutching Elmo to my chest, I took several steps closer and picked up one of the little statues. I wiped off the dust with Elmo's already dusty paw and saw that it was engraved with the name Adam Montgomery Trellis. In fact, upon further inspection, it seemed that every statue on the shelf bore this engraving, while the cups were engraved with Darwin Bartholomew Trellis.

Just then I heard floorboards creaking in the corridor behind me. I turned to see a woman standing in the doorway, watching me. It was difficult to distinguish her face in the shadows and my throat tightened as my eyes focused and refocused on her silhouette. "I thought I heard someone up here," the woman said.

"My goodness, you scared me," I said, instantly recognizing Millie's voice, and I chuckled nervously, hoping that the sound of my laughter would dispel my fear. "Teddy's been hiding up here," I continued, extending Elmo as proof. "I thought I should come up and see what he might be getting into. Actually, I think it would be safer for him if we locked up these rooms, don't you agree?"

"It would probably be safer for all of us," Millie replied in a dreamy voice. She glanced at the little statue I still held in my hand. "I see that you've stumbled upon the trophies," she said wistfully.

"Is that what they are?" I asked. "I wasn't sure."

Millie nodded. "Darwin was quite the football player and Adam was an amazing musician—a prodigy, really. He won nearly every piano competition he entered, and there was great hope that he would become a concert pianist, but he hasn't played in years."

I was stunned to hear that someone as coarse and stern as Mr. Trellis would have any interest in music at all, and it took me a moment or two to absorb what Millie had just told me. "Why doesn't he play anymore?" I asked.

Millie's bright blue eyes became cloudy. "After the accident he lost all interest for it. I don't think he's stepped foot in the music room since."

"There was an accident?" I asked, carefully placing the statue back on the shelf.

Millie started to speak and then stopped herself twice. Then she rolled her hands up in her apron and began to move them in uneasy circles. "The boys were in high school when it happened. They were on their way to Adam's recital, Mr. and Mrs. Trellis and the boys. Of course they had a driver back then, a most wonderful driver, but it had just started to rain heavily and the roads were slick. They hadn't gone more than a few blocks when a truck ran the intersection and hit them at full speed. They said that in such a downpour the driver would never have been able to avoid the collision." Millie's hands grew still. "Adam and Darwin survived the accident, but both Mr. and Mrs. Trellis were instantly killed."

"And the driver?" I asked.

"He also died," she said, lowering her head. "Most of the staff was let go after that."

"How horribly sad, and you were working here at the time?"

"Yes, but you wouldn't have recognized me," she said. "I had copper-colored hair and a proper waist, if you can believe it." She beckoned me to follow her down the hall into one of the smaller bedrooms.

"This was my room," she said proudly. "And if you look out this window you can see what a lovely view I had of the garage." She chuckled and then sighed as she took in the sight. "The first time I laid eyes on him was from this very window. From here I could see him coming and going every day. He was such a lively, handsome man—so much fun to be around. His name was Michael, but everyone called him Mick. Mick and Millie—it has a ring to it, don't you think?" She smiled fondly. "We were inseparable, and Mick used to tell me that we were just like the two peacocks on the door and at the bottom of the pool. Mick and Millie—Millie and Mick," she said, enjoying the sound of it. Then she took my arm and walked me out of the room and down the corridor.

"Where is Mick now?" I asked.

"He's gone," Millie answered with a sigh. "He was the driver who died with Mr. and Mrs. Trellis, and he was also my husband."

ive

ANA OPENED HER EYES to find her beloved watching her with sleepy eyes. She couldn't be sure how much time had elapsed, but surmised by the light in the room that it was almost noon.

"You were dreaming," he said in a hoarse whisper.

"Just remembering," Ana replied as she leaned forward to smooth a lock of hair from his forehead. He was perspiring slightly, so she pressed her hand over his, which felt quite warm.

"Remembering what?" he asked.

"Many things," Ana replied, wondering if she should take his temperature, but then she recalled the time. "I'm going to make some lunch. It's almost noon and you didn't have any breakfast."

He swallowed with effort and asked again. "First tell me what you were remembering."

Ana brought her chair in closer. "I was thinking back to the first day I came here."

His eyes glazed over as he searched for the memory.

"Remember the first thing Teddy did when he saw me?"

Adam closed his eyes and furrowed his brow. Then a small smile began to tug at the corners of his mouth. "Lucky for you he was such a bad aim."

Ana chuckled. "He made up for it later with his hugs."

"What a difficult boy he was," Adam said, suddenly energized. "We're lucky you didn't run away the first chance you had."

"He wasn't so bad," Ana replied tenderly.

Thin as he was, she saw the muscles around his eyes and mouth straining and quivering. Then tears sprang to his eyes and trailed down his cheeks. "I must see him," he said.

"You will," she replied.

"Even if he never forgives me . . ."

"He will come," Ana said softly. "I know he will, and you'll speak to him again." These words were able to calm him for the moment, and Ana turned the conversation to Sister Josepha's arrival and how well she looked in spite of the fact that she was now walking with a cane. Adam listened, his eyes glistening and attentive all the while, but Ana knew that he was still thinking about Teddy.

After a while Ana went down to the kitchen to prepare lunch. As the soup was heating through in the pan, she kept her eyes on the portion of the front drive she was able to see through the window and prayed that before the soup was ready Teddy would drive in and bound up the stairs to reconcile with his father, sparing her the most difficult decision of her life.

She returned to Adam's room with a steaming bowl on a tray.

Already, he had managed to elevate his bed with the remote, which she took as a sign that he was feeling better. She blew on a spoonful of soup to cool it down and brought it to his lips. He obediently opened his mouth and swallowed.

"Now you," he whispered, nodding to the bowl.

Ana had half a spoonful, only to appease him, and then continued to feed him.

Once he'd had enough, which was very little, she began to separate the pills that he was to take at noon, but when she handed them to him he shook his head and pressed his lips together.

"What's the matter?" she asked.

He kept his lips pressed together and widened his eyes at her.

"You don't want your medicine?"

He shook his head.

"Adam, you know you have to take it."

"Not until you've eaten more," he said.

Ana was about to protest, but then she thought better of it, put the pills down, and proceeded to eat the rest of his soup. "I'm supposed to be taking care of you," she complained in between spoonfuls. When she was finished, she showed him her empty bowl and he took his pills. Soon he was sleeping again, and Ana felt her stomach turn sour. The desire to vomit would pass. She'd eaten the soup far too quickly and she just needed to take a few deep breaths and give herself time to digest. Stretching her legs out before her, she watched the rise and fall of her beloved's chest, the slight twitching of his left eyebrow, and before she knew it, the feeling was gone.

In a few minutes she planned to check on Sister Josepha, but for the moment she was content to sit where she was and remember back to the time when everything changed, not the external circumstances of her life this time, but the inner realm of her heart.

I now understood why Millie had warned me about the party preparations in advance. It all began with the consultant, who arrived early one morning with her clipboard and briefcase in hand to meet with Lillian. While Teddy and I played in the courtyard, they sat nearby to discuss their plans for the party. It was difficult to keep Teddy from throwing cumquats at them and laughing with delight every time the tiny fruit met its mark. Eventually I ushered him back into the house and we ran into Millie, who was on her way to her room for her midmorning nap. Millie had two or three naps a day and would become quite irritable if she didn't get them. Afterward, however, she was especially pleasant, even jovial. On this particular morning, she made little effort to hide her disapproval for the whole party business. "What a fuss," she exclaimed. "What a complete waste of time and money."

"Will many people be invited?" I asked, intrigued by it all.

Millie flapped her hand about in the air. "Who knows? However many there are, you can be sure that most of them will get drunk beyond the limits of decency. As I recall, last time a few ended up in the pool." Shaking her head in disapproval, Millie continued toward her room. "You won't see me for three days before and after," she snapped.

Later that same morning, Lillian and the consultant strolled the patio area together, chatting as they circumvented the pool. All the while, the woman jotted notes on her clipboard, nodding enthusiastically as Lillian spoke.

"What do you think about the fencing around the pool?" Lillian asked.

"I'm afraid it'll have to come down," the consultant replied. "Otherwise, we should consider another place . . ."

"Oh no, I'm sure we'll be able to work something out," Lillian replied confidently.

The party was in two weeks, and until then every day would be dedicated to its preparation. Additional landscapers were hired, and workmen came to repair loose tiles in the pool and to replace some of the surrounding brick that had broken or was altogether missing. New patio furniture was delivered a week before the party, and the old furniture was carted away. Work needed to be done inside the house as well. A different woman was hired to help Lillian decide how to rearrange the furniture. They spent quite a bit of time standing about in silence as they scanned the rooms. A word or two might pass between them, and suddenly the woman would spring to life to move a chair a few feet to the left, or to reposition a table slightly back, or to replace one painting with another. And then they would again stand in silence to study the new arrangement.

I was so fascinated by this process that I made it a point to hover nearby whenever preparations were being discussed. One afternoon as Teddy and I played with his Legos in the court-yard, my attention became diverted when Lillian approached with the consultant. They were talking about what they would drape from the trees just as Teddy was talking about the truck he was building and the various bugs he planned to put inside. He asked me a question, and when I didn't answer him right away, he put both of his hands on my cheeks and turned my face to look at him. Nose to nose, he stared at me with his big brown eyes, worried that maybe I didn't find his world so interesting anymore and that he was losing me to the adult world. "Play with me, Nana," he implored with real fear in his voice.

I took his hands and lightly kissed the little palms that smelled of peanut butter, his favorite snack that he happily ate with his fingers when he could. "Let's build a really big truck," I said.

"Yes, yes!" Teddy cried, delighted that I'd come back to him, and he rewarded me with a big hug as he pressed his cheek as hard as he could against mine.

I'd never heard Adam and Lillian argue, but one evening while Teddy, Millie, and I were eating in the kitchen, Millie held her hand up to shush me and inclined her head toward the door of the sunroom to listen.

Lillian's voice was elevated and shrill. "As soon as the guests leave we'll put the fencing back up," she said.

Adam murmured his reply.

"The consultant says that it has to come down," Lillian said more loudly.

Another murmured answer.

"No, I will not calm down and I will not lower my voice. I'm trying to make this a beautiful and unforgettable evening for our friends, and you don't seem to care at all!"

Mr. Trellis said something else we couldn't make out, and

Lillian replied in the same agitated tone, "Damn you, Adam. I'll be giving birth in a few weeks, and all I'm asking for is a little understanding. But it's too much to ask for, isn't it? Of course it is, because you are quite possibly the most stubborn and boring man I have ever known!" Her ranting degraded into a coughing kind of weepy sound and then we heard her footsteps as she ran out of the room.

Millie and I were so absorbed we didn't notice that Teddy had also been listening. When he heard his mother weeping, he jumped down from his stool and ran after her while crying out, "Mama, don't cry, Mama. Don't cry! Teddy kiss your booboo. Teddy kiss your booboo."

I took off after him, but by the time I'd reached them, his mother had scooped him up in her arms and was whimpering against him as he smoothed her hair with his chubby little hand. I stood nearby not knowing what to do, but decided that it was best not to interrupt such a tender moment. As I returned to the kitchen, I saw Mr. Trellis gazing out the window toward the site of the future pool party, his eyes filled with a cold rage that frightened me. If not for his finger tapping out an agitated rhythm against the table, he was perfectly still, and so preoccupied that I couldn't be sure he noticed I was in the room. Hoping to keep it that way, I walked lightly past him, almost on tiptoe.

"I know you're there, Ana," he said, not bothering to turn around. "In fact, I know you were on the other side of the door eavesdropping on us. I'm sure that our petty arguments are greatly entertaining to such a gentle and holy creature as you. Disturbing perhaps, but entertaining just the same."

Having said this, he turned to face me and the fierce accusation smoldering in his eyes left me cold. I wanted to run away, but I could only stand before him and mutter softly, "I was not eavesdropping, but it was impossible not to hear."

He continued to glare at me for a moment or two, then he leaned back in his chair and began to nod slowly. "You must feel very relieved to have chosen a life free of romantic complications like these. I'm sure you figured out long ago that love can wrap itself around your heart so what feels like a tender embrace one moment, becomes an agonizing constriction the next. You understand how the fool becomes addicted to this endless cycle of pleasure and pain, until one day he wakes up to find that his life is nothing but a desperate attempt to please and appease the source of his misery." He focused his eyes on me again, and for a moment he appeared almost hopeful. "But you're far too wise to play such silly games and that's why you chose differently isn't it?"

Feeling anything but wise, I didn't understand why he was saying such things or how he wanted me to respond. I could only focus on his immense hands that had tightened into fists and the fine throbbing vein running down the center of his forehead. "I . . . I really haven't thought about it very much," I finally said.

He sat forward and narrowed his eyes at me, as though he couldn't believe his ears as well as his eyes. "You haven't thought about it very much?" he repeated, derisively. "Well, then, you are undoubtedly even a greater fool than I." He stood up with an impatient sigh and left the room in the direction of his study.

I remained where I was, caught in a disturbing trance until the sound of Teddy calling for me from upstairs shook me free of it. I tried to dismiss the encounter with Mr. Trellis as meaningless, but I couldn't remember ever having felt more naked and awkward in all my life. And in an effort to ease my shame, I replayed the exchange countless times over the next few days trying to come up with other ways I might have responded to him in order to prove that I wasn't the fool he thought I was. Several acceptable alternatives came to mind, and I even toyed with the idea of confronting him with what my mother had taught me about men, but in the end, I had to concede that such a feeble defense would've only made me appear more foolish. The truth is that I had avoided thinking about how it would be to love or be loved because I was afraid of where it would lead me. This door in my life had been closed long ago, and for the time being that is how I wanted it to remain.

The day of the party finally arrived, and workers spent most of the morning up in the trees stringing colored lights through the branches. When Teddy and I saw them we pretended that we were on a trek through the Amazon jungle. Teddy laughed and laughed as he pointed to the treetops, saying, "Look, monkeys in the trees, Nana. Monkeys in the trees."

Lillian Trellis was upset that her husband kept to his usual schedule. He left at eight in the morning for the office with his briefcase in one hand and his jacket slung over his shoulder, barely glancing at the men suspended high above him.

Millie stayed true to her promise and disappeared into her room, although I ran into her occasionally in the kitchen. She was glassy-eyed and worn out, as though she'd spent hours crying alone in her room. I asked her if she was upset about something. "Just tell me when it's all over," she said, shaking her head miserably.

Lillian Trellis was electrified as she pranced about the house surveying the work being done and giving orders as necessary. After the lights were strung up, the workers began to drape a transparent fabric from the tree branches to create a whimsical canopy. Earlier, I'd overheard the consultant saying that when evening fell, the effect would be like that of stars glimmering through a fine veil of clouds, and I remembered how Lillian Trellis had gasped when she heard this.

The furniture began to arrive at about noon. But before the table and chairs were artfully placed around the patio, Lillian directed the workers to remove the fencing around the pool. Once this was done, the courtyard and pool area looked much larger than before, and Teddy was so excited that he started running about in circles, and then he headed straight for the pool, but I got to him just before he was able to dip his foot in the water.

I took hold of him by the shoulders and spoke to him firmly. "Teddy must never go near the pool without Nana, or Daddy and Mommy nearby, do you understand?"

He was startled by my intense reaction and his eyes began to water, but even as they did, his little foot edged toward the pool as though to test me.

"No," I said, giving his shoulders a little shake. "Teddy is being a bad boy, and Teddy is making Nana feel very sad." I too made my eyes go sad and watery looking, and I pouted a little too.

Teddy considered me with certain fascination, his mischievousness suspended for the moment. Then he threw his arms around my neck and pressed his cheek against mine. "Teddy sorry," he said. "Teddy not make Nana sad anymore."

I wrapped my arms around him and stood up with him still in my embrace. With his legs latched around my waist we made our way to the kitchen for some lunch. Teddy enjoyed a peanut butter sandwich and half a banana, and I had the same because Teddy insisted. It seemed very important that I appease him because more yesses early in the day meant that he'd better tolerate the inevitable noes that would come as the guests arrived. Lillian had already informed me that she thought it best if Teddy wasn't present for the party.

"I don't want to take any chances with the fence down," she said. "And it'll be hard enough to deal with Adam when he sees it."

By the time the guests had arrived, at six-thirty or so, Teddy would've had his dinner and bath. Lillian wanted me to go down at around seven so that Teddy could say good night, and then we'd go back upstairs to resume our usual evening routine. Once Teddy was asleep, I looked forward to peeking through the window overlooking the courtyard so that I might enjoy the spectacle from afar.

Before Teddy went down for his afternoon nap, I made it a point to play a boisterous game with him in the back garden, during which we ran in between the trees until we were laughing and panting. We were both tired, and soon after he closed his eyes I stretched out in my own room and dozed off as well. I awoke an hour or so later and quickly went to the window to check on the progress below. The tables had been set with turquoise and white linens, accented with shells and shimmering pebbles to make it appear as though a magical wave had passed over every table, leaving behind the ocean's gleaming treasures. A small stage had been erected at the far end of the courtyard for the band, and at the other end two men were setting up the bar. Earlier, the caterers had arrived and taken over the kitchen completely. Millie had ambled between them like a ghost, looking at no one and saying nothing as she made herself a sandwich and took it back to her room. She didn't even reply to Teddy's warm greeting.

"Millie mad," Teddy said, taking hold of my hand for reassurance.

"I think Millie might not be feeling well," I said.

"Millie feel better tomorrow," Teddy said. "And she play with us."

"Maybe," I replied.

I was preparing to check on Teddy in his room when I saw Lillian Trellis emerge from the portico already dressed for the party. She wore an exquisite salmon-colored chiffon dress that swished and flowed around her ankles and made her appear as though she too had alighted from the clouds. Her hair was brushed back from her face into an elegant knot, and she wore long shimmering diamond earrings. Stunning as she was, I had no doubt that her husband would take one look at her and decide that all the expense and effort had been worthwhile.

She strolled the perimeter of the pool, surveying the tables one by one, righting a fork that wasn't quite right, repositioning a flower or two to her satisfaction. When all was in order, she looked up at the netting and lights in the trees and frowned, not too convinced by the effect. Then she turned to survey the pool, and her expression softened with obvious pleasure. Floating on the surface of the water were countless faux lily pads painted in silver and gold, and perched on each one was a votive candle. These too would be lit at twilight. She glanced at her watch, and I did the same. It was nearly four o'clock and the courtyard was empty. The caterers were busy in the kitchen and the rest of the staff wouldn't be arriving for another hour or so, but Mr. Trellis was due at any moment, as he had agreed to come home early on this day.

It was then that I heard Teddy's high-pitched voice calling out, but it wasn't coming from his room, where I assumed he was still napping. He was already downstairs.

"Mommy!" he cried when he saw his mother on the other side of the pool. "Monkeys in the trees, Mommy. Monkeys in the trees!" he said, pointing up at the lights.

He ran to her and Lillian said, "Teddy, you're not supposed to be out here. Go back inside with Ana." She looked around for me, but I hadn't moved from the window. My eyes were glued to Teddy, as I willed him to stop running. But Teddy kept running toward his mother, shrieking with wonder at the new playground.

He bumped into a couple of chairs and the stemware rattled. Lillian placed her hands on her hips. "Ana, where are you, for heaven's sake!" she cried, and I forced my feet to step away, but it was difficult because leaving meant taking my eyes off Teddy, which seemed like the worst thing I could do at that moment. He was having a grand old time running around and in between the tables, making his way closer to the pool as he went. Then all at once, he saw a clearing between the table and chairs and he took off running at full speed toward his mother.

"No, Teddy. Stop, Teddy!" Lillian Trellis called, but it was too late. Teddy did a flying leap onto one of the lily pads in an effort to walk across the pool toward his mother, but disappeared beneath the water instead. Lillian stood frozen at the edge of the pool, her face blank. The only movement was the flutter of her dress around her ankles.

"Get him, get him!" I yelled, but she was completely oblivious to my calls, and the workers inside couldn't hear me. She stood there, motionless, as though in a stupor, and I realized that she was in shock. I bolted from the window and ran down the hall. I flung myself down the stairs, tripping and falling most of the way down, and all the while calling out, "Teddy! Teddy, Nana's coming, Teddy! Hold on, Teddy!" The more I cried, the faster I ran, motivated by the horrible image of my little Teddy gasping for air as he descended to the bottom of the pool.

I pushed through the tables and chairs, knocking several over, faintly aware of the sound of breaking glass as I rushed toward the pool. Out of the corner of my eye I saw Lillian Trellis as I'd seen her from the window, frozen in time, gazing into the water as though arrested by a hideous vision. I jumped in more or less where I'd seen Teddy go in, and the water rushed in over my head as I sank to the bottom of the pool. I flailed my arms and legs about, desperately looking through the hazy water for Teddy's red shirt. I saw him at the bottom of the pool, and by the grace of God managed to get myself close enough to grab firm hold of his arm. Then I pushed with all my might with my feet off the bottom toward the surface. As soon as we broke through, Lillian came to life and grabbed Teddy's shoulder, pulling him out of the water and onto the deck. But once my task was complete, my sanity returned like a lead weight around my neck, and I was unable to keep my head above water no matter how much I flailed my arms. As I sank to the bottom my heart pounded, and my lungs exploded from lack of air, and all the while there was this strange humming all around me, as though I could hear my soul seeping out of my body.

"This is how it is to die," I thought, and an indescribable peace overcame me as the whole of me drifted away toward the beautiful birds that lived at the bottom of the pool. Their glistening blue-and-green wings beckoned me to come closer so that they might embrace me, and I would live with them forever in their soft watery world.

In the distance I became aware of a splash, seemingly on the other side of the universe. Suddenly, an alien force encircled my waist and pulled me with astounding strength up toward the surface. "This is no human," I thought in the peaceful feathery cocoon that had enveloped me. "I'm already dead and this angel is taking me to heaven, where I'll be greeted by the other angels, and saints, Jesus himself, and even my mother." The angel then touched me with such warmth and longing that I was able to breathe underwater, and his spirit flowed through me, and I sensed the exquisite tenderness of his soul, and we were flying as one beyond this world.

I was laid on a rough surface, but the angel still lingered within me. I felt it on my face, my throats, my lips.

"She's fine, she's breathing, and it doesn't look like she took in any water," I heard a voice say, and I opened my eyes to see Mr. Trellis shaking himself over me like a giant dog. His wet clothing clung to his body, accentuating his great size and height, and I sat up, blinking the water out of my eyes just as he swept the hair out of his so that he could better see what was going on at the other end of the pool. There Lillian was prostrate with Teddy on her lap, contentedly playing with her earrings that dangled in his face. Whenever she looked away from her son to meet her husband's glare, she seemed to shrink just a little bit more.

"Don't look at me like that, Adam. I know what you're going to say, so just go ahead and say it," she said, trying to sound strong, although her voice wavered.

As he spoke it seemed that every word cost him a supreme effort, and then I realized he was still winded after pulling me out of the pool. "We agreed that the fencing would not be removed," he said, between gasps.

"No. That's what you demanded, but we never agreed to anything," Lillian replied with a haughty toss of her head.

Mr. Trellis continued to glare at his wife while I sat near his feet, shivering like a worm. Certain that somehow I was guilty by association, I hoped that he'd take no further notice of me, but he tore his eyes away from his wife to consider me next.

"And you don't swim a stroke, do you?" he asked, obviously disappointed.

"No, I . . . I'm sorry," I replied.

"How are you feeling?"

I felt shaky and bewildered, but I didn't want him to see me as weak. "I feel fine," I said.

"Come with me, then," he said, extending his hand and pulling me up to my feet. He surveyed the courtyard for a moment or two and then strode away from the pool toward the newly erected stage as I followed. He began searching around and under it and eventually found what he was looking for and handed me a few metal poles, although he took the bulk of them himself.

"What are you doing, Adam?" Lillian asked, horror-struck.

Mr. Trellis didn't answer as he started to place the poles back around the perimeter of the pool, indicating that I should do the same. I watched how he did it and copied him as best I could.

"Adam, don't you dare!" Lillian cried. But he continued setting the poles in one by one, ignoring her completely.

"Ana, leave those poles!" she commanded.

I stopped what I was doing, but Mr. Trellis finished his section quickly, took the remaining poles from me, and put them in place. Then he went around back for the netting and began to clip it to the poles.

"You're ruining my party!" Lillian wailed.

Mr. Trellis addressed me calmly. "Ana, I need you to hold the netting while I secure it at the base," he said, showing me where he wanted me to hold it. I did as he asked although it was difficult to work with Lillian sobbing hysterically in the background. All the while Teddy patted his mother's head, quite confused about what was happening. As far as Teddy was concerned, he'd just gone for a wild swim with his favorite playmate, and he couldn't understand why everyone was so upset.

"Don't you touch that netting, Ana. Don't you dare," Lillian ordered once she was able to catch her breath.

I released the netting at once.

"Ana, don't let go," Mr. Trellis directed more forcefully, and I retrieved the netting.

"Ana, did you hear me?" Lillian shrieked.

Mr. Trellis straightened up and placed his hands on his hips. "I've had just about enough of you, Lillian," he seethed. "Our son nearly drowned and you're worried about your party? Do you put this party before the safety of your child?"

"You know I don't!" she retorted, crossing her arms.

"Then be quiet and let us finish," he returned.

Lillian groaned and sat sullen for a while with Teddy still on her lap, watching her with big round eyes. Finally, she stood up with some difficulty and grabbed Teddy's hand rather brusquely. "How dare you disrespect me? I am not your servant, Adam, I am your wife!" she said and then she rushed off with Teddy in tow, saying, "Mama no cry. Mama please no cry."

As we secured the netting to the poles, few words passed between us and I tried not to look at Mr. Trellis, who was as somber as he was focused on his task. Once finished, he surveyed his work, and appeared pleased with it.

"I don't think that one little fence could possibly ruin a party, do you?" he asked, his tone decidedly lighter.

I breathed a sigh of relief, glad that his anger had subsided somewhat. "I don't think so, but Ms. Lillian is very upset. I doubt she's in the mood for a party anymore."

At the mention of his wife, he appeared to tense up again, and I immediately regretted mentioning her. He sighed. "You underestimate my wife. She can be an amazingly resilient woman when she wants to be."

"Well, then, I should probably go find Teddy so she can finish getting ready," I said, eager to leave the scene of the crime for fear that there might be another explosion. I'd already taken several steps away when I heard Mr. Trellis call my name softly. I turned to find him gazing at me with an expression I'd never seen on his face before. This time he didn't appear angry or indifferent or disapproving. Instead I saw tenderness, gratitude, and something more. Was it admiration? I couldn't be sure, but for the first time, I felt that I was seen, not as a child, a nun or a nanny, but as a woman.

"You risked your life for my son," he said. "I will never forget what you did."

As I looked into his eyes, I became aware of a powerful stirring within me that I couldn't identify as anything but awe, and it made me extremely uncomfortable. Not knowing what to say or do, I nodded and quickly left the patio in search of Teddy, only to find Lillian reclining on a lounger in the sunroom, her eyes moist with tears and her dress wet from where Teddy had been resting. When she saw me enter, she gazed at me adoringly and her fine manicured hands reached out to me. "Ana," she said. I sat next to her and she took hold of my hand, pressed it to her cheek, and started to sob. "Adam was right, you saved my little Teddy while I could only stand by and watch," she said once she had composed herself.

"You were in shock, Ms. Lillian. I've seen it happen to people before," I said, remembering how some of the children in the orphanage never recovered after the horrors they'd witnessed.

"But if you hadn't been there, my little Teddy could've drowned."

"Don't think about it anymore, Ms. Lillian. Teddy is fine, and people will be here any minute for your party. Everything is beautiful and you look lovelier than ever."

"God has sent you," she said. "God has sent you to take care of us."

After his dinner and a warm bath, Teddy fell asleep almost instantly. As I ate my dinner alone in my room, I became aware of a pleasant humming sound in my ears and a tingling sensation all throughout my body that made me feel as though I were floating. Thinking back on the remarkable events of that afternoon, I could've sworn that my heart had grown to one hundred times its previous size and that, somehow, I had redeemed myself and that I was changed because of it.

In pajamas and bare feet, I left my room and went down the hall to look out the window at the pool and patio below. The sun had just begun to set, and tiny lights twinkled from the tree branches like a canopy of stars. The guests were milling about and the merry sound of clinking glasses, laughter, and the hum of pleasant conversation could be heard. I felt like an angel looking down from heaven on mere mortals frolicking in the Garden of Eden. I caught glimpses of Ms. Lillian beyond the canopy, swirling through the crowd like a graceful dancer, remarkably light on her feet despite her pregnancy and delighting her guests at every turn. It was a wonder to me how quickly she'd recovered. Looking at her now, no one could've guessed that just an hour ago she'd been despondent beyond words. Mr. Trellis knew his wife well.

My eyes scanned the crowd for him, but I was unable to find him. I stood at the window and watched for a very long time. I watched as the dinner was served and cleared away and then dessert arrived. I listened as the band played and the guests danced on the patio beyond the edge of the pool where Lillian had stood frozen only a few short hours ago. I would've easily recognized his slightly hunched posture and his thick wavy hair. Even from such a distance, I would've detected his dark brooding expression. But the party was coming to a close and I was certain that he never made an appearance.

I took a deep breath, and the whole of me shuddered with satisfaction as I pictured him reading alone in his study and then standing over me after he'd pulled me out of the pool, the breadth of his shoulders, the intensity that shone behind his eyes as he looked at me. And as I thought of him, I slowly slipped down with my back against the wall until I was sitting on the floor in the dark, gazing now at the shifting patterns of light on the wall opposite me. I stayed where I was until the guests drifted off one by one and all the lights were turned off and the shadows crept in and it was pitch-black and silent all around me. And I was in my hammock, and my mother was rocking me to sleep. "Let's imagine, *mija*. Let's imagine that tomorrow we will wake to the sound of guitars softly strumming . . ."

Teddy's screams tore through my reverie. "Nana! Nana!" he cried, and I leapt up from the floor and ran to his room. When he saw me, his arms reached out for me, and I immediately embraced him and felt his little body tremble against me.

"It was just a bad dream. I'm here, and I'll never let any-thing bad happen to you," I whispered, careful to keep my voice calm, although I too felt frightened.

"There was a monster," Teddy said, choking down sobs. "Monster eat Teddy."

"There's no monster," I said stroking his hair, which was damp with perspiration.

"Monster eat Nana too," Teddy said, and his sobs lessened. "I hate monster. I kill monster so it won't eat you." He pulled away from me and looked into my face to see if I was sufficiently comforted by his courage.

"Then I won't be afraid," I said, guiding him back to bed. And I stayed with him, singing a lullaby my mother used to sing to me, until he was sound asleep.

> *Duerme, niñito, no llores, chiquito.*
> *Vendran angelitos con las sombras de la noche.*
> *Rayitos de luna rayitos de plata,*
> *Alumbran mi niño que está en la cuna.*
>
> *Now sleep, little baby, don't cry, little darling.*
> *The angels are coming with shadows of evening.*
> *The rays of moonlight spin fine threads of silver,*
> *To shine on my baby asleep in the cradle.*

Six

ANA ROSE FROM HER chair and peered into her beloved's face. He hadn't stirred, yet she noticed that his breathing was disrupted by halting spasms that seemed to emanate from deep in his chest. He didn't seem bothered, but Ana made a mental note to discuss it with the nurse when she arrived later that afternoon. It was then that she heard sounds coming from downstairs and assumed that Sister Josepha had gone in search of something for lunch. She didn't like being fussed over and was more than capable of looking after herself, but the kitchen was in such disarray that Ana knew it would be difficult for her to find anything.

She waited for Adam to inhale and exhale a few more times, and then reluctantly left him to go downstairs, but when she entered the kitchen she was surprised to find not Sister Josepha, but Jessie up to her elbows in soapy water, washing dishes and sniffling loudly as she worked.

"Jessie, I didn't realize you were here," Ana said, and the

young woman turned around. Her eyes were puffy and red, reminding Ana of how she looked when she was a little girl, but Jessie wasn't a child anymore. She was a young woman who was studying abroad and she had a new boyfriend who she described as "special," maybe even "the one." Ana marveled at the possibility that before too long little Jessie might be a wife and mother with children of her own.

Ana went to her and although Jessie was nearly a full head taller, she collapsed into the smaller woman's arms. "Oh, Nana," Jessie cried. "I'm so frightened. I don't think I can go up and see Daddy."

"I know it's hard," Ana replied. "He's sleeping right now, but when he wakes up, he'll be very happy to see you."

Ana helped Jessie to sit at the kitchen table, where Jessie dried her eyes with a napkin. "When I spoke to Peter a few days ago, he told me that Daddy was worse. I don't know what to expect. Do . . . do you think he'll recognize me?" she asked, her lips trembling.

"Of course he will," Ana said. "He's doing well today, a little better than yesterday, and he's been asking for you and Teddy."

"How can this be happening, Nana? Daddy was always so healthy and strong. I thought he was going to live forever."

Ana pressed her lips together, unwilling to discuss the matter of her beloved's death so candidly when she herself wasn't convinced at that moment that it was imminent, no matter what Peter and the other doctors said.

Jessie took hold of Ana's arm. "Please come upstairs with me, Nana. I don't think I can go by myself."

"I'll go with you," Ana said, patting her arm. "And then you'll see that things aren't as bad as you think."

Strengthened by these words, they left the kitchen and proceeded up the stairs with Ana leading the way. When they had nearly reached the top, Ana asked, "Have you heard from Teddy?"

"Yes," Jessie replied softly.

"Do you think he'll . . . ?"

"He says he's not coming," Jessie said abruptly. "That's what you were going to ask me, isn't it?"

Ana nodded, keeping her eyes focused straight ahead. But when they reached the landing, she said, "When your father asks you about him, as I know he will, I want you to tell him that Teddy will be here shortly."

"But that isn't true. He told me he's not coming, Nana, didn't you hear me?"

"Trust me on this, Jessie."

"I trust you more than anyone, but I don't want to lie to Daddy, especially not now."

They walked down the corridor arm in arm, saying nothing until they reached the door. Ana placed her hand on the door-knob. "Teddy will come. I know he will," she said, and they entered the darkened room.

Trembling with emotion, Jessie cautiously approached the bedside and gazed down at her father's withered face and body. She gently placed her hand over his, and her eyes filled with tears as she felt his pulse throbbing weakly beneath her finger-tips. Ana brought the chair for Jessie while she stood back near the window, grateful for this space of time in which a minute could last a month and an hour a year if she needed it to, until her beloved woke and brought her back to the present.

Two weeks before Lillian was due to have her baby, I passed her on my way to the kitchen. She was leafing through a magazine in the sunroom while trying to get comfortable on the chaise longue. Teddy wasn't with me, as I'd just put him down for his nap. Without looking up, she said, "Adam is still upset with me. He hasn't recovered from the pool incident." She closed her magazine and frowned. "He's always upset with me or with somebody. I've never known such an unhappy man."

Several days had passed since the party, and I noticed an unmistakable distance between them. Almost every evening since then, Lillian had taken her meals in her room while Mr. Trellis ate alone in his study. I imagined that matters didn't improve when he went upstairs to bed, and I wondered how men and women were able to sleep together in the same bed under such uncomfortable circumstances. "I'm sure he'll get over it once the new baby arrives," I said, trying to sound hopeful.

She looked up with large melancholy eyes and then with a flick of her wrist she motioned for me to close the door leading to the kitchen. "You know how Millie's always slinking around with those giant ears of hers," she said once I'd taken a seat next to her. "Do you have time to talk?" she asked.

"Teddy should sleep for another twenty minutes or so," I replied.

All at once, Lillian's eyes began to fill with tears and she covered her face with her hands. "Oh, Ana," she said. "Sometimes I feel like the worst wife and mother in the world. I'm so sick and tired of being pregnant. I just can't wait to have this damn baby so I can get my life back, not to mention my figure. Do you think that's horrible of me?"

"I remember the mothers at the center feeling the same way toward the end of their pregnancies. Try not to be so hard on yourself."

"But I should be thinking about the new baby, and getting all excited about her room and about all the little dresses I'm going to get for her, but the truth is I don't care about any of that right now. I just don't," she concluded with a shameless pout. She sighed deeply as her arms flopped down to her sides. "I barely have the energy to hold up my head these days, but the doctor says I should make an effort to walk a little bit every day. Would you walk with me, Ana?"

I helped Lillian to her feet, and we set off together arm in arm along the garden path. It was a beautiful summer day and quite warm, so I thought it best that we head for some shade.

"I've noticed that you and Millie are getting quite friendly," Lillian said.

"She's a nice lady," I replied.

"Don't let her turn you against me, Ana."

"Of course not," I replied, chuckling.

"You know she's a drunk don't you?"

"I . . . I . . . don't know what you're talking about."

"Believe me," Lillian said with an all-knowing nod. "Every time she says she's going for a nap, she's going for a nip as well, and if I'm not mistaken, she's partial to whiskey. Adam knows all about it, but he won't let me get rid of her."

I didn't want to believe this about Millie, but I couldn't deny that it explained the strange glassy-eyed expression I'd seen in her eyes after her naps and her sudden mood changes as well. "I'm surprised that Mr. Trellis tolerates it," I finally said.

"Normally he wouldn't, but I'm sure Millie told you all about the accident." She glanced at me. "Knowing Millie, she told you all about it before you even had the chance to unpack."

"It's all very sad," I said. "Millie must've loved her husband very much and she obviously still misses him."

Ms. Lillian leaned more heavily on my arm as we crossed to the path that would take us to the shadiest part of the garden. "Adam told me they were newlyweds and that Millie was expecting a baby. She lost it almost immediately after the accident. I suppose it was the shock of it all, or maybe it was the whiskey. Anyway, the point is that she takes advantage of Adam's pity for her. She can drink herself silly and spend all the time she should be working 'napping' in her room. Anything short of burning down the house, and she knows that she'll always have a job here."

"I didn't realize," I muttered.

"And that's why I couldn't bear it if you and I weren't friends because of her. I feel such closeness to you, Ana, as if I've known you all my life and not just a few weeks."

"Don't worry, Ms. Lillian," I replied, touched by what she had said. She'd never referred to me as her friend before, but I couldn't deny that ever since the night of the party, Lillian's manner toward me had changed. Genuine warmth radiated from her eyes when she spoke with me, and she looked for every opportunity to confide in me, even to share embarrassing tidbits, such as the fact that she'd wet her bed a few nights ago when the baby put pressure on her bladder.

We walked out from under the shade of the trees arm in arm and made our way toward one of my favorite spots. The roses had just begun to bloom, and their delicate aroma drifted all around us. It was enough to make you forget anything worrisome, but I sensed that Lillian's thoughts were as heavy as ever. After several minutes of silence, she said, "Everyone who knew Adam before the accident tells me he was an amazing pianist, but no matter how much I plead with him, he won't play a single note. Imagine how wonderful it would be for Teddy to hear his father play the piano."

"It would be wonderful, but I suppose it must bring up too many painful memories."

Lillian tugged on my arm with an air of exasperation. "Life goes on, Ana. I learned a long time ago that the best thing to do is to forget about the past and move on. I tell Adam the same thing, but he doesn't listen to me anymore." She sighed and stopped for a moment to rest. "Have you ever been in love?" I was confused by this unexpected question, but already I was getting used to the way Lillian's mind flittered about aimlessly at times. To follow her thoughts and her moods one had to be willing to flit and flutter as well or risk getting left behind.

"Me, oh no," I answered, chuckling. "I don't know anything about romance."

"Well, if you ever are, you'll know it because your heart races just thinking about your beloved, and you can't concentrate on anything else but him. You'll want to be near him, talking to him, touching him, loving him every second you're alive." She was silent for a moment and added, "That's how I always hoped it would be with the man I married, but I never felt that way about Adam."

I was shocked to hear her say this. I didn't think Lillian was the type of woman who would settle for anything less than perfection.

She took my arm and we began to walk again. "When Adam sets his mind on something or someone there's no escaping him. I was powerless against him, although I must admit that to feel such devotion from a man was unlike anything I'd ever experienced before or since. Of course, now I'm worse for it because these days he hardly knows I'm alive."

"Oh no, Ms. Lillian. I'm sure that you're wrong. Mr. Trellis still loves you very much."

"How can you be so sure?"

"I see it in the way he looks at you. It's as though the love in his heart is flooding his soul and flowing out of his eyes."

Hearing this, Lillian started to laugh. "My goodness, Ana. You may know more about romance than you think."

As we walked along, I realized that I felt not only like a friend, but like the member of a family again. And as the days and weeks passed, memories of my other life and family began to ease their way back into my mind, sometimes flooding me with so many emotions and images that on several occasions I awoke confused about where I was. I could've sworn that I'd been gently rocking in my hammock and that the scent of the jungle was all around me, that Mama was asleep next to me and that I could hear my cousin Carlitos snoring nearby.

When I was a child and turned to Sister Josepha for comfort, she told me that only time could heal the wounds of the heart and that the deeper the wounds, the more time needed to pass. She also said that sometimes these wounds were so deep that no amount of time would ever heal them and only God's infinite love could offer hope. I surmised that with the years that had passed and God's grace to aid the process, my heart had finally healed enough to make me start remembering.

A few nights later, I heard a frantic knock on my bedroom door and bolted upright in bed, worried that something might be wrong with Teddy. And then I heard Mr. Trellis calling my name on the other side of the door, which caused my pulse to race.

"Ana, wake up," he said.

He opened the door and I held my blankets up around my chin, wondering what would bring him to my room in the middle of the night. In the dim light I saw that he was dressed in blue jeans and that his shirt was hanging out. "Lillian needs you," he said.

"Is something wrong?" I asked, careful to pull my nightdress down around my thighs as I got out of bed.

"Just get downstairs as soon as you can," he said abruptly, while averting his eyes.

"I'll let Millie know, in case Teddy wakes up."

"I've already done that," Mr. Trellis said. "And hurry. Lillian delivers very quickly."

I threw on my clothes and rushed downstairs to find Lillian waiting for me at the back door while Mr. Trellis pulled the car around. Her face was pale and twisted in pain, and when I took her hand, she squeezed down hard, nearly breaking my bones. "It's worse than before," she said, panting after the contraction had passed. "They say you forget the pain, and they're right. I don't remember it ever being this bad."

"I'm sure it won't be so bad once you get to the hospital," I said, starting to shake, but I tried to calm myself, not wanting to add to her anxiety.

"Thank God you're here," Lillian said, laying her head on my shoulder. "I feel such peace when you're near."

Mr. Trellis helped Lillian into the front seat while I scrambled into the back, and we took off. I'd never been in such a fast-moving vehicle in all my life. Traveling through the dead of night as we were, I felt like an astronaut pitching through infinite space, and all the while Lillian moaned and started to scream as another contraction started. I prayed with all my heart that she not deliver in the car. "Oh please, God, don't let her give birth in the car. I won't know what to do. Please, God."

Thankfully, my prayers were answered, and the medical personnel were waiting for us with a wheelchair in front of the hospital. They quickly wheeled Lillian up to the maternity ward as Mr. Trellis and I followed close behind them. His eyes were bright and shiny and his cheeks were flush, reminding me of how Teddy looked after a bad dream.

Once in the delivery room, Lillian continued to scream as the doctor examined her, and I couldn't for the life of me understand why they didn't give her something for the pain. Women in my village had always screamed as though they were being skinned alive, but this was a modern hospital, so I expected that things would be different here. I held my breath and held her hand, trying to remain composed and encouraging for her sake.

Mr. Trellis held her other hand and placed a cool compress on her forehead. He was trying his best to remain calm too, but when the nurse and other technicians came in and out of the room, I noticed him eyeing them with increasing disdain.

When her primary nurse came in to take her blood pressure for the third time, he was unable to contain himself any longer. "Can't you give her something for the pain? It's getting worse."

"It's too late for that, Mr. Trellis," the nurse replied curtly. "We can't give the mother anything when she's so advanced in her labor. It's not good for the baby."

Mr. Trellis's face was getting redder by the second. "There must be something you can do for her. Where is her doctor? Why isn't he here yet?"

"I'll see what I can do," the nurse said, and she left just as Lillian released another bloodcurdling scream that caused Mr. Trellis and me both to jump. She was writhing in agony and this time I was certain that she wouldn't survive. Mr. Trellis's previously flushed face had turned white, but he didn't leave her side. How different from the men in my village who left their women to give birth while they got drunk with the other men in the square. Sometimes it took the new father more time to recover from his hangover than it took the mother to recover from childbirth.

Listening to Lillian's groans, I became lost in the furrow between Mr. Trellis's brow and the drops of perspiration gathering along his upper lip, and I remembered that I had

experienced this before in another life and another time. I closed
my eyes and Lillian's screams became *Tía* Juana's screams that
could be heard from the banks of the river, prompting Carlitos
and me to look up from our play. Carlitos immediately turned
back to the pile of rocks he'd been collecting, knowing that
nothing would be required of him as his new little brother or sister entered the world. I was too frightened by the sound of *Tía*
Juana's wailing to continue playing. I dropped the stones I held
to the ground and waited and hoped that it was not as I feared.
Perhaps my aunt was merely upset that a dog had defecated outside the door. One time after she'd stepped into a pile of shit, she
wailed so loudly that I was certain someone had stabbed her in
the heart.

But when I heard the moaning again, I had no doubt that *Tía*
Juana was finally in labor. Mama called for me and I ran back
to our hut without a word to Carlitos. Just as I ducked into the
door, I turned to see him watching me, his eyes wide with wonder and fear. I felt exalted and strangely powerful to be crossing
this mysterious feminine threshold for the first time, but I had
no idea of the horror this complete initiation would bring.

The first thing I saw when I entered the darkened hut was
Tía Juana writhing on a blanket on the floor, naked to the waist,
with her legs spread open as the older midwife, Mama, and two
other neighbors kneeled next to her.

"Ana, bring me the blanket on the table," Mama said to me,
not looking up. I gave her the blanket and she placed it under
Tía Juana's head. *Tía* Juana's face was pale and dripping with
sweat. Her eyes rolled back in their sockets and her jaw was
clenched so tightly that I could hear her teeth grinding, certain

that they would loosen and that before long she'd be spitting them out one by one.

The women were speaking in hushed tones as *Tía* Juana moaned and wailed. At times she arched her back off the ground and her entire body shuddered. Mama had recently told me that God intended women to suffer during childbirth so that they would love their children more deeply. I didn't understand this connection, but Mama wasn't able to explain it any better. And she said that because I'd just started menstruating, she wanted me to be present when *Tía* Juana had her baby so that I would begin to understand the commitment and suffering children brought to a woman's life.

She directed me to sit near *Tía* Juana's feet, and from that vantage point I was able to see the oozing cleft between her legs. With every scream and heave of her body, it grew wider and wetter, until finally a thick dribble of blood and water began to flow. Then all at once she released a watery stool that filled the little hut with such a foul odor I nearly fainted. Mama used a rag to clean up the mess and then she tossed it to me, saying, "Don't let the dogs get to it. I'm running out of rags."

Not knowing what else to do, I placed the stinking bundle just outside the door. If the dogs got to it, I'd rip up my own blanket for rags, anything to avoid getting near it again. By the time I returned to my place at *Tía* Juana's feet, my head was spinning and my stomach was turning somersaults. Some invisible and merciless force was stretching her open until the space between her legs had grown to ten times the size it had been moments earlier. Unable to stand it, I wrenched my eyes away from the gruesome sight. And then I heard a strange gurgling sound coming from deep down in *Tía* Juana's throat as though she were drowning, and I turned to see just as the midwife separated the torn layers of flesh from between *Tía* Juana's legs to reveal a bloody mass of hair and congealed pus that looked to me like a decomposing animal. *Tía* Juana wept and wailed and writhed some more as she pushed and pushed. The two women held her legs while Mama pressed down on *Tía* Juana's enormous belly. The midwife then plunged her bloody fingers into Tía Juana's crotch, not at all deterred by her desperate screams and pleas to stop. And then a great shock of fluid sprouted out of her like a fountain, covering me with blood and a thick, smelly fluid. I couldn't help myself, I screamed even more loudly than *Tía* Juana and ran out of the hut as fast as I could. I ran directly to the river, where Carlitos was still working on his rock structure, and I dove into the river's muddy waters. Carlitos watched me with a mixture of shock and curiosity, but he didn't ask what happened. I think he was afraid to know, and I was glad because I didn't have the words to describe it.

Later that afternoon when I returned to the hut, all was quiet and the new baby lay sleeping quietly next to *Tía* Juana in her hammock. Mama was at her sewing machine and I could tell by the long look she gave me that she was disappointed in me.

"I'm sorry I ran away, Mama," I whispered so as not to wake *Tía* Juana and her baby.

She nodded and turned back to her sewing. "Seeing the birth of a child will give you strength when your time comes, and it will also remind you to wait until the time is right."

I shook my head adamantly. "That's okay because today I decided that I'm never going to be a mother."

Mama's eyebrows came together. "Really? Why not?"

I was surprised that she needed to ask, but I answered her anyway. "Because I don't want to scream in pain and bleed between my legs and feel my body splitting apart when the baby comes out."

Mama set her sewing aside. "What are you going to do if you fall in love with a man who wants to have children? What are you going to tell him?"

I crossed my arms. "I'll tell him that if he really loves me, then I should be enough for him."

At this Mama laughed out loud, causing *Tía* Juana to stir and mumble in her sleep. Then she whispered, "If you ever find this man, throw your arms around him and never let go. Of course, you'll discover that you were dreaming and that the man in your arms is your own pillow." She waved a dismissive hand and turned back to her sewing. "Such a man doesn't exist, *mija.*"

I wondered if Mama was right as I observed Mr. Trellis's frown deepen after Lillian squeezed down on his hand harder than before. Ms. Lillian squeezed my hand as well, and although I tried not to, this time I grimaced in pain. The nurse, who'd gone for the doctor before, was watching Mr. Trellis with certain interest, while the doctor, a small, bearded man, kept disappearing between the canopy of sheets over Lillian's parted knees. Deciding earlier that the baby was no longer at risk, he'd administered an anesthetic which had helped take the edge off Lillian's labor pains, but it was apparent that his calm demeanor wasn't easily disturbed by the agony of his patients. In fact, he appeared to be almost bored as he ducked in and out from between Lillian's legs.

"Would you like to see the crown?" he asked Mr. Trellis, who declined with a furtive shake of his head.

The doctor turned to me next. "How about you?

The thought of looking between Ms. Lillian's legs horrified me for many reasons, and I was about to decline as well when I was startled by a loud crash. And when I looked up, Mr. Trellis was gone.

"Yep, just like I thought," the nurse said, shaking her head. "They're never as tough as they seem." And she went to attend to Mr. Trellis, who was lying on the floor on his back with his eyes closed as if he'd just decided to take a quick nap. Stripped of his gruff defenses, he looked as vulnerable as a child, and I envied the nurse as she knelt beside him to place a pillow under his head. She then produced a tube of something from her pocket, and wafted it under his nose. Mr. Trellis came to almost immediately, blinking his eyes in a bewildered manner just as Teddy did when he was startled awake.

Lillian had just recovered from a strong contraction, but when she realized what had happened, she started to laugh. "Oh, Adam, you're so funny. You actually fainted. Isn't he funny, Ana?"

I wasn't sure what to do or say. I could see from the wounded look in his eyes that Mr. Trellis was quite humiliated and that he desperately wanted to get up off the floor. "Can you help me up?" he asked the nurse.

"I don't know. You're a pretty big guy," she said, chuckling. "And we can't have you falling all over the place. I think we'll all be safer if you stay put for a while."

"Please," he said, his eyes pleading with her.

I managed to release my hand from Lillian's grip and knelt down to help. Mr. Trellis draped one arm over each of our shoulders. He was heavier than I expected, and his torso was solid and unforgiving against me, but between the nurse and me, we managed to get him to the chair, where he surrendered a small smile of gratitude.

A few minutes later, baby Jessica entered the world, and when the doctor held her up from beneath the sheet for her parents to admire, I was speechless with awe at the writhing little creature. I helped the nurse count her tiny fingers and toes and noted for the first time the sweet dimples on her chubby cheeks. When she bellowed with the full strength of her lungs, I was amazed at what a loud sound such a small being could make.

Mr. Trellis stood nearby, but not too close, and gazed at his new baby daughter as though he were looking into the face of the Almighty.

"She's so beautiful," he muttered.

The nurse then held the baby up so that we might see her more clearly, but I was unable to look away from Mr. Trellis's face. The love pouring out from his eyes was like the sunrise, and it held me spellbound.

Adam turned to his grown daughter, his eye lids fluttering. "Who's here?" he asked.

"It's me, Daddy," Jessie replied softly while swallowing her tears.

"Who?" he asked, his eyes still closed.

"It's Jessie, your daughter," she answered in a stronger voice.

He opened his eyes and his face broke into a brilliant smile. His pale skin became infused by a peachy glow, and his entire body appeared to strengthen. "Jessie," he whispered, "how long have you been here?"

"Not long."

He struggled to sit up and Ana quickly helped him raise the bed until he was comfortable, and then she stepped back.

"You're so . . . beautiful," he said.

Jessie laughed weakly and raked her uncombed hair back with her fingers. "If you say so, Daddy."

He coughed and swallowed hard. Ana brought a cup of water to his lips and he took a small sip. Turning to his daughter, he said, "Now, tell me about . . . what's his name?"

Jessie laughed, but this time with the typical pleasure she exuded when her father teased her. "Come on, Daddy, you know his name."

"No, I swear," he said, looking to Ana for validation. "I'm forgetting everything these days, isn't it true, Ana?"

"Some things," Ana returned with a teasing smile of her own. But she was amazed by his sudden transformation.

"His name is Jacob, Daddy," Jessie said, rolling her eyes.

"Jacob Daddy," Adam repeated with a baffled expression. "That's a very strange name."

"No, just Jacob, Daddy," Jessie said, giving her father a playful poke in the arm. "I mean Jacob, just Jacob."

"Jacob Just, or Just Jacob?" Adam asked, looking more perplexed than before.

Jessie giggled and covered her face, just as she did when she was three years old. "Oh, Daddy," she said, shaking her head.

Adam was delighted by his daughter's predictable reaction and then his smile faded. "Has Teddy met him?" he asked.

"Not yet," she replied, sobering up at the mention of her brother's name. "Nobody has."

Adam's face slackened just a bit. "Have you spoken with your brother lately?"

"I spoke with him just yesterday, but you know Teddy—he doesn't like talking on the phone very much."

Adam closed his eyes and sank back into his pillows, his previous exuberance deflating with every second that passed.

Jessie glanced back at Ana, who gave her an encouraging nod. "But he sounds well, and . . . and he said that he's coming to see you, Daddy."

Adam opened his eyes and there was a glint of hopefulness beyond the fatigue. "Is he?"

"Yes," she replied.

His chest expanded as he took a deep breath and then he raised his head to look at his daughter. "How's that accounting class coming along?" he asked.

"Please don't bring that up again. I'm *this* close to dropping it," Jessie said, pinching the air with her thumb and forefinger.

"Accounting is easy," he said.

"Easy for you, but not for me."

Satisfied that all was going well, Ana slipped out of the room intent on a cup of tea, but decided to linger in the corridor to enjoy the happy sound of their conversation that was infinitely more soothing than a cup of tea. As she stood outside the door, her eyes rested on the portrait hanging before her. In it, Lillian was dressed in white with both of her children nestled at her feet. It was a charming picture, but Ana thought the painter hadn't succeeded in capturing the true essence of Lillian's character. He'd chosen to depict her as a matron and had failed to see beyond the angelic perfection of her features, the flawless complexion and graceful posture. She was a lady to be sure, but a lady ruled by complex motivations and lurid desires that Ana would never completely understand.

As lovely as Lillian was during her pregnancy, she became even more so a couple of months after giving birth, flitting between her various adventures like a magical fairy. The children and I often halted our play to watch her float across our world until she was out of sight, which she was most of time. She was so engaged in the resurrection of her social life that she now rarely had time for her morning swims.

Nevertheless, when it was time for Teddy's first day of preschool, Lillian cleared her morning schedule so she could drop him off. They were all smiles when they left, but returned in less than an hour dissolved in a torrent of tears. I had Jessie in the bath when I heard her talking with Millie about what had happened, but quickly bundled her up in a towel and carried her downstairs.

Teddy appeared to have calmed down somewhat, but Lillian was still distraught. "Oh, Ana," she said, when she saw me descending the stairs. "I can't go through with it. I just can't."

"What happened?" I asked, taking note of Teddy's shamefaced expression.

"Teddy wouldn't stop crying, and to think that he was going

to be there all alone with all those strange children for three solid hours. I just couldn't do it."

"But all kids cry on their first day," I said. "Sometimes the parents cry too, but everyone gets over it eventually."

"That's what I told her," Millie said, shaking her head. "You can't let a few tears get in the way. It's all perfectly normal."

Lillian flashed Millie a contemptuous look, and then her mouth curled into an endearing pout. "How can that be normal—all those parents and children crying their eyes out? How can that be good for anybody?"

Jessie was starting to slip from my arms, so I repositioned her on my hip and shifted my weight to the other leg. "Teddy has to go to preschool," I said. "He'll be behind the other kids when he starts kindergarten if he doesn't."

Lillian thought about what I said as she stroked Teddy's hair. Then she knelt before him so they were at eye level. "Teddy, you saw how upset Mommy was today, didn't you?"

Teddy nodded, nervously twisting his little fingers into one another.

"And you don't want Mommy to get upset anymore, do you?"

Teddy shook his head.

"Well then, how about if Nana takes you to school tomorrow?"

He shook his head and pushed out his bottom lip. "Teddy no like school. Teddy stay home with Nana and baby."

"But Teddy's a big boy now," Lillian replied gently. "And Teddy has to go to school so he can be smart and make lots of money like his daddy."

Teddy glowered at her and stomped his foot for good measure. Lillian glanced up at me and asked, "Do you mind, Ana?"

Later, when Millie and I were alone in the kitchen, she asked, "And who do you suppose will be driving you and Teddy to school every morning? Me," she answered with a stiff nod. "And will Mommy Dearest be available to watch her own baby while we take her son to school for her? No, she won't. How can she look after her baby and have her hair done at the same time?"

"Don't worry, Millie. I'll put Jessie in her car seat and she'll sleep all the way there and back, you'll see."

"Oh, I'm not worried," she said. "Disgusted is more like it."

"And while we're planning it," I said in an offhand manner, "would you mind terribly taking your afternoon nap after we pick Teddy up? It's just . . . in case you oversleep, I don't want to keep him waiting."

Millie thought about this for a moment. "I don't mind," she said, looking away. "But you should think about learning how to drive." Her eyes were twinkling when she turned to me again. "Or aren't nuns allowed to drive?"

The next morning I walked with a very somber Teddy to his classroom while Millie and Jessie waited in the car. Up until that moment Teddy had been doing pretty well. I'd kept his mind occupied by talking about a trip to the zoo we planned to take over the weekend, but once he saw the door to his classroom, he refused to take another step.

"Teddy no go today," he said, his little face set like stone.

"You can do it, Teddy," I said walking past him, but when I turned around he was standing in the same spot, glaring at me and defiant as ever.

"What should I tell Mrs. Crandall?" I asked.

"Tell her Teddy says no!" he yelled.

"Mrs. Crandall will be sad."

"No!" Teddy shrieked, folding his arms tightly across his chest.

"Oh well," I said with a sigh and a shrug. "I guess Jessie will have to take your place, and then she'll be the big kid going to school. When your daddy comes home from work tonight, we'll tell him what a big girl Jessie is and all about school." I began walking toward the car as though to get Jessie, but I hadn't taken three steps when Teddy ran up to me screaming and pushing on my legs. "No, Nana! No! Teddy big boy. Teddy big, not Jessie."

"Well then, which kid is going to school? Teddy, or Jessie?"

His lips trembled when he said, "Teddy go."

He wailed like a wounded sea lion when I left him with Mrs. Crandall, but by the end of the week he merely whimpered and was able to give me a halfhearted wave, as though he'd resigned himself to the indifferent cruelty of the world. By the end of the second week, he couldn't wait to go to school and hardly took the time to wave at all when I said good-bye.

"He's a big boy now, Jessie," I said as we watched him through the window, and when he glanced at us, "Let's wave to your brother." Jessie stared at me and gave me a toothless grin when I lifted her chubby little hand and flapped it about. Before too long, she was waving all by herself.

And by the end of the month, upon Millie's insistence, I began taking driving lessons.

From the day she was born, Jessie had always been the picture of health. I loved gazing into her bright eyes and imagining how she would be when she was all grown up. Her little body was strong, and she was able to hold her head up almost immediately and look around her crib to observe everything around her. She could stare at the tree branches swaying outside her bedroom window for long stretches of time and much preferred them to the zoo animal mobile that hung over her crib.

Despite her obvious fortitude, at six months she developed a cough that wouldn't go away. She lost so much weight that her chubby thighs were beginning to look long and drawn. She had contracted some kind of pulmonary infection that required Lillian to take her to the pediatrician nearly every week, and she was prescribed antibiotics that needed to be administered with a dropper several times a day, and special formula. I followed the doctor's orders religiously. I prayed almost constantly while she slept and placed a medal of the patron saint Bernadette on the table next to her crib.

A couple of weeks after treatment began, it seemed that Jessie was doing much better, but one afternoon after Ms. Lillian had returned from the pediatrician's office, I heard her sobbing as I passed by her room. Her door was ajar, and when I peeked in I saw her sitting at her vanity with her head down and her shoulders quivering. My heart froze. Perhaps little Jessie was not getting better after all. Perhaps her illness was even more serious than we thought. And then I remembered the multitude of tiny wooden coffins I'd seen as a child. The death of children was so common in my village that I often wondered if childhood itself were a disease. I pictured little Jessie's cherubic face tucked into the roughly hewn coffin with her pink lacy blanket framing her body and I too began to shiver with fear.

As I slowly entered the room and approached Lillian, I became aware of the overwhelming fragrance of perfume. It was coming from the other side of room and when I looked, I saw that one of her expensive perfume bottles was shattered against the wall.

"Ms. Lillian," I said, my voice faltering. "What's wrong, Ms. Lillian?"

She looked up at me with bleary swollen eyes and then forced herself to sit up as I came to her side. She shook her head wordlessly and looked past her reflection in the mirror, and then down at her hands.

I crouched next to her. "I just came from Jessie's room and she seems to be resting very peacefully."

She nodded dumbly.

"What did the doctor tell you today? Was it . . . was it bad news?"

At this she turned to me, her eyes wide with surprise, and then she shook her head and looked down again.

"Then what's wrong, Ms. Lillian? Why are you so upset?"

Without a word, she raised her hands and separated the hair at her temples, her eyes glazed over with stark resignation. I looked at the pale scalp beneath her copper hair, but had no idea what she intended me to see.

"I'm sorry, I don't understand, Ms. Lillian," I said.

She dropped her hands and scowled. "For goodness sake, Ana. It's right there in front of your face and for all the world to see. Four *hideous* gray hairs." She pulled her hair aside again. "There, do you see them now?"

I leaned in closer, squinting a bit, and then I saw the offending hairs. "Yes, I see them," I muttered.

Her shoulders fell. "I'm getting old, Ana," she said. "All of a sudden, it feels as though I've lost everything."

I gazed at her lovely face, mottled with tears, and hardly knew how to respond. "How can you say such a thing, Ms. Lillian?"

"Because it's true," she replied, gazing at herself in the mirror again. "Once the gray hairs show up, then the jowls start to sag and the wrinkles set in. Any day now I'll start losing my teeth, but that's fine. I'll just have Millie puree my food like she does for Jessie. I'm sure it won't be any extra trouble for her."

I chuckled at the thought. "Ms. Lillian, you're still a very young woman."

She rolled her eyes at me. "That's easy for you to say because you're five years younger than me. Younger women love telling older women that they're not so old. It's like a skinny woman telling a heavy woman, 'Oh you're not so fat,' when what she really wants to say is, 'You're a horrendous cow!'"

I shook my head, baffled. "Have you ever heard of ageless beauty, Ms. Lillian?"

She pouted and shook her head.

"My mother used to tell me that some women are born with ageless beauty so that the passage of time doesn't degrade their loveliness, but refines it all the more. You're very fortunate to have been blessed with such beauty."

Ms. Lillian sniffled and glanced at me. "Do you really think so?"

"I thought so from the first moment I saw you. But you have to be careful. It can be a dangerous thing to be so absolutely beautiful."

Ms. Lillian tried to suppress the smile nudging at the corners of her mouth. Then she sat up straight and lifted her chin. As she gazed at her reflection in the mirror, her earlier upset evaporated until her eyes were flashing coquettishly. Then she fluffed her hair and powdered her face. Pleased with the effect, she applied a bit of rouge and lipstick as well. It was difficult to believe that moments ago she'd been sobbing hysterically.

"I'm going to color my hair," she announced proudly. "I will not allow myself to grow old and sallow." She turned to me, fully vindicated. "I'm going to live dangerously, Ana."

From that day forward I came to understand that Lillian's moods were as fleeting as a summer storm. I felt uneasy about this at first, but soon learned how to read her temperament and predict the weather like a master meteorologist. In fact, I even became rather good at altering it after I understood that Ms. Lillian's vanity was her primary source of pleasure and pain.

Mr. and Mrs. Trellis received many visitors after Jessie was born. Most of them came to see the new baby, but I suspect that they were just as eager to see Lillian in her vibrant postpartum state. Whenever visitors were in the house I preferred to stay out of sight, and used the service stairs to get between the kitchen and the nursery. If necessary, Lillian would let me know how she wanted me to dress the baby and at what time to bring her down. If visitors arrived after the baby's bedtime, I usually wasn't called on at all.

It was nearly nine o'clock in the evening and both children were in bed when I ventured downstairs in my pajamas, intent on preparing myself a sandwich. I heard the strains of music floating in from the patio and made my way quietly into the kitchen via the service entry, as usual. I was on my way back with my sandwich in hand when I saw the reflection of a man standing at the toilet in the powder room. I would've immediately looked away if he hadn't looked so strangely familiar.

Suddenly his eyes met mine and he smiled, nudging the powder room door open with his foot and effectively blocking my way. He zipped up his trousers and in moments we found ourselves face-to-face. His thick wavy hair was almost as black as the slacks and silky shirt he wore open at the throat, and his amber-colored eyes glistened mischievously as he studied me from head to toe.

I immediately felt uneasy, and wanted nothing more than to drop my sandwich and run away, but I was unable to stop staring at his face. I could swear that I'd seen him somewhere before.

"Sneaking a little peek, were you?" he asked in teasing tone.

"I . . . I . . . apologize," I said, feeling exquisitely awkward. "I didn't realize."

"Haven't you ever seen a man urinating before?" he asked, folding his arms across his chest. "Perhaps you were hoping to see something more?"

I had no idea how to respond to such a comment, and could only stand there holding my plate.

At that moment another man entered, intent on using the facilities as well. He had light reddish hair and thick glasses, behind which he squinted curiously. The dark-haired man threw his arm around the other's shoulders. "Peter, I've caught myself a Peeping Tom. A rather cute Peeping Tom who likes to prowl around in her pajamas, but a Peeping Tom just the same. I advise you to securely lock the bathroom door behind you."

Peter rolled his eyes. "If you weren't always looking for trouble, then perhaps you wouldn't be so apt at finding it." Then he turned to me. "And who are you, young lady?" he asked.

"I'm Ana."

"Ah, the young woman who's looking after Teddy and the baby?"

"Yes," I replied grateful to be known as something other than a Peeping Tom.

At this the dark-haired man's eyes widened in an exaggerated display of awe and admiration. "This is the famous Ana?" he asked. "The heroine who rescued my dear nephew from drowning?"

And then I realized who the dark man was. "And you must be Mr. Trellis's younger brother, Darwin," I said.

He bowed. "I see that my fame precedes me. I am indeed Darwin Trellis, the wickedly handsome younger brother you've heard so much about. And this is Dr. Peter Farrell, who compensates for his lack of good looks with his professional ambitions. I assure you," he said, "that if you ever need to be rid of your appendix or gallbladder, or"—he cupped both hands over his chest—"if you should require bigger ones of these, Dr. Farrell is your man."

Dr. Farrell shook his head and eyed the other man with studied dismay. "Well, not exactly, but I am at your service just the same, Ana. Now if you'll excuse me," he said and he entered the powder room and locked the door behind him just as a pattering of little feet could be heard coming down the stairs. Teddy appeared in the hallway and when he saw his uncle, his eyes lit up and he ran swiftly toward him with arms outstretched. "Uncle Dawin, Uncle Dawin, you came to see me, you came to see me!" he cried. Darwin swept him up and spun him around over his head while Teddy shrieked with delight.

"How is my favorite little Superman in the whole wide world?" Darwin asked, gazing at Teddy with such tenderness that my initial displeasure for him was momentarily suspended.

Teddy pressed his hands on his uncle's cheeks. "Can you spin me again? Please! Please!"

"I can do better than that," his uncle replied, and he held him up and ran the length of the hall while Teddy assumed the pose of Superman in midflight.

Once they finished, Darwin asked, "Has Superman been behaving for Ana?"

Teddy frowned and squeezed Darwin's cheeks again. *"Nana,"* Teddy said. "Her name is *Nana.*"

"He likes to call me Nana," I said with a shrug. "I've tried correcting him, but it's no use."

Darwin chuckled, allowing Teddy to continue contorting his face. "Okay, have it your way. Nana," he repeated, which made Teddy throw his head back with chortles of laughter.

"Say it again, Uncle Dawin. You look funny, like a fish."

Still clutching my sandwich that was nearly in pieces, I said, "It's very late, Teddy. We should get back upstairs now."

"No, Nana, no!" Teddy wailed, clinging to his uncle's neck for dear life.

"Is this any way for Superman to behave?" Darwin said, giving Teddy a playful pout of his own.

Teddy loosened his grip on his uncle, and Darwin placed him back on the ground. Teddy then took my outstretched hand, but was unable to erase the sour look on his face.

"Good night, Sir. It was a pleasure meeting you," I said, and we made our way down the hall.

"Good night, Nana. Good night, Superman."

"Good night, Uncle Dawin," Teddy said.

We were halfway up the stairs when Darwin called out loudly enough so that Dr. Farrell, who was still in the powder room, might hear him as well. "And please keep the prodigious size of my anatomy to yourself. I don't need any more women knocking down my door."

I didn't respond, but his discomforting laughter followed us all the way upstairs, and Teddy began to cackle like his uncle. As I was tucking him back into bed, he said, "Uncle Dawin funny."

"Yes," I replied. "He's hilarious."

When I mentioned to Millie that I'd met Mr. Trellis's younger brother, Darwin, she was eager to tell me all about him, and when she spoke her eyes glittered with wonder, much as Teddy's had the night before. She informed me that he'd been a gifted athlete in high school and would have earned a football scholarship to any university he chose, but the car accident had damaged his back so severely that it ended his football career. "He took it quite hard," Millie said, "and for years he was angry at his brother and blamed him for having pulled him out of the car. I can't tell you how many times he told me that he would've preferred to die. Oh, he got over it eventually, but when he did, that darned gambling gene surfaced in a mean way and wouldn't let go of him. In a few years he managed to squander away a good portion of his inheritance. It got so bad that he tried to convince Adam to sell the house. They had some terrible arguments about it, but Adam refused to sell the house or any of the property attached to it. Instead, he bought his brother out and then Darwin left right around the time that Lillian started sniffing around, trying to get under Adam's skin and into his wallet." Millie sighed. "Ever since then, Darwin tends to come and go. When his pockets are full we won't see or hear from him for months at a time. He usually goes to Europe. He says that European women are more open-minded and less demanding than American women. How I miss him when he's gone."

Darwin showed up unexpectedly a few days later while I was in the kitchen helping Millie with the dinner dishes.

"How's the most bewitching woman in the world?" he asked, startling us both.

Millie giggled with delight when she saw him, and propped her soapy hands on her hips. "Ms. Lillian is upstairs," she said primly.

"You know perfectly well I'm not referring to Lillian," he returned, and then he embraced Millie with obvious affection, unconcerned that her soapy hands were all over his expensive jacket. When he released her, she was flush with pleasure.

"And how are you this evening, Ana?" he said with a curt and respectful nod. "Still taking care of my precious Teddy?"

"Yes, sir, and Jessie too," I replied.

He turned back to Millie. "I came to speak with Adam. Do you know if he's here?"

"He's in the study as usual," Millie said with a wave of her hand. "Be sure to come back before you leave, and I'll have some fresh-baked cookies for you."

"Oatmeal?" he asked while rubbing his hands together greedily.

"What else?" Millie replied, and Darwin left for the study with promises to return.

The moment he left, Millie's smile dropped, and she shook her head in dismay. "It's good to see him, but whenever he starts showing up around here I worry that he's in some kind of trouble involving money, women, or both." Millie continued to shake her head with infinite regret. "I don't know how many times I've told him to find one good woman and settle down, but for that boy all of womankind is like a never-ending pack of chewing gum. He'll unwrap a stick, chew on it for a while, and then throw it away as soon as the flavor starts to fade. Then he just unwraps another stick and starts all over again. He's so darned handsome and charming that he never seems to run out of a fresh supply. The only woman he doesn't seem to tire of is his brother's wife," Millie said, pursing her lips with displeasure. "The way she teases and taunts the poor man isn't right."

"Do you mean Ms. Lillian?"

"Who else?" Millie replied with a toss of her head.

I turned away, feeling the sudden need to defend Lillian. "Maybe she just feels sorry for Mr. Darwin," I said.

"Whatever for?" Millie asked.

"Because he couldn't play football after the accident, and because he has so many problems with money and women."

Millie shook her head as though ashamed for me and my ignorance. "There's no doubt that you have a gift with children, Ana," she said, "but when it comes to adults, you don't have a clue."

I learned, through Millie, that Darwin had commissioned an artist to paint a portrait of Ms. Lillian and the children as a surprise for his brother on his thirty-fifth birthday. And as luck would have it, he knew of just the artist for the job.

On an especially dreary afternoon, when Jessie was napping and Teddy and I were reading in the nursery, Millie came upstairs looking for us. She twirled her hand before her, bowing like a royal servant. "The artist has arrived and the presence of the little prince and princess is being requested in the drawing room," she announced, slightly slurring her words.

"Do you mean right now?"

"Artistic geniuses don't like to be kept waiting," she said, and when she left the sour odor of whiskey lingered in the air. I hoped that Teddy hadn't noticed her odd behavior, but he was watching Millie in a more studied manner of late, as though he'd caught on that something wasn't quite right. Sharp as he was, I knew it wouldn't be long before he figured out what it was.

Jerome was waiting in the sitting room by the largest window, bent over his artist's tools that were scattered all about him. I had decided not to wake Jessie for the time being, knowing that she would be a very grumpy subject if I did. Teddy wasted no time and raced toward the colorful paints, assuming that they were toys. I managed to intercede before he'd opened one of the tubes of paint, remembering the week before when he disappeared into the music room with a box of crayons. He was out of sight for no more than a few minutes, but in that time managed to cover one entire wall with pictures of his favorite bugs, all with wide, happy grins.

"Teddy, these aren't toys for you," I said gently. "These are for the artist to paint with."

Teddy pouted and placed his hands on my cheeks. "But I want to paint picture for you, Nana," he said, hoping this would change my mind.

Jerome cleared his throat, and I looked directly at him for the first time since I'd entered the room. He smiled, revealing a row of perfectly even white teeth. His skin was equally flawless, and his hair a brilliant shade of gold. He possessed a soft radiant beauty unusual for a man, yet his toned, perfectly proportioned body was undeniably masculine. Teddy and I stared at him for a moment or two, quite overwhelmed by his dreamlike appearance.

"What a beautiful child," he observed. "And you must be Lillian," he said, lifting discerning eyes to my face. His smile remained gracious but he was unable to disguise his disappointment.

"Oh no, I'm not Lillian," I said, coloring. "I look after the children. My name is Ana."

"Nana!" Teddy corrected, as usual.

Jerome was obviously well accustomed to painting children and understood the importance of engaging them before requesting that they sit. He had paint and brushes set aside especially for them, and he happily chatted with Teddy about the different colors he planned on using and the brushes as well, answering all of his questions even if they weren't perfectly understandable. Teddy beamed with bright curiosity as he interacted with this fascinating new visitor, while I sat near the door waiting for Lillian to arrive. She would then let me know if she wanted me to stay during the sitting.

Moments later, Lillian made her entrance wearing a white fitted dress, and I was reminded of the first day I saw her. I'd become so accustomed to her spectacular beauty that sometimes I didn't take much notice unless I was in the company of someone who hadn't yet met her. Jerome's eyes swept the length of her willowy body and settled on her face. He was clearly dazzled and perhaps even somewhat annoyed that he would have to share her canvas with the children.

Lillian smiled and offered her hand, quite pleased by the admiration she read in the artist's eyes. A blush rose to her cheeks, making her even more striking. Teddy started his drawings as they began to discuss the process for the portrait. I was happy to hear that the children wouldn't be required to sit for more than a few minutes at a time, and that Jerome was able to capture excellent likenesses by observing them in their natural environment, as well as with the use of photos.

"I can begin some preliminary sketches today if you like."

"That would be lovely," Lillian replied excitedly. "Is Jessie up from her nap?" she asked, turning to me for the first time since the interview began.

"I don't know. I'll go check," I said, standing up.

"Teddy, you go with Ana. Be a good boy."

Teddy frowned at the prospect of interrupting his drawing session, but when he saw the seriousness in his mother's eyes, he immediately dropped his brush and ran to me. We left the room together and were only a few feet from the door when I stopped to retie one of Teddy's sneakers.

"I had a silly little thought. I'm almost too embarrassed to ask," I overheard Lillian say.

"Well then, you must definitely ask," Jerome replied with such playful intimacy that it was hard to believe they'd met for the first time just moments earlier.

"Do you paint nudes?" she asked.

It took him a moment to answer, and then he replied in a breathy voice, "I paint whatever my clients request."

Jerome came to the house twice a week, on Tuesday mornings and Thursday afternoons. On Tuesdays, the children were dressed in their portrait clothes—white trousers and a white button-down collared shirt for Teddy and a beautiful embroidered white dress for Jessie. I enjoyed creating ringlets from her carrot-colored curls and arranging them all around her head. But on Thursday afternoons, the children were not present for the sitting, and I could only assume that this was the time set aside for "the nude." I made it a point to keep the children away

from the sitting room–turned–studio, and I didn't tell Millie
about what I'd overheard. It didn't seem right to share something I shouldn't know about in the first place. Anyway, Millie
didn't need any help fueling her arsenal of complaints against
Lillian. As it was, whenever Jerome arrived, Millie would fold
her arms over her chest and eye him suspiciously.

Most of the sittings began around noon and lasted two
to three hours, which meant that Jerome always left well
before Mr. Trellis came home. Lillian explained that this way
there was no chance of spoiling the birthday surprise for her
husband.

Whenever I walked by the closed studio door, I shuddered to
think that Ms. Lillian was posing naked in front of this strange
man. The only time I'd been naked in front of a boy was when
Carlitos and I played down by the river and covered ourselves
with mud. And the sisters at the convent had insisted on absolute modesty. Our showers were private, and we always dressed
ourselves completely from head to toe before leaving the bathroom. We even took care to wash our underclothes ourselves
so that no human hands but our own would ever touch what
touched the most intimate parts of our bodies.

One Thursday afternoon, three weeks after the sittings
began, I left the children with Millie in the courtyard to get
Teddy's ball from the nursery. As I passed the studio, I hesitated outside the door when I heard a loud crashing sound from
inside. The door was slightly ajar, so I peeked in, only to find
the room empty, although I could see that Jerome's canvas had
fallen off the easel, probably making the sound I'd heard moments earlier. I was contemplating entering the room to put it

back when I heard the click of the front door and Mr. Trellis's familiar footsteps coming down the hall. He was home much earlier than usual, and although I was flustered, I managed to close the door before he turned the corner.

"You're home early today, Mr. Trellis," I said, as casually as I could.

"I need to speak with Lillian about something. Is she home?" he asked.

"Yes, I . . . I . . . believe so," I stammered.

"Where can I find her?"

"I'm not exactly sure," I replied, wondering where in the world she could be. "I can look for her if you like."

"I'd appreciate it," he said with a heavy sigh. "Tell her I'll be waiting for her in the study."

The moment he entered his study and closed the door, I ran about this way and that, not certain about where to begin my search, and the frantic beating of my heart only made my indecision worse. I realized that my anxiety had nothing to do with keeping his birthday present a surprise, but with making sure that Mr. Trellis didn't discover his wife posing naked for the handsome golden-haired artist, because if he did, I was certain that something horrible would happen.

I tried to calm down and begin my search in a methodical manner. I began on the first floor, searching the rooms one by one, even the music room and the laundry room, where it was highly unlikely they'd be. I searched the second floor in the same manner and was bold enough to open Mr. and Mrs. Trellis's bedroom door after knocking and calling out, "Ms. Lillian, Mr. Trellis is home early. Oh, Ms. Lillian, your husband is here."

But every room on the second floor was empty, which led me to reluctantly go up to the third floor.

Since my first and only visit there, I'd been quite clear with Teddy that he was to stay away from the third floor when playing hide-and-seek, and that if he disobeyed me I wouldn't play this game with him anymore. It was as much for his safety as it was for my comfort. I wasn't eager to revisit what I considered to be the most disagreeable place in the house.

As I climbed the service stairs, I went briskly, trying my best to ignore the musty odor and the drapery of cobwebs that brushed my face and arms. Once I reached the landing, my throat tightened and a chill crept up and down my spine. Immediately, I sensed that I was not alone. "Is anybody here?" I muttered, nearly choking on my words, and as I tended to do whenever I felt anxious or afraid, I remained silent, hoping that whatever I feared wouldn't find me.

I took several steps into the corridor and noticed that one of the doors at the far end was slightly ajar. I stopped and listened, certain that I'd heard something, but perhaps it was nothing more than the scuttle of the cockroaches and mice beneath the floorboards. I took another step forward and then I definitely heard something—it was my mother's whispering voice: "What a man and woman do together is private, and you shouldn't be watching."

Unable to heed her warning, I peeked through the open door and saw Lillian's pale nude body reclining on the couch, her legs demurely crossed and her hands behind her head as though she were sunbathing. Jerome, also nude, was lying next to her. His bronzed muscular body made Lillian's appear childlike, and he was lightly stroking her inner thigh as though it were a pet, slowly making his way up to her crotch as she murmured with pleasure.

Not knowing what else to do, I pushed on the door and let it swing open. When Lillian saw me standing in the doorway her eyes flew open and Jerome jumped up in a flash and cried out, but all I heard was an alien buzzing sound in my head. I stood frozen, unable to move or make a sound, certain that if I did the floor beneath my feet would give way and the entire house would crumble all around us. I could only stare into Ms. Lillian's startled ethereal blue eyes, hoping for guidance. But she was frozen as well, watching me as though I were a beast that might devour her in a single gulp.

Finally I broke the unholy spell growing between us. "Ms. Lillian, your husband just came home. He wants to speak with you in the study."

The muscles in Lillian's delicate throat strained, and she swallowed hard. She was making an effort to stay calm and focused in the face of this absurd crisis. "Ana, listen to me," she said in an almost soothing voice. "We can't let Adam find Jerome in the house. Go downstairs and tell him that I'm feeling ill and that I'll be down in just a few minutes."

"Yes, Ms. Lillian," I muttered. Without a word Jerome stood up. Looking more disappointed than alarmed, he strode toward the place where his clothing lay in a heap. His semi-erect penis bobbed slightly as he walked, and I couldn't help but notice that his pubic hair was dark brown and not golden like the hair on his head. He pulled on his trousers and groaned when the zipper caught on the loose flesh of his groin. I wondered why he wasn't wearing underwear when I was certain that all men wore underwear.

Ms. Lillian stood up next and shrugged on her robe as Jerome finished dressing. "And you must keep Adam occupied until you're certain that Jerome is out of the house, do you understand?"

I nodded, but I was unable to move, prompting Lillian to harshly say, "You heard me, Ana. Go on now! We don't have much time."

I suddenly came to life and shot down the two flights of stairs, vaguely aware of Jerome's feet pounding behind me. I rushed past the sitting room and ran directly to the kitchen, where I paused for a moment to catch my breath. From there I could hear Jerome banging around in the sitting room as he gathered his things together, but I knew this would take him several minutes to accomplish. Shaking from head to toe, I went to the sink and splashed my face with cool water. Once I felt more or less composed, I proceeded to the study, where Mr. Trellis was looking over some papers at his desk. When I entered, I could tell he was disappointed to see that it was me and not his wife standing in the doorway.

"I was beginning to think you'd forgotten about me," he said.

"I'm sorry I . . . I . . ."

"What's wrong?" he asked, half rising from his chair. "Is it the children?"

"No, they're fine."

"Well, did you find Lillian?" he asked.

"Yes," I replied. "But she's not . . . she's not feeling well."

His eyes were shrouded with concern. "What's wrong with her? She seemed well enough this morning."

Somehow the words found their way into my mouth. "She has . . . she has female problems."

"I see," he said, looking away awkwardly. "Well, this can't wait, is she upstairs?"

"I . . . I'm not sure," I stammered.

"I thought you said you just spoke with her."

"Yes, but she may not be where I last saw her," I replied nervously.

He stood up and came around his desk. "And where exactly was that?"

I stared up at him for a moment or two, my mind completely blank.

"Ana, what in the world is the matter with you? You look very strange."

"I don't know."

"You don't know? How can you not know?"

"I . . . I . . . guess I'm not feeling very well either."

"You too?" he asked incredulous. "All right, I'll go find Lillian myself and then maybe she can tell me about this mysterious illness that seems to be going around." He went to the door and opened it just as I heard Jerome making his way down the hall, his easel knocking about as he went toward the front door. Not knowing what else to do, I gasped and collapsed into a heap on the floor.

Mr. Trellis rushed to my side. "Ana," he said tapping my cheeks gently. "Ana, can you hear me?" When I didn't answer him, he slipped his hands under me and carried me to the sofa.

His nearness made me feel warm and alive as if a river had suddenly forged itself through my soul. I longed for him to place his head on my shoulder and rest with me as we waited together for the danger to pass, but he didn't touch me again.

When I finally opened my eyes he was watching me, undeniably worried. "You look pale. Have you eaten anything today?" he asked, and the deep sound of his voice so close to my ear made me feel weak and wonderful all at once.

"Just a little breakfast," I mumbled.

"No lunch?"

I shook my head, wishing for him to remain kneeling next to me, breathing over me, concerned for my well-being—because all at once my life felt blissfully complete.

"You should eat more, Ana. You're far too thin."

"Yes," I said, gazing into his eyes that were so close I could see the black of his pupils against the deep brown of his irises. Until that moment, I hadn't really noticed what lovely eyes he had, so shiny and dark, so expressive.

Before he could say anything else, the door of the study was flung open. Lillian entered in her bathrobe and with her hair wrapped up in a towel, as though she'd just stepped out of the shower.

She was alarmed to see me lying on the couch and her husband kneeling next to me. "What's wrong with Ana?" she asked.

"I was just on my way to go find you when she collapsed," Mr. Trellis replied.

I swallowed my emotions as best I could. "I wasn't feeling well, Ms. Lillian, and . . . and everything went black."

She said nothing, but nodded her understanding.

Mr. Trellis said, "I'm going to ask Peter to come by and take a look at you."

"I'm sure that isn't necessary," I said, sitting up. "Once I get something in my stomach I'll feel better, and Millie's been with the children for far too long."

Lillian flashed me a grateful look and took her husband by the hand, leading him smoothly to the door. "Let's give Ana a moment longer to rest. Did you want to speak with me about something?"

Later that evening, after I'd put the children down, I was in the kitchen preparing a cup of tea when Millie entered in search of a snack. She was teetering on her feet and I detected the odor of whiskey on her breath, which always intensified at night. "Are you feeling better after your fainting spell?" she asked, sidling up next to me.

"Yes, much better."

She went to the refrigerator and after rummaging about, tossed ham and cheese on the counter and proceeded to make herself a sandwich. "You hardly ate any dinner. Would you like me to fix you a sandwich?"

"That would be nice. Thank you, Millie."

She started to slather four slices of bread with butter and mustard as she hummed a happy little tune. "It's a funny thing," she said as she worked, "after Adam got home this afternoon, I saw that artist Jerome running to his car as if he were being chased by wild dogs." Millie smiled a silly lopsided smile. "And I could've sworn that his shirt was on inside out," she said, looking at me with wide, innocent eyes. "Funny, isn't it?"

I said nothing as I sipped my tea.

"And what a fight those two had while you were resting in the study. Did you hear any of it?" Millie asked while slicing the sandwiches in two.

I shook my head, grateful for my ignorance.

"Well, I couldn't make all of it out because Lillian was more hysterical than usual, but I know it had something to do with Darwin's birthday surprise for his brother. It seems that he arranged for the portrait, but forgot to arrange for the payment," Millie said, pushing the sandwich across the counter toward me. "My guess is that the invoice was sent to Adam's office by mistake and now the surprise is ruined." Millie clucked her tongue. "Or it could be that Lillian felt sorry for Darwin, and told him to bill her husband instead. Do you think that might be what happened?"

"I don't know," I said, fingering my sandwich.

"That woman is so darned selfless," she said. "Who would ever guess that there was a saint living among us?" Millie peered at my untouched sandwich. "What's the matter, Ana, did I put too much mustard?"

"No, I'm just not that hungry after all."

"You still look a bit pale. Maybe this place is finally getting to you."

"I just need to get some rest. I'm sure I'll feel better tomorrow."

"Yes, tomorrow," Millie said with a bright cackle that ejected a few pieces of semichewed sandwich onto the counter. "Another day filled with familial harmony and bliss. You go write about it in your letters, Ana. Let the sisters know all about this nice family you're working for. And give them my regards, would you?"

Never had I yearned more for the peace and tranquillity of the convent. If I could just curl up in my little cell and sleep undisturbed until the morning prayer bells woke me, I knew that all would be well again. After breakfast, I'd tell Mother Superior that life outside the convent was not for me. It was filled with too much pain and deception, and I would never find meaning in the chaos. It was no better than the civil war of my childhood, a place devoid of God and goodness, and on certain days it felt as though I were walking barefoot along an endless road of broken glass. I couldn't make sense of what I'd seen that afternoon, and even less of the growing tenderness I felt for Mr. Trellis.

I was almost asleep, comforted by the thought that in only a few weeks I'd be back at the convent where I belonged, when I heard Teddy calling for me in his plaintive little voice. I threw on my robe and ran to him. By the glow of his night-light I saw the anxiety on his face. "Nana, my Nana," he said, holding his arms out to me.

"What's wrong, Teddy? Did you have another bad dream?" But when I stepped into his room, I became aware of a familiar foul odor.

Teddy's bottom lip quivered. "I went poopoo in my pajamas," he said.

I rushed to help him out of bed and put him in a warm tub to soak while I changed his sheets.

When he was fresh and tucked back into a clean bed, he said, "Please don't tell Mommy and Daddy, okay, Nana?"

"It was an accident. I'm sure they'd understand."

"No, Nana!" he said, grabbing my arm. "I don't want them to know. Please don't tell them."

"Okay, I won't tell them," I said, certain that he wouldn't have gone to sleep if I'd said otherwise. Even so, he whimpered for a good half hour before he was able to close his eyes again. When I got back into my own bed I could still detect the odor of excrement. I got up and scrubbed my hands again until they were raw, careful to clean under my nails and up to my wrists and elbows. I changed my nightgown for good measure and inspected my bedsheets a second time. Everything was clean, but the odor lingered through the night.

The next day, Mr. Trellis returned home from work at the usual hour and asked to speak with me in his study. Still shaky from the events of the previous day, I dreaded facing him, certain that this time he'd see the guilty truth in my eyes. Whenever I thought about how I'd partnered with Lillian to deceive him, I felt such an aching shame in the pit of my stomach that I was unable to eat.

I entered the study and realized that the man sitting behind the desk was not the same man I'd met on my first day. While he was still large and somewhat menacing, he was also vulnerable and burdened by a great sadness I didn't understand. It was odd that this man who I considered to be the epitome of masculine strength that frightened me so should also remind me of the gentle sisters who I missed so much. I was drawn to him, and trying to deny it was like trying to deceive God. But still, I could implore him to protect me from these overpowering thoughts and feelings, and this is what I did as I walked toward Mr. Trellis's desk.

Our eyes met and he was thoughtful. I knew by now that Mr. Trellis wasn't one to indulge in unrestrained emotion. He measured each moment for what it was worth and then decided what to do and say. He motioned for me to have a seat. "How was your day, Ana?" he asked.

"Very nice. The children enjoyed their time in the garden. It was such a beautiful afternoon."

"Was it?" he asked, raising his eyebrows. "When I drove to work this morning it was dark and it was also dark when I left for home, so I have no idea what kind of day it was."

"Perhaps you're working too hard, Mr. Trellis."

"Perhaps," he said, dismissing the thought. Then he turned his attention to an opened letter on his desk. "This letter just arrived today. It's from Flor. She won't be coming back as she'd planned. It seems that her sister died and she needs to stay in Mexico to look after her nieces and nephews, who are now orphaned."

"I'm sorry to hear it," I said, my stomach tightening.

"I realize that you were planning to return to the convent after these six months, but I'm hoping that I can persuade you to stay with us for a few months longer."

It seemed strange that I would be discussing this matter with Mr. Trellis and not with Lillian or even with Millie. Of course, Lillian had been avoiding me since yesterday, and I suspected that she would continue to do so for some time longer. Probably she'd asked her husband to talk to me for her on some pretext or another.

It would've been easy for me to explain to Lillian or Millie that I was expected back at the convent and that postponing my return would push everything back several months. I wouldn't be able to take my vows until the following year and I had no doubt that Mother Superior would be disappointed in me. But with Mr. Trellis I felt undone and confused about the whole matter. It was as though an invisible hand had suddenly muddled my plans and turned them inside out.

"It would just be for a few months longer," he said in response to my ongoing silence. "And I'll pay you a higher wage as well." He appeared encouraged, and looking at him I felt dizzy as though I were breathing rarefied air. And then I remembered how Lillian had described his effect on her when she first met him. "When Adam wants something, he goes after it until he gets what he wants. I was powerless against him."

He wanted me to stay and the only thing that mattered at that moment was the hopefulness I saw in his eyes. I wanted to please him, to ease whatever anxiety he felt about the children or anything else, and this feeling was stronger than my desire to return to the convent. "Very well, tomorrow I'll inform Mother Superior that I'll be staying on for a few more months," I said.

"Thank you, Ana," he replied with a sigh of relief. "Millie and Lillian will be very happy to know it, but I'm sure Teddy and Jessie will be happiest of all."

And you, I yearned to ask. *How do you feel about it?* And then I lowered my head, willing with all my heart and soul for these strange feelings to pass away. Mr. Trellis cleared his throat and

I looked up. Our talk was finished and I could see that he was expecting me to leave, so I hastily left the study and went about my usual duties. As I prepared the children for bed, my mind was preoccupied with how I'd talk to Mother Superior about my decision to stay on without giving her the impression that my conviction for a holy life was in any way weakening.

But it is weakening, a voice whispered deep in my soul. *You have found a new passion, one that makes your life not only a recompense for the past, but a reconciliation for the future.*

The next day, I called Mother Superior and carefully explained about Flor, who was still in Mexico, and her sister's death and the orphaned children, saying more about it than Mr. Trellis had, perhaps embellishing a bit more than I should have. I hoped that she would consider my decision to remain with the Trellis family to be a selfless and charitable act, but I knew that in spite of my sincere commitment to the family, it was more than that. I was indulging myself with something wonderful that I didn't understand, and until I discovered what it was, I would never return to the convent.

$\mathcal{S}$even

ANA STEPPED IN CLOSER to the portrait and traced her fingers along the outlines of the three faces she knew so well. She felt the smooth and rough contour of the thickly applied oil paint and studied the individual brushstrokes. Close up, they looked like nothing but a series of disconnected shapes and lines, splotches of color carelessly applied, layer upon layer. But as she stepped back, the picture came into sharp focus and she couldn't help but smile when she beheld Teddy's impish grin and the wide eyes that made Jessie look as though she were perpetually startled. "She's an observer," Ana would explain when Lillian noted that her daughter rarely blinked. "She's just taking it all in."

Ana was surprised when she felt a hand on her shoulder. "Ana, my dear," Sister Josepha said. "I believe that someone has just pulled up to the front of the house."

Ana went quickly to the window, hoping against hope that Teddy had finally come to his senses, but she instantly recognized the shiny bald crown of Benson's head and the requisite briefcase swinging at his side as he walked briskly to the front door.

"It isn't who you were hoping it would be, is it?" Sister Josepha asked gently.

Ana turned to the older woman and smiled. "No, but Benson is a dear friend and I'm glad he's here."

Sister Josepha took Ana's hand and tucked it under her arm as they walked down the corridor toward the stairs. "I'm sure the person you're waiting for will come," Sister Josepha said, and when Ana considered the contents of Benson's briefcase, she had no doubt that she was right.

Sensing that Ana needed to speak to this visitor alone, Sister Josepha headed to the kitchen while Ana opened the front door. Benson's cheeks were rosy and he was slightly winded after having rushed up the front steps. Ana embraced him, noting that in only a few days he'd put on more weight, or perhaps it was that she'd lost weight. He smiled, but his kindly eyes remained somber. Once in the entry hall, he swung his briefcase up to the sideboard.

"Is everything in order?" Ana whispered.

Benson looked around as though searching for imaginary spies. "Is the room bugged?" he asked.

Ana folded her arms across her chest. "No, but I don't want to take any chances."

"I'm glad," he replied. "Because if this gets out, I could lose my license and my law practice. I could even go to jail."

"I appreciate the risk you're taking . . . with all my heart."

Benson remained glum. "And do you realize that Adam would never approve of this? If he knew I was helping you, he'd disown me as a friend. Maybe he'd disown you too."

"Benson, please, do you think this is easy for me?"

He shook his head. "Do you want to know what I really think?"

"Of course," Ana replied, lifting her chin.

"I think this is far too easy for you. You haven't thought it through beyond the next few days, but when this is all over, as it must be . . ." He took her hand. "As it must be," he repeated, in spite of the anguish in her eyes. "Then what becomes of you and your future?"

"I don't have a future," Ana said.

"What are you talking about?" Benson asked, taking her other hand. "Of course you do."

Ana gently retrieved her hands. "Dear, dear Benson," she whispered.

Flush with emotion, he was about to say something more when Jessie appeared on the staircase. When she saw the old family friend, she rushed down the rest of the way and welcomed him with a warm embrace.

"Daddy and I were just talking about you," she said.

Benson grinned and tucked his thumbs into his belt. "Were you discussing my good looks and athletic prowess on the golf course?"

Jessie chuckled weakly. "Neither," she replied. Then, turning to Ana, "You're right, Daddy's doing better than I thought he was."

"Didn't I tell you?" Ana replied brightly. "You should go up now, Benson. In a little while he'll need to rest again, and I know he wants to see you."

Benson took his briefcase with him upstairs while Ana and Jessie proceeded to the kitchen.

"Did I tell you that Sister Josepha is here?" Ana asked, circling her arm around Jessie's waist. "You so enjoyed her company last time she visited."

"That was a long time ago, Nana. I don't think I was even ten years old."

"Was it that long ago?"

The two women were almost to the kitchen when Jessie said, "Nana, when I was a little girl you used to tell me that if we prayed for something with all our heart and soul, God would always listen. So, I was thinking that maybe if you and Sister Josepha and I pray together now, harder than we've ever prayed for anything, God will grant us a miracle. Do you think it'll work, Nana?"

"I don't know," Ana replied, tightening her grip on the young woman. "But I think it's definitely worth a try."

They entered the kitchen and once Sister Josepha and Jessie greeted each other, the three women sat down at the table. As Sister Josepha led them in prayer, Ana's thoughts constantly turned to Benson. Would he get Adam to sign the documents? Would he betray her confidence? Ana trusted Benson implicitly, but still she worried. She tried to concentrate on Sister Josepha's words, but as had been true since the sun rose that morning, she was unable to calm herself with anything but her own memories.

When the afternoons were mild, I often took the children to the park only a few blocks from the house. I'd pack Jessie up in her stroller, and Teddy would stand on the platform between the carriage and handles when he got tired. We spent many happy hours ambling up and around the jungle gym, running between the trees, or lying back and watching the squirrels scamper about over our heads. Upon our return, we always entered the house through the back entrance, where Millie was certain to have a snack waiting for us in the kitchen. If she felt the need for a nap, she'd leave the back door open, so I never bothered to bring my key.

On one such afternoon, the children and I had just made our way to the back of the house when I saw a man standing on a chair attempting to squeeze himself through the kitchen window, but he was stuck with half his body inside and half of it out. I didn't know what to do, but I wasn't too frightened because the pudgy intruder wore a suit and dress shoes. Teddy started to scream when he saw the man and Jessie followed his example, which caused the man to teeter on his feet and the chair to topple over, leaving him with his feet dangling several feet from the ground. He started to call out and flap his hands and feet about in the air as though he were trying to swim.

I approached slowly. I could see that his broad face was puffy and red from overexertion and that, although he looked to be only in his thirties, he was nearly bald, with a neat band of dark hair encircling his head from ear to ear.

Moments later Millie appeared in the kitchen, sleepy-eyed and irritated that her nap had been interrupted. When she saw the distressed man, she threw up her hands and rushed to the window. "For goodness sake, Benson, what in the world are you doing?"

Seeing us outside, Millie unlocked and opened the back

door, and Teddy ran into the kitchen and stared up into his face. I followed with Jessie still in the stroller.

"Uncle Benson!" Teddy cried. "Uncle Benson, you look silly!"

"I'm sure I do," he replied sheepishly.

Millie opened the window while I went outside and placed the chair back under his feet, and in moments he was free. Still slightly bent and rubbing his sore back, he chuckled and explained to Millie that Adam had invited him to dinner and that he'd come early. The back door was locked so he thought he'd let himself in through the kitchen window as he'd done so many times before.

"Didn't I unlock it? Oh, I'm getting forgetful," Millie said as she wiped the dust from his suit jacket. "But, honestly, you boys weren't more than twelve when you came in through the window like that."

"Well, I've definitely put on a bit of weight since then, and I'm nowhere near as limber, either." I was immediately set at ease by the kindly expression in his eyes, accentuated by his droopy teardrop-shaped lids.

"You must be Ana," he said, turning to me. "Adam told me how great you are with the kids."

"Thank you," I replied, wishing that I could say I'd heard Adam speak of him as well, but Mr. Trellis rarely spoke to me about anything unless it pertained to the children.

Millie put a pot of coffee on for our visitor, while Teddy rushed upstairs. I was certain that he'd return moments later with a favorite toy to show Benson. I gave Jessie her afternoon bottle while Millie and Benson chatted. From their conversation I gathered that Benson and Mr. Trellis had been friends since childhood and that they still played golf together from time to time.

Mr. Trellis arrived home a short while later and when he saw his friend sitting with us at the kitchen table, his eyes lit up. For a moment it looked as though a dark veil had been lifted from his face and that all the deep-hearted worry he carried around with him had suddenly vanished. I thought he looked astonishingly handsome. He asked Benson to join him in the study, and Benson excused himself as Millie waved him off with a cheerful smile, telling him that she'd never seen him looking so happy and well.

Once they were safely out of earshot, her smiled dropped and she said, "That poor miserable little man. You'd never know it by looking at him, but he's quite a successful attorney. Brilliant when it comes to books, but quite stupid when it comes to everything else."

"He seems very nice."

"That's his problem. He's so nice that he lets women walk all over him. He's been kicked in the head so many times it's a wonder he has any hair left at all."

"That's too bad," I said, careful to take the bottle from Jessie's mouth without waking her.

"And it doesn't help that he still lives with his mother," Millie said, shaking her head in dismay as she began to organize ingredients for the evening meal. "Can you imagine a thirty-five-year-old man who still lives with his mother?" With eyes glittering she said, "And you should see how he gets around Lillian. At the mere mention of her name his ears turn bright red, and whenever she walks in the room I'm always afraid he's going to drop from a heart attack. You'll see what I mean at dinner tonight. It's really quite amazing."

Sister Josepha placed her hand on Ana's forearm. "Ana, dear, are you all right?"

Ana widened her eyes, suddenly aware that the prayer had finished and that she'd lost track of the conversation. "Yes, I'm sorry," she muttered.

"Sister Josepha was just telling me that you're thinking about going away to New Mexico. Is that true?" Jessie asked, her eyes wide with worry.

"Well, yes, but I haven't made any final decisions yet."

"Don't you like it here anymore?"

"Of course I do," Ana said, glancing at Sister Josepha. "And there's no need to worry about any of that yet."

"But I do worry, Nana," Jessie said. "You know how I worry about you."

Sister Josepha stood up and turned on the teakettle. "Now where is it that you're planning to attend university?" she asked as she rummaged about the cupboards for tea bags.

"Vanderbilt," Jessie answered with a pout. "I'll be applying in a couple of months."

"And where is that again?" she asked, dropping tea bags into three empty mugs.

"Tennessee," Jessie replied.

"I may be wrong," Sister Josepha said cheerfully, "but isn't Tennessee closer to New Mexico than it is to California?"

"I suppose," Jessie replied, unconvinced. "But this is home, and I like to think of Nana being here and not off in New Mexico somewhere. And doesn't it get very cold there in the winter? Nana doesn't like the cold. Isn't that right, Nana?"

"Well, it depends," she said, looking up toward the ceiling. Benson's visit had lasted longer than she expected, and it was almost time for Adam's medications.

"I like warmer climates too," Sister Josepha replied, placing three mugs of tea on the table. "But you must admit that there's something energizing about the cold. It seems to make the blood run quicker through the veins, and the brain work more efficiently."

"I suppose," Jessie said reluctantly, turning to look at Ana, who again was lost in her thoughts.

After that first day, Benson visited often and we became fast friends. As time passed, I realized that in his company I felt as I did when Carlitos and I played together at the river, saying whatever came to mind, laughing at jokes only we understood and making exaggerated proclamations that made sense nowhere else but in our private universe.

"If you marry someone else, I'll have to drown myself in the river," Carlitos would say.

"And if you drown yourself in the river, I'll throw myself down from the highest mountain," I'd reply.

"And if you throw yourself down the highest mountain, I'll cover my entire body in kerosene and burn myself alive."

"How can you do that when you already drowned yourself in the river?" I'd ask.

And Carlitos would smile sheepishly. "That's right. I forgot," he said. "Well, forget about the drowning part. I'd rather burn myself alive instead."

"Ana, for the love of God, don't touch it!" Benson exclaimed. He was splayed out on the couch in the front room with his leg propped up on a pillow. Teddy stood next to me wide-eyed, clutching my hand. Benson and Mr. Trellis had just returned from a day of golf, and Mr. Trellis had gone to the kitchen for some ice.

I turned to Teddy. "Why don't you find Jessie? Millie must have your lunch ready by now." Reluctant to leave the drama so soon, Teddy took several hesitant steps toward the door and then ran off to do as I asked.

"Poor kid," Benson muttered. "He probably thinks his uncle Benson has lost all his marbles, and to think that this may be his last memory of me."

"Oh Benson," I said. "I'm sure it's nothing."

His eyes screwed up in his face, and his hand trembled as he pointed to the leg in question—a chubby, stout leg that looked comical in plaid shorts and socks. "See how much more swollen it is compared to the other leg?" he asked.

"I don't see any swelling at all," I replied.

"Of course you do," he retorted. Then he flopped his head back, already defeated. "It's a blood clot. I know it is. My father died very suddenly of a blood clot to the lung. It probably started just like this."

"Does it hurt?" I asked, taking a seat next to the injured leg.

"It's excruciating," he replied, lifting his head so that I could appreciate his agony.

"I'm sure the ice will help," I said.

"An ice pack can't save me now."

I gave his sick leg a friendly if irreverent pat on the knee. "I'd better go see if the children made it to the kitchen."

"No, stay here with me, Ana," he said. "I feel so much better when you're near. And . . . and just in case you-know-who is lurking about, I don't want to deal with her on my own."

"Well, if you mean Ms. Lillian, she's gone out shopping. And when she's been out shopping, she usually comes home in a very good mood."

"Sssh, do you want to provoke the evil spirits?" he asked, glancing nervously at the door.

I couldn't help but laugh. "Why are you so afraid of Ms. Lillian?"

He shrugged. "I guess women, especially attractive women, always make me feel ridiculous in some way. In high school Adam and Darwin always had the prettiest girls swarming them and they never gave me a second glance. But if one of them should miraculously look my way, I instantly became a fumbling idiot. Honestly, it's as if I forgot how to speak, how to swallow and breath."

"That's very sweet," I said.

"No, it's dangerous," Benson replied, his eyes round. "One time I ate twenty-seven hotdogs all at once just to impress a lovely young lady at the carnival. I spent three days in bed with a bellyache and I'm certain she didn't even know my name. It's safer for me to keep my distance." Benson lifted his head. "You know something? You may be the only woman I've known who doesn't make me feel foolish." I was about to speak when he stopped me. "And don't tell me again that you're small and plain because as far as I'm concerned you're even more beautiful than a woman like Lillian. There's something about you, Ana. Everything around you seems to glow." Remembering his ailment, he flopped back on the couch, breathing deeply as though he were at the end of life's journey. "Oh, I suppose you just think I'm a silly little man."

"Of course not," I replied, touched by his words. "I'm very fond of you, Benson."

"But not fond enough to leave all of this and go away with me, are you?"

I laughed to hear him ask such a thing, and he frowned. "Of course, I don't for a minute believe that Adam would ever let me take you away. He admires you too much to let you go."

It was overwhelming to think that Mr. Trellis would make any comment about me to his oldest and dearest friend, let alone a positive one.

"Do you doubt that he admires you?" Benson asked, lifting his head again to look fully into my reddening face.

"I don't think Mr. Trellis gives domestic matters much thought," I replied, uncomfortable with the direction our conversation was taking, but Benson persisted.

"You're wrong. Adam may not always show it, but he cares deeply about his family and his home, and he considers you to be a member of it. He's told me more than once that he and the children would be lost without you. And sometimes I think," Benson said with a furtive flutter of his bushy eyebrows, "that he's jealous of our relationship."

"Benson, the things you say."

"It's true," he returned. "As happy as I'd be if you left with me, I'm certain that Adam would be equally devastated."

I shook my head, overwhelmed and flustered by his words, and I tried to laugh it off. Just then Mr. Trellis entered the room, both amused and somewhat annoyed by his friend, who started to moan anew about his impending death. "It'll be the first time I've heard of anybody dying from a strained tendon," he said while placing the ice pack under Benson's knee. "I suppose I'll have to find a new golf partner if this continues."

Benson moped but cooperated with the first-aid intervention. "I'm telling you it's a blood clot. I'm certain of it."

Mr. Trellis wiped his brow. He'd been out in the bright sunshine all afternoon, yet he was pale. "Of course. I'll let Peter know that you won't be joining us next week. Have you considered amputation?" Despite his mocking tone there was something in his voice, an unspoken sadness just beneath the surface. I suddenly yearned to place a comforting hand on his shoulder, but of course, I didn't move a muscle.

It was then that Lillian swept into the room, laden down with several shopping bags and boxes emblazoned with the names of strange men I'd never heard of before like Tom Ford, Michael Kors, and Jimmy Choo. When Millie informed me later that these were designers and that one handbag might cost as much as five thousand dollars, I was speechless. Five thousand dollars would've fed my entire family in El Salvador for several years.

"I thought I'd find you here," she said, her face flush. "My car is absolutely crammed with bags. Would you boys help me bring the rest of them in?"

Mr. Trellis stood up with a sigh, and to my surprise, Benson immediately swung his injured leg off the couch and bounded toward the door behind him. He was hunched over and limping a bit, but he was able to keep up without too much difficulty.

"What happened to you?" Lillian asked. "You look like the hunchback of Notre Dame."

Benson chuckled nervously. "Oh, it's nothing, just a little twinge," he said.

"If you ask me, you've put on too much weight," Lillian said, scrutinizing him from head to toe.

It seemed that Benson was bloating and expanding before our very eyes just to appease her. Then he hobbled out to the car for more bags, and I noticed that his ears had turned a deep shade of red.

That same evening, after the children were asleep and the house was quiet, I lay in my bed and tried to sleep as well, but every time I closed my eyes I saw the wounded expression in Mr. Trellis's eyes. It worried me deeply, although I wasn't sure why it should. I told myself that it was because I knew about Lillian's betrayal and that I'd played a role in keeping him from finding out about it. But I sensed that there was something more.

As I lay in bed I heard a creaking sound upstairs, on the third floor. It continued for several minutes, and I got up to make sure that Teddy and Jessie were still in their beds and was relieved to find them both sound asleep. I tiptoed out of the nursery and down the corridor. From there I saw a faint light glowing in the study across the courtyard and suspected that Mr. Trellis was reading late into the night. Millie said that in order to keep making money "by the truckload" as he did, he had to keep up with all the latest financial news. "He has the Midas touch," she said. "And thank God for that or else we'd both be out of a job with the way Her Majesty likes to spend his money."

At that moment I was startled by a loud banging sound coming from up above. It occurred to me that a possum could be making a nest up there or perhaps a family of cats. And if Millie discovered them before I did, she'd immediately call the exterminator and have them destroyed.

I returned to my room for the flashlight that I kept in my nightstand drawer and proceeded toward the service stairs. I peered up the stairwell and turned on my flashlight, which instantly banished the darkness, but the murkiness that surrounded me was hardly comforting. When I reached the third floor, I heard cockroaches scuttling about and caught sight of their shiny backs as they frantically scrambled for cover. I swallowed hard and reminded myself that in El Salvador the cockroaches were much bigger and the spiders and rats made the ones here look like gnats. I pressed on.

The floorboards groaned as I walked over them, and the darkness amplified every little sound, as did my growing anxiety. I was partway down the corridor and hadn't seen or heard anything unusual when I became aware of what sounded like rustling paper. I stood very still and held my breath to determine that it was coming from the storage room and that some kind of animal was building a nest. Once I knew what it was, I'd be able to plan a humane way to get rid of it.

I cautiously walked down the corridor and slowly opened

the door. I was surprised to see a faint eerie glow emanating from behind a stack of boxes at the far end of the room. The light wavered over everything, and when I glanced at the mannequins it seemed that their torsos were twisting in an effort to wrench themselves free of their stands. My throat tightened and a cold numbness overtook me. No animal could produce a light like this—and then my flashlight slipped from my sweaty hand and crashed to the floor. I was immediately blinded by a flash of light and I stumbled back, knocking over a pile of books and disturbing some furry creature that scrambled over my feet. I shrieked and turned to run out of the room, but I hit the wall again and again, unable to find the door through which I'd just entered. All at once I felt a heavy hand on my shoulder pulling me back.

"Ana, what in the world are you doing here?" a familiar voice said. "Didn't Millie tell you that this floor and this room are out of bounds?" I turned to find myself staring up into Mr. Trellis's troubled face.

"Mr. Trellis," I whispered, my heart pounding so loudly I could hardly hear myself speak. "I . . . I'm sorry, no, she didn't tell me, and I thought I . . . I . . . heard a noise."

"You're trembling like a scared rabbit," he said and he removed his jacket and draped it over my shoulders. Then he picked up my flashlight from the floor and flicked the switch several times, but it wasn't working, which seemed to annoy him greatly.

"Do you think it's wise to go around exploring noises in the middle of the night, Ana? What if I'd been an intruder? What would you have done?"

I pulled his jacket more tightly around my shoulders. "I'm fast on my feet Mr. Trellis."

He considered me dubiously while shaking his head. "You're fast on your feet, are you? That's hard to believe when you couldn't even find the door." Before I could respond, he left me to go to the other end of the room. I had no choice but to follow him, or go back downstairs by myself in the dark. He sat on one of the many boxes in the room and proceeded to read what appeared to be a musical score. He became so caught up that it seemed he'd forgotten I was there watching him as he listened to the music playing in his head and his body rocked and swayed. And then before my eyes his face was transformed. The chiseled frown fell away to reveal an expression filled with wonder and peace, as though a beautiful river of light were flowing through his heart. As I watched him, I was enveloped by an enthralling warmth and I lowered my arms and took a step closer, careful not to disturb him until I was quite certain that he was finished.

After he lowered the score to his knees, I asked, "Did you play that piece before?"

"Yes," he replied softly.

"What is it called?"

"Most people know it as Beethoven's Moonlight Sonata."

"Is it difficult to play?"

"It's more difficult not to." He closed the score with a huff and set it aside, but the soft expression in his eyes hadn't changed, and he continued. "I used to play this piece for my mother. She said that when she heard it she was able to forget all of her worries. Today marks exactly fifteen years to the day since I lost my parents, and every year on this day, I come up here to look these things over, to read my old music and remember how it used to be."

My eyes fell upon the shelves filled with his trophies. "Forgive me, Mr. Trellis, I know that it's none of my business, but why don't you play anymore? The piano downstairs is so beautiful, and Millie tells me that you were very good."

He furrowed his brow and studied his fingers. "I can't," he said. "I don't have the heart to play anymore."

Feeling uncommonly bold, I took another step toward him and said, "Millie told me about the accident and how angry your brother was with you because he couldn't play football anymore, but that wasn't your fault."

Hearing this, he closed his eyes and my heart stopped. I was afraid that this time I'd crossed the line, and that he was going to tell me to leave him be and get back to my room where I belonged. But when he opened his eyes again, they were filled with anguish, not anger. "I'm going to tell you something that I've never told a soul," he whispered. "But you must promise to keep it to yourself. Can you do that, Ana?"

I nodded and he shoved a nearby box toward me so that I could sit down next to him.

He glanced at me and then away. "Millie may have told you that her husband was driving the day of the accident, but he wasn't." He raked back his hair with trembling fingers. "I was a young man and I'd convinced Mick to let me drive to the recital that day. Naturally, the police and everyone else assumed that Mick had been the one at the wheel and I never bothered to correct them."

"Darwin doesn't know either?" I asked, stunned by his revelation.

"He was in a coma for almost a week. He doesn't remember anything about the accident, and the driver in the other car didn't survive. I was the only witness."

We sat in silence for a while, and I searched desperately for something I might say to comfort him. Finally I said, "It was still an accident, Mr. Trellis. You didn't mean for any of it to happen. You shouldn't blame yourself anymore, and you must remember that if God planned for you to survive then you should accept his will for your life."

He considered my words for a moment or two and then the cold demeanor that always held him prisoner returned, and when he looked up at me again his eyes were so filled with rage that my trembling instantly returned and I had to take several steps back. "You shouldn't speak for God regarding things you know nothing about, Ana," he muttered. It seemed that he wanted to say more, something hateful, but he stopped himself and stood up. "It's getting late," he said curtly. "We should go."

I stood up and followed him through the corridor and down the stairs to the second floor, where I returned his jacket, and we parted ways without another word. But as I lay in bed, I replayed every moment, every word and glance that had passed between us during those precious moments that his guard was down. Now that I understood the great burden he'd been living with for so many years, I wondered what else I could've said to ease his suffering. He'd been annoyed with me, it's true, but that didn't change the remarkable fact that he'd trusted me with a secret he'd never told another soul. There was now a special understanding between us, almost like a vow, and thinking of it this way reminded me of the secrets that Carlitos and I used to keep. I remembered how he tugged nervously at the loose fibers of his woven sandals when he confessed, "I saw Papa with the other woman. Her name is Marisol."

"Did you actually talk with him?" I asked, knowing that *Tía* Juana would be very angry if she knew that he had.

"I tried not to," Carlitos said, his face contorting with shame, "but I miss Papa so much, I couldn't walk away from him." Tears slipped down his face, leaving clean, shiny trails on his dusty cheeks. "I talked to Marisol too. She was pretty and nice, and she gave me a cool drink." He glanced shyly at me. "She told me I was handsome."

"You are handsome," I said, wanting to ease his turmoil however I could. "You know, if I saw my father, I would talk to him too even though I know Mama would be so mad she might never talk to me again."

"You would?" he said, looking up with grateful eyes.

"Yes, I would. And I wish that I was brave like you so I could go find him and bring him back home."

"But he's dead," Carlitos said, forgetting his own upset for the moment.

"That's what Mama and *Tía* Juana say, but sometimes I think they just tell me that so I won't go looking for him."

Carlitos nodded his understanding. This kind of parental trickery was something we were both familiar with. "Sometimes I wish that I could run away and live with Papa and his new woman," he said, but then his eyes flew open in alarm. "Don't tell anyone, okay?"

"I won't tell about Marisol if you won't tell anyone that I believe my father is still alive somewhere in the jungle."

He nodded enthusiastically, and already I could see that he was less anxious and that his playful mood was returning. "You're going to make a good wife," he said, giving me a solid shove, which I promptly returned.

"And you'll make a good husband, but I should warn you that I'm not planning to have any babies, so I'm going to have to be enough for you."

He thought about this for a moment and then smiled. "You're enough for me."

Eight

WHEN ANA HEARD BENSON'S heavy footsteps descending the staircase, she left Sister Josepha and Jessie, who were still discussing the pros and cons of living in New Mexico. He lumbered down the staircase with his briefcase dangling loosely at his side, and it seemed that at any moment it would slip away from his fingers and tumble down before him.

When he reached the bottom of the stairs, he sighed and clicked open the latches, releasing the fragrance of fine leather, paper, and ink. He shuffled through the contents and then looked up at Ana, his expression grim. "Before I proceed any further, I must tell you one last time that in my opinion your plan is ludicrous. I think we should tear these documents up right now and forget about the whole thing."

"Did he sign them?" Ana asked.

Benson showed her the space where Adam had signed. His signature was shaky, but it was undeniably his. "I told him they were routine addendums. He didn't bother to read any of it."

Ana briefly reviewed the documents and handed them back. "Benson, I know this is difficult for you, but it's the only way I can be sure that Teddy will come."

"This is no guarantee," Benson said, shaking his head so vigorously that his jowls jiggled. "And it doesn't have to be such an extreme arrangement."

"It will be worth it," Ana replied.

Benson returned the documents to his briefcase and closed it. "When will he receive them?"

"Peter told me that Teddy's back in town and staying with his mother. I'll have them delivered to her place this afternoon," Benson replied. "In fact, I'll deliver them myself."

Ana was relieved to hear this. "Do you have time for lunch?" she asked.

"I have to get to the office." Rarely did Benson turn down an invitation to eat.

"You'll be back soon?"

"I'll swing by on my way home this evening, but I don't want to keep you now. Adam's asking for you."

Ana gave Benson a quick peck on the cheek and scurried up the stairs with renewed energy. She turned just as he was walking out the door. "Once again, thank you," she said.

"You know I'd do anything for you. Ana. I just hope you know what you're doing."

"Don't worry, Benson. I've never been more certain of anything in my life."

Adam shuddered with every breath, and Ana was angry with herself for having allowed Benson to visit for so long. She quickly counted out his pills, but he turned his head away when she brought them to his lips.

"You've waited too long already," Ana said.

Adam whispered hoarsely, "I want to talk to you."

She cupped the pills in her hand and leaned forward so that she was close enough to feel the warmth of his breath on her face. "What is it, my love?"

"It's about Benson."

Ana's heart began to beat wildly as she thought about what Benson might've told him.

"He's a good man," Adam said.

"Yes, I know. And he's a wonderful friend," Ana replied, barely able to endure her anxiety and the agony of her beloved's suffering.

"He's always cared for you."

"And I care for him," Ana replied, but all she wanted at that moment was for Adam to take his medicine so that his suffering would cease. His eyes opened wide and he stared intensely, but they were focused far away, beyond her. She took this opportunity to offer the pills again and this time he accepted. Immediately after swallowing them, he grew calmer and closed his eyes. Then he suddenly reached out and grabbed her hand with surprising strength. He opened his eyes and said, "He wants you to go with him."

"I'm staying right here with you. I'm not leaving with Benson or anybody."

"After," he whispered. "After it's finished."

Once her beloved had fallen asleep, Ana allowed her tears to flow, weeping quietly into her sleeve to avoid waking him. Then she stacked the empty glasses on the nightstand and folded the clean sheets she'd brought up from the laundry the day before. After she finished these chores, she sat back in her chair and gazed down at his face, savoring the tranquillity and quiet of the moment, and thanking God for every painless breath that entered his lungs.

Moments later, Jessie entered the room and sat at Ana's feet, resting her head on her knee. "He looks peaceful again," she said.

"He'll sleep for an hour or more," Ana whispered.

"I don't want you to go to New Mexico," Jessie said.

"I'm not going anywhere right now," Ana murmured.

"But how about later . . . after . . . ?"

Ana gently stroked the hair away from Jessie's forehead. "Let's just focus on right now."

The roses were in full bloom and Millie so enjoyed fresh flowers in her kitchen that I spent the better part of an hour selecting the most beautiful roses for a fresh water bouquet. Jessie was with me in her carriage and every time I snipped a stem with my clippers, she squealed with delight and waggled her little arms and feet in the air. Then suddenly, she became still and gazed at me with her big, curious eyes. Dropping my clippers to the ground, I knelt down next to her and gazed back. Every time I smiled, she smiled. If I grew serious, she did as well, watching me intently, trying to predict my next move. Then, just for fun, I stuck out my tongue. She appeared momentarily confused, but then much to my amazement, she stuck out her tongue too.

I nearly fell back on my heels, and she grinned as though

on the brink of madness. I plucked her out of her carriage and she chortled with happiness. At that moment I spotted Lillian watching us through her bedroom window. I waved to her and she gave me a halfhearted wave in return. She'd been avoiding me ever since I'd discovered her with Jerome several weeks ago, and for the most part I was glad. I felt awkward and ashamed for her and a deep sadness for Mr. Trellis. I also felt guilty about my role, but whenever I convinced myself that the honorable thing to do was to tell him about what I'd seen, I realized that this too would be wrong, and as my mother always told me, "What happens between a man and woman is private."

Even so, I thought the time had come for us to move on, so with Jessie in my arms I rushed upstairs, intent upon having her perform the little miracle I'd just witnessed for her mother. Surely this would ease the tension between us. I knocked on her bedroom door and entered. She was still sitting at the window, her lovely eyes alternating between sadness and the joy of seeing her little girl.

"She did something amazing just now," I said, placing the child on her mother's knee and then explained how she'd poked out her tongue at me.

"She didn't," Lillian said, duly impressed.

"I swear that she did. Try it and see if she does it again."

"Like this?" Lillian said, poking out her tongue like a schoolgirl.

"Yes, but she has to be looking directly into your eyes."

And so it was that after a few more attempts Jessie performed the little miracle for her mother, who rewarded her with a flurry of kisses all over her face. But then Lillian's delight turned to sorrow, and her tears began to flow. I brought her the Kleenex box from her dresser. She plucked several tissues out, then blew her nose.

"Oh, Ana, I don't know what to do," she said. "I feel as though I'm dying inside."

I sat down next to her. "Are you in love with the painter, Jerome?" I asked, feeling that somehow I'd earned the right to ask this question.

She threw her head back and laughed, appearing for an instant just as she did when she lay with him on the couch. Then she shrugged, and wiped her eyes. "I'm in love with his body and with the way he makes me feel, that's all."

I was shocked to silence.

"You may find this hard to believe, Ana, but when I was your age, I'd already slept with countless men."

It was ludicrous to associate such an image with a woman as beautiful and refined as Lillian. In my mind, women who did this were girls who hadn't been blessed with natural beauty. If they were going to be noticed at all, they had no choice but to engage in the most lurid behavior. But Lillian need only bat her lashes to bring an entire regiment of men to their knees.

In response to my baffled expression, she said, "Women like me aren't born, they're made, and my lessons began at a very early age."

"I'm sorry, Ms. Lillian, I don't understand."

Jessie started tugging on her mother's pearl necklace, so Lillian removed it and gave it to her daughter, while placing her on the floor near her feet, where she remained happily engaged.

"When I was a little girl about Teddy's age, the woman who took care of me was nothing like you. She was lazy and she didn't enjoy looking after children. One of the duties she least enjoyed was bathing me. I'd splash about so much that she ended up soaking wet. So when her teenage son visited one summer, she delegated bath duty to him, and I liked the arrangement even better than she did. He was a sweet, handsome boy who liked washing me in the most meticulous manner you can imagine. He didn't mind getting wet and often stripped down and got into the bath with me. Oh, how we played. I never wanted bath time to end," she said.

"That's child abuse," I said.

"Oh, I realize that now," she replied. "But at the time, the secret 'tickle game' as we called it was the most fun I'd ever known, and I missed him terribly when he went back to school."

"Didn't you ever tell anyone what happened?"

"I couldn't betray my best friend," Lillian said, her eyes round. "At least that's what I considered him to be then. He told me the grown-ups would never understand the secret we shared and keeping the secret was almost as much fun as playing the game." Lillian twisted the tissue she held, and little pieces fell to the floor. "That was just the beginning of my story, and there were many more adventures that followed," she said, her eyes darkened by regret. "I learned things I shouldn't have, and trying to unlearn them has been my undoing." She turned to me, her expression as earnest as I'd ever seen it. "It didn't take me more than a minute or two to figure out that Jerome would be open to my advances."

"What that boy did to you is wrong, Ms. Lillian. You can get professional help, and maybe if you do, your secrets won't hurt you as much as they do."

She smoothed her skirt with the palms of her hands. "Believe me, Ana, I've had so much therapy that my brain probably looks like a block of Swiss cheese."

"Does Mr. Trellis know?"

"He knows some of it," she said with a perfunctory nod. "He knows that I had a rather wild adolescence and more psychotherapy than Patty Hearst and Sybil combined. But as far as he's concerned, I've more or less overcome my addictions."

"Addictions?"

If I was baffled before, I was now completely bewildered. "Ms. Lillian, if you just keep your mind focused on your husband and your precious children and put them before everything else, that should give you enough strength to move mountains."

"You'd think so, wouldn't you?" she said, her expression toughening, but she was unable to sustain her hard demeanor and before long her tears were flowing again. "Help me, Ana. Help me change so I can save my marriage and be a better wife and mother."

"I don't know how I can, Ms. Lillian. I've never helped anybody with this kind of problem before."

"But I know you can help me, Ana. That's why you're here. That's why you haven't left us."

Looking into her pleading face, I couldn't find the words to respond, but then I thought back on how it had been for me on that early morning when I walked up from the river with a bucket of fresh water for Mama. The bucket was so heavy I feared my fingers would break under the strain of the handle, so I stopped and set it down for a moment to rest. That's when I saw Dolores's husband behind their hut urinating against the same tree he used for machete target practice. His feet were set wide apart so he wouldn't splatter his good shoes. He'd probably been out the night before. Everyone knew that Dolores's husband liked going to the dance halls in town, but never with her.

He didn't see me at first, but then he turned and stared directly at me while his urine continued to flow in a heavy stream. I knew that it wasn't polite to stare back, but I felt I should follow the same rule as I followed whenever I encountered a snake on the path: never take your eyes off it, because the moment you do, it'll strike. So, without removing my eyes from his face, I took up my bucket and slowly backed away. I wanted to move faster than I did, but the heavy bucket made this impossible.

He watched me intently all the while, and his flow of urine turned into a dribble and finally stopped. Then with his penis still in hand, he turned around to face me and he began to wave it around in mesmerizing circles, moving his fingers up and down the length of it until it was stiff as a peg for pots and pans to hang off. I stopped and stared at his rigid penis, amazed by the way he caressed it like a snake charmer, gently coaxing it, propping it up for me to admire. He began walking toward me, his mouth twitching into a filthy smile. I was desperate to run away, but my horror confused and paralyzed every part of me except for my eyes, which rapidly shifted back and forth between his face and his crotch as he continued to massage it more vigorously.

As I stood there, his feet shuffled forward until he was so close that I could clearly see the shiny skin of his penis and the red swollen bulb at the tip. His lips were moist with spittle as they stretched across his face into a hideous grin. He smelled as though he hadn't washed in days.

When he was close enough to touch me, he reached out a trembling hand, grabbed the crown of my head, and began to push me down toward his crotch while mumbling, "Tastes just like candy," over and over again. But his touch brought me back to my senses, and I released my bucket of water all over his shoes and ran back home to my hut without looking back.

Once I caught my breath, I told Mama everything that had happened and the reason I didn't have any water for her or even the bucket. As she listened her eyes narrowed, and she stared silently into the corner of the room. When she was finished thinking, she put on her good shoes and combed her long black hair back into a ponytail. Then she took one of the priest's robes she'd just finished mending from her sewing cabinet, inspected it, and refolded it before placing it in her bag. "Wait here for me, Ana," she said.

"But I want to go with you, Mama."

"No. You must wait here for me," she repeated so sternly that I knew there was no point in pressing her further. I watched from the window as she walked down the path toward the village church. About twenty minutes later, she reappeared with Father Lucas at her side, and they both turned toward Dolores's hut. They were there for a long while, but I remained at the window waiting, watching, and worrying. I thought of *Tía* Juana, Carlitos, and my other cousins, who'd left the previous day for the fair in town. I would've gone with them, but Mama wanted me to stay home and help her work. Perhaps now she was sorry that she hadn't let me go.

Eventually I saw Mama and Father Lucas walking up the path with the bucket I'd dropped in his hand, although with the light and easy way it swung from his fingers, I knew that it was empty. When they entered the hut, Father Lucas asked me many questions about what had happened that morning and what I'd seen, while Mama stood back listening, her face not revealing the slightest emotion. He asked me the same questions for a second time. No doubt, Dolores's husband had denied everything, and now Father Lucas didn't know who to believe. I told him everything that had happened again and tearfully added, "And I dropped my bucket of water and ran away as fast as I could."

Father Lucas's ears perked up. "What did you do?" he asked.

"I ran away."

"No, before that."

"I . . . I dropped my bucket."

"Was it empty or full?"

"It was full. That's why I dropped it, because it was so heavy, I couldn't run with it."

Father Lucas seemed more convinced of my story now. "Where did you drop it?"

"On the ground and all over Dolores's husband's good shoes."

Father Lucas turned to Mama. "That explains why his shoes and socks were drying outside by the front door."

Father Lucas then recited several prayers over me, some of them in Latin, and the three of us prayed the rosary together. He instructed me to light a candle at the Virgin's altar for nine days and then every Sunday from then on. "This will purify your soul and keep you as child in the eyes of God forever," Father Lucas said with such certainty that I had no doubt it would.

I refocused my eyes on Lillian's face. "Will you help me, Ana?" she asked again. "Will you help me be a better wife and mother?" In response to my silence, she said, "Oh, I realize that Millie fills your head with lies about me, but in my heart I know you don't listen to her and that you don't judge me, not even now."

"I don't for a moment approve of what you did, Ms. Lillian, and I feel very badly for helping you get away with it."

Lillian gazed desperately into my eyes. "But you did help me, and I believe you did it because you know that I'm a good person and that I'm capable of changing. God knows that Adam deserves a better wife than I've been to him."

"Yes, he does," I replied softly.

"I told you before that I didn't love him, but I do. This crazy obsession may control my mind and my body, but it doesn't control my heart." She took my hand and said, "I know that with your help I can change."

"I'm not sure how I can help you, but for the sake of your marriage and your children, I'll try my best."

Overcome with gratitude, Lillian pressed her forehead to my hand, and when I looked over at baby Jessie, she gave me another one of her beautiful toothless grins.

Dear Sister Josepha,

I'm writing you this letter with a heavy heart because, unfortunately, my plans have changed again. I was fully expecting to join you in a few weeks, but my obligations here make it impossible for me to leave now. I know that you need my help as you set up your school and as always, I remain deeply inspired by the idea of working with you. I also know that, as you suggested, it would do me good to get away and reevaluate my conviction about a religious life. And what better way to do that than working side by side with my dearest friend and mentor? Nevertheless, I fear that if I abandon the Trellis family now, harm will come to them and most especially to the children. Although I try, I don't understand what provokes the destructive spirit that lurks within the walls of this beautiful and elegant home. Perhaps if you were here you would be able to help me understand how people who are blessed with so much can be so unhappy. And then perhaps I would better know how to help them.

I often think about the pain and suffering of my country and I hope that one day soon the world will know the truth about what happened there and that the evil will stop. If there is hope for a nation to heal, there must be hope for a family as well. Until then, I pray that your offer to work with you at your new school will still be open to me once this situation has been resolved. . . .

Ms. Lillian and the children began attending church with me on Sundays while Adam and Benson played golf, and when the mass was finished, we always lit candles at the Virgin Mary's altar. Afterward Lillian knelt and prayed for a very long while, and we often lingered until we were the only ones left in the church. When the children got fussy and their whining echoed throughout the cavernous building, I would tap her on the shoulder, only to find her eyes moist with tears.

As the weeks and months passed, Lillian's time spent in prayer lessened somewhat, but her general demeanor was greatly improved. She was fresher, lighter, and lovelier than ever. Her social life blossomed again, and she scheduled lunch meetings and shopping excursions with her girlfriends several times a week, assuring me all the while that keeping busy was good for her.

Soon after Lillian's revelation, I had lent her the rosary Sister Josepha had given me when I first entered the convent. I instructed her to pray the rosary every morning and every evening until she felt peace in her heart. Then she was to do so only once a day. About three months later, I found the rosary in an envelope under my door with a note that read, "I have found my peace. Thank you, Ana."

I took the rosary out of the envelope and kissed the crucifix before placing it back in my drawer. I was overall pleased with the changes I'd seen in Lillian. She seemed less prone to bouts of anger and not so controlled by passions pulling her in so many directions. I could swear that she was dressing more modestly and that she wasn't as obsessed with her appearance or so easily manipulated by flattery. She was kinder toward Millie, and she seemed to enjoy spending more time with her children. She made an effort to play with them in the afternoon after they woke up from their naps, and more than once she'd come in to help me with them during bath time. When Jessie flapped her arms about, drenching Lillian's new silk blouse, she was only moderately perturbed, whereas she would've been livid before. I could only guess that her marriage had also improved because I hadn't witnessed any more arguments, but I didn't feel comfortable asking about this directly. As it was, I was more than content to know that the remedy Father Lucas had prescribed for me all those years ago seemed to be working for Ms. Lillian as well.

Nine

BY THE TIME JESSIE was three years old, she preferred selecting the roses herself as well as picking the wildflowers that grew near the perimeter of the garden wall. We enjoyed making mini bouquets of tiny purple and yellow flowers that we carefully tied with ribbon before presenting them to Jessie's growing collection of dolls. We could spend most of Saturday afternoon occupied in this way while Teddy flew his motorized airplanes over our heads, often coming far too close for comfort.

Teddy had developed a keen interest in airplanes. He proudly announced as often as he could that one day he planned to become a pilot so he could fly the big jumbo jets across the sky and all over the world. No matter what he was doing, if he should hear the rumble of a jet engine overhead he'd stop to look up and wouldn't turn away until the aircraft was completely out of sight.

"Nana, tell him to stop," Jessie cried when Teddy's plane grazed the top of her head for the third or fourth time.

I turned to Teddy, who was standing at the far end of the

garden with his remote control in his hand and a devilish grin on his face. It was difficult not to smile in return, but if he was going to take me seriously, I had to be stern. I picked up the plane that landed nearby and promptly deactivated the motor.

"Okay, Nana, I'll stop," he said, his big eyes still glittering with mischief. "I'll go show my plane to Uncle Darwin instead."

"Uncle Darwin? Is he here?" I asked.

"I saw him talking to Mommy by the pool," Teddy said. "I'll fly my plane over the pool. He'll like that."

"And I'm going to give Mommy these flowies," Jessie happily declared.

"I'm sure they'll both be delighted, but first we must have lunch."

Teddy scowled and hunched his shoulders forward in protest as we walked back to the house. "I hate lunch, Nana," he said.

"Even when lunch is peanut butter and jelly?"

"I hate peanut butter and jelly the most," Teddy grumbled.

"I love peanut butter and jelly the most," Jessie said, slipping her hand into mine.

Upon Teddy's insistence, we walked by the pool on our way to the kitchen, but his uncle and mother were nowhere in sight. He ate lunch with his toy plane beside him on the table and once he'd finished he took it up again and began to search for his uncle in earnest. I left Jessie at the table to load the dryer as she rearranged her bouquet. I was away for no more than a minute or two, but when I returned she was gone. I called for her, but it was Teddy who came running back looking distraught. "I can't find Uncle Darwin anywhere," he said, "and I want to show him my plane."

"Are you sure he's still here?"

Teddy pointed out the window toward the front of the house. "Isn't that his red sporty car?" he asked.

It was indeed Darwin's car. "Have you seen Jessie?" I asked.

"Nope," Teddy answered, absorbed again by his plane and the movable wing flaps.

I began my search for Jessie on the ground floor, but all was silent except for the soft rhythmic rumble of Millie's snores. Sometimes Jessie amused herself by looking in on Millie while she slept. I was hoping to find her there, but Millie was alone. The second floor was also empty. With my heart in my throat, I climbed the rear flight of stairs toward the third floor, and when I neared the landing, I spotted Jessie standing in the corridor with her bouquet of flowers hanging limply from her hand. I called to her softly, and when she came to me her expression was strangely pensive and faraway. As we descended the stairs, I suggested that we make mud pies, one of her favorite activities. She readily agreed, but as we mixed the mud and constructed our pies she seemed less enthralled than usual, as if understanding for the first time that the brown gooey concoction we so carefully decorated with rocks and flowers was not really pie.

Darwin left as surreptitiously as he'd arrived, and Teddy was disappointed when he looked outside and discovered that his uncle's car was gone. Later that same evening as we sat around the dinner table Jessie was quiet, her attention focused entirely on her drawing, while Teddy talked nonstop to his father about his remote control plane. All at once, Jessie jumped off her chair and ran around the table to show her mother what she'd drawn. "I drew a picture of you, Mommy," she said, quite pleased with herself.

Lillian looked at the picture and blanched. "My goodness," she muttered.

"May Daddy see it?" Mr. Trellis asked. Before Lillian could say anything, Jessie happily plucked the picture from her mother's hands and ran to show her father.

Mr. Trellis stared at it for a moment or two and glanced warily at his wife. "This is quite interesting," he said.

"Do you like it, Daddy?" Jessie asked.

"You're quite the artist," he said tersely.

Jessie took the picture from her father and showed it to me next. When I saw it I blushed, and then I suddenly remembered how relieved I'd been that Jerome's secret painting of Lillian had never materialized. I had interpreted this as a sign of Lillian's heartfelt commitment to living a moral life. I was preparing to return the picture to Mr. Trellis, but didn't realize that Teddy had already left his chair and was looking over my shoulder. "Jessie," he said harshly, "you shouldn't draw Mommy naked. It's wrong. Isn't it, Daddy?"

Mr. Trellis seemed at a loss for words. "Many artists paint their subjects in the nude," he replied, coloring a bit as his disapproval seeped through the calm demeanor he was trying so hard to maintain.

Teddy shook his head adamantly. "I don't care. Mommy shouldn't be showing her boobies."

Jessie's bottom lip began to quiver. She ran over to me, snatched the drawing away, and ran out of the room. We heard her footsteps pattering upstairs to her room, and I knew she would immediately store the picture in her treasure box, where she kept her favorite drawings, stones, leaves, ribbons, and other odds and ends she considered uncommonly beautiful and worthy of collecting.

Teddy was preparing to run after his sister and right the situation with a few shoves as he tended to do when he was upset with her, but I stopped him at the door and led him back to the table. "You stay here and finish your dinner, Teddy."

"I don't want to, Nana," Teddy said, glowering at me. "Jessie is a stupid and bratty kid." He'd been coming home from school with these expressions of late.

"You go on, Ana," Mr. Trellis said sternly. "We'll deal with Teddy."

Just as I expected, Jessie was in her room on the floor with her treasure box open next to her. The drawing of her mother was at her feet, and although she was still sniffling and grim, she was for the moment preoccupied with some of the treasures that she hadn't visited for a while.

I sat down next to her and asked, "Are you going to put this picture of your mommy in the treasure box too?" I asked.

She nodded and sniffed some more.

"Well then, how about if I fold it up for you so that it doesn't get ruined? May I?"

She nodded again and I took up the drawing. After carefully folding it, I placed it at the bottom of the box. Then one by one we put all of her other treasures over it. Jessie was calmer once this was done and the box was closed. Then she turned to me, her eyes wide with wonder. "I saw Mama naked with Uncle Darwin," she said. "He has a poky peepee just like Teddy's."

I sat back, unable to speak or move for several moments. A tremor began to invade my hands and my face grew hot.

Jessie placed her little fingers on my face. "Nana, why are you crying?" she asked. I took her little hand and kissed it, trying my best to smile.

"I'm fine, Jessie. How about we go downstairs now and finish our dinner?" As far as I was concerned, if Jessie wanted to talk about what she'd seen, there was absolutely nothing I would do to stop her.

When we arrived to the dinner table, all was back to normal. Teddy was calm, and soon Jessie started to chatter on about her many treasures. All the while Lillian's eyes focused on mine, pleading with me to understand, but I avoided her stare and tried to concentrate on what Jessie was saying.

"I have one rock shaped like a heart. That's my favorite," she said, enjoying the rare privilege of her father's undivided attention.

"What other shapes do you have?" he asked.

"I have hearts and rainbows. Many, many rainbows," she replied, arcing her arms over her head.

"I like rainbows," Teddy added, eager to get in on the conversation and steal a portion of his father's interest. "And tarantula spiders too."

"I don't like spiders," Jessie retorted.

"Have you ever seen a tarantula?" Mr. Trellis asked, turning to Teddy.

"Only on TV," he replied.

"Would you like to see the ones they have at the pet store?"

"Yes," Teddy said, nearly falling off his chair with excitement. "Can we go right now?"

"Not now, but maybe tomorrow I'll take you. I happen to know that some people keep them as pets."

Jessie made a face.

"I don't want a pet tarantula here," Lillian said sternly to her husband. "This house isn't big enough for the two of us. I'm sure you feel the same way, don't you, Ana?"

Reluctantly, I turned to look at her. "I used to find tarantulas in my little house in El Salvador all the time."

"Wow," Teddy said, duly impressed. "Were you scared?"

"Yes. I was especially scared of the female spiders. They were even larger than the males and could get as big as your hand."

"My goodness!" Lillian said, turning her nose up in disgust.

"Did you squish 'em dead?" Jessie asked, both horrified and fascinated at the same time.

"Not exactly," I explained. "My cousin Carlitos was just a year or two older than Teddy when his mother gave him a big plastic bag she'd saved from market day and directed him to collect all the spiders he could find around the village. There had been a drought, and an army of brown tarantulas had crawled down from the hills in search of moisture. Every day we heard women screaming when the spiders turned up in shoes, under blankets, and just about anywhere a big hairy spider could think of to hide. Carlitos was delighted to be assigned this task, and it mystified me how a boy with such a tender heart could take pleasure in such ugliness.

One evening as I lay in my hammock, he crept up to me, held the bag up to my face, and shook it. The plastic crinkled and puckered in places as the tarantulas crawled over one another inside. It gave me the shivers to think of so many ugly hairy spiders in one place, but I also pitied the poor creatures because I had no doubt that Carlitos had devised horrific plans for their demise.

"What are you going to do with them?" I asked with a shudder.

He gazed pensively at the bag for a moment or two. "I'll probably drown some of them and burn the rest. Or I might just stick a big sewing needle in the center of them and see how long it takes for them to die. The last one I tried this with took half a day, but it wasn't as big as some of these," he said, his eyes glittering with promise.

"Father Lucas says that all animals are God's creatures and that we should respect them."

Carlitos shook the bag again. "God doesn't care about big hairy spiders."

I turned away from him. "He cares about everyone and everything, even if they're ugly," I muttered.

"Don't be mad at me, Ana," he said. "I'm just following Mama's orders. She said that I had to destroy them or they'd come right back to the village and maybe next time they'll crawl into your bed and"—he stroked the back of my neck—"right down your back."

I swatted his hand away without turning around. "It doesn't matter. You don't have to enjoy killing them as much as you do."

Carlitos was too honest to argue the fact, so he left with his rustling bag of spiders and went to his hammock without another word.

That night I was unable to sleep. All I could think about was those poor spiders destined to be destroyed the following morning. When I was certain that everyone had fallen asleep, I crept out of bed and found the bag of spiders under Carlitos's hammock. Quiet as a mouse, I tiptoed outside and walked to the edge of the village, grateful for the full moon illuminating my way. Several hungry dogs followed me out, thinking that I was discarding trash, but their noses soon told them I carried nothing of interest to them.

Because of the drought, the river was low and I was able to cross with the water only reaching up to my knees. Once on the other side, I quickly untied the bag and tossed it away from me. The spiders must have been lethargic or perhaps somewhat stunned because they didn't run out of the bag delirious with their newfound freedom as I expected they would. I prodded them out with a long stick so that I could return the bag to *Tía* Juana, and they slowly crawled out and disappeared into the night. Only two were dead, and I was certain that the rest wouldn't be seen in our village again, as everyone knew that spiders couldn't swim across the river.

The next morning when Carlitos discovered that his bag of spiders was missing, he immediately suspected me. When I admitted to releasing them, he was angry and refused to play with me, but his anger didn't last for long. It was easy for me to change his bad moods by tickling his feet, and once he was his lighthearted self again, he said, "Anyway, my spiders will be back."

"No they won't. I released them on the other side of the river, and everybody knows that spiders can't swim."

"Of course they can swim," he said. "I've seen them."

"You're making that up."

"No I'm not. They float on all eight of their legs like this, see," he said, making his hand look like a spider. "And then they move their legs back and forth and then before you know it—" Quick as a flash he put his hand over my face, and I jumped and screamed, which caused Carlitos to laugh so hard he almost fell off his hammock.

After I finished my story, Teddy was the first to speak, "If I found a tarantula I wouldn't put it in a plastic bag," he said. "I'd keep it on a leash and tie it next to my bed. Then I'd take it for walks and scare everybody with it. Wouldn't you, Daddy?" he asked, his color high at the mere thought of it.

Mr. Trellis folded his napkin and placed it on the table thoughtfully. "I think I would release it somewhere safe just like Ana did when she was a little girl," he said, giving me an approving nod, and the slightest hint of a smile.

"Me too," Jessie said, clapping her hands.

The conversation moved on to the proper care and feeding of snakes, and Jessie never said a word about what she'd seen that afternoon.

Jessie started preschool only a few months later, just as Teddy entered the first grade, and that's when Darwin began showing up at the house once or twice a week in the middle of the day. While in the garden, I often heard the sounds of their seductive laughter drifting out from one of the many open windows. It seemed they were taunting me with their perverted version of musical chairs, daring me to look up toward the sound and discover them, but I didn't want to see any more than I'd seen already. It sickened me to think that Ms. Lillian could betray her husband and family in such a blatant and perverse manner, and try as I might, I couldn't understand it. Even when I thought back on all she'd told me about her abusive past, it still made little sense to me.

So that I wouldn't have to look into her eyes and pretend to understand as I knew she wanted me to, I avoided her. If I heard her voice in the entry hall after a shopping trip, I turned and went in the opposite direction. She often spent time with the children in the afternoon after their naps when they were in happy, playful moods. At these times, I dressed them in their play clothes, fed them their snacks, and left them with Lillian alone in the back patio or in the sunroom.

One afternoon as I was leaving them with her on the pretext of needing to tidy the nursery, she said, "I was thinking of going to church with you this Sunday. It's been such a long time and I miss it. Would that be okay with you, Ana?"

Both Teddy and Jessie were playing in the corner with their toys, so I was sure they couldn't hear me when I replied rather sternly, "You don't have to ask my permission to go to church, Ms. Lillian."

She was taken aback by my response and studied me for a moment or two.

"Fine, I won't go if that's the way you feel about it," she said, folding her arms across her chest and pouting prettily.

I wanted nothing more than to get away from her and was almost to the door when I stopped and turned around, my arms also folded across my chest. "You may think that I'm very stupid and perhaps I am, but God isn't stupid. He sees everything. He knows everything, and he isn't fooled by a person who goes to church on Sundays and then lives their sinful life as usual every other day of the week."

Ms. Lillian narrowed her eyes at me and then smiled slyly. "So are you saying that I should go to church *every* day?"

"I'm afraid that not even that will help you now," I said.

At this, her face broke out into a big easy grin. "My good-ness, Ana, you make it sound as though I'm the most wicked person you've ever known."

When I didn't deny it, her smiled dropped instantly. "You should remember your place here and try to show me a little more respect."

I remained silent, and she sat up in her chair. "If I wanted to I could have you fired, and you'd be packing your bags tomor-row. But, of course, I know that if I did that you'd tell Adam everything you know about me."

"You can rest assured that I'll never tell Mr. Trellis any-thing," I replied. "And if you like, I can leave tonight. There's no need to wait until tomorrow, I have very few things to pack."

"That isn't what I want," Lillian said, her eyes watering. "I want you to . . ." Her lips started to tremble. "I want you to be my friend and confidante again," she said in a whimper.

"You know very well why I can't do that anymore, Ms. Lil-lian," I replied sadly.

She then set her jaw and looked away.

"I'll be back for the children in an hour or so," I said, and I left the room.

For the first time, I would've been grateful for the opportunity to gossip with Millie about what was going on because at least then I wouldn't be dealing with the situation alone, but Millie had been spending more time in her room and emerging from her naps with a thicker glaze over her eyes and the ever-more-pungent odor of whiskey on her breath. She usually recovered sufficiently to prepare the evening meal, but in the middle of the day, she was oblivious to what was going on in the house.

One afternoon while sitting at the fountain with a letter from Sister Josepha, I detected movement out of the corner of my eye and turned to see Darwin and Lillian watching me from Lillian's bedroom window. They stood shoulder to shoulder within the frame of the window, as though posing for a picture.

I turned my attention back to my letter and tried my best to concentrate on its contents. Sister Josepha wrote to me of her joy in knowing that finally, with the help of the United Nations, the peace accords had been signed in El Salvador. What's more, several high-ranking officers implicated with plotting the murders of priests and peasants during the war had been detained, pending an investigation. It was cause for great celebration in my country, and I was grateful that my prayers for peace had finally been answered.

Sister Josepha also wrote about the great challenges she was facing at her school. There wasn't enough classroom space for the children, and they were in desperate need of a playground so that the children wouldn't have to play in the dirt. Given the difficult conditions and measly salary, it was difficult to recruit teachers, and she hoped that before too much longer I'd be available. There was more, but I couldn't focus properly on what I read when I knew that Lillian and Darwin were watching me all the while. When I finally yielded to their stares and looked back to the window, with a disapproving scowl cut across my face this time, they were gone.

Several nights later I was awakened by a frantic muttering next to my ear and opened my eyes to see Lillian kneeling next to my bed. I immediately sat up and turned on the light. Her hair was disheveled, and smeared makeup darkened the hollows of her eyes. "I know that you're not my friend anymore, but I need to speak with you anyway," she whispered. "You're right. God knows everything and he sees everything, and I don't know how much longer I can live this crazy charade. Sometimes I think that I should just tell Adam the truth and leave before I destroy my family. But when I think about leaving my children and this house and my life, I get so afraid. I don't think I could ever survive on my own."

"Then you must try harder," I said. "To resist this temptation, you have to focus all of your heart, mind, and soul."

"I try, Ana. Believe me, I do. I pray all the time like you taught me, but why is it that when I do manage to resist temptation, I don't feel any better? Why do I feel like I'm all tied up in a knot? Shouldn't I feel liberated?" she asked, her eyes pleading. "Instead, I only get more annoyed with Adam. I can't stand the sight of him, the sound of him, the smell of him, and least of all his touch. But when I give in to temptation with others, Adam becomes my noble prince, and all of a sudden I love him again."

"I don't know why you're feeling this way, but if you're going to stay in the marriage, you have to keep trying."

"But how?" she asked, pressing her hands together. "If I pray any more than I have been, I might as well become a nun, and you and I both know that no convent would ever accept me."

I covered her hands with my own, my mind whirling in many directions at once as I searched for another solution. "My mother used to tell me that positive thoughts are like the sun that can banish the darkness of wicked thinking."

"I must stay positive," Lillian muttered, closing her eyes. "I must think positive thoughts." She opened her eyes. "What positive thoughts should I focus on, Ana? Should I think about angels and saints and all those holy kinds of things?"

"No," I said, vigorously shaking my head. "We tried that already and it didn't work. Now it's time to think about something closer to home. I believe that it would be better for you to think about your husband and all of his good qualities."

"Yes, of course, he's a very good man and he has many good qualities doesn't he?"

"Of course he does."

Lillian closed her eyes and tried to relax. "My husband is very skilled at managing money," she said. "That's one good thing I can say about him."

"What else?" I asked with an encouraging nod.

She closed her eyes tighter, but when she opened them again she looked more fearful and anxious than before. "I can't think of anything else. I'm sorry, but I just can't."

"Ms. Lillian," I replied, unable to disguise my disappointment, "Mr. Trellis has so many good qualities that you should be able to list dozens without having to think very hard."

"Fine, then why don't you continue where I left off?" she said in a challenging tone.

I sat up straighter in bed. "He's a loving father and a hard worker. It's true that he can be stern at times, but this is only because of the unbearable tenderness in his heart. He has a strong character and definite opinions about things, but he's open and curious as well. He has a brilliant mind, yet he's patient and understanding with those who aren't as gifted as he.

He is courageous, and noble, and he puts his family first above everything else."

Gazing up at me with misty eyes, she said, "I'm not sure we're talking about the same man, but hearing you speak about him like that does make me feel better."

"I'm only speaking the truth as I see it, Ms. Lillian."

She lowered her head contritely. "Do you . . . do you think he's handsome and desirable? I don't mean to ask you such an awkward question. It's just that I . . . I used to think he was very handsome, but lately, unless I'm misbehaving, I don't feel attracted to him at all."

I felt a sudden chill steal up my spine, well aware that what I felt for Mr. Trellis would be considered more than reverent admiration, but then I banished the thought. "Ms. Lillian, the other day when your girlfriends were here, didn't you notice the way they looked at your husband when he walked into the room?"

She shook her head. "I wasn't even sure they noticed him."

"They noticed all right. In fact, they couldn't take their eyes off him. And the blond lady . . ."

"Gina?"

"Yes, she unbuttoned the top button of her blouse when she realized that he was out in the corridor."

"You're kidding me," Ms. Lillian said, her eyes glittering.

"Be careful, Ms. Lillian, or someone might steal your husband away from you. Maybe they would have by now if he weren't so devoted to you."

"Yes, yes," she said, breathing deeply, her understanding suddenly restored. "I will be careful, and I will think positive thoughts, and I will get involved with positive people and positive activities, and I will continue praying just like you told me to."

"Good. Now go to sleep. It's very late."

"I will, but first tell me something else your mother said."

I lay back in my bed, feeling quite weary as I sifted through my memories of her. "She said that good can come from the worse things that happen in our lives and that we have to be patient if we're ever going to discover what they are."

"Ana, do you think it's possible that despite everything that's happened to me and everything I've done, I could find peace and happiness?"

"I have no doubt, Ms. Lillian. You just have to be patient."

Lillian left much calmer than when she'd entered, and I couldn't help but wonder what she'd do once she returned to her room. It was so late that even Mr. Trellis would be sleeping by now. No doubt she would quietly change into her nightgown and crawl into bed with him. This thought sent a guilty shiver down my spine. To be with the man you love so close in the darkness with nothing between you but a thin layer of fabric was an over-whelming thought. But would she find the warmth of his body under the blankets and the sound of his steady breathing reas-suring and desirable, or repulsive? If she found him desirable, then perhaps she would snuggle up next to him and wrap her arm around his shoulders, and then in a delicious state of semi-sleep he'd mutter something that would let her know he was glad of her presence. His hand would reach for hers and when their fingers came together, all would be well again because no matter what happened before, they still belonged to each other. That's how it is with holy matrimony, and it should never be broken by conflicts within or without. That's what I'd been taught by the church and that's what made sense to me.

What didn't make sense is how Lillian didn't feel like the luckiest woman on earth to have a man like Mr. Trellis for her husband. But then, perhaps behind closed doors he wasn't as I saw him. Perhaps I had invented a person who didn't really exist and I had deluded myself into believing that he could rescue my dreams and correct all the wrongs I had endured.

That night I dreamt that the moon was shining through the rough slats in our wall. As we rocked in our hammocks, soft beams of light swept across my mother's face, and I could see that she was still awake and thoughtful. This had always been the best time to ask her the most difficult questions.

"Mama, why is it that all our heroes are destroyed?" I asked. "It seems to me that if the world doesn't destroy them, they destroy themselves."

When Mama turned her eyes to me they were glistening like stars. "Maybe it's because nobody really wants to be saved, *mija*," she said, and then she turned away from me so that I wouldn't see the tears in her eyes, and I wrapped my arm around her shoulder and rested my face against her back.

"I'm sorry if you're sad," I said.

"Just tired," she replied. "So very tired."

Ten

JESSIE LIFTED HER HEAD from Ana's lap. "Are you tired, Nana?" she asked.

Still in a semidaze, Ana replied, "Just a little, I suppose."

"Maybe we should go outside and get some fresh air. It doesn't look like Daddy's going to wake up for a while longer."

Although Ana knew Jessie was right, she hesitated and leaned in closer to make sure he was still sleeping comfortably. Satisfied that all was well for the moment, she allowed Jessie to lead her downstairs and out to the courtyard, where they sat together beneath the umbrellas shading the loungers. It was a warm day, but the breeze was refreshing.

"When I was a little girl, this was my favorite place," Jessie said. "Remember how we used to pick flowers and make little bouquets for my dolls here?"

"Yes, I do. And enough mud pies to open our own bakery," Ana said, smiling, and when she turned she saw that Jessie was also smiling at the memory.

Then she saw her smile fade. "I wish we could go back to the way things were." Tears began to stream down her cheeks. Ana took hold of her hand, knowing exactly how she felt, yet words of comfort eluded her, so they sat in silence for some time.

Eventually Jessie spoke. "I've been thinking about this ever since the trouble with Teddy began." She turned to Ana, restraining her emotions as best she could. "I think we should tell him the truth about everything."

"Exactly what truth are you referring to?"

"You know, about Mom and Uncle Darwin."

Ana felt a heaviness press against her chest, making it difficult for her to breathe. "A son shouldn't know such ugly things about his mother and an uncle who he loves dearly. No, Jessie, I don't want you tell him."

"What about me?" she asked, somewhat exasperated. "I've had to deal with the ugly truth for as long as I can remember. In fact, I still have that picture I drew of Mom when I saw them together, and as painful as it is, I force myself to look at it every now and then so I can remind myself of everything I don't want to be."

"You're being very hard on your mother," Ana said. "She tried to make things better."

"She didn't try hard enough, and if Teddy understood that, maybe he wouldn't judge Dad so harshly . . . and you."

Ana turned her face back to the sun. "We all make mistakes, Jessie. Maybe if you find a way to forgive your mother, it will inspire Teddy to forgive his father . . . and me."

Jessie's chin began to quiver. "I may tolerate her better than I used to, but I'm not ready to forgive her for what she did to

Dad." She suddenly stood up, eager to end the conversation. "I'm going to go look for Sister Josepha. Are you coming?"

"I'll be there in a moment," Ana said, feeling the tightness in her chest begin to ease. "I just need to rest a little while longer."

Jessie walked across the courtyard, and Ana watched her until she was out of sight. Then her eyes fell upon the light reflecting off the peacock pool as brilliant triangles of blue and green light danced before her eyes.

Ms. Lillian became an active member of the local women's charity league during the same year Teddy celebrated his eighth birthday and joined Little League. I'd never seen mother and son so excited about anything before. She happily explained to me and anyone who'd listen that her league was composed exclusively of dignified women of good social standing who were inspired to dedicate their time and energy to charitable causes. Ms. Lillian was especially thrilled because she'd been appointed chair of the yearly gala, which meant that she would be applying her magnificent party organizing skills to a worthy cause. It was wonderful to see her valued for something other than her charm and beauty, and it seemed that this also helped her to transcend her insatiable appetite for other men.

Because of Ms. Lillian's frenetic schedule I took Teddy to all of his Little League practices and to most of his games. Occasionally Mr. Trellis was able to make it to the games, but his investment business continued to thrive and required more and more of his time. If he made it home for dinner twice a week, we considered ourselves lucky.

I enjoyed watching Teddy's games, although when it was his turn up at bat, or when the ball was anywhere near him out on the field, I became extremely anxious and had to repeatedly remind myself that I was watching eight-year-olds playing baseball and not a professional world championship.

I sat with the other parents on the bleachers and heard them shout out encouragement when their sons were at bat. Things like "Hey slugger, show 'em what you're made of!" and "Shoot the moon, buddy!" Although their sons rarely acknowledged them with anything more than a stiff nod, they seemed to stand a bit straighter and to swing their bats with more confidence and power as a result.

When Teddy walked up to home plate, I wanted to call out something too, but as the only nanny present, I felt awkward, so I sat with my anxiety balled up like a silent fist in my throat instead.

When Jessie accompanied me, she usually lost interest midway through the first inning and headed off toward a nearby grassy field to practice her cartwheels where I was able to keep an eye on her. She was enrolled in a gymnastics class with twenty or so other five-year-olds who all dreamed of becoming Olympic stars even though only one or two of them had mastered the cartwheel.

On the drive home Teddy liked to review the game and his performance with me.

"Did you see how I caught that line drive, Nana?" he asked excitedly.

"Yes, that was a wonderful catch," I replied, not quite certain what a line drive was. "And you threw it back so well too."

"Yeah, I have a good arm," Teddy said. "But I'm not a very good hitter. The coach says I need to step into the ball and not be afraid of it."

"What do you think?" I asked.

"I think he's right, but when the ball hits me, it hurts really bad, Nana."

"I bet it does."

Sometimes I pitched to Teddy in the backyard and assigned Jessie the task of chasing after the errant balls. Teddy complained about my pitching skills, which I had to admit were horrendous, but whenever I suggested that we go out back to practice, he never turned me down. A few times when Mr. Trellis saw us and he had the time he took over as pitcher and Jessie and I ran the imaginary bases just for fun as we fielded the balls. His pitching skills were quite good, and it was a pleasure to see him with his shirtsleeves rolled up and a catcher's mitt on his right hand. Sometimes I'd stop running after the balls just to watch him for a while, and if he should throw the ball my way, as pitchers do to test their basemen, and if I caught it, I felt that I held the world in my hands.

After practice one afternoon, I approached the bench from behind as Teddy was talking with one of his teammates. "Who's that short lady who brings you to the games all the time?" the other boy asked.

"She's my nanny," Teddy replied.

"You're a liar. I bet you a million dollars she's your mom."

"She's not my mom," Teddy returned more forcefully.

"Yeah she is," the other boy taunted. "The short ugly lady is your mom!"

Without another word, Teddy stood up and punched the boy in the face as hard as he could. The boy fell off the bench and rolled one or two revolutions after hitting the ground. Teddy stood over him with his fists still clenched. "She's not ugly." He seethed.

The coaches, players, and several of the parents came running over to find out what had happened. By that time the boy was already sitting up and bawling as he held his bloody nose. The sight of blood intensified everyone's upset, and the mother of the stricken boy, whose name was Joseph Waller, wagged her finger in my face and told me that she intended to call Teddy's mother. The coaches, however, were much more sympathetic to Teddy. Apparently Joseph Waller had a history of provoking arguments, and this wasn't the first time he'd been smacked because of it.

On our way home Teddy asked, "Nana, how come Mom doesn't come to any of my games?"

"She has many meetings to attend these days, but I'm sure that if she had more time she'd come."

Teddy thought about this for a moment. "Maybe you can go to her meetings and she can come to my games."

"I'll talk to her about it," I said.

We were almost home when Teddy said, "I punched Joseph Waller because he said mean things about you."

"Were you protecting me?"

Looking straight ahead, he nodded, his earlier rage gathering again.

"Do you feel bad about punching Joseph Waller?" I asked.

His eyes filled with tears. Then turning to me, he lifted his baseball shirt to reveal the Superman T-shirt his uncle had given him for his birthday underneath. He insisted on wearing it to all of his games, and I'd washed it so many times that the S was beginning to fade. "I felt bad, but I also felt strong, like Superman," he said.

"Well, I happen to know that even Superman cries sometimes," I said, and this seemed to make him feel a little better.

Teddy's team made it to the league semifinals, but as luck would have it, the game fell on the same day as Ms. Lillian's charity gala, which both she and Mr. Trellis were expected to attend. Although Millie, Jessie, and I tried to be enthusiastic cheerleaders, Teddy was sullen all the way to the game. But soon after the first pitch was thrown, I saw Mr. Trellis making his way across the parking lot toward the bleachers in his tuxedo. And when Teddy spotted him, it was as though an invisible pair of hands had straightened his shoulders and lifted his chin. He elbowed the boy standing next to him and pointed to his father while grinning ear to ear.

Mr. Trellis sat between Millie and me and propped Jessie on his knee. "I'm sure I'll have time to make it to Lillian's event. Hopefully she won't notice if I'm a little late," he added with a guilty smile. All at once the picture was complete, and the game took on a heightened significance.

Nobody was quite sure how it happened, but we were at the bottom of the sixth inning when the accident occurred. The players had always been instructed to keep a safe distance from the batter and Teddy wasn't one to disobey orders, but perhaps he was so excited to have his father present that he forgot to put on his batting helmet, and when he reached for his bat to begin his practice swings, he didn't see the batter.

I'll never forget the horrible sound of the bat slamming into Teddy's skull. Immediately he collapsed and began twisting and writhing on the ground. Mr. Trellis leapt up and rushed to him. He ran off with his son in his arms while frantically calling out for me to follow him, and while running after him I directed Millie to take Jessie home. As Mr. Trellis drove like a fiend to the hospital I sat with Teddy in the backseat and cradled him in my arms. I spoke to him in the language of my heart and he shuddered. *"Tienes que ser fuerte, mijo. No te olvides que siempre estamos contigo y que te queremos mucho. Usa nuestro amor como tu coraje y tu fortaleza."* You have to be strong, my son. Don't forget that we're always with you and that we love very much. Use our love as your courage and your strength.

But I felt him slipping away, and we were in my black sewing cabinet, hovering between life and death, waiting for our fate to be determined by the stomp of a boot or an angry cry. But unlike before, I would've traded my soul for Teddy's life.

When we arrived at the hospital Teddy was swept from my arms. Mr. Trellis ran and I tried my best to keep up. They were wheeling Teddy's now motionless body away into another room at the end of a long corridor, while a flurry of doctors and nurses appeared to attend to him.

Mr. Trellis began to argue with one of the nurses who refused to let him go any farther. "I need to be with my son," he said. "I don't care about the regulations. I need to be with him."

"I can't make any exceptions," she replied in a calm and professional tone. "Your son is in good hands."

After she left us, Mr. Trellis collapsed into a nearby chair as I helplessly stood by. Then he placed his hand on the empty chair next to him. "You might as well sit down, Ana," he said. "I'm sure we're going to be here for a while."

I sat down, and as orderlies and nurses and grumbling patients filed past us, Mr. Trellis hung his head and wept. Not thinking about it, I wrapped my arms around his broad shoulders and held him close as I'd held Teddy moments ago. And as I took in the fullness of his strength and sorrow, I felt suddenly fortified as I did when Sister Josepha and I escaped through the jungle all those years ago. Then as now, I was certain that all will be well. "Teddy will be okay. I know he will," I whispered.

He stiffened in my arms and with faint derision in his voice, he asked, "How do you know? Have you been talking to your God?"

"Yes, and he's been talking to me."

"Well, if he's still listening," he said sarcastically, "tell him that I'll do anything he asks as long as he saves my son."

"He will save him," I replied.

Mr. Trellis turned to me, his hand curled up in a fist between us. "I don't need or want your platitudes. You ask him, damn it, and tell me what I should do."

I reached for his fist and cradled it my hands. "Forgive yourself, Mr. Trellis. My God is begging you to forgive yourself, that is all he asks of any of us."

He grew still and his hand softly opened into mine. Then he retrieved it and turned away. Feeling suddenly embarrassed to have behaved in such an unseemly and forward manner, I was preparing to stand when he whispered, "Don't go, Ana. I need you here with me."

And so I sat back in the chair and waited with him until Ms. Lillian burst into the ER, wearing a spectacular crimson gown and calling out for Teddy in a hysterical panic. Several of the nursing staff told her to calm down and take a seat, but she was too upset to listen to them. When she spotted Adam, she rushed to his side and dropped at his feet, although I'd already risen from my chair so that she could take the seat next to him.

"How is he? How's my baby?" she asked.

"We don't know yet," he answered soberly. "He sustained a significant blow to the head."

The delicate veins on her throat bulged beneath her jeweled necklace. "How could you let this happen? Who did this to him?"

"It was an accident, Lillian," he said. "There's no one to blame."

Moments later, we saw one of the physicians who'd rushed in after Teddy walking down the corridor toward us. His expression was guarded, but not defeated.

"Are you Teddy's mother?" he asked, addressing Lillian first.

"Yes, yes," she wailed. "How's my little boy?"

The physician nodded. "Follow me, please."

They left me to go with him through the double doors at the end of the corridor. I waited where I was as patients of all ages were wheeled past me on gurneys and as the nurses and technicians took their breaks. I noticed that some of them walked away from their stations hastily, eager to get away and make a phone call or have a cigarette just outside the emergency room doors. Others didn't take any breaks at all and seemed to be enthralled by their work and their patients, and I wondered what kind of nurse I would be if given the opportunity. And then I prayed that a nonsmoking nurse be assigned to Teddy, only because it seemed to me that they were happier and I wanted Teddy to see a smiling face when he opened his eyes as I knew he would.

I waited as the janitor mopped the entire corridor from end to end and I lifted my feet from the floor when he neared me so he could pass his mop under my chair. Eventually, new nurses came in to replace those ending their shifts, and that's when I caught sight of Mr. Trellis walking down the corridor in my direction. He sat beside me. "They haven't found any bleeding, which is very good news. They're going to watch him for a few days, but it looks like he's going to be okay."

"Thank God," I said while clasping my hands together.

"Which reminds me," he continued, looking straight ahead. "I was wondering if you'd do me favor."

"Of course."

He glanced at me and then away. "Tell your God that I'm going to seriously consider his request."

"I'll let him know," I replied.

I was allowed to see Teddy a short while later, and he appeared so much like himself that it brought tears to my eyes. "Nana," he said frowning, "they cut up my lucky shirt." He pointed toward a pile of clothes on the chair. I held the shirt up and saw that it had been neatly cut right down the middle, separating "Super" and "man."

I folded up the shirt and tucked it in my purse. "Don't worry, I'll fix it for you."

Teddy gave me a dubious look. "How can you fix that, Nana?"

"You'll see," I said, giving his nose a little squeeze.

Adam and Lillian had left the room momentarily, and when they returned Lillian made her way to her son's bedside. "Sweetheart, Mommy is exhausted and my feet are killing me. I'm going to have to leave and soak them in a hot tub, but I'll be back first thing tomorrow."

"That's okay," Teddy replied brightly and he gave his mother a kiss and a smile, but the moment she left he turned to me and his smile dropped. "You're not going too, are you, Nana?" he asked.

"Don't worry, Teddy. I'll be right here."

Teddy came home from the hospital a couple of days later and Jessie hovered nearby with wide, curious eyes, staring at her brother as though he'd just returned from another planet. She was unusually considerate and brought him several of her favorite toys to play with. Normally, Teddy would've rejected these girlish toys, but he appreciated her kindness and made an effort to respectfully consider each one she offered. It was only when she left the room that he asked me to place her dolls on the chair away from him.

One evening a week or so later, when the children were asleep and all was quiet throughout the house, I moved my chair closer to the reading lamp beside my bed and threaded a sewing needle. I placed a thimble on my right middle finger as my mother had taught me and I began to mend Teddy's Superman shirt.

For years I believed that if I took up a needle and thread, I'd feel my mother's absence more acutely, but I was wrong. I felt her presence in the room as I worked, guiding my hand and watching me, speaking when she thought my stitch wasn't quite right or massaging my hands if they grew stiff. "You must be patient, *mija*. Mending a garment requires focus, and you can't rush it. In this way, the threads are able to find each other, and the fabric heals itself in your hands."

It was nearly midnight by the time I finished, but when I surveyed my work I was pleased. The stitching was not as refined and precise as my mother's, but it was quite good. And I thought the mended line running down the center of the shirt was interesting, like a scar that Superman had sustained in a cosmic battle. I could only hope that Teddy would see it the same way.

When I went to bed and turned out the light, I drifted back to swaying in my hammock. "Let's imagine, *mija*. Let's imagine that beautiful music is raining down from the heavens and flowing over us and everything we see, washing away all our fears and doubts. Do you hear it?"

"Yes, I hear it, Mama."

And as I slept, the melody drifted and swirled all around me, as though plucked from an angel's harp, and it carried me through much of the night. Although I'd gone to bed later than usual, the next morning I awoke feeling very rested. After checking on Teddy and Jessie, who were still sleeping soundly, I went to the kitchen for some coffee, but Millie was already waiting for me, her eyes bright. "Did you hear the music last night?" she whispered excitedly.

"Yes," I replied, amazed that she'd heard it too, when I was certain that I'd been dreaming.

Millie's cheeks quivered with emotion. "To hear him playing again after so many years"—she clasped her hands together—"it took my breath away."

At that moment, Ms. Lillian entered the kitchen dressed in her yoga clothes. "What are you two whispering so mysteriously about?" she asked as she poured herself a cup of coffee.

"Didn't you hear the music last night, Ms. Lillian?" I asked.

She froze with the rim of her coffee cup poised on her lips. "What music?"

Millie glanced at me warily. "Ana and I are certain that we heard piano music last night. I can only assume that it was Adam."

"Don't be ridiculous," she said with a toss of her head. "You know as well as I do that Adam hasn't played in years. In fact, I have a good mind to sell that piano or give it away." She gulped her coffee and stuffed a banana into her tote bag. "I'd say you were both dreaming. Or maybe," she said, her eyes round with imaginary fear, "it was a ghost."

After Ms. Lillian left, Millie and I went directly to the music room.

The furniture was scattered about in disarray as usual, but when we approached the piano, we saw that the cover over the keys that was always kept closed had been lifted. And the felt strip of fabric that lay over the keys had been neatly folded and placed on the floor next to the piano bench.

"Well, well, well," Millie said, crossing her arms. "It appears that we're being haunted by a musical ghost who forgets to put things back where he found them. And," she continued, nodding toward the mug on the table, "our ghost seems to have a taste for coffee."

After dropping the children off at school, I arrived home to find Millie hard at work in the music room. She'd thoroughly dusted the piano so that every inch of it shone, and rearranged the furniture so that it faced the piano as it would during a recital. That evening when Mr. Trellis came home from work he found us gathered around it. Teddy had settled himself on the piano bench and was pounding away at the keys while Jessie sat below him, pressing the pedals with her hands, fascinated by its mystical effect on Teddy's notes. When we saw Mr. Trellis standing in the doorway watching us, Millie and I held our breath. Even Teddy and Jessie were silent. Finally Teddy asked, "Do you want me to play a song for you, Daddy? Millie and Nana think it's very good."

Mr. Trellis took a moment to consider his son's offer. Then he shook his head, obviously disappointed. "Before you place your hands on the keys, you have to learn how to sit properly on the bench. Look at how you're slouching, son. Sit up, lift your chin," he commanded.

"But then I can't see the keys," Teddy complained.

"That will come later," he said, and in three strides he was sitting next to Teddy and demonstrating appropriate posture and hand positioning.

"Millie says you used to play really good. Will you play for me, Daddy?" Teddy asked.

"Me too!" Jessie chimed in. "Play for me too!"

He flashed Millie and me a look that was not altogether sour, then he placed his fingers on the keys and closed his eyes. The notes he played were tentative at first, as though he were searching for his music through a storm of broken memories. But once he found what he was looking for, he created a sound so lovely that I was transported to a realm I'd never experienced before. As I listened, it felt as though my spirit were flying beyond this time and place into an eternity I couldn't comprehend. And as he swayed to the sound of his music, I was able to see into the deepest recesses of his soul, and the beauty I saw there brought tears to my eyes.

When he finished, we were silent, overwhelmed by the mastery of what we'd just heard. And then Ms. Lillian, who unbeknownst to us had come into the room while he was playing, began to applaud and exclaimed, "Darling, that was spectacular! I insist that you play for the guild event I'm planning next month. The theme is 'An Evening in Salzburg,' and you would be perfect!"

Ms. Lillian was relentless. Whenever I saw her with her husband she was talking about "An Evening in Salzburg," and the fact that she'd already told the gala committee he would perform, and how important it was that he play, and how it would elevate her status at the guild, and on and on. Despite her enthusiasm, Mr. Trellis remained stoic and uncommitted.

"I don't understand it, Ana," Ms. Lillian complained one afternoon as I folded the children's clothing in the kitchen. "Adam has been blessed with an extraordinary talent and he's positively stingy with it."

When she pressed me for an opinion, I simply said, "I agree that it would be nice for him to share his talent with others, but perhaps it's too soon. I think you should be more patient with him."

"Ana, I've been waiting for years to hear him play," Lillian fumed. "How much more patient can I possibly be?"

Mr. Trellis preferred to play late at night after everyone had gone to bed. I made a habit of leaving my bedroom window open so I could hear the music more clearly as it drifted through the courtyard. One particular night, I was so mesmerized by the beauty of his playing that I found it difficult to sleep. I heard the melancholy strain of his notes, how they lingered as though drifting and searching for hope. Sometimes it sounded as though he were weeping inconsolably through his music, at other times that he was soaring with unrestrained joy.

One Saturday morning I was on hands and knees collecting some toys that Teddy and Jessie had left in the foyer when Mr. Trellis strode up and announced, "I've decided not to play at the guild. I just told Lillian and I wanted you to know as well." In response to my baffled expression he added, "Lillian told me that you thought I was being selfish."

"I'm sure she misunderstood," I replied, flustered.

He folded his arms across his chest and set his chin firmly. "Perhaps I am being selfish, but I . . . I don't feel comfortable displaying myself in such a manner. When I was a boy, I did as I was told, but I'm no longer a boy," he said with defensive bluster that I found endearing. "And if I don't enjoy performing for strangers like I'm some kind of trained monkey, then that should be explanation enough."

"Of course," I replied, "and Ms. Lillian will eventually understand."

"How about you? Do you understand?"

"Mr. Trellis I . . . I have no idea how it must be to play as you do, but when I listen to you it's like . . . it's how you described it when you saw your father perform heart surgery for the first time."

"All I remember saying was that it smelled very bad. Are you saying that my playing stinks?" he asked with a teasing smile.

"Oh no, of course not," I replied. "But you said something else too, don't you remember? You said that it was like life struggling with its own mortality. And that's what I hear whenever you play. So as far as I'm concerned, it's up to you when and how and to whom you choose to reveal it."

He was thoughtful for a moment and then he knelt down before me so we were at eye level, and while gazing at me, he gently touched my cheek with his fingertips. Then, as though suddenly remembering who he was and where he was, he stood up and left me to my task without another word. But I was hardly able to see what I was doing for the tears in my eyes and the pounding in my ears that his touch had provoked. I looked up just as he entered his study, his head hanging and his broad shoulders stooped as though burdened by an enormous weight. And then I came to fully accept what I'd been denying for years.

I begged God to forgive me as I realized how I truly felt about this awkward, brilliant, and remarkable man. I loved the children, there was no doubt about that, and I'd developed a deep affection for Millie and Ms. Lillian too. But the real reason I hadn't returned to the convent, or gone to New Mexico to work with Sister Josepha, was that I couldn't bear the thought of leaving him.

I was hopelessly in love with Adam Trellis.

$\mathcal{E}$leven

ANA'S REVERIE WAS INTERRUPTED by the sound of foot-steps, and she looked up to see Millie walking briskly across the courtyard toward her. It lifted Ana's spirits to see her smiling face and twinkling eyes. Although her hair had gone from gray to white, it suited her and she seemed more youthful somehow.

"Jessie told me I'd find you here," she said as they embraced. Her sharp eyes took in Ana's thin face and pale complexion, but she said nothing about it.

"How is he?" she asked.

"He seems weaker today," Ana replied, knowing that it was useless to slide into her wishful platitudes with Millie. She looked about to see if Jessie were anywhere in sight. "Dr. Farrell came by early this morning. He doesn't think there's anything more he can do, but I think we still have some time left."

Millie nodded soberly, and then her face screwed up with sadness and a touch of anger. "Whatever time is left, it isn't fair."

"I'm grateful for every second—"

"It isn't fair," Millie said, shaking her head resolutely. "All the gratitude in the world doesn't change that, Ana."

The two women entered the house and climbed the stairs side by side.

Before entering Adam's room, Ana hesitated outside his door. "I'm sure that he'll ask you about Teddy."

Millie nodded and squared her shoulders. "What should I say?"

"Tell him that you're certain he'll come," she replied without hesitation.

Millie frowned. "Are you sure? Last time we spoke you said nothing had changed, and that was only yesterday."

Ana closed her eyes. She felt suddenly faint and reached out to the wall for support. "For goodness sake!" Millie cried, helping her to one of the chairs in the corridor. "You told me you were taking care of yourself, but look at you, you're a walking cadaver. How much weight have you lost?"

"I don't know," Ana muttered.

"You don't know?" Millie replied, her eyes bugging out. "Well, if you continue this way, we'll have to bury you next."

Ana stared wide-eyed at Millie, shocked to hear her say such a thing, but Millie didn't back down. "You wouldn't mind, would you? It would be just fine with you if we buried you and Adam together side by side."

Ana brought her hands to her face, and Millie sat down next to her as she wept. "That's okay," she said, circling her arm around Ana's thin shoulders. "You go right ahead and cry your eyes out until there's nothing left. And when you think you're all done, you won't be. You still have a lot of crying left to do."

"Oh, Millie," Ana said once she was able to catch her breath. "I'm dying with him. I know I am."

"Of course you're not," she said. "You've lost a bit of weight, that's all."

Ana shook her head. "It's more than that. I read somewhere that when someone you love dearly is seriously ill and dying, you're at risk of getting ill yourself, and I can feel it inside of me. You're the first person I've told, but I don't mind telling you that I'm glad I'm sick because I can't live without him."

"Now, now," Millie said, taking hold of Ana's hand. "I've been where you are now, and I know that when your heart is breaking it can feel like you're dying inside. Only time can ease the pain and make it better. You have to be patient."

"Yes," Ana said, hastily wiping her eyes. "Time is all I have left."

Once Ana felt more composed, she and Millie entered the sickroom. Adam's eyes fluttered open and he smiled when he saw them. "Millie," he whispered.

She sat next to him and took his hand. "I can see that Ana's taking good care of you."

"Always," he replied.

Millie chatted about her retirement and how busy she'd been, sounding so cheerful and casual that it was possible to forget that she was talking to a dying man. Ana was grateful that for a moment or two she could pretend that all was well, and she took several steps away toward the window. She spotted Sister

Josepha sitting on the ledge of the fountain, enjoying the breeze and the sound of the water. It seemed to be singing to her, and when Ana closed her eyes, she could hear it too.

Now that he had brought music back into his life, Mr. Trellis was less angry than before. He smiled more easily and, although more than ten years had gone by, he appeared younger than he did on the first day I met him. He began keeping normal hours, and the best time of day for the children and me was at around six o'clock in the evening when we heard the crunching of his tires on the gravel in the driveway. We usually waited for him at the front door, Jessie with one of her art projects in hand to show him and Teddy with his favorite board game tucked under his arm. Now that Teddy had started junior high, his father had taken to playing a game with him after dinner as a reward for having completed his homework, and Teddy liked to give him a preview of what it would be as soon as he walked in the door.

The joy in Mr. Trellis's eyes when confronted by such a welcoming committee was a beautiful sight to behold, and I'd gaze at him spellbound, always standing at a respectful distance, yet ready to lend a hand should the children hang on him for too long as he made his way to the study.

Sometimes I pretended that he was my father too. I was the older sister who'd come home from college to enjoy a few days with my younger siblings. My father might call me into his study to discuss my future plans, my hopes and dreams. Or perhaps he was delighted to find his dear sister enjoying the afternoon with her niece and nephew. Sometimes I was his mother looking down on him from heaven. I would appear in a vision and tell him how proud I was, what a good father he was, and that he needed to be careful with his wife. I did not allow my secret visions to take me any further than this.

I always knew what kind of day he'd had by the way he held his jacket. If it was slung over his shoulder, he'd had a fairly pleasant day—if it was flung across his arm, only moderately so. If his hair was disheveled, the thick waves ruffled by several rakes of his fingers, and he forgot his jacket in his car, I knew it had been a stressful day.

"How's the brood, Ana?" he'd ask. "How near to the edge of insanity were you driven today?"

"I'm miles away from the edge today, sir," I'd reply. And then once, when he looked particularly weary, I asked, "And you?"

He was thoughtful, and when he lifted Jessie, who at nine still enjoyed being carried about by her father, he said, "Precariously close today, but all of a sudden I've taken several steps back. By later this evening I'm sure that I'll be miles away, just like you."

Lillian, who remained busy with her women's meetings and events, wasn't likely to greet her husband until dinnertime, and lately we'd all been eating at the table together as a family, which I enjoyed very much. But Millie had been excusing herself early and spending most of her time in her room. Some days I never saw her at all, and when the housekeepers arrived from the service, I'd be the one to direct them. Once or twice I discovered her passed out on her bed with an empty whiskey bottle nearby.

On these days I ordered food out and had it delivered, or put something together for dinner as best I could.

One evening as I was preparing a cup of tea before bedtime, Mr. Trellis entered the kitchen. Whenever I found myself alone in his presence my heart began to beat more rapidly and I became aware of a pleasant hum at the base of my neck that radiated warmth all throughout my body. Over time I'd learned how to manage my feelings for him and resigned myself to appearing red-faced whenever we spoke. If he noticed my discomfort or suspected the reason for it, he never said anything about it.

He removed his glasses and rubbed the bridge of his nose. "I'm worried about Millie," he said. "She's been drinking more than ever, and yesterday I saw her stumble as she was going down the stairs."

I'd seen her do the same on a number of occasions, and was surprised that he should bring it up now. After all the years that Millie had been taking her "naps," Mr. Trellis and I never discussed it.

Mr. Trellis continued. "I'm sure you're aware that Lillian's wanted Millie out of the house for years, but I've always felt an obligation to her. Nevertheless, I understand Lillian's concerns regarding the children. Teddy notices everything now and Jessie's not far behind," he said with a sad smile. "It's going to be hard on them, which is why I wanted to let you know first."

The cup and saucer in my hand began to rattle as I realized what he was saying, and I placed it back on the table. "Maybe if we talk to her about it . . ."

"I've lost count of the number of times I've talked to Millie about her drinking. And each time I have, she's promised that she's going to see a doctor and attend AA meetings—the whole nine yards. In fact there's a meeting within walking distance from the house, but she's never gone, not even once."

"I wish there was something more we could do."

Mr. Trellis sighed. "Hopefully one day Millie will be ready to stop on her own accord, but I can't wait for that someday any longer. It wouldn't be fair to the children." Mr. Trellis put his glasses back on. "We'll need you to step in for Millie until we find a suitable replacement. I realize that in many ways you've already done that, but this would be in a more official capacity and we'd pay you additionally for your help. I . . . I hope you don't mind."

"I don't mind," I replied as a heaviness settled over my heart. "When are you going to tell her?"

Mr. Trellis shook his head, clearly pained at the prospect. "I'm not sure. I was thinking about telling her tomorrow, but tomorrow I have a very late meeting and I'm not sure when I'll be home."

"And tomorrow Jessie's trying out for the school musical."

"Is that tomorrow?" he asked.

"Yes, and you know how upset she'll be if she doesn't make it."

"Well," he said, somewhat relieved. "It doesn't look like tomorrow's the right time to take care of this, but soon. I can't let it drag on for much longer."

That same evening I noticed light under Millie's door and I hesitated outside. I didn't know what to say to her or how to say it, but I knew that I had to do something. After praying for the words and the wisdom that would reach her, I took a deep breath and knocked lightly. To my surprise, she answered right away, and when I entered the room, I was immediately struck by the sweet and pungent smell of whiskey.

She was sitting in her rocking chair watching TV, entranced by a police drama of some kind.

"Can I sit with you for a while, Millie?"

She nodded and patted her bed, while keeping her eyes glued to the set, holding her drink below her knee, perhaps thinking that I wouldn't notice it there. She seemed to be in a good mood, but I knew it wouldn't last when she heard what I had to say. Nevertheless, I dove right in. "Millie, they're going to ask you to leave here if things don't change," I blurted out.

She turned slowly, a shifting pattern of light from the TV moving across her face as she stared at me for a moment or two. "What things?" she asked, her glass no longer hidden.

I glanced at the glass and then at her face. It was cold and challenging. I took a deep breath and continued. "Mr. Trellis told me that he and Ms. Lillian are worried. They don't want the children to see you this way," I said, nodding toward her glass.

She turned away to stare at the television, her expression distant and pained. The police actors were yelling at someone they'd just pinned to the ground, their weapons drawn. The villain struggled against the officers, but it was clear he wouldn't get away.

"Have you ever tried to stop drinking, or at least cut down?"

Her fingers gripped the glass so tightly that I was concerned it would shatter in her hand. "What right do you have to ask me these questions?" she asked.

"I don't have any right, but I don't want you to go away."
When she didn't respond, I added, "I know that drinking can
help to ease the pain when life gets difficult."

She turned to glare at me, her lips twitching into a smirk.
"That's an impressive insight, but let's face it, you've lived most
of your life locked away in a convent and since you've been here
you act as though you've never left. What could you possibly
know about life and its difficulties?" She chuckled derisively
and turned back to the TV. Together we watched as the officers
shoved the struggling villain into the back of the police car.

"I had a life before the convent, Millie."

She turned to me, her eyes wide and cynical. "Oh really?
I just figured the stork lost its way when you were born and
dropped you there by accident." She turned back to the TV.

"I know I haven't been willing to tell you very much about
it, but if you want, I'll tell you now."

Millie turned around again, took a long and bold swallow of
her drink, and turned the TV off with one click of her remote. Then
she crossed her arms over her chest and gave me a stiff nod.

Hesitantly at first, I told her about my village and everything I could remember about my mother and my family and
how the war began. After so many years of silence, hearing myself say these words out loud emboldened me and I began to
speak even more freely about the massacre, and how my mother
hid me away in her sewing cabinet to save my life. My mind became flooded with the horrific sounds of war, the sight of bodies
scattered about like laundry blown off the line, and the bleeding
scabs in the soldier's eyes. I felt the fear and pain rip into my gut
as though it had happened only yesterday. And then I told her

about my days at the orphanage, my love for Sister Josepha, and how we escaped into the jungle. I told her too about the peacefulness of the convent, and how even today I sometimes hear my mother's voice when I'm afraid.

Millie's face grew slack and she stared at me with unblinking eyes. I was concerned that perhaps she wasn't able to make sense of all I'd told her. It was such a jumble of events and people, and I wasn't sure I had explained it all in the right order.

"I had no idea," she muttered.

"When I was younger I hoped that if I didn't talk about it, the memory would fade and eventually I could make myself believe that these things had happened to somebody else."

"Is that why you entered the convent?" she asked. "So that you could forget?"

I lowered my eyes, feeling suddenly ashamed. "I wanted to be somewhere safe and I wanted the hurt inside to go away. The peacefulness I felt in the convent made it easier, and as the years passed it became part of me. Sometimes I wish that I could still wear my veil and feel the weight of it on my shoulders protecting me. It may sound silly, but I miss my veil most of all."

Millie reached for her glass, but she didn't take a drink this time. Instead, she swirled the golden liquor and watched it spin round and round, enjoying the way it moved and flowed. "Who would've ever guessed that you and I were so similar?" she said, as a strange sad smile played on her lips. "I always thought that we couldn't be more different, but for years we've been living exactly the same life. It's really quite amazing when you think about it."

"What do you mean, Millie?"

"I've been hiding behind my God," she said, nodding to the glass of whiskey on her knee. "And you've been hiding behind yours."

Two days later, Millie and I found ourselves sitting in a room with thirty or so strangers, men and women of all ages and backgrounds. We sat more or less in a circle, although Millie and I had placed our chairs a bit farther away from the rest. People began to speak of their experiences and to share testimonials of their lives, but only after introducing themselves one by one. "Hello," they'd say, "my name is so-and-so and I'm an alcoholic." The group would respond, "Hello, so-and-so."

I didn't think Millie would say anything during this first meeting, but to my surprise, when it came time for her to introduce herself, she said, "Hello, my name is Millie and I'm an alcoholic. I've been an alcoholic for more than thirty years, give or take a few." The group welcomed her warmly. When it was my turn, I felt at a loss. I was not an alcoholic, yet I felt at one with the wounded souls in the room, as though we'd all come from the same village and experienced life's cruelties together.

I tried to speak, but I was so overwhelmed with emotion that I wasn't even able to say my name. Millie placed her hand on my back and spoke for me. "This is my friend Ana. She is one of the kindest and most courageous people I have ever known. She agreed to come here with me because I was afraid and ashamed to come by myself. Thank you, Ana," she said.

Millie attended her meetings every night, and although my responsibilities with the children made it difficult for me to attend every meeting, I went with her when I could. Before long, she didn't need a chaperone. Not only was she comfortable attending on her own, but she looked forward to it. She began to tell me about a special friend she'd made there. His name was Fred, and when she spoke of him more it became obvious that their relationship was evolving into something beyond friendship. Sometimes he drove her home from the meetings and sometimes she invited him in for a cup of tea.

It was easy to like Fred. He had a full head of snow white hair and a cropped white beard. He was an uncomplicated, happy man with a soulful laugh that could tenderize the tensest of moments. Even Ms. Lillian liked him, and his presence seemed to make Millie more tolerable to her.

One day Jessie said to me, "Millie's in love."

"Do you really think so?" I asked, amazed by how perceptive a ten-year-old could be.

Jessie nodded, her eyes round and serious. "When she looks at Fred, it's like her insides are melting. That's how I feel when I look at Joey Robinson." She'd had a crush on Joey Robinson for two years in a row and she didn't care who knew about it.

"And do you think that Fred is in love with Millie too?"

"Of course," Jessie answered confidently. "That's why he laughs at everything she says. That's what I do with Joey Robinson. Joey Robinson is very funny, Nana."

"Oh, I know he is," I replied.

"The other day I told him that he was the funniest boy in school."

"Really? And what did he say to you?"

"He said . . ." She looked down at her shoes, unwilling to finish.

I lifted her chin to find her eyes filled with tears. "Jessie, what did he say to you?"

"He said I was the ugliest girl in school."

"That is a horrible lie," I said, embracing her. "Joey Robinson doesn't know beauty when he sees it."

"Joey Robinson loves Tiffany Michaels," Jessie muttered. "She's the beautiful one, not me."

A few months later, when the holiday season was approaching, Millie surprised us all when she came home from a weekend in Las Vegas with Fred and announced that they were now husband and wife and that she planned to move out a few days before Christmas. We were all delighted for Millie, and it was wonderful to see her so happy, but it was a somber day when Fred pulled up the drive in his truck and loaded Millie's things into the back.

Ms. Lillian left to do a bit of Christmas shopping, but Mr. Trellis, the kids, and I helped Millie with her things. We were almost finished when Millie appeared with a tray of fresh-baked cookies. As we sat on the front steps to enjoy them, the children chatted with Fred about what they hoped to receive for Christmas this year.

"So I take it you've already mailed your list to Santa Claus?" he asked seriously.

Teddy rolled his eyes, and Jessie gave him a friendly nudge on the shoulder. "We figured out years ago that there's no Santa Claus. I was still in diapers when I figured it out, wasn't I, Nana?"

"Not quite that young," I replied.

"What is this?" Fred asked, properly shocked. "Don't tell me that after sixty-odd years of believing in Santa Claus, I've been wrong all this time."

Teddy nodded, not buying a word of it. "I'm afraid you have, Fred. *Very wrong.*"

"Well then, if there isn't a Santa Claus, how do you explain all the presents under the tree on Christmas morning?"

"Simple," Jessie replied, happy to solve the mystery. "Mom and Dad buy the presents, and Nana wraps them up and puts them under the tree."

"And how about my Millie? Doesn't she have a role in this charade?"

"She sure does," Teddy chimed in. "When we put out the cookies for Santa Claus, Millie's the one who eats them." And everybody broke out in laughter.

Once the truck was packed and they were ready to go, Millie climbed in next to her new husband with many promises to return on Christmas Eve so she could eat Santa's cookies. Teddy and Jessie gave her hugs, as did Mr. Trellis, who quickly disappeared into the house so that we wouldn't see his tears. Even Teddy, who'd acquired a new stoicism now that he was entering his teenage years, shed a few.

"I'll miss you most of all," she said when we embraced.

"I'll miss you too, Millie."

Then she held me at arm's length, and whispered softly so that only I could hear, "Take care of Adam. He needs you as much as you need him."

To think that Millie knew of my true feelings for Mr. Trellis left me speechless. I could only nod as my eyes filled with guilty tears.

The children and I stood out front and waved to her as they drove down the drive and out the front gates. Once she was out of sight, Jessie buried her head on my shoulder and began to whimper. "It's not going to be the same around here anymore, Nana. Who's going to make dinner now that Millie's gone?"

"I am," I returned as brightly as I could, although I shared their concern.

"You?" Teddy said incredulously. "You've got to be kidding."

"I'm very serious."

Teddy and Jessie eyed each other nervously. "No offense, Nana," Jessie said, "but you're not exactly a good cook. Not that you're horrible . . ."

"Yeah she is," Teddy said.

"Come on, you guys. If Millie can get married again after all these years, don't you think I can learn how to cook?"

They thought about it as we walked back into the house. "I'm not sure," Jessie said.

"Maybe you should just get married too," Teddy added.

"No way!" Jessie cried, wrapping her arms around me. "She's not going anywhere. We'll just order takeout every night until we hire a new cook."

I was in the kitchen a couple of nights later, navigating my way around as best I could while following a recipe for spaghetti and meatballs that Millie had simplified for me, when Mr. Trellis came in looking for a predinner snack. Sometimes Millie would prepare a small fruit and cheese plate for him and take it to his study, so I offered to do the same.

"Yes, thank you, Ana," he said with an awkward nod, but he lingered in the kitchen as I prepared his plate. I felt him watching me as I worked, and the warm, tingling sensation erupted all over my cheeks, more intense than usual. I hoped that he wouldn't notice me blushing, but the more I willed myself to stop, the worse it became, until I was quite certain that my face was as red as the strawberries I was slicing.

"I've been meaning to tell you for some time now that Millie shared with me what happened," he said softly.

My knife became still and I looked up at him, completely perplexed.

"Millie has many wonderful qualities, but I think you would agree that keeping secrets has never been one of them," he said. "Anyway, I just wanted you to know that if there's anything I can ever do to help . . ." Then he looked away as though suddenly ashamed. "Listen to me," he muttered, shaking his head, "talking as though there was something anyone could ever do to make up for what you've suffered."

And then I realized that he was referring to what I had told Millie about my life just before she started attending her AA meetings. "Thank you, Mr. Trellis," I whispered, overcome by the deep caring I felt from him and for him. And to my great embarrassment, tears sprung to my eyes, and I hastily wiped them away. I finished preparing his plate and handed it to him.

He took the plate from me, and when I looked into his eyes I saw tears there as well. "If there's anything I can do, I'll do it . . . for you . . . you just let me know," he muttered, looking even more embarrassed than me.

"I'll let you know," I said, smiling to keep myself from weeping.

He mumbled something unintelligible and left the kitchen with his snack. I heard him walk down the hall toward his study and close the door behind him. And as I continued preparing the evening meal, forming one meatball after another, I thought about his offer to help however he could, and what I might ask of him if he weren't a married man and I were a courageous woman.

"I just thought of what you could do for me, Mr. Trellis," I imagined myself saying to him "Hold the seed of my love in the palm of your hand and when you're ready, plant it in your soul, where it will bloom and grow forever, and then . . ."

At that moment, Jessie entered the kitchen. "Oh my God!" she exclaimed, startling me out of my reverie. "That has got to be the biggest meatball I've ever seen in my entire life!"

I looked down to find that my meatball was the size of a small melon and I started to laugh.

Jessie laughed with me. "You're so silly, Nana," she said, breaking off a piece to make a normal-sized one.

"Yes, I am," I said, doing the same. "I am a very silly woman."

Twelve

IT WAS EVIDENT BY Jessie's eleventh birthday that she would never be the great beauty Ms. Lillian was. Often, Jessie watched her mother while she dressed to go out, and more than once I caught a flicker of resentment shadow her expression. I suppose she was asking herself why it was that her mother, now near forty, had such an exquisitely smooth complexion when her own was blotchy and freckled, and why she hadn't had the good fortune to inherit her mother's slim hourglass figure, and why, when her mother's auburn hair was the texture of silk, hers was so coarse and unruly. These were agonizing questions for a young girl to ponder, and Ms. Lillian's explanations were of little help.

She surmised that because of an unfortunate twist of genetic fate, Jessie had inherited the physical attributes of the women on her father's side, who were all known to have difficult curly hair, thick waists, and very big breasts. But Ms. Lillian was quite cheerful about it, saying, "Don't worry, honey. When a girl has big boobs, it makes up for everything else."

I usually fixed Jessie's hair before she went to school in the mornings. I enjoyed it and even purchased a book that taught me how to make a variety of complicated braids. Jessie was happy to wear her hair this way and often told me about the many compliments she received at school. It seemed that everyone was eager to see what new hairstyle she would wear the next day, and we would study the braid book the night before to decide.

One morning I entered Jessie's room and found her glaring at her reflection in the mirror. Her red hair was sticking up all around her head, making her look as though she'd been caught in an updraft of turbulent wind.

"What's the matter, Jessie?" I asked, taken aback by the sight of her. She didn't answer me and I walked toward her and crouched down to meet her eyes in the mirror. I placed a comforting hand on her shoulder, but she shrugged it off and scowled at me.

"Don't you want me to do your hair?" I asked. Still no answer. I went to her bathroom and tidied up a bit. Her sour mood wasn't typical, and I needed time to figure out what to do. I glanced at the clock on Jessie's nightstand while making her bed. We had to be out the door in ten minutes, or we'd be late for school.

I approached her again. "Jessie, you'll be late for school if we don't hurry."

Jessie glowered at me again and then her hands flew up to

her face and she began to sob, her big orange hair bouncing about like a powder puff. I kneeled down before her and placed my hand on her shoulder again. This time she flung herself into my arms and sobbed for a good five minutes.

"Nana, why am I so ugly?"

"You're a beautiful girl, Jessie," I replied, passing my hand across her back as I did when she was an infant.

"No, I'm not. Mom is beautiful and I look nothing like her." She pushed herself away from me, blinking away her tears. "Nana, I've been thinking about it for a long time and I'm pretty sure that I was adopted."

It took every effort to keep from smiling. "Really? What makes you think you were adopted?"

"It's only obvious, Nana. I don't look like Mommy or Daddy. And I don't even look like Teddy, and everybody says that he looks just like Daddy."

I couldn't deny that it was true. One look at Teddy and there was no doubt he was their child, but it wasn't so apparent when you took in Jessie's red hair, her freckles, and such a smile that it took my breath away. Although she didn't have classically beautiful features as her mother did, she had the most expressive face I'd ever seen. Of course, I knew that eleven-year-old girls didn't want to be told they had expressive faces. They wanted to be told that they looked like princesses or supermodels. Nothing less would do.

I searched my heart and mind for the right words, but came up short.

"You see?" she said, taking my silence as confirmation. "You think I'm adopted too."

"Oh, believe me, you weren't adopted. I know for a fact that you weren't."

"How do you know?" Jessie asked, challenging me.

"Because I was there the day you came into the world."

Jessie's eyes flew open with wonder. "You were?"

"Yes, I was, and I have no doubt that the little baby I saw on that day was you."

Jessie pouted. She was somewhat disappointed to be denied her self-pity, but more intrigued than anything else to hear what I had to say. "How can you be sure, Nana? Maybe when my real mother saw how ugly I was she switched me for a prettier baby when nobody was looking."

At this I smiled. "There was no prettier baby than you. And I'm sure it was you because of your beautiful dimples. You even had them as a baby, although you weren't smiling then, you were making quite a fuss just like you are now. But if you smiled," I said, touching her cheek, "I'd see them."

"I don't feel like smiling, Nana," she shot back with a sniffle.

"I know you don't," I replied. "It's probably the worst thing you could do. In fact, I think you should try your hardest not to smile."

She looked back at me, ready to accept the challenge. And then her lips started to twitch.

"Don't you smile, Jessie," I said. "Don't show those dimples, not now before your breakfast. Oh my goodness, no!"

Unable to resist, she broke out in a beautiful grin that touched me deeply as always. I wiped the tears from her face and said, "We only have time for a simple braid today, is that okay?" She shrugged, feeling a bit defeated, but willing to get on with her morning.

As far as I could tell, Ms. Lillian had been managing her impulses fairly well. Her activities with the charity league continued to keep her busy, she was enrolled in a variety of exercise classes, and she went shopping with her friends several times a week. It was a wonder to me that she had any energy to spare, but what energy she had she devoted to Jessie. She was constantly frustrated by her daughter's "frumpy appearance," as she called it, and she fussed over her incessantly.

"Jessie dear," she'd say. "Why don't you let me take you to the hairdresser, and we'll cut your hair into a cute short style."

"Hey, sweetie," she announced as she walked through the door with a multitude of shopping bags. "Wait until you see these lovely Betsey Johnson dresses I bought for you."

But Jessie didn't like wearing designer dresses. She preferred to wear slacks and shorts so she could run after her brother and play the games he enjoyed, anything just to keep up with him, which wasn't always easy.

"Oh, Ana, will you look at her?" Ms. Lillian said when she spotted her daughter swinging from the branch of a tree or throwing dirt balls with remarkable accuracy. "She looks more like a monkey than a girl."

"I think it's wonderful they get along so well."

Ms. Lillian put her hands on her hips and shook her head, "You're not helping, Ana." But whenever she turned her eyes on her son, all disappointments vanished. She was able to gaze at him for hours. As the years passed and Teddy grew, there was no denying that he was indeed a beautiful child, and as successful in academics as he was in athletics. He'd inherited both beauty and brilliance, and when anyone spoke of him there was a certain hush in their voice, as though they knew they were speaking about someone who would one day achieve greatness.

One afternoon, after Jessie had finished her homework and chores, I spotted her in the front garden with the bike she'd received the previous Christmas. It was purple with a mesh basket hanging from the handlebars decorated with plastic flowers. She loved her bike and often rode it to her friend's house a few blocks away. She hadn't had it long, but already the basket was dented in several places because she liked to ride fast and often fell or crashed into things. More than a place to put her belongings, the basket served as an effective shock absorber, and it seemed that I was constantly applying bandages and antiseptic ointment to elbows and knees. She wouldn't allow anyone else but me to apply these treatments.

As Jessie sat on the seat of her bike, she kept glancing at the kitchen window, obviously hoping that someone would notice her. She hadn't asked permission to ride her bike to her friend's house, so I wiped my hands on a dish towel and went outside to find out what she was up to.

She was balancing precariously off the seat of her bike, with one foot on the ground and teetering from side to side. Her face was set in a formidable frown, as though she were preparing for a fight she had no intention of losing.

"Where do you think you're going, Jessie?" I asked, noting

that her basket was filled with clothing and a couple of her favorite stuffed animals.

Her chin trembled as she put her foot on the pedal. "I'm running away from home. I don't like it here anymore. In fact, I *hate* it here!"

I saw the anguish in her eyes, her genuine desire to find her place and her dignity within the family. And in her eyes, I also saw myself as a child so many years ago.

It was after the rainy season had passed that Carlitos and I decided the time had come to make our move. Our plan was to search for my father first, and then once we found him, we'd proceed to the nearby village where *Tío* Carlos was living with his new family. Somehow we'd convince them both to come home with us. We weren't certain how we'd do this, or how we'd recognize my father—because neither of us could remember him—but these details didn't trouble us too much. The way I imagined it, we'd find him whittling under a tree, perhaps making a toy for me, as he waited to be found. When our eyes met, it would be like gazing into a mirror tarnished by time and regret, but our undeniable connection as father and daughter wouldn't be altered.

I convinced Carlitos that this was how it would be, and trusting soul that he was, he didn't need any more convincing than that. Anyway, his mind was occupied with the more practical matter of our survival in the jungle. He would hunt daily to keep us fed, and we would gather all manner of fruits and make certain to keep our water jugs filled. We would sleep in the trees at night and follow the river by day. Carlitos couldn't wait to get started on our adventure, and I too was eager to get on with it.

Because we had no doubt that they would do everything in their power to stop us, we thought it best to leave without informing our mothers. Also, *Tía* Juana, being more excitable than my mother, would probably beat Carlitos for good measure.

The day of our departure arrived and we were collecting a few essential items when Mama walked into the hut and asked what we were doing with the sack she used for her marketing. Carlitos and I glanced at each other and said nothing, our faces burning with shame. *Tía* Juana entered moments later with baby Lupita perched on her hip and immediately sensed that something was up.

"What's going on?" she asked, her eyes hot with suspicion.

Carlitos was always rendered speechless by his mother's anger so I knew that this explanation would be up to me. I kept my face turned toward my mother, as *Tía* Juana could make anyone's tongue tangle up in seconds. "You might as well know that Carlitos and I are running away from home."

I heard Carlitos groan behind me. He was hoping that I'd make something up, but when surprised in this manner, I could never be anything but truthful.

"You're what?" *Tía* Juana asked.

I turned to her and shuddered when I saw her eyes bugging out at me. "We're running away from home," I repeated somewhat less boldly.

"Why are you doing this?" Mama asked, her voice calm and measured as always.

I took a deep breath, knowing that answering this would be hardest of all. "I'm going to look for my father, and Carlitos is going to convince *Tío* Carlos to come home with us. If he doesn't want to come, then Carlitos might stay with him."

Tía Juana gasped and nearly dropped her baby. She began to sputter and stamp her feet as her rage gathered like a hurricane in her chest. Already she was looking around for something she might use to beat Carlitos. *Tía* Juana didn't usually waste any time. She liked to get right to it.

"Your father is dead," Mama said. "You know that."

I shook my head. "You say he drank himself to death, and other people tell me he was hit by a car, but what I feel in my heart is that he's alive in the jungle, waiting for me to find him."

Tía Juana couldn't contain herself any longer. "Oh, you stupid girl!" she cried. "Your father was so drunk he didn't realize he was on the main road in the middle of the night, and a truck ran him right over. They found him the next day flattened out like a tortilla. It was so dark, the driver thought he'd hit a dog, and he was right."

"I don't believe it," I said, taking hold of Carlitos's trembling hand.

"And you," *Tía* Juana said, pointing her finger at Carlitos's face. "After everything your father's done to us, you would abandon me and your brothers and sisters to go live with him and that whore he's taken up with?"

Carlitos said nothing, but his silence was more than enough to confirm it.

"You little shit." *Tía* Juana seethed. "You're just like your miserable father. I bet she seduced you as well, didn't she? That whore Marisol with her big *tetas* and dainty manners. But I'm not worried. She'll kick you out as soon as she realizes how much you can eat."

"I can hunt too," Carlitos muttered.

Tía Juana started to shout obscenities, but Mama quieted her down with a hand to her shoulder. As *Tía* Juana grumbled under her breath, Mama began to rummage around through some of her things and returned with a light, finely textured blanket. "I was saving this for the day you left the house. I was hoping that it would be under different circumstances, but I'll give it to you now. And I'll leave word with Dolores if we move so you'll know where we are when you return, *if* you return."

"You're moving?" I asked, taking the blanket from her.

Mama shrugged. "You'll be gone a long time searching for someone who can't be found, so who knows what will happen?" She turned away and began to sort through the beans she would cook for dinner, deftly removing the tiny rocks she found and tossing them aside.

Tía Juana, who was still fuming quietly while glaring at Carlitos, turned away too and began to breast-feed her baby with inflated tenderness that was not typical of her, as though to emphasize that her maternal affection was only for those who still belonged to her.

After a while, Mama looked up from her work surprised to find us still standing there. "If you don't leave soon, the night will catch you," she said.

I felt like collapsing at her feet and begging her forgiveness. How could I have ever hoped to live a day without my dear mother? Yet I had no idea how to bridge the great chasm I'd created between us, and Carlitos seemed even more lost than I.

"Maybe we should just go tomorrow morning," he whispered nervously.

"Yes, I think tomorrow morning would be best," I said loudly enough so that Mama and *Tía* Juana could hear, but if they did, they didn't seem to care. I understood at that moment how a mother's worry can keep you safe and warm, and how her indifference will leave you so cold that you may not care whether you live or die.

I took the blanket Mama had given me and placed it on my hammock. I lay down over it and stayed there until morning, not daring to move even for a meal. I was afraid that if I left it for too long, my place would be taken from me, and suddenly the only thing that mattered was this little corner of the world, the slat in the wall through which I could see the first rays of dawn, and all of the dear people who shared this little hut with me.

Carlitos did the same as I, although he watched his mother with big eyes as she went about the hut taking care of this or that, grateful, I'm sure, that at no point did she discover a stick or some item that reminded her she owed him a beating.

The next morning, just when we thought that the rainy season had ended, we were blessed with more rain. It would be a bad idea to run away in such conditions, and we never mentioned it again. Carlitos did his chores without being asked and with such exuberance that anyone would think he was being paid to do them. I did mine with a newfound sense of commitment as well, and when Mama wasn't looking, I put the blanket she'd given me back among her things.

"Where will you go?" I asked Jessie, who was taking her time repacking her basket.

She shrugged and then said, "To Disneyland, probably."

Like most children, Disneyland was Jessie's favorite place.

"Will you live at Cinderella's castle?"

She shrugged again, more forlorn than ever. "Probably," she muttered.

"Wait," I said, and I rushed into the kitchen and returned with a box of cereal and tucked it into her basket amid everything else. "You'll be hungry in the morning," I said.

She gazed at me with large, luminous eyes. "Aren't you going to miss me, Nana?" she asked.

"Oh, I'll miss you terribly. I'll cry every night and so will your mommy and daddy. I'm sure that Teddy will also be very upset."

She opened the cereal box and popped a few nuggets in her mouth, but she kept her foot planted firmly on the ground. "Do you think they'll call the police?" she asked.

"Once they realize you're gone, I'm sure they will, but if you go straight to Disneyland now, you can probably get there before the police start looking for you."

She nodded thoughtfully and popped a few more nuggets into her mouth. "They might think I'm dead or that a bad man stole me away," she said, "and then they'll be sorry."

"I'm sure they will," I replied.

"I know what," Jessie said, her face lighting up. "Why don't you come with me? How about we *both* run away from home?"

I thought about this for a moment or two. "Well, I would go with you, Jessie, but the truth is that I really like it here and I'd be sad if I left."

She nodded wisely and closed the cereal box with a sigh. "You're scared, aren't you?" she asked.

I nodded, trying my best to look a bit ashamed. "I guess I am . . . a little bit."

Looking rather relieved, she swung her leg up and jumped off her bike. She walked it to the garage, glancing back once or twice to see if I was following, which I was. Once she'd parked her bike, she pulled her things out of the basket and handed them to me one by one. As we walked back to the house, she said, "I'm not going to run away after all, but if you ever decide that you're not scared anymore, let me know."

"I'll remember that," I said.

Thirteen

WHEN ANA TURNED AWAY from the window, Millie was no longer chatting casually with Adam about her retirement. She had her face buried in her hands and she was weeping. In all the years she'd known her, Ana had never seen Millie weep in such a manner, and it frightened her.

Millie lifted her face and said, "Tell me again, Adam. Please, I want to know exactly what happened. Where was Mick sitting in the car? How did you persuade him to let you drive?"

Adam nodded to Ana, letting her know in his way that he was fine. She decided to leave them and go outside where Sister Josepha was still sitting on the ledge of the fountain.

When she saw Ana approaching, she smiled. "It seems that over the last year or so these knees of mine have been getting worse. I don't think they're going to get any better," she concluded with a chuckle.

Sister Josepha leaned on her cane as she attempted to

stand but was having difficulty, so Ana helped her to her feet. "Maybe you're working too hard, you should slow down a little bit."

Sister Josepha leaned on Ana's arm. "If I didn't have my work, it would be the end of me, but when you come . . ." She corrected herself with a conscientious nod: "I mean *if* you come, you'll see for yourself how infectious the work can be. The children are so grateful and they'll love you, but I must tell you, in spite of the many improvements we've made over the years, the conditions are nothing like they are here. It will be quite an adjustment for you."

Ana stopped to face Sister Josepha, her expression incredulous. "Sister, do you forget where and how we met?"

"Oh, I'll never forget," Sister Josepha replied, lowering her eyes.

"Nor will I. And this," Ana said with a grand, sweeping gesture, "is all very beautiful, but it's not who I am, and it doesn't belong to me. It never has . . . not really."

Sister Josepha appraised Ana for a moment or two, surprised by her impassioned reaction. "My dear, I didn't mean to upset you."

"No, of course not, I . . . I'm not upset," Ana replied, flustered and embarrassed about having expressed herself so forcefully, when Sister Josepha was only being considerate.

They headed toward the house and when they entered Sister Josepha said, "You go on up now, I'll be fine."

"Are you sure?"

"I'm quite sure," Sister Josepha said with a kindly smile.

Ana rushed upstairs and by the time she reached the top, she was winded. "Time is passing too quickly, and I can't keep up," she thought. "I just can't keep up with it."

"There is always time," came the reply in the stillness between each breath.

"But what if there isn't? What if I'm left behind again?"

"Trust yourself, *mija*. When you follow your heart, you'll have all the time you need."

On her way down the hall back to Adam's room, Ana hesitated outside Teddy's bedroom door. After the children had left for school, Ana would often go into their rooms to remember the many conversations they'd had over the years, the happiest moments as well as the difficult ones, and for an instant she was able to alleviate the loneliness she felt in their absence.

For several months, she hadn't dared peek into Teddy's room, knowing it would only bring her additional sadness and strain during an already difficult time. Nevertheless, feeling that it was all she had left of him, she opened the door and peeked in. The first thing that met her eyes was Teddy's extra-long single bed in the corner of the room beneath the window. When he was in high school and had grown several inches in one year, it became apparent that a regular-size bed would no longer suffice. How they'd laughed when he lay down with his feet sticking out beyond his blankets.

They'd rearranged this room many times over the years, from a nursery to the room of a schoolboy and now to a young man's room. Each time, Ana had been involved in the task, helping Teddy select new furniture, curtains, and bedclothes to achieve the look he wanted. The poster of his latest athletic hero still hung on the wall. Ana couldn't remember the name of this man, who was one of the best pitchers of all time, only that Teddy worshipped him for the better part of his four years in high school.

Feeling surprisingly better than she thought she would, Ana took several tentative steps into the room, and the memories flooded her before she could step out again.

Lillian watched Teddy and his new "little floozy," as she liked to call her, through the sunroom window as they sat out sunbathing by the pool. Maggie was a sweet girl with short brown hair and a wide, easy smile. I thought she was lovely and down-to-earth, the kind of young lady who was just as comfortable in a pair of old blue jeans as she was in a strapless gown. Teddy boasted that she was not only pretty but smart, as evidenced by the fact that she was applying to Harvard in the fall. She hoped to become an international journalist and tour the world to write about the exploits of presidents, kings, and underworld spies. I could easily imagine her in such a role, and when I watched the news at night, I thought that her pretty, smiling face and intelligent gaze would be very well received by the viewing public.

"There's something about her," Lillian said, narrowing her eyes at the young woman, "something that makes me uncomfortable, but I can't quite put my finger on what it is."

I couldn't imagine what it could be, and when I turned back to them, Maggie was giggling while applying suntan lotion to Teddy's muscular shoulders. He was teasing her about something as she rubbed his back, and they were both obviously enjoying the process immensely. "She seems like a very nice girl to me," I muttered.

"Oh, you would say that, Ana," Lillian said, rolling her eyes. "But then again, Teddy could bring home a stripper with nipple rings and you'd probably say, 'She's such a nice girl, isn't she?'"

I cringed at the thought of what nipple rings might be and shook my head. But if what Lillian said about me was true, then she was the complete opposite. She heartily disliked all the girls Teddy brought home and had no difficulty indentifying their faults no matter how subtle they might be. There was one girl who she thought of as sallow and with a watery personality to match. Another was, in her opinion, too manly, and yet another was so syrupy sweet that it made her sick to her stomach.

"I think I know what it is," Lillian said, turning to me with a start. "This young woman with her highbrow ambitions, impressive SAT scores, and modern short haircut is really nothing more than a common trollop who wants to snare my son and tie him down for her own sick amusement."

"So," I said, nodding in understanding, "you think she'd like to marry Teddy and make a life with him, is that it?"

Lillian turned to me, disappointment clouding her expression. "One has to read between the lines, Ana. As a mother, I have to remain vigilant. Teddy is an extremely good catch, and any girl would happily sell her soul to the devil to get her hands on him."

"Teddy will make someone a wonderful husband one day," I said.

"You miss the point entirely," Ms. Lillian snapped.

"Forgive me, but what exactly is the point, if you don't mind my asking?"

Ms. Lillian shook her head as though my profound lack of insight made it difficult for her to speak. She glared at Teddy and Maggie, who were now feeding each other frozen grapes, and scowled. "If you don't know," she muttered, "then I'm certainly not going to spell it out for you." She continued to stare at the scene before her, and her lips began to tremble with rage. "I can't take this anymore," she snapped and she walked away in a huff.

I wasn't put off by her remarks because I'd long understood that the sexual obsession Lillian had finally learned to control had been replaced by the persistent and irrational fear that her son would end up with someone just like her. I admired and pitied her at the same time.

Several nights later, I was awakened by the sound of yelling somewhere down the hall. I realized that it was Lillian's voice, and she was so hysterical that I became frightened the house might have caught fire. I threw on my robe and ran out into the hallway, expecting to confront a cloud of smoke and flames. Instead, I found Lillian standing in front of Teddy's bedroom door, with Mr. Trellis trying his best to calm her down.

"Call the police, Adam!" she yelled. "Call them now!"

"I'm sure that isn't necessary," Mr. Trellis said in a measured voice, although I could see that he was also upset.

"I don't want her in this house, do you understand me? I want her out of here!" She attempted to reenter Teddy's room, but Mr. Trellis held her back. Then he turned to me, his face coloring a bit as he explained, "It seems that Teddy has a visitor."

Lillian glared at him, looking as though she might claw his eyes out. "A visitor? Tell the truth, Adam. This girl tries to impress everyone with her high-and-mighty ideals, but now we know the truth, don't we? She's trying to trap him." Ms. Lillian was speaking loudly at the door so that Teddy and his visitor would be sure to hear her.

Mr. Trellis led Lillian down the hall toward their room. She struggled against him at first, but eventually she gave in and went with him, muttering all the while. Once they had closed the door to their room, Teddy peeked out to see if the coast was clear. When he saw me, his face colored much as his father's had moments earlier, but he seemed relieved that it was me standing there and not his mother. He was at a loss for words, and I was preparing to return to my room as well when he whispered, "Can you help me, Nana? Maggie's really upset right now."

I followed Teddy into his room to find Maggie sitting on the edge of his very long bed with her head hanging. In her blue jeans and long T-shirt she looked all of thirteen, and it was hard to imagine that she'd snuck into Teddy's room with scandalous intentions. As I went to her, Teddy quickly grabbed something from his nightstand and stuffed it into his pocket, but not before I saw that it was a package of condoms. It gave me some comfort to know that at least they were taking precautions.

"I'm so embarrassed, Nana," she said, looking at me with anguished eyes. "I don't know what to do." Her fingers were trembling as she wiped tears from her cheeks, and I could only imagine the scene she'd endured with Lillian. "I want you to know that I don't make a habit out of sneaking into guys' bedrooms in the middle of the night."

"I'm sure you don't, Maggie," I said. "Where do your parents think you are right now?"

She stared at me with wide, imploring eyes. "That's the problem. They think I'm spending the night at Lisa's house or I'd go home right now, but then they'll know I wasn't there, and if my Dad finds out, he'll kill me." Her shoulders slumped and she glanced at Teddy, who was equally despondent. "And I obviously can't stay here," she muttered.

"Can you help, Nana?" Teddy asked as he used to do when he'd broken a toy. "You know how crazy Mom gets. If Maggie isn't out of here in a few minutes, she'll call the police, no matter what Dad says."

I nodded, not sure of what I could or should do to help out. I thought it was wrong for Teddy and Maggie to go sneaking around, and for Maggie to lie to her parents about her whereabouts.

"No matter what we do, I'm screwed," Maggie muttered, and she began to whimper, something that I'd never expected this strong-minded modern girl to do.

I wrapped a reassuring arm around her shoulders. "You can come with me to my room for the rest of the night. Ms. Lillian has a yoga class tomorrow morning that she never misses. Once she's gone, I'll take you home."

"Oh my God, thank you, Nana," Maggie said, giving me a hug. And then she gazed at me adoringly. "Teddy and I are going to name our first child after you. Isn't that right, Teddy?"

Teddy shrugged, looking a bit uncomfortable. "What if it's a boy?"

"Our first girl child, then," she replied happily.

I ushered her out of Teddy's room while giving him a stern look. "You two have plenty of time for that sort of thing. Let's concentrate on getting through the night and home tomorrow, shall we?"

The next day Lillian refused to speak with Teddy. As difficult as it was for him to bring up the subject, he tried his best to apologize, but every time he did, she turned up her nose as though he smelled of rotting fish, and if he persisted she left the room entirely.

One weekend afternoon several days later, I was preparing a fruit salad for lunch when Teddy came into the kitchen looking especially bereft. I hadn't yet spoken to him further about the incident because I wasn't sure what to say. Nevertheless, I was preparing to tell him that I thought that Maggie was a nice girl and that he should consider that whenever he invited a nice girl to his room in the middle of the night, he was opening the door to many other possibilities as well, or something like that. I was thinking about how to begin when Lillian swept into the room, her smile ablaze and her mood so buoyant that she seemed to be floating several inches off the ground. "There he is," she said, gazing adoringly at Teddy. "My sweet, wonderful prince of a son."

Teddy blushed, but where his mother was concerned, he was much more at ease with this particular brand of discomfort. I stopped what I was doing to wonder at Lillian's sudden transformation. By that time I was well accustomed to her mood swings, but I had fully expected her upset with Teddy to last much longer than this.

"We're going car shopping," she said, her eyes glittering. "I believe that Teddy has his eye on a shiny yellow Porsche. It's not brand-new, but new enough, isn't that right, sunshine?"

Teddy blushed profusely and shrugged. "I guess," he muttered, avoiding my eyes.

They returned that very afternoon with the car, and Teddy parked it in front of the house and invited me and Jessie to go outside with him to admire it. We oohed and aahed and told him how striking he looked behind the wheel, and he happily gave us each a ride around the block. He was eager to show his friends his new car as well, and informed me that he'd be in a bit later than usual for dinner.

"Oh, I almost forgot," I said as I got out of his car, "Maggie called this afternoon while you were out with your mother."

Teddy's face grew somber, and he revved the engine. "If she calls again, tell her that I'm not home."

"But what if you are home?"

"I don't want to talk to her," he said

In response to my baffled expression, he said, "All this talk about children was just too much for me, so I broke up with her yesterday."

"I didn't think she was serious about that, at least not now. A smart girl like Maggie with so much ambition . . ."

"Nana, please, I don't want to talk *with* her and I don't want to talk *about* her." Then he drove off and didn't return until much later that night.

Ana walked out of Teddy's room feeling the same disappointment she'd felt all those years ago. She had no trouble believing that Lillian would bribe her son with a new car, but it pained her to think that Teddy would allow himself to be so easily manipulated. And then she remembered how years ago she'd been able to motivate his good behavior by promising him a game of hide-and-seek or an extra story before his nap. In many ways, as intelligent and capable as he was, Teddy was still a little boy in a grown man's body. But Ana knew that despite his immaturity he had a good heart. Then as now, she loved him unconditionally and could easily forgive him his faults.

Often she wondered if Maggie had gone to Harvard after all and if she was still pursuing a career in journalism. She had wanted to ask Teddy about her several times, but knew that forcing him to talk about Maggie would be like bringing up the time he'd soiled himself in the middle of the night—both were smelly shameful incidents that he wanted to forget.

Fourteen

ANA RETURNED TO ADAM'S room, and although it was barely midafternoon, she was already dreading the night. She feared that death would come in the dark, when mystery prevails and the spirit is most alive. Because of this, she understood that she needed to be most vigilant at this time. She often stayed awake, taking comfort from the fact that at least it was more difficult to perceive the passage of time in the dark. For a few hours she could pretend that it had actually stopped and that she and her beloved were suspended within an endless and eternal void.

These wakeful nights forced her to sleep in the afternoon instead, so once Adam began sleeping in a hospital bed she took to sleeping in a cot next to him. Lying upon it now, she watched the play of shadow and light against the wall and felt herself rocking back and forth. Everything became hazy as Adam's breathing kept time with the mild gusts that moved the branches to and fro outside the window. She was almost asleep when she heard voices outside. She opened her eyes and sat up slowly. Her heart began to race at the thought that Teddy had finally come home. She listened more carefully and realized that it wasn't Teddy after all. Not only could she hear who it was, she could also feel it in her bones and smell it in the air. She wondered if this is how it was in ancient times when people could sense an approaching pestilence or plague. Perhaps this knowing allowed them the time to prepare and garner the strength they needed to survive the ordeal.

She'd always hoped that the passing years would wash over everything and impart its veil of indifference, as only time can do. But if anything, her negative feelings had only grown stronger. She wasn't able to shrug his behavior off and chalk it up to the adventurous spirit of reckless but goodhearted people. Ana was unable to forgive Darwin and she doubted that she ever would.

"I hear voices," Adam said, his own voice weak.

Ana quickly left her cot and went to him. "Your brother is here. Do you want to see him now? I can ask him to wait if you like."

Adam swallowed, but it was difficult for Ana to discern whether he was nodding or shaking his head. If he were to tell her that he didn't want to see his brother, Ana would have no difficulty sending Darwin away.

"I want to see him," he said, his eyes shining.

Downstairs, Ana found Darwin and Millie embracing in the foyer. She waited a few moments to announce, more somberly than she'd intended, that Adam was awake and wanted to see him.

Darwin bowed in Ana's direction and sarcastically muttered something about how convenient that was, since that's precisely the reason he'd come. After a few more kind words to Millie and a kiss on her forehead besides, he proceeded up the stairs. Ana followed several steps behind him.

"I've never seen you look so pale," he said. "It seems that this romantic adventure has depleted you."

Ana felt herself tremble with loathing. She was unable to think of anything to say to him, as every word that came to mind was more hateful than the next.

"What's wrong?" Darwin said. "Do you hate me so much that you can't even speak?"

"I don't hate you," Ana said. "I pity you."

"Really?" Darwin replied, stopping to look down on her. "You're a terrible liar, Ana. I've always been able to see in your eyes just how much you despise me."

Ana looked away, and Darwin proceeded up the stairs alone. Not sure whether to go up or down, she sat right where she was and rested her head on her arms. She could hear people in the kitchen, but she didn't have the energy or desire to join them. Neither did she think it appropriate to be present while Adam spoke to his brother. But from this central place she could keep tabs on everything going on in the house. It was a wonder she'd never sat there before. It was an unexpected discovery, and as she listened to Jessie's voice drifting in from the kitchen, she felt herself drifting away.

Jessie appraised herself in the full-length mirror, turning round and round in her lavender prom dress. She looked lovely, although she was obviously not completely pleased with what she saw. Ms. Lillian entered the room with a pair of earrings that she wanted her daughter to consider. She then stood next to Jessie in front of the mirror. Jessie didn't have her mother's willowy figure and graceful neck. She had a thicker waist and her limbs were chunky, making her look instantly plain and awkward by comparison. It was all Jessie could do not to push her mother away.

"Jessie, your hair looks beautiful with that dress," I observed.

"Should I wear it up, or down?" she asked.

"Definitely up," Ms. Lillian replied before I could answer. "It'll give you height and make you look slimmer."

"I think I'll wear it down," Jessie said.

"But think of how lovely these earrings will look with your hair up," Ms. Lillian said, holding them next to her.

Jessie shrugged. She clearly had no intention of wearing them. "Nana, will you brush out my hair for me and curl the ends with the iron like you do?"

Immediately I went to the bathroom for the iron and plugged it in. That's when the argument began. "Put your shoulders back a bit, Jessie. Notice what happens to your tummy when you stand up straight." Jessie said nothing. "You've put on a few pounds, dear. When we bought this dress, I told you that you couldn't afford to gain an ounce, but it's definitely pulling at the seams."

"It'll be okay, Mom," Jessie muttered.

I touched the iron—not hot enough—and I crossed my arms, hoping and praying that there wouldn't be another explosion, today of all days.

"I don't know," Ms. Lillian replied, and through the door I saw her shaking her head with the most discouraging expression clouding her face.

"Mom, can you please stop?"

"Stop what? I'm not doing anything."

Jessie started to pace in front of the mirror and then rushed to her vanity to get away from her reflection and her mother. "Yes, you are, you're doing that thing you do, that 'You'll never be good enough' thing you do."

Ms. Lillian glared at her daughter. "I have no idea what you're talking about."

"Nana," Jessie cried. "Nana, get in here, now."

I rushed in ready to announce that the iron was hot enough, but I didn't have the opportunity.

"Nana, tell her to stop." Jessie's face was twisted, and already her carefully applied makeup was beginning to run at the corners of her eyes, makeup that her mother had insisted she wear to make her eyes look bigger and brighter.

Ms. Lillian turned to me, her own face beginning to color. "I don't know what she's talking about. I'm not doing anything. I'm simply standing here, and she's treating me like I'm a piece of shit stuck to the bottom of her Salvatore Ferragamo shoes that I bought her, not easy to find in a size ten, I might add."

At this Jessie took off her shoes and threw one after the other against the wall. "Here are your fucking shoes, Mom. You can take 'em and shove 'em up your ass!" That said, she ran out of the room, tripping on the hem of her lavender skirt as she left. I glanced at the clock. Jessie's prom date, Charlie Winston, was due to show up in a few minutes and he was always on time.

Ms. Lillian's face had drained of all color. The arguments between them had been growing in intensity and frequency, but Jessie had never resorted to such crude language before.

"That little bitch," Ms. Lillian said. "I do everything I can for her, take her shopping, get her the dress and the shoes she wants. Do you think she's taking drugs?" she asked, jerking her head around to look at me.

"I don't think so, Ms. Lillian."

"But this is exactly what they say happens when kids take drugs. They have outbursts that make no sense, and they act crazy just like Jessie's acting right now."

"She's not taking drugs," I said with more certainty.

Ms. Lillian glared at me, her fists clenched. "And what do you know about it? That girl has you wound so tight around her finger, it's a wonder you can breathe, Ana. Honestly, sometimes you act as though you're her personal slave."

"I realize that I indulge her at times, but that's because I know that she's sensitive, and she's at a difficult age."

"And does that give her the right to be rude and profane to her mother? Tell me, does that give her the right?"

"No it doesn't," I replied. "Jessie was very wrong to say what she did."

But Lillian wasn't listening to me. She was fuming and yelling, hoping that wherever Jessie was she could hear her. "She has everything she wants whenever she wants it and she's never happy. She's nothing but a spoiled brat."

Mr. Trellis came into the room. "Why has Jessie locked herself in the powder room downstairs?" he asked.

"Because your daughter's an ungrateful pig!" Ms. Lillian replied, throwing the rejected earrings still clenched in her fist onto the bed.

Mr. Trellis glanced at me. His eyes told me to go downstairs and look after Jessie, while he attended to Lillian. We'd had to proceed in this manner several times before, and it seemed to be the most effective strategy.

I rushed downstairs and knocked lightly on the powder room door. "Jessie, it's me. It's Nana."

"I don't want to talk to her," she said. "I don't want to see her face."

"I'm alone," I replied.

Jessie unlocked the door and let me in. She'd already washed off most of her makeup, and the front of her dress was soaked.

"I don't know what to do, Nana," she said. "I don't want to go to the prom. I don't want to wear this stupid dress or those ridiculous shoes. I'm not the prom type. And I'm sick of doing things to make her happy. I'm sick of her, Nana." She stared at me with red-rimmed eyes. And then she said softly, almost reverently, "My mother is nothing but a slut—a beautiful, glamorous slut."

I stared at Jessie, not knowing what to say.

"Don't act so shocked, Nana. I know that you know. Everybody knows except Daddy and Teddy. And Mom thinks she's so slick, but believe me, people talk. Do you know that none of my friends' mothers will let their husbands anywhere near her? If Daddy knew, it would destroy him. That's the only reason I don't tell him." She sighed and shook her head. "But sometimes I get the impression that he does know and that he's just pretending for our sake. I wish I could find a way to tell him to stop pretending."

I could only gaze at her dear freckled face, shocked to hear that Lillian hadn't recovered from her past as I thought she had. And I was amazed by Jessie's insight and her ability to live through this for so long without falling apart.

We heard footsteps approaching and a knock on the bathroom door. I opened it and Mr. Trellis peeked in, looking rather awkward. "There's a young man in the foyer wearing a tuxedo and holding a beautiful corsage that would match very nicely with a lavender dress," he said quickly and then closed the door and left us.

Jessie shook her head sadly. "Look at me, Nana. I'm a mess and I don't want to go to that stupid prom. Do you think that if I tell Charlie I'm having a really bad day, he'll understand?"

I shrugged. "I suppose he might, but remember, you're still a junior and Charlie's a senior this year. He won't get a chance to go to the prom next year."

Jessie sighed. "Will you go upstairs and get my shoes, Nana?"

On my way up, I passed Mr. Trellis, who was chatting politely with Charlie in the foyer. I commented on how handsome he looked in his tuxedo and gave Mr. Trellis a nod, which we both understood to mean, "Another catastrophe averted."

I finished Jessie's hair and thought she actually looked better without all that makeup. Charlie lit up when she made her entrance, and Jessie gave him a lovely smile as he slipped the corsage on her wrist.

I couldn't help but feel that I'd failed Jessie by not better protecting her from the truth about her mother. And as Mr. Trellis and I waved Jessie and Charlie off, I remembered my mother's words from long ago.

"The less you know about your father, the better," she said.

"But why, Mama? Why won't you tell me about him?"

She set her sewing aside and thought about it for a moment.

"Because the truth will only destroy the dream, *mija*. And if you continue dreaming about the father you wish you had, then perhaps one day you'll find him."

Once Teddy was away at college, it was decided that Jessie would spend her senior year of high school studying abroad in Italy. Ms. Lillian had pushed for it, telling her daughter that it would be an awakening unlike anything she'd ever experienced. But I figured that Jessie agreed to go so that she could get away from her mother, and Lillian's motives I would discover soon enough.

With both children away the house became filled with a deep, lonesome silence as thick and cold as a winter fog. The stillness reminded me of my years in the convent, and I often strolled the grounds and the house with my hands folded before me, as though I were participating in a holy procession of one.

I missed the children terribly and spent much of my extra time writing letters to them. I wrote to Sister Josepha as usual and even to Millie once in a while, although she'd call me back on the telephone to tell me that it didn't make sense to write when the cost of a call was less than a stamp. Teddy and Jessie wrote back occasionally, apologizing that they'd taken so long to write back, but I was always joyful to receive their letters and would read them many times over.

When Mr. Trellis arrived home in the evenings the fog lifted and the house became filled with light and life. I felt his shimmering presence no matter where I was. And when he played the piano in the evenings, the lilting melody of his music comforted my lonely heart. I know that he missed the children terribly as I did, yet he appeared as though he'd been relieved of a heavy burden. His steps were lighter when he strode down the hall toward his study, and his laughter was brighter and more frequent than ever before.

I was compelled to do whatever necessary to make him comfortable. I saw to it that his mail was neatly stacked in his office and that dinner was always ready when he arrived home. Ever since Millie's departure I had frequently consulted with her about matters in the kitchen so that my cooking skills gradually improved. Ms. Lillian's life had become increasingly busy. It was difficult to keep track of her activities, and she no longer called home to say she'd be late, so Mr. Trellis often ate alone.

Sometimes he invited me to join him, and we'd talk until long after we'd finished our meal. There was so much to discuss regarding the children, and I happily shared the contents of their recent letters and listened to him recount their latest phone call. Teddy was considering premed, and Jessie had an Italian boyfriend, which made us both a little anxious. We also discussed the details regarding repairs for the house and the condition of the garden. Mr. Trellis appreciated my concern for the maintenance of his beloved estate, and together we planned a number of renovations, some more urgent than others. A few weeks earlier, I noticed that the east garden wall had required replastering to keep it from crumbling. I'd told him about the cracks I'd seen while strolling the perimeter of the grounds, and together we'd inspected the progress of the repairs. I lived for these precious moments with him.

But this tranquil, pleasant space in our lives ended abruptly one sweltering summer afternoon when Ms. Lillian came home laden down with shopping bags from Neiman Marcus and Williams and Sonoma. I met her at the front door to help her bring them in, but she immediately dropped them and pulled me with her into the kitchen. Her cheeks quivered with excitement as she spoke.

"I did it," she said breathlessly. "I finally did it."

"What did you do?" I asked.

"I left him. I finally left him."

"I don't understand, Ms. Lillian. Who did you leave?"

Ms. Lillian stared at me incredulous. "Adam, of course. Who do you think?"

It took me a moment to respond. "But everything is so peaceful. We've been making repairs on the house, and the children are happy at their schools . . ."

"Ana," Ms. Lillian said, grabbing my shoulders. "Don't you see? I've only been waiting for Teddy and Jessie to leave so I could do the same. It will be less painful for them this way." She dropped her hands. "I found a fabulous loft in the city a few weeks ago and I signed the lease this morning. I can't wait for you to see it."

"Does Mr. Trellis know?" I asked, bewildered.

"We've been talking about it for some time now, but we didn't want Teddy and Jessie to find out prematurely, and since you're so close to them, we thought it best to keep it from you too, but I've been dying to tell you about it, and since I signed the lease today, I thought that now was the right time to let you know."

I sat down at the kitchen table, stunned to silence.

"Ana, why do you look so upset? You of all people must've seen this coming."

"I thought . . . ," I said, looking up. "I thought that things were getting better."

"They're just great as long as we stay out of each other's way. And that hasn't been too difficult to do," she said rolling her eyes. "Adam and I haven't been living like man and wife for years."

My head was spinning with all she was telling me, and I couldn't take in anymore. The fact that she'd found another place to live and that there had been no intimacy between them for years was more than enough for me to digest at the moment. And most confusing of all was Mr. Trellis's behavior of late. He seemed so happy and content with his life. Perhaps he was suffering from some kind of extended shock as he tried to manage the grief of losing his wife. "Mr. Trellis must be very upset," I said.

Lillian sat down so she could look me straight in the eye. "Ana, you're not hearing me. I have a beautiful loft in the city. It's the kind of place I've always dreamed of, and tomorrow I'm having a few things delivered. Best of all, I'm taking you with me. Now that Teddy and Jessie are gone, there's nothing much for you to do here, and I need you with me, Ana. I need you now more than ever."

Stunned by this revelation, I asked, "Does Mr. Trellis know?"

"Yes, I told you, we've been planning this for months."

"I mean, does he know that you want me to go with you?"

Ms. Lillian shrugged, somewhat put off by my question. "Of course he does, and he's fine with it as long as I help him find another housekeeper, which I've already looked into." Lillian gazed admiringly at me. "But from now on I don't want you to think of yourself as a nanny or a housekeeper or anything like that. I want you to think of yourself as my personal assistant."

"And the children," I muttered. "What about the children?"

Mrs. Trellis folded her arms across her chest and narrowed her eyes at me, disappointed that I wasn't as overjoyed with my promotion and this new turn in life as she was. "They're not children anymore, Ana. They're adults, and I think it's best that we start treating them as such."

"Yes, you're right," I muttered and I stood up to gather the packages that were still in the foyer. And as I helped Lillian organize her luxurious purchases for her new home, one-thousand-thread-count Italian sheets and hammered copper cookware among them, I felt the life dripping from my veins. I couldn't imagine living away from Mr. Trellis, and it hurt me to think that he could so easily imagine living without me, that after all these years I was nothing more than a housekeeper to him. I chided myself for the rest of the day and tried to rid my brain of these preposterous thoughts, but they crept back in like a trail of hungry ants. If I couldn't stop them, I could at least modify them somewhat. Perhaps Mr. Trellis didn't need me the way I needed him, but he was certainly in need of my services at the house. It had taken me twenty years to understand what was required to look after it and him, and a replacement for me wouldn't be so easy to find.

I resolved to speak with Mr. Trellis that very evening. I wanted him to know that I would continue working for him if he wanted me to stay, even if it would upset Lillian. I planned to talk with him during the evening meal just as we'd discussed so many other household matters, but for the first time in weeks, Ms. Lillian stayed home for dinner, and I couldn't possibly bring the subject up with her present. I had cleared the dishes and was rinsing them in the sink when I heard her shrill voice above the running water.

"First you tell me to take my time, and now you can't wait to get rid of me."

He muttered a reply, and although I couldn't discern his words, the gruff impatient tone was the same as I remembered.

"No, I haven't found anyone to take Ana's place," she replied. "Fine, if you prefer I'll leave tomorrow, and Ana can stay here until I find someone."

As their chairs screeched across the dining room floor, I fell to my knees and pressed my hands together in desperate prayer. "Let me stay here forever, dear God. Please, I don't want to go with Ms. Lillian to her new loft. I want to stay here with Mr. Trellis."

At that moment, Lillian came into the kitchen and found me prostrate on the floor before the kitchen sink. "What in the world are you doing, Ana?"

I stood up hastily and wiped my soapy hands on a dish towel. "I . . . I dropped a fork, but I can't seem to find it."

"Finish up as soon as you can," she said. "I need your help."

After I finished with the dishes, I went upstairs and found Ms. Lillian in her room packing her things with a vengeance and muttering to herself all the while. "I can't wait to get out of this rat trap," she said. "Tomorrow can't come soon enough for me."

I helped her fold her fine clothing while saying very little. I was worried that perhaps I'd overheard her incorrectly. Maybe after we were finished with her things, she'd direct me to pack my things as well.

"There's been a change in plans," Lillian announced casually as she appraised her collection of silk scarves in every color of the rainbow. "You won't be coming with me right away as I hoped. Adam's being difficult, but as soon as I find a replacement I'll send for you."

The muscles in my face quivered as I willed myself not to smile with unadulterated joy and relief.

Lillian turned away from her scarves to look at me with sympathetic eyes. "I'm sorry, Ana. I know you must be very disappointed."

I nodded, trying my best to appear valiant and resigned. "I'll be fine, Ms. Lillian. You shouldn't worry about me when you have so many other things to think about now."

Ms. Lillian sighed with contentment as she tossed the scarves into her open suitcase. "I'm finally going to make my own life," she said. "Oh, Ana, remember all those years ago when you told me that if I was patient I'd find my happiness?"

"I remember."

"Well, you were right, and this is the moment I've been waiting for."

I smiled and said nothing, but as I helped Lillian finish her packing, I realized, even as I prayed for God's forgiveness, that this was the moment I'd been waiting for too.

Fifteen

ANA STOOD UP AND slowly made her way to the top of the stairs. From there she could see that her beloved's door was open. When she approached, she saw Darwin kneeling at Adam's bedside with his head hanging down and Adam's hand resting on his crown, as though conferring a blessing.

Ana hesitated and then decided not to enter. She wandered back downstairs and found herself in the music room. The late afternoon sun spilled in through the window, filling the room with a hazy golden light that inspired her recollection of the beautiful music she'd heard here. Sitting in the chair closest to the piano, her eyes traveled over the graceful contours of the instrument. With its lid propped open, it reminded her of an eagle on the wing soaring through the sky. The next moment it was immovable and timeless as a mountain range, always true to itself and its beauty. It represented the strength and depth of her beloved.

She slowly approached the piano, pulled out the bench,

and sat upon it. She carefully lifted the cover to reveal the keys.
The ivory was slightly yellowed, but the black keys hadn't lost
their luster. Her fingers gently brushed their tops without making a sound. She dared not press down and disturb the peace in
the room.

Pulling a tissue from her pocket, she began to wipe away a thin
layer of dust from the glossy surface, leaving a discernable streak.
She worked her way down the legs of the instrument, along the
broad sides, and across the back in a gentle and caressing motion
until every inch of the piano gleamed. She then studied the intricate internal construction, the golden strings and white hammers
that looked like a harp neatly fitted within the piano's wood frame,
as beautiful and delicate as jewelry. How she'd enjoyed watching
the hammers dance across the strings as her beloved played, and
whenever she stood as close as she was at that moment, she could
feel its vibrations traveling through her body.

After Lillian left the house, the weeks that followed were a
dream. Mr. Trellis played for me every night, and for well over
an hour I was with him as the music soared around us. I spent
most of my days supervising the cleaning staff or working in the
garden. In the evenings I prepared simple meals for Mr. Trellis
and Benson, who was a regular dinner guest now that Lillian
was gone. We often sat around the table in the sunroom with
candles lit until late into the evening. I enjoyed waiting on them
and listening to their conversation and joining in from time to
time, especially if the discussion veered toward the children. I
was floating on such a sea of contentment that I didn't notice the

passage of time. If Teddy and Jessie had come through the door at that moment, my life would have been perfect and complete.

The subject of Mr. Trellis's divorce came up often in conversation. The most contentious issue involved the house. Mr. Trellis was willing to compromise on everything but that. On several occasions I heard him say to Benson, "I'll give her whatever else she wants, but I won't give her the house, or any part of it." They never curtailed their conversation because of me, but I kept my distance at these times. I didn't feel comfortable talking about Lillian, and although my heart had secretly aligned itself with Mr. Trellis years ago, I didn't want to be put in the position where I would have to openly take sides.

It wasn't getting any easier explaining to Sister Josepha why, once again, I had changed my mind about going to New Mexico. There had been so many reasons over the years that I was starting to feel like an irresponsible child who kept inventing clever reasons for why her homework wasn't done. Nevertheless, I wrote that my services were once again required at the house and that considering the upheaval the divorce was causing for all family members, I'd have to wait until the situation had stabilized before leaving. As always, her response was gracious and kind. "When the time is right, you will know," she wrote back. "Until then, I will always hold a place for you here as I do in my heart."

As Christmas approached, I took great pleasure in decorating the house. By then, Teddy and Jessie were aware that their parents had separated, so I wanted things to be as pleasant as possible for them when they returned home for the holidays. I put wreaths in every window and selected a tree for the main room that was more than ten feet tall. I needed a ladder to decorate it and even then, Mr. Trellis had to put the star on the very top. More than ever, I wanted Teddy and Jessie to feel that they were coming home to a house filled with warmth and love.

One evening, just a few days before they were due home, I was listening to Mr. Trellis play the piano when he stopped abruptly and said, "Ana, I don't believe I've ever seen you look so content."

"I always feel happy when I hear you play," I replied.

"Would you like to learn how to play something yourself?"

"Oh, I don't think I could. It's probably too late for me."

He slid over to make room for me in the bench. "It's never too late," he said with a stiff nod.

I sat next to him, intensely aware of his thigh so close to mine. He placed his hands on the keys and asked me to copy him. I tried very hard to imitate the arch in his hands, but this was difficult to do with quivering noodles for fingers.

"Ana," he said, somewhat surprised, "why are you trembling so? Don't you feel well?"

I was so overwhelmed that it took me a moment or two to find the words to answer him. "I'm afraid that I'm going to disappoint you and that you'll think I'm stupid and dull."

"I could never think that about you, Ana," he replied. "You should try to be more confident."

My vision became blurry, and I felt the blood racing through my veins. His nearness was affecting me so intensely that I felt the need to get away from him or risk appearing even more foolish. "I'm sorry, Mr. Trellis. I suppose that I'm not feeling very well after all. May I go now?"

He hesitated as though perturbed by my question. "Of course, Ana. You're free to come and go as you like. You know that."

"Thank you," I said and I left as quickly as I could.

He continued to play for some time after that, and as I listened from a safe distance through the open window, I imagined myself still sitting next to him on the piano bench, our hands crossing over each other and bridging beyond the rapture of the notes we played.

Benson arrived early for dinner the next afternoon, although this in itself was not unusual. He enjoyed following me about, chatting while I finished my chores. But on this day, he was distracted by a guest he brought with him, an attractive woman with a neat blond bob. She was an attorney who'd recently joined his firm. I was in the kitchen reaching for the wineglasses off the top shelf that he'd requested when Benson entered to help me while his friend waited in the sitting room. "Now, Ana, I don't want you to get jealous," he said with an exaggerated frown. "Sandra and I are just friends, although I'm hoping that Adam takes a liking to her."

I nearly dropped the glass in my hand. "Mr. Trellis? But he's not even divorced yet."

"That's true," Benson replied with a devious flicker of his bushy brows. "But it'll be good for him to get his mind off the divorce, and in the meantime, life goes on."

"Does Mr. Trellis know about your plan?"

He glanced warily over his shoulder. "Actually, neither of them do. We'll just have to see what happens, won't we?"

Nodding somberly, I handed him the glasses, and he left the kitchen with a wine bottle tucked under one arm.

Sandra was a decidedly elegant and self-assured woman who shook my hand as though I were one of her colleagues. She made every effort to include me in her conversation with Benson, which was difficult to do since I wasn't up on current events and I had nothing clever to say about the news last night, or the state of international affairs. I was only servile and quick to understand that a glass was empty, or that Benson would like the window open because it was starting to get a bit stuffy. But I did as necessity required and smiled politely whenever Sandra turned to me as her graciousness demanded that she do. And all the while, I was unable to shake the sadness that had fallen over me since Benson told me of his intentions for Sandra.

The more I observed her, the more perfect she seemed to be. She was intelligent and lovely, yet clearly not overly concerned with her appearance. In fact, I noticed that there was a loose thread hanging from her sleeve and that she probably hadn't refreshed her lipstick for several hours.

In spite of my sadness and upset about the whole situation, I liked her. I liked her very much and I knew Mr. Trellis well enough to know that he would like her too. In the span of a half hour or so, I had convinced myself that they were perfect for each other.

When Mr. Trellis arrived home he looked especially weary. I informed him that Benson had brought a friend for dinner, and he wasn't very pleased to hear it, although I suspected that he'd find fresh energy when he met Sandra, and I was right. Within minutes I could see that he was captivated by her. I hovered about the periphery and filled wineglasses. I floated in and out of the room, checking on this or that, trying my best not to disturb or interrupt.

After I'd served the meal and refilled the water glasses, Mr. Trellis noted that I'd set only three places.

"Ana, you won't be joining us?" he asked.

"I've eaten, thank you," I replied, eager to leave them and go to my room. The longer I stayed in their presence, the more I felt myself shrinking away. As I climbed the stairs, I realized that although I was a simple woman, with simple thoughts and desires, over the years I'd managed to tie myself up into so many knots that I hardly knew who I was anymore. My mother's voice followed me all the way to the top of the stairs and down the corridor to my room: "I was the greater fool to believe that a man's sweet words and caresses could ever banish the harsh realities of life."

"I didn't listen to you, Mama. Why didn't I listen? How could I ever allow myself to hope that a man like Mr. Trellis could ever be interested in a woman like me?"

I took a hot bath and climbed into bed. All was silent, and a sense of peacefulness came upon me when I heard the strains of piano music coming in through my open window. It meandered like a river, haunting my dreams, washing over me and threatening to drown me in my sleep. I saw his face, his dark, stormy eyes; I heard his voice, and I felt the warmth of his thigh running along the length of mine. I inhaled the wonderful perfume of his body, his hair, his hands, and I felt the stir of his soulful music filling me up. And I imagined Sandra swaying to the sound of it, her eyes closed as she allowed him to seep through to the depths of her soul as well.

When I couldn't take it anymore, I bolted out of my bed and yanked the window closed with such force that I was afraid I'd shattered it, but my tantrum had produced nothing more than a tiny fissure in the glass that was almost as invisible as I felt.

Sitting alone in the front room late on Christmas Eve, I gazed at the blinking lights on the tree. Teddy had returned from college the day before, and Jessie from her first term abroad just that morning. The two of them had spent the afternoon with their mother and were now fast asleep in their rooms. They informed me that Ms. Lillian had found a new "personal assistant," who sprayed her sheets with lilac water, and that because of this she was no longer so upset that I wasn't able to go with her to her new loft. Teddy and Jessie, on the other hand, were delighted that I was home to greet them when they arrived. Thinking back on how they'd embraced me at the door, I felt it was almost as if nothing had changed.

Millie and Fred would be coming by the next day, and Millie had promised to make her Christmas morning coffee cake. Benson would come too, and we would open presents before preparing the meal, as we did every year. Sandra and Mr. Trellis had been out once or twice, but she had family back east and would be spending Christmas with them. I had started to doze, anticipating what a perfect day it would be, when I felt movement and was startled to find Mr. Trellis sitting next to me, watching me with sad and curious eyes. He and Dr. Farrell had spent quite a bit of time earlier that day talking in the study, and his mood had remained somber ever since then. He appeared distracted, and even when Jessie announced that she'd broken up with her Italian boyfriend, he didn't appear to be listening very well.

"You're up late," he said.

I straightened up. "Yes, I . . . I . . . was just thinking about how good it is to have Teddy and Jessie home again." I left the sofa and began to rearrange the gifts under the tree, trying to appear as preoccupied as possible. Ever since Sandra's visit, I felt it wiser to keep my distance from Mr. Trellis. My head was clearer, and my heart felt lighter when I did.

"I've always admired you, Ana," he said. "You have such a fresh and uncomplicated way of seeing things, but we haven't had much opportunity to talk lately."

"The holidays are such a busy time," I said, smiling awkwardly.

"I've been meaning to ask you something."

"Yes, of course." I turned away from my organizing to look at him.

"What is your honest opinion of Sandra?"

His question assaulted me, but I managed to respond in a casual, offhand manner. "I only met her a few times, but she seems very nice."

"How do you think Teddy and Jessie would like her?"

I swallowed my upset and answered as best as I could. "I don't know, but . . . but they need to accept that sooner or later you have to get on with your life."

"And how about you?" he asked. "Do you accept it?"

I turned away from him, nearly blinding myself with a tree branch. "Who am I to accept or reject something like that?" I answered, feeling suddenly indignant.

"Why, Ana, you should know by now that you're a member of the family," he said. "And your opinion matters very much to us."

"That's very kind of you, Mr. Trellis," I replied, aware of an unbearable heat burning behind my eyes. "Well then, my opinion is that you must get on with your life. We all have to get on with our lives," I said as I rummaged through the presents.

"Is something the matter, Ana?"

"Yes," I returned, not sure how to explain my irritation. "I was positive that I'd finished all the wrapping this morning, but now I can't seem to find my gift for Millie."

Mr. Trellis helped me search through the pile of presents under the tree and then he reached for the box that was just next to my knee and read the attached card. "Here it is, Ana, it was right next to you all the time," he said, handing me the box.

I took the box from him, and when I looked at his face, I was certain that I'd never seen him look so pale.

My perfect day was not to be. Now that Mr. Trellis had brought up the possibility of Teddy and Jessie meeting Sandra, my mind would be flooded with images of the loving couple walking hand in hand through the garden, while Jessie and Teddy followed close behind, laughing over something terribly clever Sandra had said. I feared that the entire day would be consumed by the novelty of their father's new girlfriend and that I would have to endure hearing her name over and over again. But I began to understand that none of the weeks, months, or years that I'd spent with the Trellis family had been real. I'd been living in a fantasy, pretending to belong while I hovered about the periphery of my life, still waiting in the sewing cabinet for my mother to rescue me. This was no longer enough. I had to break free of this delusion or risk living the rest of my life with my knees pressed into my chest and my head bent over the whole of my body.

I slept fitfully that night. I was once again running for my life with Sister Josepha as gunshots rang out all around us. We skimmed over the surface of the jungle, moving like leopards searching for the faint glimmer of light that would lead us away from death and toward life. I awoke the next day understanding for the first time that the sooner I left the Trellis house, the better it would be for everyone. I'd wait until the holidays were over and a normal schedule had resumed, and then I would join Sister Josepha in New Mexico once and for all. I was physically tired after a restless night, but my soul was again at peace.

It turned out to be a lovely holiday. Millie and I worked happily side by side in the kitchen, and Teddy was always nearby, tasting whatever we had cooking on the stove, talking excitedly about his plans to go to medical school, as his grandfather had. He was such a striking young man that every time I looked at him, my eyes lingered. He'd inherited his father's height and distinguished manner, but he possessed a playfulness that made him especially attractive. It's no wonder that his cell phone was continually ringing, and from what I could tell, the callers on the other end were usually girls.

Jessie's charm was far more understated. She swept her red hair back in a ponytail at the nape of her neck and wore modest clothing in muted colors. She seemed somewhat self-conscious of her broader hips and wore her sweaters over them. She'd gone on a few shopping trips with her mother over the break and emerged from the car with many boxes and bags, but didn't seem particularly thrilled with her purchases.

"Oh, you know Mom," she'd say with a smile and a good-natured roll of her eyes. "She says a girl can't ever have too many clothes."

"Well, I hope they're not all in various shades of black and brown," Millie said.

A few days before Jessie was due to leave for school, she came into my room and sat on my bed as I hemmed a pair of trousers she'd received for Christmas. I suspected that she wanted to talk about her ex–Italian boyfriend again and the fact that he'd called her several times over the holiday break with the intention of winning her back. I listened and advised her as best I could, but she soon surprised me with a different topic altogether.

"What do you think of that Sandra woman?" she asked. Jessie and Teddy had met her briefly when she stopped by to drop off her Christmas gift for Mr. Trellis.

I glanced up and noted her furrowed brow. "She seems like a nice lady," I replied.

"Do you think Daddy likes her?"

"It certainly seems that way to me."

Jessie fell back on the bed and gazed up at the ceiling. "Uncle Benson thinks she's perfect for Dad, but I'm not so sure. Maybe it's because she's too perfect."

"Perfection isn't usually a problem," I said.

"Oh, but it is, Nana. Perfection stifles life. Just think about it—even the earth isn't perfectly round." She stared at me with so much conviction that she almost had me convinced.

I shook my head in wonderment. "You're getting far too smart for me, Jessie. Pretty soon I won't understand anything you say."

At that moment Teddy strolled in and promptly stretched out on the bed as well. "Why all the long faces?" he asked.

"I don't think Sandra's right for Dad," Jessie said.

"Of course she's not," Teddy replied while resting his head on my shoulder. "Mom and Dad are just going through a midlife crisis. I'm sure once they get it out of their system, they'll patch things up."

Teddy took every opportunity to express his belief that his parents could eventually reconcile, and while I knew this was highly unlikely, I said nothing as I continued to work on Jessie's trousers.

"Nana," Jessie said, giving me an inscrutable look, "I've been giving it a lot of thought and I think you should marry Benson."

Once I got over the shock, I had to laugh.

"Don't laugh. You know he's crazy about you, and I'm sure Daddy wouldn't mind if he moved in here with you. He practically lives here as it is."

"You're insane," Teddy said. "Nana's not the type to get married. She was planning to be a nun once, don't you remember?"

Jessie dismissed him with a wave of her hand. "But I don't think you should have children. You don't want to complicate your lives with that nonsense."

Teddy added, "At least we agree on something."

"What do you think, Nana?" Jessie asked. "We have your whole life planned out for you."

I chuckled as I started on the other trouser leg. I had managed to more or less neutralize the jealousy I felt whenever I thought about Mr. Trellis with Sandra, and I was looking forward to spending some real time with Sister Josepha. In some ways, she was the only family I had left. "Your plans are very interesting, but you shouldn't worry about me. Everything's going to work out just fine," I said. And I finished my sewing with Jessie draped across my legs and Teddy's head resting on my shoulder.

After Teddy and Jessie left for school and the house grew quiet again, I knew the time had come to make my move. Every night before bedtime, I prepared a cup of tea for Mr. Trellis and took it to him wherever he might be in the house, which was usually in his study or the music room.

The evening I decided to tell him about my plans to leave, I took a long hot bath to calm my nerves. Dr. Farrell had been by after dinner, and once I was certain that he'd left, I quickly dressed and made my way downstairs. In the kitchen, I steeped the tea for a long while and added plenty of sugar. With two cups in hand, I proceeded down the long corridor toward Mr. Trellis's study. The door was ajar so I entered and approached his desk, careful not to spill a single drop. He was working on the computer, and even with the glow from the screen illuminating his face, the dark shadows that rimmed his eyes made them look especially black and foreboding. I took a deep breath, realizing that this would be even more difficult than I had anticipated. I had spent so many years understanding, admiring, and loving this man that to simply tell him I'd be leaving in a month would be like ripping out my heart. I didn't want to leave him, yet I knew that it was the only choice left to me if I wanted to stay sane.

"Excuse me, Mr. Trellis. I can see that you're busy, but I was hoping to have a quick word. I would've come earlier, but I didn't want to interrupt your meeting with Dr. Farrell."

He pushed himself away from his desk. "That's quite all right, Ana," he said.

I handed him his tea and stood before him, feeling tongue-tied as usual. "This is very hard to say, but I've given it a lot of thought and I think it's for the best."

He smiled, trying to make light of it. "Don't tell me that after all these years you've decided to go back to the convent?"

"Not exactly," I replied, attempting to smile as well, although not very convincingly.

He studied me for a moment and placed his teacup down on his desk. "Ana, are you leaving us?"

I swallowed hard. "For years Sister Josepha has been asking me to go work with her at her school. If I don't accept her invitation soon, I don't think I'll get another opportunity."

"I see," he said, his expression darkening. "And where is this school?"

"In New Mexico."

He nodded. "And when do you plan to leave?"

"At the end of the month."

His voice was faint. "Well, I guess it would've been foolish to think that you'd stay here forever. Do Teddy and Jessie know?"

"You're the first to know. With everything else that's going on, I didn't want to upset them over the holidays."

"Wise decision," he said, turning back to his computer screen.

I stepped back toward the door, unsure of what to do or say next. I had intended to express my gratitude, and to say more about how much the family meant to me, and how much I was going to miss everyone, but I was disappointed and hurt by Mr. Trellis's indifference. After all, we'd been living under the same roof for twenty years, and even if he didn't feel about me the way I felt about him, he didn't have to be so dismissive. He could at least pretend to care a little bit about me for the sake of common courtesy if nothing else.

"I'm going to the music room before I retire, would you care to join me?" Mr. Trellis asked.

"I suppose," I replied, rather flatly. I followed him to the music room, and he sat on the bench as I settled myself on the nearest sofa. Once he began to play I closed my eyes, hoping that the sound of his music would ease my upset, but he'd only played a few bars when he suddenly stopped. I opened my eyes to find him watching me strangely.

"Is something wrong, Mr. Trellis?"

"I'm not feeling very well. I think I might have a fever," he said, bringing his hand to his forehead. "What do think, Ana?"

I stood up and walked over to where he was. Then I gently placed the palm of my hand on his forehead, my pulse racing all the while.

"Your hand feels cool," he muttered, closing his eyes.

"If you have a fever, then it must be very slight," I replied, removing my hand, but he quickly grasped it.

"Ana, what would you do if I told you I was ill? Would you leave for New Mexico then?"

"I hope and pray that you're not ill," I replied, overwhelmed and startled by his touch. And I tried to retrieve my hand, but as he spoke his grip on me tightened.

"The truth is that I don't understand why you would leave us now after all these years. I know the children are grown and out of the house, but surely you could tell what a difference your presence made over the holidays. I'm not sure that Teddy and Jessie would've come home if you hadn't been here. They may have skipped Christmas altogether this year if not for you."

"Excuse me, Mr. Trellis," I said, nodding toward my hand that was beginning to throb.

He released it instantly. "Forgive me," he muttered, dropping his chin to his chest.

I rubbed my fingers, flustered and confused by what he was saying. "Of course, if you think that my presence will be of some use to the children, then I'll stay as long as they need me, but please tell me what's wrong with you? What did Dr. Farrell say?"

Mr. Trellis raised his head to look at me, his eyes blazing. "Are you worried about me? I've always envied Teddy and Jessie for the infinite reservoir of love you have for them, and even Lillian and Millie have benefited from your unceasing devotion. Ana," he whispered, "don't you see how you've woven your gentle spirit through me and softened my coarse heart? Don't you see how you've changed me?" He studied my startled expression for a moment, and appeared bemused. "You seem surprised to hear me say these things, and yet I always thought you knew."

"All I know is that I'll do whatever you ask of me. If you want me to stay, of course I'll stay."

"I can see that I'm going to have to be more direct," he said with a troubled sigh. "Let me put it to you this way. When Lillian told me she was leaving me, for reasons that I'm sure you're well aware, I was glad. But when she told me that she was planning to take you with her, I became despondent."

I stared at him too overwhelmed to speak.

"Say something, Ana," he said, his eyes pleading.

"I don't know what to say. I . . . I . . . wouldn't want you to feel despondent about anything."

At this he stood abruptly, and began to pace the room. When he turned to face me his expression was grim, and his voice firm. "For all these years I believed you to be the gentlest, most beautiful and noble creature to walk the face of the earth, but I never expected you to be this . . . this difficult."

"I don't understand, Mr. Trellis." I said, completely at a loss.

"There you go again, being coy and pretending that you don't know what I'm talking about when I'm laying myself at your feet, a sick and desperate man."

"But Mr. Trellis . . . I . . ." I couldn't deny that he did look desperate, and that his agitation was growing with every second of confused silence that passed between us. "If you must know, I decided to go to New Mexico because I thought it would be easier now that you've found Sandra."

Hearing this, Mr. Trellis's expression softened, and he took a step toward me. "Easier?" he asked. "Easier for who?"

When I didn't respond, he asked again. "Please, Ana. What does Sandra have to do with anything?"

I shook my head and began walking toward the door, but

he met me in the middle of the room and took my hand, gently this time. His fingers felt like feathers across my palm that sent a wave of satisfying shivers down my spine. "Ana, please," he whispered, and I felt his warm breath on my ear, and my whole body tingled with pleasure. "What does Sandra have to do with anything?"

"Well, obviously," I said, turning away from him, "you're in love with her—any fool can see that. Not that I blame you, she's a very lovely woman, and I think you two make a very lovely couple."

Mr. Trellis stepped in closer to me and tipped my chin up so that I had no choice but to look at him, and the longer those dark penetrating eyes bore through me, the more flustered I became, and I felt my insides squirming and the blood rushing to my feet. "You're jealous of Sandra," he mumbled to himself, mildly amused. But he was quite serious when he said, "Ana, I'm going to be completely honest with you. I've always been content to have you near me, but nearness isn't enough anymore. I want to touch you and kiss you, and love you completely."

"Mr. Trellis," I muttered, my heart pounding so wildly that my ears were ringing, and I was certain that at any moment my knees would buckle beneath me.

"If you don't feel the same, then you can go to New Mexico with your dear Sister Josepha, and I'll never bother you again. But if you have any feelings for me at all, then I beg you to stay here with me."

I closed my eyes as tears streamed down my face, as the scarred layers of my life pulled apart little by little, to reveal my naked heart.

"Ana," he said touching my cheek. "Can't you say that you love me just a little?"

I shook my head, not able to speak, hardly able to breathe.

"I understand," he said sadly. "That's okay. Please don't cry anymore."

I opened my eyes to gaze at him fully. I took in the dark eyes, the beautiful and familiar face I had adored for so many years, the soft contour of his lips that I longed to feel against my skin. I couldn't hold back any longer, the desire I felt for this man was like a flood pushing against my rib cage. "I can't say it because it isn't true, Mr. Trellis. I don't love you just a little, I love you so much that every time I'm near you, as I am now, it feels like my heart is going to explode, and every time I speak your name, I can taste you on my lips."

He was momentarily taken aback by my words, but then he cupped my face in his hands and gazed into my eyes for a very long time, and as I gazed back, I swear that I could see eternity. Then gently, tenderly, he kissed away my tears one by one and then brought his mouth over mine, and his lips pressed against me with such ardor that I feared I would melt away before I could take another breath. But with this spark of new life he breathed into me I was suddenly emboldened and I flung my arms around his neck and returned his kiss again and again, and each time my lips found his, I felt a stirring in my soul, my womanhood emerging like the sunrise, brilliantly tracing its path across my life, branding me forever as a flesh and blood human being who needed only to love and be loved. All at once, I could see beyond the fears and apprehension that had blinded me for so long.

"You wanted me to be jealous of Sandra, didn't you?" I asked breathlessly. "That's what you wanted all along."

He chuckled, breathless himself. "You know I did," he whispered. "And just say the words I need to hear, and I'll never see her again. I'll never even mention her name."

"What words should I say?" I asked, trembling in his arms, certain that I'd found my heaven.

"Say, 'Adam, I belong to you and I will never leave you.'"

"Adam, I belong to you and I will never leave you," I whispered. "And do you belong to me too?" I asked, already knowing the answer.

"When we first embraced at the bottom of the peacock pool, all those years ago I was yours," he whispered softly. "My beloved Ana."

Ana sat at the keyboard and brought her hands to the keys. Her fingers pressed down hesitantly so that a couple of errant notes floated away like singular tears. Then she looked up to find Jessie standing in the doorway.

"Uncle Darwin left and there's a nurse here to see Daddy," she said. "And Benson's waiting for you on the phone."

Ana sighed and closed the keyboard cover. She walked across the room, slipped her arm through Jessie's, and together they left the music room, closing the door behind them.

Sixteen

I SUPPOSE THAT I should've felt more conflicted than I did, and perhaps I would've if the circumstances had been different, if I thought that I could indulge in the luxury of time. Even so, when I looked in the mirror, I sometimes didn't recognize myself, and at other times it seemed that I was able to see myself for the first time. But regardless of where I might be on this moral roller-coaster ride I had willingly embarked upon, I had to admit that we'd been growing into each other so gradually over the years that the next step felt completely natural for us. As one does when a plant gets too big for its container, we transplanted our relationship into fertile ground, where the roots began to spread and deepen instantly. And so it was that in the evening after we'd had our tea and it was time for bed, we now slept together in the same room, on the same bed, and in each other's arms. And it is here that I discovered that a man's sweet words and caresses could not only banish the harsh realities of life, but create a whole new reality I eagerly embraced.

The first time I lay with my beloved and felt his body wrap around and through me with such tender desire, I knew that I'd never be the same woman again. I was breathless with yearning as he caressed me in places that only God had seen, and when his lips, softer and more exquisite than a prayer, kissed my quivering soul, there was no one else in the universe but me and him. After we made love, I could gaze at him for an eternity as he slept next to me, and I was nothing more than a wisp of smoke curling blissfully up toward heaven.

"This is what men and women do together when they want to forget, *mija.*"

"If this is how it is to forget, Mama, then I never want to remember again."

The only real difficulty I experienced during the first few days and weeks of our new life together was learning how to call my beloved by his first name and not "Mr. Trellis," as I had for the last twenty years. I cringed a bit whenever I said, "Adam, would you like some tea?" or, "Adam, would you play for me?" And the truth is that the words "Mr. Trellis" had acquired a unique sweetness I didn't want to relinquish.

We decided not tell people right away about us, or the fact that Adam was sick. We needed time to strengthen our hearts and our own understanding about how best to proceed. And naturally, we were most concerned with how to soften the blow for Teddy and Jessie.

Benson was the first person to hear the news about Adam's illness and our relationship. I have no idea how Adam told him because he thought it was best to talk with his friend privately. An hour or so after Benson entered the study with Adam, he emerged with a dazed look in his eyes. He didn't come into the kitchen as he normally would've, but sat in the front room with his chin resting on his chest for almost an hour as Adam sat next to him, also in silence. It was painful for us to see the shock and betrayal in Benson's kindly eyes. He left without a word to me, and we didn't see him for several days after that. Every time I suggested to Adam that we call him, he told me that we needed to respect his need to stay away for a while. Unlike me, Adam had no doubt that our friend would return.

Almost two weeks to the day after he and Adam spoke, Benson entered through the back door as usual and placed his briefcase on the kitchen table. I was rinsing the dishes in the sink.

"Would you like some coffee?" I asked.

"Only if it's made," he replied.

"It's not, but it will just take a moment."

"Don't trouble yourself."

"It's no trouble," I said.

As the coffeemaker dripped and sputtered, Benson tapped his fingers on his briefcase.

"I'm making chicken for dinner tonight. I hope you can stay," I said.

His fingers stopped tapping, and when I turned to him, his mouth was turned down in an endearing frown. "I'd like to, but I feel like a third wheel now—round, ridiculous, and completely useless."

"Benson, how can you say that when you know how dear you are to both of us? And Adam needs you now more than ever."

"Of course he needs me," he said, still frowning. "I'm handling his estate, and it would be a hassle for him to look for another attorney."

"You know that isn't the reason," I said. "Adam has another appointment with the oncologist tomorrow, and it would do him such good to see you tonight. We're both very worried."

Benson shrugged. "I'll make a bargain with you. I'll stay for dinner as long as you promise to call me tomorrow and let me know what the doctor says. Adam doesn't like talking about it."

I promised that I would and proceeded to pour the coffee. Knowing that Benson was back in our lives made me feel more hopeful than I had in days.

Benson took up his coffee cup and then placed it back on the table. "Ana, I'm going to ask you this once and then I'll never bring it up again," he said, "but I want you to be completely honest with me." I nodded and sat across from him. "Did I ever have a chance with you?"

I stirred my coffee as I searched for the right words. "Benson, I believe that God brought me here for many reasons. One is that Adam is the man I was meant to fall in love with and another is that you—you are the man I was meant to love as a brother. I'm very blessed to have you both in my life."

Benson's brooding expression eased somewhat. "A simple 'No, Benson, you never had a chance in the world' would've done." Then he smiled. "But I guess I like the way you put it much better."

The sublime joy Adam and I experienced in our new life together was overshadowed by the grim reality of his illness. I prayed as never before for a miracle to come upon us. When I accompanied him to the hospital for his treatments, I prayed. As I organized his medications in their little compartments, I prayed. And in the evening when he played the piano and I sat next to him, I prayed. But despite my prayers, my beloved weakened as our love and devotion for each other grew.

One afternoon while sitting with him in Dr. Farrell's office, I was so lost in my thoughts and prayers that I wasn't paying much attention to what was being said. When my eyes refocused on Dr. Farrell's face, he seemed less somber than usual. In fact, he was actually smiling and the tone of his voice was decidedly upbeat.

"That's wonderful news," Adam said. "Don't you think so, Ana?"

"Yes," I replied, embarrassed to admit that I hadn't been listening.

Dr. Farrell said, "We'll need to wait a bit longer to surgically remove the tumor, but if it continues shrinking as it has been, it might be sooner than we think."

"And then he'll be cured?" I asked, hoping that the miracle I'd been praying for had finally been delivered.

Dr. Farrell looked dubious, but he clearly wasn't closed to the possibility. "It's difficult to make any predictions at this stage," he said. "But this is a very good sign."

I left the clinic overjoyed by the news. As far as I was concerned, Adam was as good as cured and before long this nightmare would be behind us so that we could better face the challenges that still lay ahead.

"Your love has made all the difference," he whispered that evening as we lay in each other's arms. "I'd marry you tomorrow if I could, but Lillian's making things very difficult at the moment. Even so, I want you to know that no matter what happens to me, you'll be well taken care of."

"Nothing's going to happen to you," I replied. "You're going to be well again, and that's all that matters."

I placed my head on his chest and listened to the beating of his heart. It sounded strong and vibrant, a heart that would beat steadily for many years to come.

And then he sighed and I heard a whirlwind blowing through a canyon deep in his chest. "I should warn you that it's just a matter of time before Lillian finds out about us, and when she does, things are going to get even more difficult," he said.

"Ssh. Sleep now and don't worry anymore," I said, on the brink of sleep myself. And I heard my mother's voice from that deep knowing in my heart. "Let's imagine, *mija*," she whispered. "Let's imagine that we're sleeping in a grand house with arched windows and tiled floors and that in the morning we'll wake to the sound of guitars softly strumming."

"It's the piano you hear, Mama," I whispered back. "And it's even more beautiful than I imagined."

A few days later we were awakened in the early morning hours by the sound of the front door opening and closing. My first thought was that Lillian had come home to confront us. Then we heard a rush of footsteps pounding up the stairs, and before we had the opportunity to react, Teddy burst in through the bedroom door expecting to find only his father. When he saw Adam and me in bed together, he froze and stared incredulously at us for what seemed like an eternity. For the first time since Adam and I had openly declared our love for each other, I felt shame flooding into my heart, and I brought the blankets up to my chin, too horrified to move or speak.

Teddy's eyes became filled with disbelief and rage, and he began to shake his head as though beset by a sudden and severe headache.

"Son, we can explain," Adam said, moving slowly to get out of bed.

He looked away as he muttered, "Peter told Mom you were sick, and I came as soon as I heard."

"Please, Teddy, let us explain," I replied weakly.

He took a step back. "You don't have to explain. I understand everything now, the real reason our family fell apart. But you waited for the right moment, didn't you? You waited until my father was sick and vulnerable to make your move."

"That isn't true, son," Adam said, getting out of bed. "Let's go downstairs and we'll talk about this calmly."

"No!" he yelled, taking another step back. "You've been cheating on Mom for years and that's why she left you."

"That's a lie!" Adam countered more forcefully.

"What I see now isn't a lie. God only knows how long you've been sneaking around together. Who knows, maybe you paid her a bit extra for her services . . ."

"I won't allow you to disrespect this dear woman."

"*Dear woman?* Are you such a fool that you can't see the truth when it's under your own nose, or in your own bed?" He glared at me hatefully for a long while before turning back to his father. "You're not only a fool, you're a liar, and I have no respect for you—for either of you."

"You want to know the truth?" Adam said, his own face quivering with rage. "The marriage ended because your mother is and has always been an unfaithful woman. And you're right, I was a fool. I was a fool to marry her and tolerate her as long as I did."

"I don't believe you," Teddy said, his eyes narrowing to slits. "I don't believe a word you're saying. Mom isn't like that. She was never like that."

Adam took a step toward Teddy and held his hands out to him. "I didn't want to believe it either, son, but as shameful and ugly as the truth can be, sometimes we have to accept it."

Teddy glared at Adam for a moment or two. "And am I suppose to accept that you and Nana are sleeping in the same bed you shared with my mother for more than twenty years? I won't accept it, not ever!" he yelled, his body trembling. "But here's another shameful and ugly truth that you'd better accept—I don't care if you drop dead tomorrow or next week, you'll never see me again as long as you live." He turned and ran down the stairs and out the front door as swiftly as he'd arrived, and the room and the entire house became eerily silent.

Adam stood motionless for a moment and then sank back down to the bed and put his head in his hands. "What have I done, Ana?" he muttered. "What have I done?" He crawled back under the covers and pulled them up over his head. There he stayed for the rest of the morning. In the afternoon I was able to persuade him to go downstairs and sit outside in the courtyard before dinner, but he ate very little and said even less.

I understood his despondency and was reminded of those times years ago when my village was nearly swept away by a flood. After the waters receded we'd gaze at the damage done in a state of hopeless stupor, not knowing where to begin. Every time I remembered Teddy's accusation and the hatred in his eyes when he looked at me, I felt an ache I'd never felt before that started in my heart and spread throughout my entire body. This and the distance I felt from my beloved was almost intolerable. I wanted desperately to reach him and to bring him back to me, but I knew that I'd have to be patient. I could wait an eternity for him if I needed to.

The next few days that followed were similar. He got out of bed later and later every morning and he refused to play his music or visit the garden. He was slipping away from me, and only when I held him in my arms at night did I feel that he was near. He called Teddy countless times, but Teddy never returned his calls. He wrote notes and left messages, but Teddy never replied.

"I've lost him," he said to me one afternoon when I was able to persuade him to sit with me in the garden. "I've lost my son."

"You don't know that, Adam. Maybe he just needs time."

Adam sighed. "I shouldn't have said those things about Lillian. As true as they are, I shouldn't have said them. And I shouldn't have waited so long to tell Teddy and Jessie about us. If I'd told them right away, then maybe I could've avoided this."

I took Adam's hand. "After Teddy stormed off, I wrote him and Jessie each a letter, explaining about us. It was the most difficult letter I've ever written in my life I . . . I didn't know how much to include, but I felt that I had to let them know how I felt about you and the family and how much I love them," I said. "Teddy's letter was returned unopened yesterday, but I'm certain that Jessie read hers. Maybe you should call her."

"Yes, I'll call her," Adam said. And that evening when he did, he was greatly relieved. Jessie was shaken, to be sure, but she didn't completely accept Teddy's view that her father and I had been sneaking around for years. She'd read my letter and told her father that she wanted some time to think about things, and that when she was ready, she would come home and talk with us.

A few days later, I was in the front garden snipping the dead rose heads when Ms. Lillian's car roared up the drive. She didn't notice me crouched in the flower bed as she marched straight into the house, using her own key to let herself in.

Adam was in his study resting after his final round of chemotherapy, and I had no doubt that this was the first place Lillian would look. After a few minutes I went around back and walked softly across the courtyard so that I could be nearby in case Adam needed me. I heard Lillian screaming through the open window of the study. "You deserve to die a miserable death. After what you've done to me, I don't pity you at all."

"I didn't think Teddy would waste any time telling you what he saw."

"Don't flatter yourself, Adam. I don't care who you choose to sleep with, but this house belongs to us. And don't you dare pretend that you don't know what I'm talking about because I just spoke with my attorney and he informed me that you recently made a rather significant change to the trust."

He coughed. "You and the children will never want for anything. And as far as this house is concerned, it's been in my family for generations, and I will give it to whomever I choose. Besides, I know that if you got your hands on this house, before they started digging my grave, you'd sell the land and then auction off the rest of it brick by brick to the highest bidder until there was nothing left. But I'm certain that Ana will honor my wishes to keep the house in the family."

"We'll see how Teddy and Jessie feel about this new development. It's just one happy surprise after another, isn't it?"

"It's my place to speak with them."

"And exactly when do you plan to do that?"

"I'll speak to them soon," Adam replied weakly.

"I'm going to fight you on this until I've breathed my last, and I have many more breaths left in me than you do."

"I'll let my attorney know that he'd better start polishing his armor. Are you quite finished?"

After a pause, Lillian said, "I just have one question. Why did you choose to lower yourself in such a cowardly and predictable manner? Are you that desperate for affection that you'd turn to the hired help to get it?"

"Lower myself? I'd happily trade twenty years of misery with you for just twenty hours of bliss with Ana."

"I take it back," Lillian said. "I do pity you because it's obvious that the cancer has spread to your brain, which will only make my job in court easier." I then heard the clicking of Ms. Lillian's heels and, moments later, the roar of her engine in the drive. Once I was certain she'd left the grounds, I returned to the rose garden, but my hands were trembling so terribly that I had difficulty maneuvering the clippers.

Adam hadn't told me about his plans for the house, and I was frightened about what this meant. Why was he rearranging his affairs now? Had he had another conversation with the doctors that I didn't know about? And how would the children react? I knew that Lillian wouldn't wait for Adam to speak with them. Now that she'd confirmed it, she would tell them about the change in the trust immediately, and this would only serve to alienate them further.

The clippers slipped and as I went to catch them, the blade nicked the palm of my hand. I sat back and watched the blood pool and then run down my wrist and spill to the earth, where it was absorbed almost immediately. I don't know how long I would've sat there watching myself bleed, but when I heard Adam calling for me, I hastily wiped away the blood with a tissue I found in my pocket and went to him.

"I saw Lillian drive off," I said, nervously. "She seemed very upset."

Adam nodded regretfully and slipped a reassuring arm around my shoulder. "We need to talk, Ana," he said, and then he told me about the conversation he'd had with Lillian and the changes he'd made to the will. When I told him that I didn't need or want the house and that I thought he should change the will back to the way it was before, he kissed me and said, "That's exactly what I thought you'd say, but my mind is made up. And there's nothing Lillian or the children, or even you, can say to change it."

Jessie showed up a couple of weeks later. I was in the kitchen preparing a light supper, and I was so relieved when she said that she'd be eating with us, and not leaving in a burst of anger as Teddy had, that tears of gratitude sprung to my eyes as I chopped the vegetables.

She sat at the kitchen table for a while, saying very little. Finally she said, "Teddy believes that you and Dad were lovers for years and that that's the real reason the marriage broke up. I have to admit that there were moments when I wondered as well. They way you and Daddy spoke to each other and looked at each other sometimes . . ."

I dropped my knife. "I swear to you, Jessie. Nothing ever happened between us. Your father never disrespected his marriage and neither did I."

"I believe you, Nana. And I'm not upset about the house and the trust like Teddy is. I know that Daddy will always take care of us." Jessie fingered the napkin on the table. "But Teddy believes that by giving you the house, Daddy's putting you before us, and it just strengthens his belief that you were sneaking around together for years. But I've thought about it and I see it differently," she said, setting the napkin aside and gazing up at me. "I believe that Daddy wants you to have the house because even though neither of you did anything about it, he's loved you and you've loved him for years. Isn't that the truth, Nana?"

I nodded, unable to deny the truth, no longer wanting to.

Tears welled up in Jessie's eyes. "I see how happy you and Daddy are together, and I know he wants to live now more than ever, but he's so sick, Nana," she said, tears streaming down her cheeks. "I'm glad he has you."

All the way to Dr. Farrell's office, Adam was silent. He insisted that he felt well enough to drive, and that it helped him to feel useful. We waited in Dr. Farrell's office for some time, and when he finally entered the room with the usual manila folder tucked under his arm, we both sat up eagerly in our chairs. He never spoke a word without referring to his folder, but we always knew whether the information contained within was good or bad by his expression. On this day his face was grim.

He spoke at length about the specific kind of cancer Adam had and how difficult it was to predict its course. Depending on an individual's general health and response to treatment, some were able to survive for years after diagnosis, and others merely months. We'd heard all this before, and I realized that Dr. Farrell was stalling.

Adam's hand reached out to mine as we listened to Dr. Farrell go on in agonizing detail about the treatments that had already been tried and the tests performed. Then Adam interrupted his friend in order to spare him and us. "Peter, I believe you're trying to tell us that you've discovered another tumor, is that it?"

Dr. Farrell looked up from his folder and nodded, his glasses foggy and his lips trembling slightly in spite of his effort to remain stoic. "I'm sorry, Adam," he said. "We'll need to proceed with another round of chemo before we consider surgery. And then we'll just have to wait and see what happens."

Adam squeezed my hand and nodded his understanding. I, however, was numb. And after we left Dr. Farrell's office, I became despondent and wept all the way home. Adam tried to comfort me, and I tried to compose myself and be courageous for his sake, but I couldn't find the strength. I was losing my precious beloved and that's all I could see, think, or hear at that moment.

When we got home, I leaned on Adam all the way to the front door. Anyone watching us would've thought that I was the one who was ill. Later that evening, I prayed the rosary for the first time in years, and when I was finished, I told Adam that I thought we should get a second opinion.

"Peter's one of the best oncologists in the country," he said. "I don't think we'll get any better news if we talk to someone else."

"But you heard what Dr. Farrell said today. He said that the kind of cancer you have is very rare, and that researchers are learning about new treatments every day. Maybe another doctor will know something Dr. Farrell hasn't heard about."

Adam appeared dubious as he considered this possibility.

"Please, my love. It's worth a try. We can proceed with the chemotherapy just as Dr. Farrell ordered and talk to another doctor in the meantime. What have we got to lose?"

A few days later I had just set potatoes to boil on the stove when I heard the front door and the familiar clicking of heels coming toward the kitchen. I turned to find Lillian standing in the doorway, her hair cascading like an auburn waterfall over her shoulders. The darker tone at her temples let me know that she'd recently had it colored.

"Hello, Ana," she said smoothly. "How are you doing on this glorious afternoon?"

"I'm fine."

"And how's the patient?"

"He's resting and I don't want to disturb him," I replied, feeling exquisitely awkward to be keeping Lillian from her own husband.

"Don't worry, it's you I want to speak with," she said coolly, taking a seat at the kitchen table. "My goodness, Ana, you look like a scared rabbit. If you think for one moment that I begrudge you your intimacy with my husband, then you're very mistaken. Anyway, I know better than anyone that you're not sleeping with a man, but with the shadow of a man who is only able to please you with his music, and perhaps not even that."

My face colored deeply. I was embarrassed to admit, especially to her, that despite his illness, Adam remained a very sensual and loving man. "There are more important things than physical love, Ms. Lillian," I replied.

Her eyes narrowed. "That's precisely why I'm here." She produced an envelope from her bag and placed it squarely on the kitchen table. "My attorney assures me that any last-minute changes Adam may have made to his will can be revoked with little difficulty. He's a dying man, emotionally unstable and easily manipulated by any opportunists that may be around him."

"He knows I don't want anything from him."

"Well then, this should be an easy decision for you to make," she said, placing her hand on the envelope. "These documents state that you unequivocally surrender all claims to the Trellis estate. In exchange for your signature, you will receive a handsome sum of money. The only other condition is that you leave this house immediately and never return."

"You're paying me to go away?"

Lillian smiled sweetly. "You know how principled Teddy is. As long as you're here, he would never agree to see his father again. But if you leave, I think there's a good chance he will. In fact, I'm sure of it. I understand that Jessie's already made up her mind about it," she said with a dismissive little shrug.

I stared at the envelope. "But I promised Adam I wouldn't leave him."

"Who do you think he'd rather have at his side now, you or his children?"

I stared dumbly at the envelope.

Ms. Lillian sat back in her chair and folded her arms across her chest. "Ever since Teddy made his unfortunate discovery and stormed out of here, Peter tells me that Adam's taken a turn for the worst. He needs his children more than anyone or anything. He needs them even more than he needs you." She leaned forward and pushed the envelope toward me. "Take the money and go make your own life so that Adam can end his with his family by his side. It will be the kindest thing you ever did for anyone and the best thing you ever did for yourself."

That said, she took up her purse and strode out of the house.

I sat there for some time, staring at the envelope in front of me and before long I became aware of a whispering in my heart. "Angry words are difficult to take back, *mija,* and more words are seldom enough to make it better."

"Then what do I do, Mama?"

"Exactly," she said. "You must *do* something and leave the words to the priests and the poets."

Before the potatoes were tender, I knew what I had to do.

$\mathcal{S}$eventeen

ANA SHOWED THE NURSE up to Adam's room. He was just beginning to wake, and it took him a moment or two to comprehend that she'd come to draw a blood sample. He obediently extended his arm as Ana left to take Benson's call in the next room.

"Teddy has the papers. I dropped them off not twenty minutes ago," he said.

"Are you sure he understands what they mean?"

"I don't see why he shouldn't," Benson replied. "I clearly explained that his father thought it over and decided to change his will and bequeath the house back to his children. I showed him the signature and urged him to go and see Adam as soon as possible."

"Thank you, Benson. I'm sure he'll be here shortly."

"I hope you're right," Benson said, his voice shaky. "Lillian was there as well and, as you can imagine, she wasn't very happy to be left out of the will. I'm sure she's filling Teddy's head with more venom as we speak."

"He'll come," Ana said.

"I hope you're right, Ana. Because if you're not . . ."

"I know him," Ana said. "He'll come."

She hung up and made her way back to her beloved's room. The nurse was finishing up and packing her bag as quietly as she could so as not to disturb her patient, who was resting peacefully again. "Oops, I almost forgot," she whispered. "Dr. Farrell wanted me to take a blood sample from you as well."

"Me? But why?"

"He's concerned that you may be anemic. It's easy to correct if you are, but he wants to be sure before he prescribes anything."

Ana nodded, remembering their conversation earlier that morning. He wanted her to rest and eat something right away, which of course she hadn't done. She had no doubt that the blood test would reveal a condition far more serious than anemia; nevertheless she obediently extended her arm as Adam had moments earlier. The nurse tied a band around her arm to expose the vein and prepared the syringe. Ana closed her eyes and waited for the needle's stick.

For several nights after Teddy stormed out, Adam was unable to sleep. He'd toss and turn fitfully, occasionally crying out. I asked him to tell me about his nightmares, but he didn't want to. I heard the wheezing deep in his lungs and sensed the waning strength of the muscles in his arms and chest and all throughout his body. And when he coughed, the sound echoed from somewhere so deep that it seemed he was coughing up bits of his soul.

Once or twice after dinner we retired to the music room, and I sat next to him on the piano bench as he played, hoping that this would revive him, but he was unable to play for more than a few minutes without feeling exhausted, and I would help him to the couch, where we would sit together in silence for a long while.

"Tell me truly, Ana," he said on one such occasion. "Do you have any regrets? Do you look back on your life and wish that you'd left this place long ago?"

"I have no regrets," I said, resting my head on his shoulder. "Well, maybe just one. I wish that we could've been together like this sooner. And you?" I asked. "Do you have any regrets?"

"Aside from what you just said, only one," he said with a sigh.

I knew he was referring to his outburst with Teddy, who still refused to return his calls or his letters. Only once did Adam hear from him, and that was indirectly through Lillian. She'd left her cruel message on the answering machine while we were away at the clinic.

"Stop harassing Teddy with your pitiful apologies, Adam. As far as he's concerned, you're already dead."

I lifted my head and repeated what I'd been saying to him for several days. "I don't need or want this house, Adam. Give it back to the children. If you do, Teddy will understand that no matter what you said and what happened before, he's still your son and you love him."

"Ana," he said, taking my hand, "when my parents were killed, the love in this house died with them. But when you came, you brought the love back and made it a home again. Maybe you

don't need this house, but it needs you. I can't completely explain why or how, but I know that this is the right thing to do."

"But Adam . . ."

"That's what my God is telling me to do. You don't expect
me to go against his wishes, do you?"

"No," I muttered.

"Then please don't ask me again."

It was a beautiful afternoon when we drove home from Adam's
appointment a few days later. The sun cast a shimmering light
through the trees, and its warmth was deliciously mild. Even
so, our hearts were heavy. Adam had agreed to a second opinion only to appease me, but he'd already resigned himself to the
dark reality that I was unwilling to accept.

We were about midway home when he pulled the car to a
stop at the side of the road and turned to me, his eyes gray with
fatigue. "Ana, do you mind driving?" he asked. "I'm tired and
I'm afraid I might nod off."

We exchanged seats and as I drove, Adam fell asleep with
his hand on my knee. Before long his fingers began to flutter
slightly, and I realized that in his dream he was playing the piano. I was pleased to know that at least in his dreams he was
still able to play, and when we drove past the gate and into the
drive, his fingers were still moving. I hated to wake him, so I
turned the motor off, intent to stay where I was until he woke,
but the sudden stillness prompted him to open his eyes with a
start. I came around to his side of the car, and he leaned on me
as I slipped my hand around his waist.

"Ana, for such a dainty little sparrow you're very strong," he observed as we entered the house.

I expected that he'd want to go to his study, but he hesitated as we passed the stairs.

"I think I might like to lie down for a bit," he said.

"Now? If you sleep now you might not be able to sleep tonight."

He considered what I said, for my sake more than his, but didn't make a step toward his study.

"Of course, I can wake you at dinnertime, and then you'll be more rested and you'll probably have a better appetite."

"That's a good point," he said, and we proceeded up the stairs, more slowly than we ever had before. I helped him get undressed and into bed, and he was asleep before I finished hanging up his slacks.

"Ma'am? Ma'am?"

Ana opened her eyes to find the nurse all packed up and ready to go.

"I just wanted you to know that I'm leaving and that I'll be back in a couple of days," she said.

"Yes, thank you," Ana replied, surprised that she'd nodded off.

"Hopefully Mr. Trellis will sleep through the night so you can rest as well."

It was then that Jessie rushed into the room, her eyes big and round as plates. "He's here, Nana," she said.

Ana stood up, nearly knocking over the nurse's bag. "Who's here?"

"Teddy. He just drove up."

"Are you sure it's him?"

"I know his car."

Adam heard the commotion and opened his eyes. "What is it, Ana?"

"He's here, my love," Ana said, kneeling beside him. "Teddy's come to see you."

$\mathcal{E}$ighteen

BY THE TIME JESSIE and I made it to the top of the stairs, Millie was already at the front door. When she opened it, she was momentarily speechless and then she pulled Teddy into a hearty embrace. After so many months of not seeing him or hearing from him, I longed to embrace him as well and tell him all about his father and how our hearts were breaking with every hour that passed without him and how much we'd been thinking about him during this vigil. But I knew that he wasn't ready to hear these things from me and that he probably never would be.

I stayed where I was, and Jessie rushed down the stairs to greet her brother. "Teddy, thank God you're here," she said, taking hold of his hand. "Daddy's been asking for you. He's waiting for you, Teddy."

Teddy and Jessie rushed up the stairs together arm in arm, but when they passed me Teddy didn't acknowledge my presence with so much as a word or even a glance in my direction.

After they entered their father's room, I joined Millie, who was watching me with sad, weary eyes.

"How did you know he'd come?" she asked.

"Teddy's always had a good heart," I said, taking hold of her arm.

We walked together toward the kitchen. "While you were upstairs I made a big pot of spaghetti. I'll serve you some now, and you'll sleep much better with something in your stomach, you'll see."

Millie served me a plate, and I managed to take a bite or two, but then dropped my fork when a terrible thought occurred to me. What if Teddy mentioned the documents to his father? Incredibly, Benson and I hadn't discussed this possibility and how to prevent it. I was frantic by the time Benson appeared at the back door moments later. He lifted the pot lid to inspect its contents, and Millie promptly served him a plate, explaining that Fred was expecting her home within the hour, but that she'd be back the following day.

"Is that Teddy's car in the drive?" he asked once Millie left.

"He's here now," I replied. "But I'm worried, Benson, very worried. What if Teddy mentions the documents to Adam? I hadn't thought about that until just now. How could I be so stupid?"

Benson set his plate aside. "Don't worry, Ana. When I delivered the documents the same thought occurred to me, so I told Teddy the only thing that came to mind—that he shouldn't mention the changes while he was here because you didn't know about them yet and Adam didn't want you to find out any sooner than necessary."

I placed my hand over my chest. "I hope it works," I muttered.

Benson ate two full plates of spaghetti and was contemplating a third when Jessie entered the kitchen, her face flush with emotion. "He's calling for you, Nana," she said. "You should come now."

I left Benson and rushed upstairs with Jessie just as Teddy was coming down. This time he stopped when he saw me. His eyes were large and glistening with tears. His sorrow had carved deep furrows into his face that made him look much older than he was. His eyes met mine, and for an instant it was as if nothing had changed between us. I was once again comforting him in the middle of the night, wiping away his tears and telling him that all the monsters were far away and couldn't hurt him. But then a shade of resentment fell over his eyes again, and he looked past me.

Nevertheless, I said, "I'm glad you came, Teddy. It's good to see you again."

He focused his cold eyes upon my face and said, "I came for my father, not for you, Ana."

"You don't have to be rude," Jessie said. "That doesn't help things."

"Leave it be," I said, placing a hand on her shoulder, and I quickly left them on the landing, realizing that for the first time in his life, Teddy had pronounced my name correctly.

The evening had descended, and the night-light glowed next to my beloved's bed, faintly illuminating his face. It had been days since I'd seen him look so peaceful and serene. His eyes fluttered open when he heard me pull up a chair, and when he saw that it was me, he smiled. "Ana," he whispered, his eyes glistening. "Teddy was here."

"Yes, I saw him," I said, taking his hand, and it felt so cold that I shuddered.

"I have my son back, and I know in my heart that I have you to thank for it," he said.

"Teddy came because he loves you. He loves you very much."

His eyes struggled to stay open as he weakly squeezed my hand. "You've taught me so much," he whispered. "My life is complete because of you, and now all I wish is that we had more time."

"Adam, please," I said, unable to control the grief tearing through my heart. "Don't say anymore."

"But I must," he said, squeezing my hand again. "Neither of us had the chance to say it before, and we can't let this opportunity slip away, no matter how difficult it is."

Although we'd never spoken about it before, I knew exactly what he meant, so I nodded as I kissed his hand and held it to my cheek, bracing myself as best I could.

"I know the reason," he whispered. "The reason why you survived the war in your country and came here to us."

"Why is it, my love?"

"Because we couldn't have survived without you. We've always needed you to show us the way, Ana. And my children still need you now."

"And I need you, my love," I replied.

He shook his head and was about to speak again, but I placed my fingers over his lips to stop him. "No, Adam," I said, know-ing and dreading what would come next. "Please don't say it."

He took my fingers away from his mouth. "Then you say it," he whispered.

"I can't," I replied, shaking my head and fully sobbing now. He waited until I had stopped crying, and when I saw him gaz-ing tenderly at me, I realized that he was prepared to wait for-ever in agony if I needed him to, but I couldn't stand to think that he would suffer one more second because of my cowardice. So I gathered myself together as best I could, looked into his eyes, and said what I wished I could've said to my mother and Carlitos the last time I saw them: "Goodbye, my darling. I will always love you."

He smiled and responded, barely above a whisper, "And I will always love you, Ana. Tell me that I'll see you again."

"Yes, you will see me again. I promise that you will."

He closed his eyes and sighed contentedly. "Goodbye," he whispered.

That very night my beloved and I strolled hand in hand through the streets of my village. It had just rained, and the air was fresh as our feet sunk into the moist earth. Despite the recent storm, the sky was the brightest blue imaginable and the ground, the huts, and the trees shimmered with golden light so that even ordinary rocks appeared as polished jade. And in the distance, the river that had always been muddy was a flowing ribbon of clean, clear water. Never had my little village looked so pristine and beautiful.

Villagers peeked out their windows and stood in their doorways to look at us. Some smiled and waved while others stared, trying to figure out who we were and why we were there. Stray dogs wandered about, but unlike the way I remembered them, they appeared well fed and content.

I saw Dolores sitting on her porch relaxing when her husband suddenly appeared from inside and handed her a cup of coffee to enjoy in her repose. When she saw me, she pointed toward a small shop with a glass window displaying many different colored dresses. "You'll find her there," she said.

Two boys were playing dice on the front step of the shop, and I recognized Carlitos and Manolo at once. Manolo's white tennis shoes looked brand-new, and when Carlitos saw me, he waved his arms exuberantly and beckoned me to come quickly as he always did when inspired by a new game. When we walked up to him, he wrapped his skinny arm around my shoulders and shook my beloved's hand in a manly fashion, although he still looked like the same little boy I'd vowed to marry so long ago. "She's been expecting you," he said and my beloved simply nodded.

We entered the shop and found Mama sitting at her sewing machine, focused on her work. When she looked up, her eyes gaped in wonder at us and then she smiled broadly. I immediately ran to her and embraced her. "Mama," I cried. "You look so well, and what a beautiful shop you have. It's even more beautiful than I imagined it would be."

"Thank you, *mija*," she replied, pleased by my reaction. "Do you like the dresses I've made?"

"They're beautiful."

"I'm glad you like them because they're all for you—each and every one. Why don't you take a closer look and see which one you like the best?" she said, giving me an encouraging nudge toward the window.

Then she turned to my beloved. "And who is this?" she asked, her eyes glittering as they did when she already knew the answer to her question. "Oh, I know. You must be the one I've heard so much about—the one who's made a liar out of me. Come and sit down," she said, pulling out a chair only for him. Deciding that I'd have plenty of time to admire the dresses later, I looked around for a place to sit as well, but there was no other chair in the shop. There was only the sewing machine and cabinet. This would have to do.

As Mama and my beloved began to chat, I pushed it toward the table and leaned upon it. All at once the shop, the window full of dresses, my mother, and my beloved became enveloped by a gray misty cloud that thickened before my eyes until I couldn't see them any longer. I was surrounded by a chilling darkness and I felt myself falling away from them at a fantastic speed. As I fell, the darkness surrounding me became solid as a stone wall that I tried to push away with my hands and my feet, but the harder I pushed, the harder it pressed down upon me, until I was barely able to breathe. Still, in the distance I heard the faint sounds of Mama and my beloved talking and laughing. Their voices were whirling away from me as I called out to them, "Don't leave me here again. Please . . . don't leave me here again." But I couldn't hear them anymore, and they could no longer hear me, so again I pushed away the darkness with all of my strength until my muscles ached and my bones nearly splintered.

Then all at once, a flash of light burst against my eyes, and I found myself lying next to my beloved just as the first ray of sun slid through the window shade. My arms were still wrapped around him, but his chest was no longer rising and falling against me. I kissed his cheek and stayed with him until dawn's faint glow filled the room.

Nineteen

I LEFT THE TRELLIS house immediately, knowing that this is what Teddy wanted. Sister Josepha insisted that I move back to the convent with her for a few days. Once I felt stronger, we would go to New Mexico together where I would begin a new life. I agreed to this plan because I needed to be near her and because I lacked the strength and clarity of mind to propose any other.

Mother Superior was happy to see me again and made it a point to look in on me from time to time. It seemed that the years had softened her, or perhaps they'd hardened me, because when she stared at me silently for those long discerning moments as she used to do, I met her gaze knowing that whatever she saw in me now, there was very little I could do to change it. I was who I was. And although I was deeply touched by her interest and concern, I was always relieved when our brief meetings came to an end, because it was becoming increasingly difficult to pretend I was on the mend.

The truth is that never in my life had I known such profound and utter silence. It melted through my skin and sunk down into the pores of my bones like molten lava. It hardened into a thick black crust that sealed me off from the rest of the world. Disembodied voices floated about the periphery of my dark island, well-meaning voices talked at me about the sensibility of grief as though it were a benign illness that needed to run its course. "Only time can heal the wound of such a loss," they said, and, "You must take care of yourself now." "Pray and give your pain to the Lord. He will never abandon you." "Go ahead and cry and let your feelings flow. You can't stop them any more than you can stop a raging river." "Death is a part of life."

I knew that all of these things were true, but I had lost not only my beloved, but the pillar that held the roof up over my life. And I yearned for death like a new day. It was the dark sun rising on the horizon, and when I pictured my skinny corpse lying next to my beloved in a bed of decay, I felt peace envelop me like a silken shroud. "Take me, dear Lord," I prayed. "Take me so that I can be with those I love and those who love me." But my heart continued to beat, and I was unable to stop myself from breathing.

The day before my beloved's funeral, Benson came by to see me. I could tell by the way he dragged his feet and hung his head that there was something he'd come to say to me and that it was difficult for him.

"What is it, Benson?"

"Am I that easy to read?" he asked with a sheepish smile that only accentuated the sadness in his eyes. He sighed. "Teddy called me this morning, and he asked me to ask you not to come to the funeral. Lillian is quite hysterical. It seems that she's suddenly become the grieving, inconsolable wife," he said with a roll of his eyes, "and Teddy's concerned that your presence will be an unbearable humiliation for her in front of her friends and that it just might push her over the edge."

"I see," I replied, not at all surprised to hear it. Lillian typically caved in like this after she'd misbehaved, and even if she wasn't willing to admit it to anyone else, I knew that she felt badly for how she'd treated Adam those last days. What's more, I knew that she couldn't resist the dramatic role of the still young and beautiful widow.

"I'm not saying that you shouldn't go, Ana. I'm just relaying his message, that's all."

We sat down on the bench that was situated beneath a willow tree. "What do you think I should do?" I asked.

"I think you should do whatever is right for you," Benson replied. "If you want to go, I'll be by your side and we'll face Lillian's insanity together. How bad can it be?"

Knowing how Benson felt about Lillian and what little help he'd be, I couldn't help but smile. "Thank you, Benson," I said. "I'll think about it and see how I feel tomorrow. Perhaps she won't notice me."

"That's a distinct possibility. From what I understand, there will be hundreds of people in attendance. Lillian's hired musicians, and the caterers are already preparing food for the reception." He paused when he saw the expression on my face. "What is it?"

"It sounds like another one of Lillian's grand parties that Adam always tried his best to avoid."

Benson nodded sadly. "This time he has no choice."

Jessie showed up later that same afternoon with a very different message. "I don't care what Teddy and Mom want," she said, clinging to my arm as we sat together in the garden. "I want you there, Nana. I *need* you there."

"But if your mother gets upset, it could make the situation very awkward for everyone," I replied.

Jessie shook her head and shut her eyes tight. "Why does everyone always tiptoe around my mother as though she were some kind of porcelain doll that might break into a thousand pieces? The truth is that she's made out of fortified rubber. She's always bounced her way through life without a scratch and she always will. Now that Daddy's gone, she breaks down in tears every five minutes and says that he was the most tolerant and wonderful man in the world. Just last week she was calling him every name in the book. I think she's full of shit," she concluded with a *humph*.

"I agree with your mother. Your father was the most wonderful and tolerant man in the world," I replied.

"I know he was, but—"

I gently pressed her arm. "Jessie, there are some people who can't appreciate what they have until they lose it. Knowing your mother, she's suffering just as much if not more than we are because along with her grief, she has to contend with her guilt."

Jessie shook her head fervently, refusing to accept my words, and then she broke down and I held her as she wept. "I want to hate her but I can't," she said.

"Hate is never the answer," I replied, remembering Sister Josepha's wise words from long ago, but I lacked the strength to say anything else.

Jessie gazed at me, her eyes pleading. "Please come tomorrow," she said. "I miss you so much, and it feels like I'm losing you too."

"I'll try my best," I said.

But the next morning I was unable to get out of bed without nearly collapsing. Sister Josepha stationed herself next to me and prayed, but this was unable to quell the sour feeling in my stomach and the incessant aching in my bones. I felt that I would be unable to keep down food or water, but Sister Josepha insisted on bringing meals to my room, which was frowned upon at the convent. Only the most elderly sisters enjoyed such a privilege and then only when they were ill and unable to come to the table. Since she had broken the rules for me, I made an effort to eat a little more, but I was only able to keep down a few bites. I was sinking through the layers of darkness one at a time, and a strong hand was leading me to my death. I was unable to attend my beloved's funeral, but I knew that I'd be with him soon. And when I closed my eyes and held my breath I could almost hear his music playing in my heart.

In this state, it was difficult to know how many hours or days had passed. I had no doubt that Benson and Jessie would be by to see me eventually, but I hoped that they'd stay away for a few days. I needed time to rest my mind and body, to meditate and pray and find my bearings again. Sister Josepha was content to spend long stretches of time with me in my room or in the garden. We prayed the rosary together and sometimes we sat in the garden and listened to the birds. She watched me as one would an egg that is beginning to hatch. I knew she was waiting for the fog to lift from my heart and soul, knowing that healing such as this couldn't be rushed. She brought me broth and tea and kept the other sisters away with kindly assurances that I was fine and had suffered a great shock and that all I needed was time to recover, time to find my way back to my life again. When she said these things, I listened to her as if she were talking about somebody else, for more than ever I felt that I was caught up in a current that would take me far away forever, and I was happy to go.

She rarely left me, but one afternoon she had to leave the convent to run an errand, and I found myself alone for the first time in days. I sat in a chair in my room, and my eyes settled on my bedside table. It was odd to see it clear and not cluttered with a multitude of Adam's medications and half-empty water glasses. It was odd to no longer be waiting, and it seemed that finally time had found a way to stand still, but now I wanted it to rush by as quickly as possible. There was nothing to wait for, nothing to hope or live for. Sister Josepha had been gone only for a few minutes, but already it felt as though she'd been away for hours.

I heard a light knocking on the door, and one of the young novices informed me that I had a visitor who was waiting for me in the lounge downstairs. I thanked her, assuming that it was either Jessie or Benson, both of whom would be upset that I hadn't attended the funeral. But when was it? Was it yesterday or the day before? Could it have been a week ago? I put a comb through my hair and tried my best to remember. I didn't want them to worry about me. And suddenly I felt a gust of something hopeful blow through me. "I'm going to leave this world soon," I thought. "I don't need to worry about going anywhere or beginning again. The weakness that has overcome me is much more than grief." And this thought filled me with peace as I made my way downstairs.

When I entered the lounge, I was shocked to see an elegantly dressed woman with ethereal blue eyes and auburn hair rise from her chair.

"Ms. Lillian," I muttered, unable to disguise my shock.

She walked toward me as her eyes swept me from head to toe. "What's happened to you, Ana?"

"I'm tired, that's all," I replied, noticing that her own lovely face appeared drawn and that her lipstick had been applied with a shaky hand. She walked back to the sofa by the window and sat down. I waited for a moment and then sat in the chair across from her. I felt a flutter in my heart, and it was difficult to catch my breath.

"I'm told that you'll be going to New Mexico soon," she said, crossing her legs at the ankle.

"Yes, in a few days, I'll be going with Sister Josepha to her school."

"You must relish the thought of getting away," she said, with a courteous nod. "I would love to do the same if I could. I truly envy you."

I watched her as she fingered the latch on her purse, her fingers trembling all the while. The dimples around her mouth and the strain in her eyes let me know that she was trying very hard not to weep.

"Why have you come here, Ms. Lillian?" I asked.

She glanced up at me and then away again. She set her purse aside and folded her hands on her lap. "I've come to ask for your help," she said. "Not for me, for Teddy."

"What's wrong with him?" I asked as the flutter in my heart grew stronger.

"He's been very upset since his father's funeral. I understand that it's perfectly normal for a son to be upset at a time like this, but there's something else. Darwin spoke to him after the funeral. I have no idea what he said, but ever since then Teddy's been behaving very strangely and he won't tell me what they spoke about."

"Have you asked Mr. Darwin?"

Ms. Lillian waved her hand in a disparaging gesture. "Oh, you know Darwin, he's off on one of his escapades and God only knows how long he'll be gone and when we'll see him again. I guess it depends on how quickly he goes through the money Adam left him."

"He'll be back," I muttered.

Lillian leaned forward in her chair. "But in the meantime, Teddy won't come out of his room and he won't talk to anyone. Not me or Jessie or anyone."

"I'm sorry to hear it, Ms. Lillian, but I still don't understand why you're here."

"I want you to talk to him, Ana."

I felt my hands slip one against the other and I became aware of a ringing in my ears, and I was shaking my head as the ringing grew louder.

"He'll talk with you, I know he will . . ."

"You're wrong. I'm the last person in the world Teddy would talk to right now. If I went there, it would only make things worse."

Lillian began to wring her hands, and her chest seemed to cave in on itself as she struggled for the words to go on. "You don't understand, I'm losing him, Ana. I'm losing my precious Teddy. And I've come here to ask—no, to beg you—to come to the house with me now." Tears ran down her cheeks as she rustled through her purse for a tissue and blew her nose hard. "I realize that I have no right to ask this of you after all that's happened, but I know that if he hears your voice on the other side of that door, he'll answer. You've always been the one he loves the most." She held her hands out to me. "Please, Ana. I beg you to forgive me for all of my stupidities and come with me now before something terrible happens."

I felt pressure gathering inside of me as though a churning storm had landed in the very center of my chest, and my hands began to quiver with rage. "I forgive you, Ms. Lillian, but I can't come with you," I said.

"Please," Lillian pleaded. "I know my son, and I know he'll—"

"You don't know him!" I sprang up from the chair and walked away from her. "You've never known him!"

"But I still love him," she said, hanging her head.

"Then you'll find a way to talk with him yourself."

"I've been trying, but I don't know how!" Lillian wailed. "I don't know how, Ana. That's why I'm here." She wept into her tissue for some time.

I walked toward the door. My head was throbbing, and I could feel the pressure gathering behind my eyes. Another migraine was coming on, and I could tell it would be worse than any other. For the first time in my life I couldn't set my grief and my pain aside to attend to somebody else's. That part of me had died with Adam, and try as I might to bring it back, to empathize with Lillian and her struggles with Teddy, I couldn't find the heart and the will to do it.

"I'm trying," Lillian whimpered again. "I'm trying so hard."

"You've never really tried," I said. "You've always given in to your weakness and you walked away from your family when they needed you most. If you really love Teddy, you'll find a way to reach him now."

"But Ana . . . he's not in his right mind."

"And I'm not his mother, Ms. Lillian, you are!" I said loudly, almost yelling.

Lillian stared at me with gaping, wounded eyes.

"You're his mother," I repeated softly. "And he needs you, not me."

I left her hunched over and weeping in the lounge. And when I closed the door behind me, the throbbing pain in my head prompted me to rush upstairs to my room and remain in the darkness until Sister Josepha returned.

I opened my eyes sometime later to see Sister Josepha standing over my bed, but she wasn't alone. To my surprise, Benson and Dr. Farrell were standing next to her. Benson's jowls were quivering and Dr. Farrell was somber, a manila folder tucked under his arm.

"Under the circumstances, I thought it was best that these gentlemen see you here," she said in a hushed voice "But please, let's keep our voices down. Men are not allowed in this section of the convent and if you're discovered, Mother Superior will be quite irritated with me."

Dr. Farrell sat in the chair next to my bed and considered me with those fateful eyes I knew so well. "Ana, I have some news I should probably give you in private."

Sister Josepha gasped faintly upon hearing this, and I understood that leaving a man and a woman alone together in the dormitory rooms was unthinkable. "I don't mind if Sister Josepha and Benson stay, Dr. Farrell. In fact, I prefer it."

"Very well," he said with a beleaguered sigh. He opened the manila envelope and adjusted his glasses. "If you recall, I asked the nurse to draw your blood a few days ago." He looked up, his eyes overflowing with regret. "I must admit that with everything that's happened I didn't look at the results until just this morning, and when I did, I was quite shocked. I . . . I'm sorry, Ana, I should've reviewed them immediately and called you. I want you to know that I don't make a practice of this."

"For God's sake, Peter," Benson said, his face puffing up. "You're scaring us half to death."

"I'm sorry, that certainly isn't my intention."

I sat up in bed feeling calmer and clearer than I had in days. "Dr. Farrell, I know what you're going to tell me. I've suspected for quite some time."

"Yes," he replied, nervously fingering the folder on his lap. "I thought you would."

I looked to Sister Josepha and Benson, who were watching me with grave concern. I could see in their eyes that now they understood what I'd known all along. "I have a cancer growing inside of me," I said. "I didn't want to say anything so that Adam wouldn't worry, but I'm so glad you're both here with me now."

Benson sat down at the foot of my bed and put his head in his hands while Sister Josepha reached for her rosary.

Dr. Farrell stared at me for some time, blinking ceaselessly behind his spectacles. "I must inform you that it's not a cancer that's growing inside of you, Ana—it's a baby."

"A what?" Benson said, looking up with a start.

Peter closed the file. "A baby," he repeated. "According to these results, Ana is just entering her second trimester."

"Sweet Mother of God," Sister Josepha cried, and her rosary slipped from her fingers and fell to the floor.

"Are you sure?" Benson asked.

"Blood tests are very accurate," Peter replied. "I'm as certain of Ana's pregnancy as I am about your elevated cholesterol."

Sister Josepha came to the bedside and shook me gently. "Ana, are you all right?" When I didn't reply she turned to Dr. Farrell. "I think she's in shock, Doctor."

Dr. Farrell placed his fingers on my wrist to check my pulse. Once satisfied, he asked gently, "Ana, didn't you notice that you'd stopped menstruating?"

"I . . . I was so busy looking after Adam, I didn't pay much attention, and then, since I thought I was sick, I . . ." I refocused my eyes onto Dr. Farrell's face. "How could this happen?" I asked, and all three faces staring at me blushed in unison.

As we talked about this remarkable revelation and what it meant and what I should do next, my black watery grave began to churn and tiny light-filled bubbles swirled all around me, tickling my nose, exploding in tiny bursts about my ears and rousing me from my slumber. And then slowly, ever so slowly, my body began to rise from the bottom of my grave and my arms reached for the surface as I submitted to the force of this new life growing within me.

"Life will be better than what you've known so far, little one. I promise you that."

Benson returned the next day, but this time I felt well enough to meet with him in the reception area downstairs. He noticed the difference in me and remarked upon it.

"This may sound rather clichéd, but you're positively glowing," he said. "I can hardly believe that I'm looking at the same woman."

"Dr. Farrell said that if I don't start eating and taking better care of myself I'll lose the baby, and I'm not going to let that happen." I grasped his hand. "Oh, Benson, the deep sadness I felt just yesterday has been completely filled with the greatest joy I've ever known. And something tells me that Adam knew . . . in his heart he knew all along."

Benson nervously fingered the latch of his briefcase. "And if I didn't know you as well as I do, I'd be tempted to believe that you planned this all along."

"What in the world are you talking about?"

"The papers Adam signed, they specifically stated that the house was to go to his children, and if you continue taking care of yourself, in six months there will be another Trellis child . . . another heir to the estate."

I sat back in my chair, shocked by his words. "I don't care about the estate. I'm going with Sister Josepha to New Mexico. She tells me that it's a wonderful school and a lovely place to raise a child."

Benson leaned forward and squeezed my hand. "I'm sure that if Sister Josepha says it's wonderful, it is, but in a few months you'll be a mother. Just think about what that means, Ana. You have to consider your baby's future, and don't you think that Teddy and Jessie should be told that soon they'll have a new brother or sister?"

"I suppose so," I muttered. "But I don't know how they'll react to the news, and this may sound selfish, but I don't want anything to disturb my happiness right now. If my baby is going to get stronger, he or she needs to know and feel that their mother is happy."

Benson released my hand and sighed. "You may not want to hear this, but I took the liberty of calling the house yesterday just to get a read on how things are going over there. I spoke with Jessie and she told me that Teddy's very depressed. He's locked himself in his room, hardly eats, and refuses to talk with anyone, but she thinks he may be willing to talk with you."

My mouth felt dry and I took a sip of water. "Yes, I heard, but you know as well as I do that if I go over there right now, it would only make matters worse."

Benson shrugged. "That's what I told her. Maybe she's just looking for a pretext to get you back home."

"That isn't my home anymore. Sister Josepha and I will be leaving in a few days. I've been putting off joining her for twenty years, and I don't intend to make her wait any longer."

Benson smiled tenderly. "I know how she feels," he said.

Twenty

I AWOKE TO THE sound of howling in the middle of the night. It ripped through my heart and stole down the length of my spine, taking me back to a place I'd been trying to forget all my life. "Oh, Mama, tell me what to do now," I whimpered. "What do I do? Where do I go?"

I waited for an answer, but there was only silence and a heaviness in my womb I hadn't felt before. I lay for a long while in the stillness with my palms pressed to my abdomen. "I'm afraid, little one," I muttered. "And you should know before you come into this world that when your mother is afraid, she has a tendency to hide until the danger has passed. Maybe you should choose somebody more courageous to be your mother."

The next morning I left the convent before Sister Josepha brought me my breakfast. The taxi dropped me off at the outskirts of the cemetery, and I inquired at the office to locate Adam's grave. I expected to find his name engraved on a flat slab of stone imbedded in the lawn like all the others, but I was directed to an impressive mausoleum that looked like a small house, with an ornate gate blocking its entrance. Over the gate the family name, Trellis, was carved. It was locked and a single candle burned in the farthest corner of the small dark space. By the faint wavering light I was just able to make out the names of the various family members who were Adam's parents and grandparents, and then I saw it: carved on the crypt nearest to me was the name Adam Montgomery Trellis. I stared at it with my face pressed against the gate's bars for a long while. Although it had barely been a week since I'd held him in my arms, it seemed like a lifetime ago, and many times I wondered if I'd ever really known him and if we'd ever truly loved each other. But now with this life growing inside me, there was no doubt.

"I hope you can forgive me, my love," I whispered. "Now that you know what I did, I hope you understand that I did it because I love you and because I couldn't bear the thought that you'd leave this earth without seeing your son one last time."

The flame of the candle wavered in response. "We're going to have a baby, you and me. I hope and pray that you're as happy about it as I am and I want you to know that I'm going to tell our child all about you and how much I loved you and how you made me believe in the goodness that can exist between a man and a woman."

A mild breeze blew through the trees, nearly extinguishing the flame, but then it sparked and burned steadily again. "I've decided that I'm going to go with Sister Josepha to her school in New Mexico. I know you wanted me to stay in your beautiful house, but that isn't possible anymore, and this is what I must do."

And a new voice answered me. It was pure and innocent, un-fettered by the pain of this life, yet wise beyond my understand-ing. "There is no need to be afraid anymore," it said. "Together we will face the world and together we will find our strength."

Packing the few belongings I planned to take with me to New Mexico took very little time, and when I tried to assist Sister Jo-sepha with her packing, she refused to let me help, insisting that I rest in the garden for the remainder of the afternoon instead. In a few hours a car would be arriving to take us to the airport, and even though she tried very hard to appear impartial, I knew she was worried that I would change my mind about going. The previous day I overheard her talking with one of the other sis-ters: "I've put this matter in God's hands for the past twenty years. If it's his will that she come with me, then so be it."

"You seem very happy that God's will is finally in keeping with yours," the younger sister observed.

Sister Josepha chuckled with delight. "If truth be told, I don't believe I've ever been happier in all my life."

I chose a seat near the fountain and found myself gazing at the winding bougainvillea that grew along the arbor, while con-templating possible names for my baby. There was no doubt that if my baby were a boy, I would name him after his father, but if I had a girl I had no idea what to name her. I smiled as I considered this happy dilemma. I planned to tell Jessie about my pregnancy in a few weeks, when I was certain that all was pro-ceeding normally. Perhaps then she and Sister Josepha would help me decide on the best name, and Benson could help us too once he was in a better mood and not feeling so sour about my decision to leave. He was due to show up any moment to bid me farewell, and I had no doubt that he wouldn't pass up one last opportunity to try and persuade me to stay.

This too made me smile. Just the day before, he'd come by looking very solemn. He was perspiring profusely and drank two full glasses of lemonade before he was able to speak about anything except how much he disliked it when the days got so warm. He mopped his forehead with his handkerchief while glancing at me and smiling nervously. "I have a proposition for you," he said, "and I want you to think about it before you give me an answer."

"Very well, Benson. What is your proposition?"

He took a deep breath and stuffed his handkerchief in his pocket. "That you marry me, right now, today. Your baby will have a father, although I'll make legal arrangements for the paternity to be well established for the sake of the inheritance, and you won't have to go through life as a single, unwed mother."

"That's very kind of you . . ."

"You're answering before you've thought about it, Ana. Take your time. Sleep on it," he said while patting my arm.

"Benson, I . . ."

"I won't make any physical demands on you, if that's what you're worried about. Our relationship won't change. The only difference will be that you can be assured that you and your child will never want for anything for the rest of your lives. I'll even arrange for my mother to move out," he added, his ears flaming red.

"I would never ask that of you," I said, deeply touched. "You've lived with your mother all your life."

"For you I would do it, Ana. Only for you."

"I will sleep on it," I said, and earlier today when I called to tell him that I had to decline his offer and go with Sister Josepha as I had planned, I heard the sad resignation in his voice and pictured his kindly eyes filling with tears.

I became aware of footsteps approaching and Benson appeared just beyond the arbor. He was even more agitated than he was the day before, and when he saw me he quickened his pace.

"I was looking for you everywhere," he said, panting. "I was afraid that you'd already gone."

"You know I wouldn't leave without saying goodbye."

He was literally gasping for air as he brought his hand to his chest.

"Sit down and catch your breath," I said. "Our plane doesn't leave for a few hours. We have plenty of time."

Benson sat down and took several deep breaths, but his expression remained tense. "Ana, Teddy called me just now as I was leaving the office."

"Teddy?"

Benson nodded anxiously, still out of breath. "I don't know what's going on, but he was yelling and"—he grasped my hand—"he said that if I didn't tell him the truth about everything, the documents and how I'd obtained his father's signature, he was going to call the police and report the fraud. Ana," he said, trembling, "I could lose everything."

"But how could this be? You and I were the only ones who knew, and I'm positive that Teddy never spoke about it with Adam. If he had, Adam would've said something to me."

"I have to go see him, Ana. I have to find out what's going on, and you have to go with me."

I informed Sister Josepha that I was going to the Trellis house with Benson, but that I'd be back shortly. Fifteen minutes later we arrived at the gate. I punched in the code on the keypad, hoping that it hadn't been changed, and thankfully the gate opened for us. My heart was beating fiercely and I tried to calm myself with thoughts about the baby, but it was difficult to do with Benson gasping for air and continuously muttering his fatalistic predictions one after the other.

"I'm going to lose everything," he said. "My practice, my house, my license . . . I just know it."

"It will be fine, Benson," I said. "Don't worry."

And each time he answered, "You don't understand, Ana. I could go to jail. You could go to jail too," he said. "It doesn't matter that you're pregnant. The prisons are filled with pregnant women."

After he parked the car, we rushed up the stairs and rang the doorbell. Its melancholy tones lingered, increasing my agitation and the trembling sensation in my knees. Even so, as though greeting an old friend, I turned to admire the garden, and as always, took pleasure in the way the blanket of greenery and flowers undulated in graceful lines all the way to the wall that ran along the perimeter of the estate. I turned back to Benson and placed my hand on his shoulder, hoping that this momentary peace I'd acquired would help steady him.

"Maybe nobody's home," Benson said, his voice cracking with despair. "Maybe they've all gone to the police station to report the fraud."

"That doesn't make any sense," I replied. "Why would they do that?"

Then we heard the click of the latch and the door slowly opened. Lillian stood before us, her hair in disarray as she gaped at us with vacant, bleary eyes. Wordlessly, she stepped aside so that we could enter. At that moment Jessie came in from the kitchen and when she saw us she rushed to my side. "Nana," she cried. "You came home."

"I came to keep Teddy from calling the police," I replied, receiving her warm embrace. "I hope that we still have a chance to explain."

"Explain what?" Jessie asked, taken aback. "And why would Teddy call the police?"

At this, Benson took my hand and shook his head mournfully. "Forgive me, Ana, but I didn't know what else to do."

"What do mean?"

"I lied to you. Teddy never told me he was going to call the police."

I stepped back and pulled my hand away from him. "But why? Why would you do something like that?"

Benson hung his head and Lillian stepped forward. "It was my idea," she said. "I had to get you over here somehow and I knew that you'd come if you thought it would prevent Benson from getting into trouble."

"So you know about the papers," I said, turning back to Benson, incredulous of his betrayal. "Did you tell *her* about the papers as well?"

Lillian folded her arms over her chest and shook her head sadly. "Benson didn't have to tell me anything. I figured it out on my own. It's true that Adam and I hadn't lived as man and wife for many years, but I knew him pretty well, and he wasn't the sort of man who'd change his mind about something so important at the last minute. And I know you too, Ana. You'll do anything for the people you love, even if it means giving up a generous inheritance, which is why I have no doubt that you'll talk with Teddy now that you're here."

"Mom, what in the world are you talking about?" Jessie asked, her hands on her hips.

"I'll explain it all to you just as soon as Ana goes upstairs to talk with Teddy," she replied.

Still reeling from the shock of being tricked in this manner, I shook my head weakly.

"I beg of you, Ana," Lillian said. "I'm Teddy's mother, and as his mother I know that he needs you right now. But if I'm wrong, I'll never bother you again and you can go off to New Mexico and forget that you ever knew us."

I took several steps toward the landing. I could feel the three of them watching me, willing me to take one step up and then another, and as I ascended the staircase, the reluctance and dread I'd been feeling began to transform into something warm and familiar. I became aware of the deep desire to see my dear Teddy again, to hold him in my arms and tell him that everything was going to be okay. Just being back in the house gave me strength of heart, and I heard the voices and the laughter drifting in from the past, the sound of Adam's tires on the gravel when he came home from work, and the back door slamming when the children went in search of a snack in the kitchen after playing in the yard. I heard Lillian calling for Millie to prepare her morning coffee and Adam playing the piano in the music room. But once I reached the top of the stairs, everything was quiet again. And as I walked down the length of the corridor and stood before Teddy's door, breathing in the air that was thick with sadness, I realized that life and happiness were gone from this house.

I knocked and whispered Teddy's name. When he didn't respond I spoke more loudly, "Teddy, it's me. Your mother asked me to talk with you."

I heard a rustling and then footsteps heading toward the door. In moments it was opened, and Teddy stood in the doorway appraising me with wounded eyes. He appeared ruptured and tattered, as though he hadn't slept or eaten in days. "How about *you?*" he asked. "Do you want to talk with me, or are you here only because of *my mother?*" he asked cynically.

"I want to talk with you too, Teddy," I replied. "I've been wanting to talk with you for a long time now."

He turned away and dragged his feet across the room toward his bed, where he lowered himself down, moving slowly like an old man whose joints were stiff and aching.

The only chair in his room was hidden by a mound of dirty clothes, so I sat at the foot of his bed. "Your mother tells me that you've been very upset and that you haven't left your room since you spoke with your uncle a few days ago."

Teddy grunted and closed his eyes. "I'm sure you'd like to think that this has everything to do with Uncle Darwin, because you've always hated him." He raised his head and opened one eye to look at me. "You can't deny it, can you?"

I turned away and said nothing, but at that moment I caught sight of the Superman shirt I'd mended for him years ago on the floor. I hadn't seen it in ages, and was surprised that he still had it, but then as I picked it up from the floor I remembered that this had been a gift from his uncle and he'd never allowed me to throw it away. *"Tienes que ser fuerte, mijo,"* I whispered, remembering the day I held him in my arms as Adam rushed him to the hospital. *"No te olvides que el amor de familia es tu fortaleza."*

"Well, I loved my uncle Darwin," Teddy said, ignoring my words, snatching the shirt away from me and balling it up in his hands. "I loved him more than anyone. I loved him even more than I loved you."

Turning back to him, I said, "You talk as though you don't love him anymore."

Teddy dropped his head back down to the pillow and tossed the shirt back to the floor. He stared blankly up at the ceiling, and when he spoke again, his voice was more subdued. "After the funeral, Uncle Darwin told me that the day before he died, Dad forgave him for all that had happened, and Uncle Darwin said that he couldn't live with himself unless he told me the truth, the real reason that Mom and Dad split up. It seems he should know, since he's been Mom's lover on and off for years," he said in a tone that was at once flip and derisive. "He said that you had nothing to do with breaking them up and he didn't want me going through life believing a lie about my father. So I guess now I can spend the rest of my life hating my mother and Uncle Darwin instead of hating you and Dad."

Amazed to hear about Darwin's noble confession, I needed a moment or two to respond. "The answer isn't for you to hate anyone, Teddy, but to understand the reason things happened the way they did, and to find a way to forgive."

"But it's true, isn't it, Nana?" he asked as he shuddered with disgust. "Mom was cheating on Dad for years, and under his roof, with his own brother."

I nodded and lowered my eyes, ashamed for Lillian's sake.

"I don't want her here," Teddy said, his fists clenched. "That's why I haven't left my room. It's my house now. Dad gave it to me and Jessie and I want her out. The problem is that I . . . I just don't know how to kick her out, but I'll figure out a way, believe me I will."

I placed my hand on Teddy's knee. "I realize how upsetting this is for you, and it's true that your mother made many inexcusable mistakes, but she never meant to hurt you. She always loved you and Jessie, and I know that you've always felt her love and that you feel it even now."

Teddy shook his head. "How could I have been so stupid? Why didn't I see it? Even Jessie tried talking to me about it, but I wouldn't listen to her."

"We all see things when we're ready to see them, Teddy," I replied softly.

Eventually, Teddy unclenched his fists, and we sat together in silence for some time.

"I'm sorry for all the cruel things I said, Nana. Do you forgive me?"

"I've already forgiven you, Teddy," I said. "Just as I hope you'll find a way to forgive your mother, and your uncle too. I'm sure that's what your father would've wanted."

He nodded while gazing at me, his eyes wide and imploring. And then he sat up on his elbows. "Maybe I will forgive them, but on one condition."

"What's that?"

"That you stay here with us."

"Teddy!"

"You can't leave us now, Nana. This house isn't a home without you."

"Oh, my dear Teddy," I said, flustered and overwhelmed. "I've made plans to go with Sister Josepha. Our plane leaves in a couple of hours."

"You can change your plans. Sister Josepha will understand—she always has before."

"But she's waiting for me now."

Teddy continued to gaze at me with those dark smoldering eyes that reminded me so much of his father. "You can't go, Nana. Nothing will be the same without you. It will never be the same."

I stood up and knelt next to him. "Teddy, even if I could stay, it would never be the same, you know that."

"Of course, I realize that without Dad things will be different, but if you stay it'll be easier for all of us. You know how Jessie and I feel about you, and Mom misses you too. You're the best friend she ever had."

I lowered my head. Could I tell him? Was now the right time? "Teddy, something has happened, something I wasn't aware of until very recently. And because of this, I'm certain that it will be more difficult for everyone if I stay." I took a deep breath and told him, but even as I said the words out loud, I found it difficult to believe. I pressed my hands gently over my abdomen as I spoke, trying to be gentle, hoping against hope that this revelation wouldn't further wound my dear Teddy.

As I spoke, he sat up fully, his mouth hanging open, his eyes incredulous.

"I know it's a shock," I concluded, folding my trembling hands in my lap. "It was a shock for me too. I couldn't believe it at first, and I knew . . . I knew it would be upsetting for you and for Jessie, which is why I wanted to wait until . . ." I glanced at him, his eyes now blank, his brow furrowed. "I was going to tell you once things had settled down a bit."

All at once, Teddy sprang up from the bed and grabbed my hand, yanking me to my feet. He ran out of his room at breakneck speed, pulling me behind him. And as he ran, he yelled at the top of his lungs, "Hey, she's going to have a baby! She's going to have a baby!"

We ran down the length of the corridor and when he reached the stairs, he rushed down these as well, pulling me behind him as I stumbled and tripped, barely able to keep up with him. Benson was white as a ghost and Lillian and Jessie were more troubled than ever to see him so agitated.

"Teddy, what are you yelling about?" Lillian asked.

"Don't you have ears in your head? Can't you hear what I'm telling you?" he said, jumping in place like a madman. "She's going to have a baby!"

Jessie grabbed Teddy's arm. "Teddy, calm down, you're not making any sense. Who's going to have a baby?"

"Nana," Teddy said excitedly. "Nana's going to have a baby."

Ms. Lillian pressed her hand to her forehead. "He's lost his mind," she muttered. "My boy has literally lost his mind."

Teddy took firm hold of his mother's shoulders, shaking her

as he spoke. "Mom, listen to me. Nana's pregnant. She's pregnant with Dad's baby."

"Oh my God. Oh my God," Jessie said, taking several steps back.

Lillian stared dumbfounded at her son and then she angrily swiped his hands away from her shoulders. "You're crazy," she muttered.

"No, I'm not. She told me just now," Teddy said.

"Is it true, Nana?" Jessie asked tremulously.

I nodded. "Yes, it's true."

Jessie gasped, but when I looked into her eyes they sparkled with wonder and awe.

Lillian stared at me and took several steps toward me, which prompted Teddy to step in between us. "Leave her alone, Mom. We don't need any more trouble."

"Look at her." She seethed. "She's skin and bone. Do you really think Ana can carry a child to term in that condition?" She pointed an accusatory finger at Teddy's face. "And when you were pulling her down the stairs behind you like a raving lunatic she could've stumbled and lost the baby. It doesn't take much, you know. It's a wonder she hasn't lost it already."

"I . . . I didn't realize," Teddy stammered.

Lillian pushed him aside and stood before me. "How far along are you?"

"Dr. Farrell says I'm almost three months."

She shook her head in dismay as she looked me up and down. "We're going to have to put some meat on your bones. Benson!" she said, twisting herself around to face him.

Benson snapped to attention. "Yes, Lillian," he replied.

"Call Millie—tell her to get over here right away. There's absolutely nothing to eat in this house."

"Should I tell her the news?"

"For God's sake, Benson, tell her whatever you want, just get her over here," she barked.

Lillian linked her arm smoothly through mine and led me to the bench in the foyer. "Let's get you off your feet so you can catch your breath," she said sweetly.

"But Sister Josepha is expecting me. Our plane leaves in a couple of hours." I put my head in my hands and suddenly the entire house was lurching and dipping like a boat sailing on the high seas, and my thoughts were spinning away from me. When I looked up at the four of them standing over me, they were spinning as well, and I feared that I'd vomit all over their shoes.

"Tell her she has to stay, Mom," Teddy said.

"Of course she has to stay," Lillian replied. "She can't go off to the wilds of New Mexico in her condition. It's ludicrous."

"That's what I've been trying to tell her," Benson added.

"It's not a wilderness. It's a very nice school," I muttered.

Jessie knelt before me and took my hands into both of hers. "Nana, you've been taking care of us for so many years, now it's our turn to take care of you and the baby," she said, already enchanted by the idea.

"Nothing would make me happier, Jessie, but Sister Josepha needs me and I can't abandon her now. Please understand," I said, looking up at all of them. "I have to go."

$\mathcal{T}$wenty-one

SISTER JOSEPHA WAS WAITING for me in the hospitality room, where visitors are greeted and potential novices are interviewed before entering the convent. She was seated in a chair by the window, and the light falling across her face accentuated the crisscrossing lines around her eyes and cheeks. When she saw me, they fanned out into a happy smile.

"My dear," she said as she reached for her cane, "I'm so glad to see you."

"I'm sorry if I made you worry," I replied, taking the seat next to her. "It took longer than I expected."

She shifted in her chair to face me. "There's very little that worries me these days. Now tell me, is Benson okay? Did you get a chance to speak with the family?"

"Yes, we spoke," I said, looking away. "The situation with the family is . . . well, it's complicated . . . especially now."

Sister Josepha took firm hold of the handle of her cane and leaned forward so she could keep an eye out for the car. Then she sat back again and sighed. "This may sound odd, but whenever life gets complicated for me, I recall our escape through the jungle and I'm reminded that with God's intercession, tragedies can lead us to unexpected triumph." Sister Josepha's beautiful round face appeared almost as it did on that day. "I was certain that we would perish in the jungle, but God gave me you to look after and I realized that I had to be as strong for you as you were for me. Every day I thank him for bringing you into my life, which is why this is so difficult for me to say." She turned to me, her chin set firm. "My dearest Ana, forgive me, but I've decided that it's best I go on to New Mexico without you."

Her words hit me like a blow to my chest, and she continued. "I know that we've been dreaming of working together for many years, but I can't ignore God's voice in my heart any more than I can this pain in my knees," she said, chuckling and trying to make light of it.

"But why? Why don't you want me to go with you anymore?"

Gazing at me tenderly, she said, "Ana, you're going to have a baby in a few months. How do I explain your situation to the boys and girls at the school and to their parents? It isn't proper that we have an unmarried mother as one of our teachers."

"But we already agreed to tell everyone I'm a widow. That should take care of any impropriety."

"And is this how you want to start the next phase of your life? Predicated on a lie?" She gave my arm a friendly pat and looked beyond me out the window. "Oh, look, the car just arrived—and right on time too." She stood up and made her way to the door to separate her luggage from mine, all the while humming a merry little tune. She struggled a bit with the heavier cases, but I made no move to help her.

"You're not being honest with me, Sister. I'm disappointed in you and deeply hurt. Lillian called you, didn't she? Or maybe it was one of the children."

She didn't answer me and remained silent as the driver put her bags in the trunk. When he was finished, I walked outside with her and stood nearby as she slowly lowered herself into the backseat while leaning on her cane. She motioned for me to come closer, and I crouched down before her. She took her time arranging her skirt and the black veil over her shoulders and when she spoke, her voice was grave and her expression severe. "The day before Adam died, you asked for my advice about something, do you remember?"

I lowered my head and said nothing.

"You asked what I would advise someone who had to choose between love and honesty. I didn't answer you then because I didn't really understand the question, but now I do. Now I understand very well, and we both know the answer, don't we?"

I raised my eyes and looked up into her beautiful face that was shining like the moon. Then she placed her hand gently on the crown of my head. "You belong with your family, *mija*," she said. "And I know that you will be a wonderful mother."

Twenty-two

THAT EVENING THE TRELLIS house glowed with a warm and welcoming light that spilled out through the windows and across the surrounding gardens like a fountain overflowing. Millie had prepared her pot roast for dinner and Benson stayed as well, although he made certain to sit near me and as far away from Lillian as possible. Peter Farrell stopped by to see if Teddy had come out of his room and was delighted to find him sitting at the table with the rest of us and looking like himself again. He was also pleased to see that I was back at home and that color was returning to my cheeks.

After the dishes had been washed and put away, Benson and Millie went home with promises to return the next day. Lillian announced that she'd had one glass of wine too many and would sleep at the house that night rather than drive back to her loft in town. After some consideration, she chose to sleep in the guest room, and eventually Teddy and Jessie drifted off to their rooms as well.

I was the last one up and as usual I took it upon myself to turn out the lights throughout the house one by one. I started in the kitchen and then proceeded to the sunroom just beyond. Through the window I gazed at the blue-green lights of the peacock pool that shimmered against the portico, and although I couldn't see them from where I stood, I imagined their glorious feathers waving up at me from the bottom as though to let me know that all was well. I gently pressed my hands to my abdomen and whispered, "This is the place where in your father's arms I was born a second time." I turned out the pool lights and proceeded to do the same in dining room and foyer.

I was preparing to go upstairs, but stopped and walked down the darkened corridor leading to the study. I hesitated outside the door for a moment and when I opened it, I was surprised to see that the lamp was lit, illuminating the empty desk and the entire room with a soft amber glow. I stood in the center of the room and looked around at the bookshelves and the anatomical reproductions scattered about, remembering how it was on the first day I arrived. I walked toward the desk and turned off the light. Standing in the darkness, I felt a chill and then a stirring in my abdomen. "This was your father's study," I whispered. "When I first met him, I thought he was so cold and frightening I couldn't look him in the eye without trembling, but I was wrong about him, so very wrong."

Next, I went to the music room. It was dark so I flicked on the light and stood in the doorway, admiring the majestic instrument that gleamed in the corner. But my eyes lingered on the bench, and I remembered how my beloved and I had sat upon it not so long ago. "Your father was a gifted pianist," I whispered.

"The first time I heard him play, I thought I was dreaming. Perhaps you'd like to learn how to play someday." I then turned off the light and left the room, closing the door behind me.

The house was completely dark as I ascended the staircase to the second floor. I walked down the length of the corridor toward the service stairs and proceeded up to the third floor. And as I did, I realized that for the first time I wasn't afraid, quite the contrary. A courageous, loving force was lifting me up, holding my hands and guiding my feet as I steadily climbed. Once there, I made my way toward the storage room, and as I put my hand on the doorknob I felt a light pressure on my shoulder and a warm breath on the back of my neck. I opened the door to find the room glowing with a soft, silvery light. It swirled in brilliant beams all around me. "Adam," I whispered. "My love, are you here?"

I waited for an answer and when none came, I went directly to the stack of books and papers in the corner and immediately found what I'd come for—Beethoven's Moonlight Sonata. With the score tucked safely under my arm, I returned to the second floor and went directly to my bedroom. The children had insisted that I sleep in my old room because it was closer to their rooms and they'd be able to hear me if I needed them in the night.

Touched and amused by this reversal of roles, I began to turn down my bed, but then realized that I'd forgotten something. I dropped my blankets and immediately went to my window to open it as wide as I could. Finally, I crawled into bed, certain that I'd never felt more deliciously exhausted in all my life. And when I closed my eyes, I was swinging to and fro and the breeze that drifted in from the garden carried with it the scent of wet earth and gardenias. On the verge of sleep, I heard my beloved's music wander in from the courtyard through my open window. Sweet melodious fog swept into my room, filling my heart and even the spaces of my dreams, taking me to that place in the soul where time stands still and life and love are eternal.

And I was running for my life through the jungle alone. It was dark, but I could still make out the gray silhouette of trees that rose up against the mist from the jungle floor, and I could feel the branches and the twisting vines reaching out and brushing my face and shoulders, sometimes snagging my clothes in an effort to hold me back. But I was determined to survive, and as I scrambled and leapt over every obstacle before me, my feet barely touched the ground. I could run forever if I had to.

But this time I wasn't running from harm. Something was pulling me forward, something that existed beyond my fears and all the years of yearning and waiting. And so I kept running until I could no longer see even shadows, until the air became thick and difficult to breathe. In such stifling blackness, I had no choice but to slow down, and when I did, the jungle closed in and grappled with me from all sides. Soon my face was covered in stringy moss and spiderwebs, and my skin was crawling with insects as snakes twisted around my ankles. Just when I was certain that the jungle would devour me, I saw the faint glimmer of light in the distance, which I thought to be the rising sun, and this gave me the strength to free myself from my entanglements, and I was running even faster than before, almost flying above the ground, and I ran until light filled the jungle with warmth and color and my path was clearly visible.

I slowed to a walk and remained on the path until I arrived at a small bright clearing in the deepest heart of the jungle. And in the very center of this, to my great surprise, I saw my mother's sewing cabinet. The shiny black enamel of the machine gleamed in the sunlight, and as I stepped toward it I realized that I yearned to run my fingers along the pretty floral carvings on the door and to look upon the magnificent priestly robes that I knew would be carefully folded inside. How wonderful to see them again, to feel the silken wonder of God's magnificence between my fingers. I knew this would heal me as nothing else could.

I reached eagerly for the door handle, but when I opened it only partway a powerful shock of blue light burst forth, flinging open the doors and knocking me off my feet to the ground. When the light had subsided and all was still and quiet again, I peeked inside the open cabinet but the beautiful priestly robes were nowhere to be found. Instead, I saw a small girl curled up inside with her knees pressed up to her chest and her head bent over the whole of her body. The poor child had obviously been in that agonizing position for quite some time. Nevertheless, when she looked at me, her eyes were filled with unspeakable love. And then, with great effort, she wrenched her hand free from underneath her legs and reached out beyond the cabinet toward me.

I took her hand and ever so carefully pulled her out of her confinement one limb at a time. Once she was free, I wiped away her tears, held her tiny broken body close to my breast, and murmured, "I'm sorry to have left you alone for so long, *mija*, but I promise that I'll never leave you again."

"I always knew you'd come back for me," she replied, and we walked out of the jungle together, hand in hand.

Acknowledgments

ONE THING I'VE LEARNED since I started writing is that when crafting a novel, effective collaboration during all phases of the editing process is essential. It's about getting the words right, keeping the plot tight, making sure that the characters are well drawn and that the prose flows smoothly. The guidance I have received from my editors, Amy Tannenbaum and Johanna Castillo, reaches far beyond the usual definition of collaboration. They have given me the kind of insightful and inspiring feedback that makes not only for better novels, but for better writers as well. I am extremely grateful for the partnership and understanding that has evolved between us, and for Judith Curr's confident and discerning leadership. If ever there was a dream team, this is it, and I'm delighted to be a part of it.

Without the support and encouragement of my husband, Steve, my parents, my sisters, and my entire family, it would be very difficult for me to continue on this somewhat introverted adventure. The wonderful people who live with me day to day accept that at times I need to go into "my cave" to be productive, yet when I come out of it, sometimes as grumpy as a sleepy old bear, this too they understand as part of the process. Their unconditional love, patience, and good humor are the greatest blessings in my life.

Finally, I must express my heartfelt gratitude for my friend, agent, first reader, and advocate, Moses Cardona. He's had the vision and confidence to take me by the hand and lead me across the threshold to that place where dreams become reality. I am extremely fortunate to have found him.

Vigil

CECILIA SAMARTIN

Reading Group Discussion Guide

INTRODUCTION

As Ana sits at her husband's deathbed, she thinks back on the incredible journey of her life. Ana's story takes her from war-torn El Salvador to a convent in the United States and finally to a California estate where she is employed as the nanny for the wealthy Trellises, a dysfunctional family caught up in the throes of a decadent life. Despite her own emotional wounds, she is able to bring love and healing to her affluent yet spiritually bereft employers—gifts that no money could ever buy.

Ana's emotional attachment to her young charges leads to her staying on at the Trellis home for longer than she ever could have imagined. As she grows to love Teddy and Jessie as if they were her own flesh and blood, they grow up and move out of the house, and her abiding affection for their father is transformed into something deeper and more powerful. Faced with many challenges to her own sense of morality, Ana must confront her own spiritual longings and reconcile them with her understanding that love may have found her in the very place she least expected.

QUESTIONS AND TOPICS FOR DISCUSSION

1. "My father's only saving grace was that before he disappeared he'd given my mother a magnificent sewing machine complete with a foot pedal and a carved wooden cabinet beneath." (13) What important roles does this sewing machine play in Ana's and her mother's lives? How does its presence in their simple hut elevate Ana's awareness of the presence of God? How does the absence of her

father impact Ana's physical safety, and what role does it play in her connection with her mother?

2. How do the memories that Ana revisits during the course of *Vigil* give you a better sense of her character, and what has shaped her emotional development as a person? To what extent does the appearance of these memories throughout the novel distract you from the illness of Adam Trellis and its inevitable progress? Why do you think the author chose to fuse past and present in this manner, and how does her decision to do so complicate and enrich the narrative?

3. "Why? Why were my mother and all my family dead? Why had every man, woman, and child in my village been brutally murdered?" (31) How would you describe Ana's experience of survivor's guilt, and how does the mass murder that she alone survives imprint itself on her consciousness? What does her ability to adapt to life in a convent, and then in California in the Trellis home, suggest about her resilience?

4. What role does Sister Josepha play in Ana's early life? What accounts for the kinship that develops between them? To what extent is Sister Josepha's friendship with Ana her link to her original desire to become a nun? What does Sister Josepha's patient willingness to wait for Ana to join her in New Mexico reveal about her character and her feelings for Ana?

5. "It's much easier to ponder the mysteries of life and death, to meditate in prayer while kneeling in your pristine sanctuary . . . [T]his is the antiseptic God that you worship,

isn't it, Ana?" (92–93). Why does Adam Trellis challenge Ana's faith in their first encounter? To what extent is this initial exchange revealing of the nature of their future relationship? What accounts for Adam's dismissive attitude toward God? Why would the prospect of an employee who aims to become a nun unsettle someone who is a committed atheist?

6. How does Ana succeed in taming Teddy Trellis? What role does Teddy's mother, Lillian, play in this transformation? How does the near-drowning accident in the pool change the dynamic of Ana's employment at the Trellis home? Of the two women, who exerts more of an influence on Teddy's social and emotional development—first as a young boy, and much later as a young man—and why?

7. "When I didn't answer him, he slipped his hands under me and carried me to the sofa. His nearness made me feel warm and alive as if a river had suddenly forged itself through my soul." (175) Why is Ana willing to deceive Adam? To what extent is Ana's effort to stall Adam motivated by an innocent desire to obey Lillian and protect her infidelity with Jerome from discovery? How does Ana conceal her attraction to her employer, even from herself?

8. Why does Cecilia Samartin leave the explanation for Teddy's absence from his father's deathbed until the end of the book? To what extent should Teddy feel justified in his reaction to his father's relationship with Ana? What do Ana's efforts to repair the relationship between Adam

and Teddy reveal about the true nature of her character? Do you think she should she feel conflicted about these machinations?

9. "Even so, as though greeting an old friend, I turned to admire the garden and, as always, took pleasure in the way the blanket of greenery and flowers undulated in graceful lines all the way to the wall that ran along the perimeter of the estate." (385) How does the Trellis house function as a character of its own in *Vigil*? What does it have in common with other memorable houses in literature—like Manderley in Daphne du Maurier's *Rebecca* or Thornfield in Charlotte Brontë's *Jane Eyre*? What does the house represent to each of the protagonists?

10. How does the closing image of the child at the sewing machine affect you as a reader? Who is this child? What does she represent to Ana? How does Ana's calling her *"mija,"*—"my daughter"—in the same manner that her mother used to speak to her complicate the identity of this anonymous girl? How is her sudden appearance connected to Ana's own recent discovery of the baby she will deliver?

A CONVERSATION WITH CECILIA SAMARTIN

You fled Cuba and arrived in the United States with your family at an early age. To what extent do you feel a kinship with characters like Ana, who find themselves separated from their cultural heritage and place of birth?

I relate in many ways to people who have left their countries regardless of which country they may be from, especially if they were forced to leave because of war or political turmoil. Of course, Ana experienced a tragedy far worse than anything I ever experienced. I have a great admiration for her because despite the horrors she witnessed, she remained open and relied on her spiritual strength to guide her and keep her belief in the goodness of mankind alive. I don't think I could have been as noble and courageous under similar circumstances.

What kind of research did you do about the religious formation of a character like Ana, who intends to become a nun?

I briefly attended a convent school when I was a teenager, but I knew that my memory of this wasn't enough. Fortunately, there is a Carmelite convent very close to my home, and I contacted one of the sisters, Sister S., who was kind enough to speak with me candidly about her life as a nun and to offer me the opportunity to spend some time at the convent. I will always cherish the day I spent with the sisters from sun up to sun down, as though I were a novice. It was an extraordinary experience that gave me some wonderful insights, not just for the book, but for life. Sister S. has become a dear friend, and I maintain a connection with the convent that I hope will last for a very long time.

Why did you decide to set the opening scenes of *Vigil* in El Salvador?

As Ana was looking back on her life, it made sense to me that she would begin in El Salvador, the place where her story began. At the beginning of the novel she is feeling vulnerable and afraid, and I've found that people often remember back to times in their life when they feel similarly. It's a natural reaction, especially when it comes to loss. When people prepare themselves for the loss of a loved one, they remember previous losses and in some way experience them all over again.

How does your training as a psychotherapist inform your writing about relationships?

So much of my work with clients focuses on the strength and health of their relationships. In fact, my discipline of marriage and family therapy is considered to be one that focuses most intensely on relationships, and I guess it's only natural that my stories and characters rely heavily on relational issues. But even as a child I was fascinated by relationships, which led me to become a therapist, which then inspired me to write novels, so it all works together.

With its grandeur, hired help, and gothic feel, the Trellis estate seems anachronistic in many ways. At any point were you tempted to set your novel in an earlier era?

I was never tempted to set the novel earlier because I wanted to include issues related to the civil war in El Salvador. If Ana was to be in her early forties at the conclusion of the novel, I was tied to a current time frame. Nevertheless, as I wrote *Vigil,* I got the sense that the Trellis family was living in a bubble or a time capsule of sorts. I think this stemmed from the fact that they all had their hurts and lingering regrets that kept them distant from one another and stuck in their misery. It felt like somebody needed to open a window and let in some fresh air, which thankfully Ana was finally able to do, literally and figuratively, but it took her a while.

What led you to weave Ana's memories of her childhood in El Salvador and her past at the Trellis home with scenes set in the present day?

I see life as a circular rather than linear journey. Ana's memories are multilayered and tangential, as I believe they are for most of us. Experience prompts us to think back on a similar experience, which reminds us of another, and yet another. In this way, the richness of the present moment is colored by the past, and it's beyond what a simple phrase, no matter how well crafted, can express. I was hoping to offer a glimpse of this complexity without interrupting the momentum of the narrative too much.

Ana's mother haunts *Vigil*. Did you intend her to be a voice from Ana's past, or a real-life spirit in the literary tradition of magic realism?

Both. Ana sanctified the memory of her mother and she continued to influence her life in a powerful way, even after she died. I wanted readers to understand that over time Ana had internalized her mother's strength, wisdom, and courage. She had become the best of who her mother had been, and eventually she was able to grow beyond her, so that had she lived, Ana's mother would have been able to learn quite a bit from her daughter.

At what point in your composition of *Vigil* did you decide that the explanation for Ana's physical deterioration during Adam Trellis's illness would have a joyous rather than tragic outcome?

I knew that I wanted the story to evolve in this direction very early in the writing of *Vigil*. I'm rather shameless about my preference for happy endings, but I don't want them to be too predictable because that isn't how I've experienced happiness in my life. I have found happiness to be quite tricky and unpredictable, and often it disguises itself as trouble at first. Of course, my very wise mother tells me that this is because I over-complicate things, and she's probably right!

Vigil is your third work of fiction. What did you learn about yourself as a writer this time around that was entirely new to you?

I learned that when it comes to writing a meaningful and moving story, there are no magic formulas, and it doesn't get any easier. The process involves plenty of heartache, self-doubt, and a good dose of anxiety. But at least when I stray from my path, I'm better able to realize it and get back on track. I guess that means I'm getting to know my writing self a bit better, and that's a good thing.

How did you arrive at the closing image of the book, and what do you hope your readers will take away from that arresting final moment?

First, I must credit my talented editors, Amy Tannenbaum and Johanna Castillo, for suggesting that I conclude with a scene that included the sewing cabinet in some way, but I had no idea how to do this at first. Finally, after several days of fruitless pondering, it came to me. On a deeply emotional and spiritual level, throughout the entire novel Ana has been waiting for her mother to return for her while she hides in the sewing cabinet, and this circle needed to be closed. I hope that my readers will take a moment to reflect on the power of maternal love and devotion in their own lives and how this love can give us the strength and courage to rescue ourselves. It is only when Ana learns how to do this for herself that her vigil ends.

TIPS TO ENHANCE YOUR BOOK CLUB

1. Are you interested in knowing more about Cecilia Samartin and her other novels? If so, you may want to visit her website: www.ceciliasamartin.com. Here you can read reviews of her earlier novels, learn more about her life as an author, and read about what inspired her fictional creations.

2. Ana's story of finding her true family in the Trellis home is not a unique one. Think about people in your life who are not blood relatives, but who feel like your family. What are the characteristics that make them stand out? How have they become part of your family's history? Ask yourself if there are any constants in the types of people who become family—are they usually caregivers, do they tend to be women or men, and how do they interact with other members of the family? You may want to share your thoughts on these important people with members of your book club.

3. Did the scenes of bloodshed and anguish in Ana's childhood El Salvador stay with you long after you finished reading *Vigil*? Would you like to understand more about the civil war that gripped the country? If so, visit: www.pbs.org/itvs/enemiesofwar/story.html to learn about how governments like the United States and the former Soviet Union lent support to both the National Guard and the insurgent-led rebels. This site offers an informative timeline and a detailed explanation about atrocities committed against locals like those in Ana's home village.